I0596851

THE LONG ARM OF FANTÔMAS

BEING THE SIXTH OF THE SERIES OF THE
FANTÔMAS DETECTIVE TALES

BY PIERRE SOUVESTRE & MARCEL ALLAIN

Bibliographical Note

This Antipodes edition, first published in 2016, is a republication of the work first published by The Macaulay Company, New York, in 1924. The original translation has been slightly altered to reflect modern spelling and usage.

ISBN 978-0-9966599-1-8

Contents

THE LONG ARM OF FANTÔMAS

1. A Promising Job

". . . Six, seven, eight, nine, ten. There you are!"

"And there's your bill back in exchange. Monsieur Moche, I thank you."

"It's *I* should thank *you*."

"Not at all, not at all! . . . Your leave, Monsieur Moche, to count them over again on my side? Ten thousand francs, quite a sum of money!"

"My word, yes, my man. So that clears your budget, eh?"

"Please don't think I mistrust you because I check the notes. It's the usual thing."

"Go on, go on. Don't apologize."

The bank collector deposited his peaked cap on a straw-bottomed chair beside him, mopped his streaming brow, and moistening his thumb with a rapid, eminently professional movement, passed one by one between his fingers the ten big blue bank notes his debtor had just paid over to him.

The heat was stifling. It was the 15th of May—settling day, and about four o'clock in the afternoon.

Bernard, an employee at the Comptoir National, was nearly at the end of his day's round when he reached M. Moche's abode, which lay at the far end of the *quartier*, No. 125 Rue Saint-Fargeau.

The man had climbed the stairs slowly. On the fourth floor right was a door with a brass plate on which was inscribed:

MOCHE, ADVOCATE

The description was only roughly indicative of the professional status of the tenant of the fourth floor. M. Moche was indeed an advocate, but not an advocate borne on the rolls of the Cour d'Appel, a pleader affiliated to the Paris bar and consequently bound by the strict rules of the profession. He was an *advocate* in the bare, literal sense of the word, leading persons of some perspicacity to surmise that M. Moche was in actual fact merely an ordinary business agent.

Nor was the impression produced on a visitor entering M. Moche's domicile such as to modify the supposition. A real barrister's chambers are in the main very much like any middle-class private house, whereas M. Moche's office, or to be more precise, M. Moche's offices, bore the unmistakable stamp of a place of business.

The first room you entered was divided in two by a partition pierced by wicket-windows, the lower portion being solid, the upper consisting of a latticework of stout bars. Behind could be seen rows and rows of deed-boxes and bundles of papers ranged on big shelves. In this room M. Moche generally sat, and whenever the outer door opened he would follow suit by throwing open a little window and popping out his head to take stock of the visitor.

Anyone who had ever seen M. Moche, or even just his head framed in the window opening, could never forget the man, for the advocate of the Rue Saint-Fargeau possessed a physiognomy that was highly characteristic.

His features, prematurely wrinkled, betrayed his age to be a good fifty. Following the fashion of ministerial officers of former days, M. Moche wore on his cheeks a pair of short, bushy whiskers, of a reddish hue that made them strongly resemble a rabbit's paws. His rather prominent nose, under which a black smudge of snuff was invariably to be found, carried a pair of enormous, round, gold-rimmed spectacles. Atop his skull, which one guessed to be completely bald, was perched a badly made, badly kept wig, ragged at the temples and unduly flattened at the crown, whereon the wearer found it necessary from time to time to balance a little velvet skullcap.

Had it not been for the shifty eyes that were never at rest for an instant, M. Moche might have been taken for a perfectly honest man; yet his old-maidish manner, his soft, silky address, his often exaggerated politeness, his trick of rubbing his hands and bending his back before visitors, somehow modified any such favorable impression. Still, as a matter of fact, despite his unpleasing exterior, M. Moche had earned an excellent reputation in the *quartier*. He was a serviceable, obliging old fellow, occasionally over-inquisitive about other folks' business, but as a rule ready enough to do a kindness. Many in the neighborhood had had recourse to him at one time or another for little loans of money, granted, it is fair to say, at quite reasonable rates of interest, and none had come to any harm at the hands of the old businessman.

The truth is, M. Moche was richer than people might suppose, judging by the appearance of his abode on the fourth floor, a quite modest set of apartments. Apart from the outer room with the barred and windowed partition, the accommodation included a second apartment, a trifle larger, a trifle more pretentious, which was honored with the title of drawing room. One or two armchairs of worn and faded leather and a round table with a gas chandelier over it made up the furniture. The room had two windows looking on the street, affording a superb view over the northern parts of the city and the fortifications running parallel with the Boulevard Mortier.

The third room of the flat was M. Moche's bedroom, a chamber rarely occupied, however, for its tenant frequently slept at home, and appeared to utilize his quarters in the Rue Saint-Fargeau merely as a place for interviewing callers and conducting his business affairs in general. M. Moche, in fact, was entitled to use more than one address, and it was matter of common knowledge that he was owner of a house in the La Chapelle district.

. . . The collector had finished his verification of the total, and declared it to be correct. Then he added, as he turned to take leave of M. Moche:

"There, my day's work is done, or as good as done. I've only another flight to climb in your house, and then back to the bank as fast as I can go, for I'm behind my time already."

At these words, M. Moche looked at the man with an air of surprise.

"You have a payment to collect on the floor above?" he asked. "And from whom, may I ask?"

Bernard consulted a little notebook dangling by a string from a button of his uniform.

"From a Monsieur Paulet."

"Oh, ho!" laughed M. Moche.

"Yes, that's so," affirmed the other. "Oh, a mere trifle, a matter of 27 francs!"

"Well, good luck to you," concluded the old man philosophically, closing the wicket, as the bank employee took his leave with a bow and a final word of politeness:

"Hoping to meet you again, sir!"

Left alone—he kept neither housekeeper nor office-boy—the old fellow stretched himself in one of the old leather armchairs in the dining room. Through the open window came a breath of cool air. M. Moche sat in his shirtsleeves, enjoying the evening freshness, and presently took advantage of his momentary leisure to inhale a huge pinch of snuff. Not a sound came from outside—vehicles are few and far between in the Rue Saint-Fargeau—and only faint and far away in the distance could be heard the occasional tinkle of the bells of the electric trams that, in this remote quarter of Paris, link up the outer suburbs with the central districts of the capital.

Suddenly, M. Moche started violently. From the floor above a dull, heavy thud reached his ear. He found no difficulty in identifying the sound—it was that of some heavy object falling on the floor above his head. The old man scratched his chin and muttered half aloud:

"It's a piece of furniture overturned . . . or a body!"

For a minute or two he stood hesitating, but M. Moche was a man of a curious and inquiring turn of mind.

Abandoning the siesta he was proposing to enjoy, he crept cautiously from the salon, and crossed the outer room of the flat, which opened directly on the landing. Then, stepping noiselessly in his felt slippers, he climbed the stairs leading to the upper floor without a sound.

On the fifth floor of No. 125 Rue Saint-Fargeau, there had

been residing for some weeks, in a pretty enough, albeit cheap, set of rooms, two individuals who appeared at first blush to be just an amiable pair of turtledoves.

They were quite young—the united ages of the two would barely have equaled that of M. Moche! The man looked twenty-three at most. His companion, a dainty, slim little thing, a brunette with great dark eyes, had seen no more than sixteen summers.

They were lover and mistress. His name was Paulet, hers Nini. The pair had set up house together in the Rue Saint-Fargeau after their union one Easter eve in the tenderest, but unconsecrated bonds of love. The two had known each other from childhood. Paulet was the son of a worthy woman who kept the porter's lodge at a big house in the Rue de la Goutte-d'Or. Nini lived in the same house, where she had come as a child with her mother, a respectable working woman, Mme. Guinon by name, widow of a railroad worker.

Nini was the youngest of a large family. They had been five brothers and sisters, but two having died at an early age, Mme. Guinon had only three surviving children. The two elder, Firmaine and Alfred, were employed—the former at a mantua-maker's in the Rue de la Paix, the latter with a book-binder in the Rue des Grands-Augustins. But Nini, a child of an uncontrolled and capricious temper, with a venturesome and vicious disposition, could never acquire the habit of regular work, no matter how light. Forgoing apprenticeship, the girl had preferred to run the streets with the most outrageous young scamps of the *quartier*.

This was the very thing to attract and fascinate Paulet, the concierge's son, who also, as the phrase goes, had a wild "bee in his bonnet," and who from his teens onwards had been told over and over again by the flash girls of La Chapelle that he was far too pretty a boy ever to do any work.

For all that, Paulet was scarcely to be styled an Adonis. Slenderly built and below average height, he had into the bargain a pasty complexion, colorless hair, and a pair of pale, watery eyes. Still, the features were well cut, almost refined. It was a common saying in the Rue de la Goutte-d'Or that certainly his mother must have gone wrong one day with a man of quality to have brought such a piece of goods into the world.

In a word, Paulet was the women's darling, because not only had the lad pretty manners of his own, but an inexhaustible fund of high spirits and an amazing gift of the gab—a typical "ladies' man" in all the abomination of the term . . . and in all its beauty!

The whole La Chapelle quarter was stirred to its depths when Paulet seduced little Nini Guinon and resolved to set up house with the girl. There had been some violent scenes with the child's family. Mme. Guinon, in particular, had been profoundly grieved at the catastrophe. But there, one must learn to take things as they come—and she had resigned herself to the inevitable.

As a matter of fact, for the two months the pair had been living together as man and wife, the lovers appeared to have grown quite well behaved. Nini kept her little home in decent order; Paulet worked now and then as a stonemason, a trade he had learned once upon a time in a rather haphazard fashion. Such at any rate was the official, ostensible occupation of the tenant of the fifth floor. But his real business, one which sometimes of evenings he constrained his pretty mistress to follow, was, may we surmise, of a less reputable sort.

A certain angle enabled anyone looking out from the staircase window to see what was going on in the kitchen of the flat occupied by this dubious couple. At the moment M. Moche reached this window, Paulet and Nini were engaged in a highly animated conversation; and, to be sure, the old man looked on and listened with all his eyes and ears.

M. Moche was lost in astonishment at the strange attitude of the two and the amazing things they were saying! Bending down over the sink, Nini and Paulet were letting the water pour over each other's hands, which they were soaping in feverish haste, while red soapsuds dripped between their fingers into the trough.

Paulet was saying:

"Buck up, Nini! Don't let the flies grow on you . . . once the stuff dries on our fingers, it'd be the devil's own job to get it off afterwards!"

"I know that," muttered Nini in a trembling voice. Then she added:

"But, look, I've got some on my apron, too."

"Lather it well," her lover told her, "and if it won't come off, we'll chuck the thing in the fire."

Paulet half turned round and took down from a shelf a heavy hammer stained with blood, which he set to work sponging carefully.

"That's mighty dangerous, too," he observed, "if it's not wiped clean."

M. Moche could form a pretty shrewd notion of what had occurred before he arrived. Mechanically he mounted the three or four steps that still separated him from the landing of the floor occupied by Paulet and Nini.

The door stood ajar—a crazy piece of imprudence! M. Moche pushed it open softly and made his way stealthily along the little passage at the end of which was the kitchen.

Suddenly, in the half dark, his foot struck against something. M. Moche, his sight getting accustomed to the dim light, gazed down at this "something" with haggard eyes—it was the body of a man lying quite still, face down on the floor!—the body of the bank collector! At the back of the neck showed a fearful wound.

The thing was beyond a doubt—Paulet had murdered the employee from the Comptoir National.

The unfortunate man's wallet lay beside him, wide open, and M. Moche could see that its contents had not yet been touched. The bank notes stuck half out of the case, like the contents of a parcel that has been ripped up; you had only to stoop to help yourself. It was plain Paulet and Nini, their victim once dead, had merely shut the door, without making sure it was fastened, calm and confident in their conviction that nobody in the house, empty at this hour of the day, would come in to surprise them.

The deed once done, they had deemed the most urgent thing was to set to work instantly to cleanse their hands and clothes in order to get rid of the evidence of their guilt at the earliest possible moment. The corpse lay absolutely motionless. No doubt the bank employee had been killed outright with one blow.

During the few seconds M. Moche stood hesitating before the ghastly sight, he could still hear the two accomplices discussing the details of their cleansing operations. But there was something else that, even more than his curiosity to overhear what they were saying, held the old advocate's attention—to wit, the bank notes that overflowed from the wallet, that were all but out of their receptacle, that seemed to be actually offering themselves to whosoever cared to appropriate them.

It was a strong temptation—and M. Moche did not resist it!

Creeping like a cat, hiding in the semi-darkness of the little passage, with a thousand precautions, he advanced step by step. He reached out his hairy hand, his fingers shook as they touched the brass fittings of the open wallet. Then his hand fell on the bundle of notes. Suddenly he sprang back in alarm—Paulet and Nini had stopped talking. Had they heard him?

But presently the same excited conversation began again. Whereupon M. Moche, with an ugly smile on his face, crept down again to his own floor, bolted his door and counted his spoils. Yes, it was a fine stroke of business: not only did he recover his own ten thousand-franc notes, but with them were ten others of the same denomination!

"Ha, ha! Money well invested, and that brings in a hundred percent on the nail, or I don't know what I'm talking about!" M. Moche muttered in delight, his eyes sparkling with greed.

But next moment, the old man turned ghastly pale. The front-door bell had rung! Instinctively, M. Moche crammed into his pocket the notes he had just stolen so audaciously, and with the aplomb of a hardened thief.

Then he stood stock-still, waiting. Would the visitor insist? Yes, he would—the ring was repeated. M. Moche had nothing to fear, for the moment at any rate. Had he not taken the precaution to double lock the door? Still, he must find out what was afoot. In a second the old fellow had decided the line of behavior he must adopt.

"Bless my soul," he thought to himself, "it can only be a caller, a client, and there is no reason why I shouldn't receive him. If by any chance it were Paulet, I need only refuse to open and leave him to kick his heels till the police arrive."

At the third repetition of the summons, M. Moche put the tentative question:

"Who is it? What do you want?"

Through the door the old advocate caught the sound of a fresh young voice asking timidly:

"Is this M. Moche's?"

"Yes, madame . . . mademoiselle, but I don't know if he can be seen. What is it about?"

"A lady wishes to speak to him—about a flat to let in the Rue de l'Evangile."

Rue de l'Evangile, that was where M. Moche owned a property. Most certainly it would never do to send away this inquirer who appeared anxious to take rooms in his house.

So M. Moche turned the key in the lock and half opened the door to make sure his visitor was alone, and that no one suspicious accompanied her. Evidently there was no cause for alarm, and the old man stepped back and threw the portal wide open.

"Please come in, mademoiselle," he said with a bow, and ushered her into the little salon.

His visitor was a young woman, quietly but elegantly dressed. Twenty-four at most, she was a tall, fair, pretty girl. A heavy veil partly masked the brilliance of her complexion of lilies and roses. She wore mourning weeds.

Moche, after a brief survey, pointed to a chair and invited her to state her business.

"Sir," began the unknown, "at present I am living in the Rue des Couronnes, but on account of my work—I am employed in the correspondence office of a factory at Aubervilliers—I am anxious, very naturally, to make my home nearer the place where I work. Well, I have been to see a flat in your house in the Rue de l'Evangile that would suit me, provided you would consent, as the concierge led me to hope you would, to make a trifling alteration."

The girl spoke simply, equally without exaggerated timidity and undue assurance.

Moche looked at her with interest, preoccupied as he was. Still he forced himself to attend to the conversation. Meantime, to gain time and recover his equanimity, he asked:

"Whom have I the honor to address?"

"True," the young woman apologized, "I have not told you my name yet. I am called . . . Elizabeth Dollon."

The girl had pronounced the name only after a momentary hesitation, a fact which did not escape M. Moche's perspicacity. He said nothing, but cast a long, scrutinizing glance at his visitor. He saw that she was coloring.

"*Mademoiselle Elizabeth Dollon,*" he repeated. "Now it's a curious thing, but somehow the name strikes me as not unfamiliar."

The young woman had risen, and her brows contracted. She seemed agitated and spoke with difficulty.

"Forgive me, sir, but I always feel strangely moved whenever I have occasion to mention my name."

"Why, pray?" demanded M. Moche, courteously.

"Why? Oh, sir! Some years ago my name acquired a sad notoriety through the tragic, the lamentable deaths of the dearest of my family. First, my father was murdered under mysterious circumstances in a railroad car. Then it was my brother who disappeared, struck down by an odious criminal, who furthermore caused him to be accused, even after his death, of the commission of atrocious crimes."

These statements, succinct as they were, sufficed to reanimate M. Moche's recollection.

"I have it," he cried, "yes, I know . . . Dollon . . . the Dollon case . . . Jacques Dollon . . . so he was your brother? Jacques Dollon, whom they called the 'Messenger of Evil.'"

The girl, greatly agitated by this reminder of a terrible past, merely nodded her head affirmatively, while great tears filled her eyes.

M. Moche expressed his sympathy: "I am truly sorry, mademoiselle," he said, "to have recalled such mournful memories to your mind, but as landlord of the house where you wish to take rooms, I was bound to know your name. But I assure you that henceforth . . ."

He broke off, but presently resumed:

"You spoke just now of a small alteration in the flat you wish to rent." He had guessed from the first what it was and was quite ready to agree.

"You think, mademoiselle, that the five rooms of the vacant flat are really more than you require, and you are asking me, I'm convinced, to divide the premises in two by having a party-wall constructed?"

Elizabeth Dollon assented: "That, sir, is what the concierge led me to expect."

"Consider the matter settled," declared M. Moche, "and accordingly, the premises being only one half as big, the rent will be proportionately less—I will ask you 400 francs. When do you wish to move in?"

"As soon as possible."

"The rooms are empty; as soon as ever the partition is built, you can take possession."

Moche went into the adjoining room and returned with a form of contract he had taken from one of the pigeonholes.

"Sign this paper, mademoiselle, if you please."

Elizabeth Dollon was preparing to do so when he asked another question in a tone of fatherly interest: "You are alone, eh? Quite alone?"

"Why, of course," replied the girl, whose look of surprise clearly showed that she failed to understand what her prospective landlord was getting at.

The latter explained: "The house in the Rue de l'Evangile is let out to very desirable tenants—only respectable families. . . . It is not for me to judge your character, my dear young lady, but if you did happen to have a 'friend,' or several 'friends,' why, you must not let them come to see you—or not too often, at any rate."

Mademoiselle Dollon drew herself up.

"Sir," she declared, a good deal offended, "I don't know what you take me for, but I am an honest woman—"

"Well, well, I felt sure of it the moment I set eyes on you; but there, it's as well to understand one another from the beginning. So please sign your name there, mademoiselle," and with his great hairy finger, M. Moche pointed out the place.

This formality completed, she bade a hasty farewell to M. Moche, who escorted her politely to the door.

"Brigand, scoundrel, blackguard, thief!" A torrent of insults, followed by a torrent of blows . . . M. Moche was on the point of recovering his threshold when he was struck, full in the face and fell to the ground. As he lay there, he felt the weight of a man's body crushing him, holding him forcibly down.

But Moche, for all his years, was a wonderfully active man, and quite unexpectedly nimble. In one second he had shaken off the incubus and leapt to the other end of the room, where he stood glaring at his assailant.

It was Paulet he saw, but Paulet changed beyond recognition—eyes starting out of his head, mouth set hard, features convulsed, muscles taut.

The lover of Nini Guinon, knife in hand, was hurling himself at M. Moche, when suddenly he came to a halt. The sharp click of a cocked pistol stopped him where he stood.

Moche, quick as lightning, had not only dodged the villain's furious onslaught, but had whipped a revolver from his pocket and pointed the weapon straight at the scoundrel's breast . . .

"Not another step," he shouted, "or I shoot you like a dog!"

At the same moment a cry of anguish rang out. Behind Paulet appeared the face of Nini Guinon, pale and agonized. Her two hands clutched her lover, whom she was holding back with all her strength.

But the man had realized the risk involved in a fresh attack, and was ready to parley. The voice shook that came from between his clenched teeth: "Brigand!" he repeated, looking furiously at Moche, "brigand, give me back my money!"

For a moment the old advocate entertained the idea of shamming ignorance, pretending not to know what the murderer meant by the demand. But a half-dozen words that fell from Nini's lips decided him. "I saw you fumbling in the money-bag," she declared, and he knew at once that dissimulation was useless. The wisest policy was to take the bull by the horns there and then—and he had his plan all ready, cut and dried. Best to play the cards face upwards on the table.

"No," he declared, grimly, "I will not give you back the money."

"Ruffian!"

"One minute . . . !"

A sardonic smile curled the old man's lips. He cast a searching glance at Nini, pondering with which of his adversaries he should open the attack. They were two to one—was it not judicious to win one of them over to his side so as to reverse the superiority of numbers?

"Poor little Nini," M. Moche murmured in softened, honeyed tones, "my poor little girl, you're in a nasty hole. Whatever is to become of you?"

The girl looked superciliously at the old man: "I don't understand," she told him.

"Oh, yes! you do," returned the advocate. "Nothing easier to understand, my dear child. You'll be left all alone in life now, it is only a question of days, perhaps hours—your lover will be arrested by the police and in six months from now guillotincd at the back of the prison of La Santé. To do a man in to steal his money is always a bad business!"

Beside himself with rage, Paulet screamed:

"But it was *you* who stole the money, *you* will be turned off, too."

But Moche, in the same quiet voice, yet all the while keeping his revolver leveled at the scoundrel's breast, retorted:

"Impossible! How prove it? Bank notes can be made to disappear. There's nothing more like a thousand-franc note than another thousand-franc note, while the dead body of a bank messenger, a body stretched on the floor of a lodging, fifth floor No. 125 Rue Saint-Fargeau, the residence of one Paulet by name, that's a thing that's not so easy to stuff away in a pocketbook . . . Now, what are you proposing to do with the corpse in question, eh, my young friend?"

Paulet turned ghastly pale. Since he had done the deed, and especially since he had discovered there was nothing to be gained by it, the money having vanished, the scoundrelly apache had completely lost his head. If only things had gone according to plan, the affair might well have been highly advantageous. Paulet had arranged it all with Nini—to kill the collector, to appropriate his takings and fly right away to foreign parts. It was good business, a job well worth the trouble. But, lo and behold! the unlucky and unexpected interference of old Moche upset all their plans, for the old ruffian had left in the wallet nothing but a few small notes—just enough and no more, to pay for a little spree.

It was M. Moche, no doubt, who had stolen the money . . . Paulet was to pull the chestnuts out of the fire and the other was to reap the benefit . . . Nini, in fact, had actually seen the man making off! If at that very moment the old man had not had a visitor, Paulet would have hurried down at once and had it out with him there and then.

In broken phrases and a breathless voice, Paulet detailed all this to the old advocate, who only smiled enigmatically. After a pause, the latter spoke again:

"You are a fine, brave fellow, Paulet—a bit of a scamp, too, but who can blame you? It's just your little way, you know. . . . Now, my man, I'm going to make an offer: put your knife back in your pocket, I will clap my revolver in its case—we'll be more comfortable talking. Let's sit down across the table, and perhaps we can come to some arrangement."

The young brigand was at a loss, as he gazed alternately at the old lawyer with the sharp eyes and at Nini, who was prompting him in hurried, urgent tones:

"Don't be a fool, Paulet, do what the old ape says. He's an artful, knowing beggar, he'll find the trick to get us out of the hole we're in . . ."

Moche had caught what Nini said. He stepped up boldly to Paulet, with outstretched hands, though the young man had not yet pocketed his weapon:

"There, you see, I trust you," he declared. "I offer you my hand, mate, as a good comrade—shake, my man, we'll fix things up yet."

Paulet gave in. Ten minutes later, seated at the round table in M. Moche's dining room, the advocate and his two visitors, Paulet and Nini, were just finishing a bottle of wine together.

They clinked glasses for the last time:

"Well, then," demanded Paulet, "it's a sure thing, Moche, old man, you're going to help me?"

Moche, with a superb and impressive gesture, laid his heavy, hairy hand on Nini's tousled curls, where she sat beside him:

"I swear it, on your lady-love's glorious tresses, Paulet, and that's as binding as the Blessed Sacrament!"

"All the same," Paulet warned his mistress with an air at once peremptory and timid, "you'll have to shut your jaw tight and not go gassing about the job in hand."

Nini nodded, laid a finger on her lip, and with a shrug and a look of scorn:

"D'you really suppose," she scoffed, "I should be such a silly goose as all that?"

She said no more, for the two men were deep in confabulation.

Moche was asseverating:

"I tell you this, Paulet, we're in for a gorgeous fine thing. Don't you imagine I've come to my present respectable and respected age without seeing a thing or two and learning pretty thoroughly what's what in this world of ours! A smart customer like you, with a smart chap like me to help him, why, we'll play some fine games together!"

Paulet agreed, smiling a well satisfied smile. But one detail still troubled him:

"The body," he asked, "the fellow's body . . . upstairs. What's to be done with it, eh?"

"Never you worry, Paulet, there's more tricks than one in papa Moche's pack, trust me. If you do what I tell you, the 'cold meat' upstairs in your passage will be fixed up, never fear, so he'll never come back again: it'll take a mighty clever devil to find him, I can tell you!"

"But I don't understand," objected Paulet.

"What's that matter?" snapped the other.

The old scamp got up, stuffed his hands in his pockets—an ordinary enough gesture seemingly, but in reality to make sure his revolver was still safe in the inside-pocket of his breeches.

Paulet had risen, and he, too, thrust his hands in his pockets, in one of which he mechanically felt for his knife, which lay there open. All very well to have made peace, to have concluded a treaty of alliance over a bottle of wine—prudence is a virtue all the same!

But neither Paulet nor M. Moche had any warlike intentions. The two malefactors had made up their minds it was to their mutual advantage to help one another.

"As a matter of fact, you are a mason by trade, Paulet, aren't you?"

"Hmm, that depends . . ."

"Could you undertake to build a wall, a stone wall, a brick wall, a lath and plaster partition, any contraption of the sort?"

"Bless my soul, yes," laughed Paulet, "provided you give me the needful supply of stone or brick or plaster and lime for the job."

Moche clapped his arm on Paulet's shoulder:

"Well, my boy, that settles it. There's not a minute to lose, I engage from tonight."

Nini Guinon, who had been waiting the result of the colloquy with no small anxiety, Nini, whose gaze fixed first on one, then on the other of the speakers, tender and passionate on Paulet, questioning and admiring on M. Moche, and who had kept her curiosity forcibly in check for all this time, could no longer restrain the question:

"But what are you going to do?" Moche looked first at her, then at Paulet:

"You'll see what we're going to do all in good time," he announced, "but I can tell you one thing—what we're going to do is a mighty promising job."

2. A Night Affray

The Boulevard de Belleville at nine o'clock at night presents a grim and forbidding aspect. Long rows of flickering gas-lamps cast wan reflections over the far-stretching pavements, on which sinister figures—drunken men, dejected-looking street-walkers and apaches—appear momentarily in the ruddy glow from the lighted window of barroom of the sort Belleville used to build or American bars of a later fashion.

Along the sidewalk, with slow steps and head bent in deep thought, moved a young man of twenty-five or so, with a fine, intelligent face, but so preoccupied an air he scarce seemed to know where his feet were carrying him. The man was talking to himself. Anyone overhearing his monologue, or reading, if that could be, the thoughts that surged within, would have been amazed, perhaps terrified.

"An odd thing, life! An odd thing and repulsive!" he was muttering. "Six months ago, seven months at most—God knows how I have lived meantime—I was a King, I was greeted with a string of pompous titles. Gold jingled in my pockets . . . Six months ago I was on the path to glory, the highest glory I could conceive of; was on the road, with my old friend Juve, after saving the Sovereign of Hesse-Weimar, to share the honor of Fantômas' arrest! In a word, I was in the full tide of success. Then the luck changed, that devil Fantômas eluded us—more than that, he contrived that Juve was nabbed in place of himself. Juve in prison, I am myself liable to arrest as an accomplice, forced to fly, to take to hiding. The good days are over and done for me. I, ex-King of Hesse-Weimar as I am, find myself, this eighteenth day of May, starving, without a penny in my pocket, and in imminent danger of being jailed . . . oh, instability of human fortune!"

The young man was Jerome Fandor. The excellent journalist's history to date was summed up in the few words his despair had just wrung from his lips. By Juve's arrest under the guise of Fantômas, and thanks to the deep duplicity of the Grand Duchess Alexandra, Jerome Fandor had been plunged into the most alarming embarrassments.

That Juve was really Fantômas, Fandor had not, of course, for one moment admitted. To him the thing was a sheer impossibility, a supposition not only inconceivable, but positively insane. But alas! the conviction he held as to his friend's innocence, and even the hope he entertained that Juve would soon succeed in exposing the monstrous error whereof he was the victim, did little or nothing towards bettering Fandor's personal predicament.

On leaving the Gare du Nord, as they were carrying off Juve to prison, the young man had clearly realized that he must disappear unless he wished to be clapped in jail, too. Now it would never do for him to be arrested, in the first place because, if still at liberty, he could perhaps help Juve to get out of the mess, secondly, because now Juve was under lock and key, he, Fandor, was the only one left to fight Fantômas and paralyze the machinations of the brigand whom he still held to be at liberty, inasmuch as he refused to believe Juve to be Fantômas.

At the time the journalist had some money in his possession. Without a moment's delay he had changed his costume, and dressed out as a "ragged rascal," had plunged into the underworld, the social stratum where an artful and wary fugitive can most easily cover his tracks. This done, he had waited events. Day followed day, however, without bringing him any further information. Juve was in prison, the authorities still believing him to be Fantômas, and this evening Fandor, who had hitherto been living by casual odd jobs, was penniless and starving. What was he to do, he asked himself.

The young man continued to follow the Boulevard de Belleville, hesitating between the notion of going to find a night's lodging under the arch of a bridge and his fear of being run in by a police patrol—an eventuality he was far from desiring— when his attention was attracted to a passerby, a woman who brushed past him, walking very fast, rapidly outdistancing him.

"Hello!" muttered Fandor, looking after the form of the young woman. "Doubtless a Paris working girl. Now, if I were really what I seem, an apache, I should profit by the opportunity. A little woman of this sort would be better in bed at this time of night than out and about on the Boulevard de Belleville! And she carries a bag in her hand—how imprudent! I'd wager something will happen to the girl."

Jerome Fandor possessed something of that extraordinary instinct to be found in some veteran detectives. He seemed to have a presentiment of crime, to divine beforehand the possibility of acts of violence; and being a man of courage, he never failed to forestall and try to prevent the mischief. Mechanically, Fandor followed the young woman, keeping some distance behind, and as he went, took stock of her appearance. Small black toque, black jacket, a flowing veil, a slim umbrella, small shoes, a quite simple frock.

"A working girl, a respectable working girl, on her way home after doing a bit of overtime . . . Good! But, well, one may be mistaken!"

The young woman Jerome Fandor was following had just been accosted by a streetwalker, a little dark-haired creature with a tousled head, outrageously powdered and painted, clad in the typical spotted corsage of her class, the swaying skirts, the apron with scarlet bib, its pockets bulging, stuffed full of silk handkerchiefs.

"Hello! hello!" thought Fandor, "so here's my working girl in very odd company! Oh dear, oh dear!"

Next moment the young fellow darted forward at a run. From the shadows two men had just sprung out on the women. Seizing them roughly by the arms, they were hustling and dragging them away.

The streetwalker put her head down, fighting hard, but without uttering a sound. The working woman gave a piercing shriek for help.

To fly to the rescue, to save the woman in this perilous strait, Jerome Fandor's mind was made up in an instant.

Someone else came hurrying up behind him at the same moment. A voice shouted:

"Have at 'em mate!"

"A gallant working man," thought Fandor, as he caught a glimpse of a young man running across the road dressed in a blue jacket, the sort plumbers wear. "There's still honest folk left who won't let women be molested."

But the time for action had come. He was level by now with the two women, who were still struggling, and cried in a peremptory voice to the assailants:

"Let the women go, or I strike!"

At this the two bullies, finding it was their turn to be attacked, suddenly loosed hold of their victims and wheeling round to face Fandor and his companion, stood on the defensive.

In an instant Jerome Fandor realized the state of affairs: one of the fellows was putting a hand in his pocket—his purpose was clear.

"By God!" yelled the young man, "none of your tricks here, or you'll make me angry!"

Fandor was wrestling savagely, locked in a close embrace with the fellow who had first laid hands on the working girl. Behind him he could hear the labored breath and fierce cries and oaths of the working man who had hurried to the rescue, and knew that the same battle was raging between him and the second ruffian.

A few seconds, and all was over.

At the very moment Fandor, with a masterly trip, stretched his adversary on the ground, where he held him down by force, he heard the workman give an exultant shout of victory:

"Ah, ha! I've got you, you hound!"

Jerome Fandor looked round.

"Bravo, mate!" he cried, "so you've downed your man, too?"

A thick, hoarse, common, ignoble voice replied:

"Downed him, have I . . . yes, by God! and what's more I'm busy fixing the bloke up workmanlike, I am!"

"*Workmanlike,* eh?" Fandor looked, and could scarcely believe his eyes. In the calmest way possible, but with surprising dexterity, the man he had taken for a working man had whipped a coil of rope from his pocket and tied up the victim of his prowess.

"And now for your man!" he cried, pointing to the wretch Fandor held captive under his knee, and who had now ceased to offer the slightest resistance.

"Must truss him up, too—but I think we'd best not do 'em in . . ."

"Well and good!" thought Fandor. "Why, by God, this beats cock-fighting. It's just the finest scoop I've ever been in!"

The other went on: "It's the street officers, look—the swine! I just love it when I can spoil their little game. And it's all to the good for our gals, eh?"

"For sure it is," Fandor agreed, getting to his feet, for his companion had by this time roped up his man, too, and rolled him into the gutter, not without planting a shrewd kick or two on his carcass, the journalist proceeded to scrutinize his companion.

He was not a working man at all! True, he wore a plumber's short blue jacket, but one only needed to note his flat cap, his brown muffler, to say nothing of the broad red sash round his waist, his velvet Zouave breeches, his elegant, down-at-heel shoes, the whole vicious cut of the fellow, to guess his vile trade.

"A pimp!" thought Fandor. "A fancy-man, a bully, was my ally! . . . and the two we've just planted on the sidewalk are purely and simply a couple of police officers!"

But once more the other broke in on his reflections.

"Upon my soul!" he burst out, drawing Fandor away with a friendly grip on his shoulder, "it's a rum business, this here! . . . all the same let's pad the hoof, mate, the boulevard ain't a healthy place for us just now, if more cops should turn up."

So Fandor and his companion raced down the street at top speed and dodged in and out of a maze of dark alleys . . . In five minutes the apache called a halt.

"Easy does it now," he panted, "they'll never nab us here."

And then, suddenly confidential: "You know, don't you, why my donna stopped the wench?"

Fandor, without showing a trace of surprise, replied emphatically in the negative.

"Why, look, old chap, I'd told Nini—Nini my doxy's called—I'd told her when I saw your girl go by, 'Look, sure as my name's Paulet, there goes a wench who is bound to have a bit of money in her bag! . . . you go and talk to her, pitch her a tale, tell her you have a sick brat at home, some jeremy diddler or other, eh? and entice her down a dark street—and you and I'll deal with the baggage."

Spitting on the ground to give more weight to his words, the apache Paulet—for Paulet it was—added: "I take my oath I never dreamt she was a night-bird, I took her for a working girl by her duds."

Fandor was far from liking the state of affairs, as he realized more and more clearly the nature of the mistake made.

His companion, Paulet, evidently the "bully" of the street-walker Nini who had accosted the young working woman, took him, Fandor, for the latter's protector, while the two men, whom he had supposed to be apaches, were just simply guardians of the peace wanting to arrest the two women . . .

To tell the truth, Jerome Fandor was half sorry he had rescued the two unfortunates, but, for all his philosophy, he was still more amazed to have involuntarily become the antagonist of the officers of the law and the accomplice of a Belleville "ponce."

"What's dead certain," Paulet summed up the matter, "it's another evening wasted, old boy. Our two wenches took their hook during the fight, and I'll wager they'll say they're too shaken up to put in another stroke of business tonight—above all as Nini's none too fond of work at the best of times. And so, hang it all! We'll just go drink a glass and have a snack, eh?"

This last proposal was eminently agreeable to Fandor. It was thirty-six hours since he had broken his fast, and a supper, be it in company of an apache or no, was so much to the good.

"The fact is," he put in, however, for he had no desire for a quarrel with Paulet after their liquor, "the fact is, for the moment I'm stone broke, cleaned out, not a penny to my name."

But Paulet was in a generous mood. "Right O!" he cried, "I've got dibs. It's my turn this time . . . to Korn's, is it?"

For a bite of bread the unhappy young man would have gone anywhere whatsoever. "That's the ticket," he agreed, at once, adding by way of acting up to his role: "Maybe we'll meet some of the boys there."

At the *Rendezvous des Aminches,* the famous tavern kept by old man Korn, the two portals of which opened respectively on the Boulevard de la Chapelle and the Rue de la Charbonniere, Fandor did not at first notice any of the "boys"—or rather he made a pretense of knowing nobody.

In the low-ceilinged, smoky room, where seated in state, old Korn was rinsing out glasses stained with the lees of red wine in a basinful of greasy water, his shirtsleeves rolled up to the elbows, his bald bead shining in the gaslight, Fandor had recognized, with a surprise that bordered on stupefaction, a whole gang of people whom he knew very well. Paulet was pushing him along towards a little table where an extraordinary-looking individual sat, head like a broken-down tipstaff surmounted by a well-worn wig, nose decorated with an enormous pair of spectacles, frowzy mutton-chop whiskers framing the face.

"Good day, Moche, old cock!" the apache greeted him.

Fandor had been taking stock of the other customers.

Later on, Paulet, after ordering a liter of "Red Seal," bread, cheese, and Bologna sausage, was describing the late encounter to old Moche and his meeting with the "new chum." Fandor seized the opportunity to scrutinize the group of persons gathered at the far end of the boozing-ken.

So, the old gang had come together again? Again the same lot haunted Père Korn's tavern? Fandor was dumbfounded to meet once more at the *Rendezvous des Aminches* the very same ill-omened crowd of apaches that had over and over again been mixed up in the crimes and wild adventures of Fantômas. He could only just contrive to play up to his assumed character and pay decent attention to what Paulet was saying, who meantime was praising him to the skies to M. Moche.

"To be sure," Paulet was asseverating, *"you'll* pay for drinks, M. Moche . . . yes, yes, your Honor, never say no! . . . But look here, that man there—I don't so much as know his blessed name—well, there'd be something to be made out of him, eh? . . . There's no flies on that bloke, you bet. Why, in two shakes—crack!—he'd downed his gentleman, let me tell you that, sir. Two constables, sir, and we chucked 'em both in the gutter. Cost me a bit of good rope, it did—but there, I don't care."

M. Moche, sipping an extraordinary mixture of brandy and absinthe, applauded Paulet's narrative, and then turning to Fandor, asked:

"So, young sir, things going well with you, eh?" The question roused Fandor from a deep fit of abstraction. The old fellow repeated his remark.

"Hmm, no!" Fandor confessed, "by no means! . . . Cleaned out!"

"And you can write?"

With the utmost seriousness the journalist declared he could—"and none so badly either," he added, "I write quite a good hand."

For some seconds the old man sat lost in thought, then he brought out his proposal: "Now, what would you say if I asked you to come and work with me? I am a business agent, yes, a business agent—in *every* kind of business, you must understand. . . . In a word, if you care to sleep tonight at my place, why, there's a pile of papers in the garret, where you'd be comfortable enough . . . say, does that suit you, lad?"

For the moment Fandor hesitated. He asked himself who and what was this dreadful person, and for what shady work was he engaging him—on Paulet's recommendation, Paulet a common "bully," and that after he had just heard how he had been an active participant in an assault on officers of the law.

But Paulet gave him a nudge: "Go on," urged the young blackguard, "you're cleaned out, ain't you? So you risk nothing, and you'll rake in the dough at the old man's—he's rolling in it, ask any fellow here."

So it seemed old Moche, who frequented Korn's tavern, knew all the crew that met there.

Jerome Fandor's mind was made up. No matter what adventures might befall him if he agreed to "work" for M. Moche, he ought by no means to neglect the opportunity thus offered for renewing his observation of the machinations of this amiable confraternity.

"M'sieur Moche," he gave his answer, purposely exaggerating his vulgar affectation, "as you might say, sir, your offer does me proud. As for sleeping in your garret, I won't say no, after all it's May, and none too cozy bedding down under the stars."

M. Moche, who wore an enormous ring on his finger, hammered noisily on the zinc-topped table.

"Korn," he commanded, "another go of the same all round, it's my treat. I've just enlisted a new clerk."

3. Shady Schemes

Elbows resting on the handrail of the bridge, a man stood gazing down pensively at the flowing water.

It was M. Moche. The old man was even dirtier than usual, his hat crammed down over his ears—a huge topper, all dinted and dulled. His brow was wrinkled in deep and serious thought. It was eleven in the morning when the usurer of the Rue Saint-Fargeau had taken up his position on the footbridge thrown across the narrow sluice-gates separating the basin of La Villette from the Canal de l'Ourcq and connecting the two sections of the Rue de Crimée. Heedless of anything passing about him, M. Moche looked down at the current, in which the man's common, cunning features were reflected as in a mirror. But at the same time he kept occasionally casting furtive glances towards the bottom of the street.

At last the old fellow shook off his lethargy. From the far end of the Rue de Crimée he had caught sight of a man dressed in a long white blouse who was pushing before him a wheelbarrow loaded up with a workman's tools. The barrow bumped up and down over the uneven pavement as the man advanced slowly along the road, for the load seemed a heavy one. Still, in time the modest vehicle reached the bridge. The workman let go of the handles, mopped his brow—it was a blazing hot day—and then, after a glance round, he saw M. Moche and stepped up to him.

It was plain enough the two had met by appointment, for they seemed in no way surprised at the *rencontre*. The pair began talking in low tones:

"You were waiting for me, M. Moche?"

"Why, yes, I was waiting for you, waiting without much hoping you'd come. Still I waited."

The workman mopped his forehead again, muttering in a

weary voice:

"I've had the devil's own job of it this morning, I can tell you!"

"Poor fellow!" observed Moche, a note of ironical commiseration in his voice. Then the old businessman went on: "It's uncommonly seldom, all the same, one sees you sweating; when a man has a 'bee in his bonnet' like you . . ."

The workman laughed:

"Say a hiveful of 'em, Père Moche, and you'll be nearer truth. God! I can't deny it, hard work's not my strong point."

But old Moche, suddenly putting on an air of sternness and anxiety, questioned:

"Tell me, Paulet, how goes the work in question?"

The young apache, who for the occasion, bore the stamp of the most respectable of working men, replied eagerly: "The work's done, M. Moche. Oh! I give you my word I've put in a desperate hard four hours over the job. I've never in all my life done such a day's work for the masters. True," added the pale-faced young loafer, "it was no ordinary job I had on. . . . Just you think . . ."

But Moche interrupted him:

"That's all right, that's all right, Paulet. No need to go gassing here about matters that concern only you and me. You shall tell me the whole story by-and-by if things have gone well. Come along and have a glass with me."

"And my barrow?" asked Paulet.

"Bah! Leave it on the sidewalk. No risk anybody'll come and pinch it. And besides, if they did make off with it, I guess you'd never care—you strike me as the very image of a workman out-of-work."

A good quarter of an hour later the two men were coming out of the barroom, looking at once well satisfied and mysterious.

The barrow was still there. Paulet buckled to again and towed it slowly up the slope of the Rue de Crimée, while Père Moche, keeping to the sidewalk, stumped along in a line with the working mason.

The two confederates, who forty-eight hours earlier had

come near slaughtering each other over the tragic murder of the bank messenger, presently reached the top of the incline and stopped a moment to take a breath behind the Parc des Buttes-Chaumont at the opening of the Rue Botzaris. The place was admirably chosen for people wishing to talk without fear of eavesdroppers. The street was empty and even in the park not a soul could be seen afoot.

Père Moche, pointing to a bench set against the palisade surrounding a piece of waste ground—the very same where some months before a woman's body had been found hacked to pieces—was saying to his companion:

"Sit down there, my boy, we've got to talk."

Paulet was not sorry to rest a while, for his barrow was heavy. He gladly obeyed, and the two men faced each other. "Paulet," began M. Moche, "I told you the day before yesterday we were going to make a mighty fine thing of it, unless you proved a coward."

The apache lifted his right hand as if to take an oath. "Never," he asseverated, "I've never had cold feet, and you saw yourself how I downed the bank man with a crack on the dome. He was dead and done for quicker than it takes to tell."

Père Moche smiled, and resumed:

"Very true, my boy, you know your job. But as you are so clever, d'you think you could run a man in trying the epileptic fake, eh?"

"What's that?" demanded Paulet. "What's that mean?"

"That means," M. Moche went on, "you've got to upset your client, tie him up to rights, and pop him in a wheeler before he has the time to say 'knife.'"

"It's nothing so very formidable," remarked Paulet. But the old man proceeded.

"That depends on the place where the thing's done. Don't you go and suppose I'm proposing to do the job in a faraway corner at night when there's nobody around—that'd be elementary. My dear fellow, the man we're to pack away—for you may be sure I've got an idea at the back of my head—we're out to do his business in broad daylight, in the open street, in the middle of Paris!"

"That's a bit more difficult—but not impossible," Paulet declared.

Père Moche nodded approvingly.

"For sure, you've got the guts, my boy, and I begin to think you'll do fine for yourself yet. But just tell me how you'd go about it?"

Paulet, who in his braggart way had declared the problem old Moche set him as simple as A B C, seemed a trifle nonplussed. He scratched his nose, fingered his chin and growled out some unintelligible remarks, then finally admitted:

"Well, to tell the truth, M. Moche, I have the best will in the world, but I don't quite know how to tackle it."

Père Moche had expected the avowal: "No matter, my boy. Now listen carefully to what I'm about to say, for the little scheme I'm talking about must be carried out this very afternoon. Now look here—we're going to stage the fine old play of the *epileptic seizure*. Presently, after feeding time, we shall come along, nicely dressed up to look like honest bourgeois, into the high-life streets, say the grand boulevards or the Tuileries—I can't tell yet exactly where. We must shadow the individual I shall point out to you. We'll both walk behind him without any concealment, so that he'll notice us and forget to pay attention to two other crooks who'll be stumping along before us. At a given moment I'll give a signal, and one of the two in front will turn sharp round and come into collision with our man, then beg pardon civilly for the blunder. That's the time, Paulet, for you—you'll be behind, you know—to play up. A neat trip, and you'll roll your gentleman in the mud. Then, like the other chap, you must pretend to beg pardon, and meantime, when the guy's got his head down and his heels in the air along of the sudden tumble, you'll shove a stopper in his mouth."

"A stopper, you say? But I don't understand."

"You're going to understand," Père Moche went on, and adding demonstration to description, he drew from his pocket for his accomplice's inspection a sort of small india-rubber ball, the size of a walnut. Paulet examined the contrivance with interest.

The old man proceeded: "Soon as the client's got this chest-nut in his chops, he won't be able to say boo to a goose, for look, Paulet, it's made of elastic rubber you can swell out as you choose." So saying, he pressed a spring, while Paulet stood gazing in wonder and admiration at the extraordinary torture implement—nothing more nor less than an ordinary choke-pear or elastic gag.

M. Moche continued his explanations: "You can imagine, when he's got that between his jaws, how the beggar will kick and dance like a cat on hot bricks; but he won't be able to ar-ticulate one word, and to make the fake more lifelike still, we'll take care to soap the rubber ball a bit beforehand. Coming in contact with the saliva, the soap will lather, and I bet you a pint of red our friend, what with his wild contortions and the froth all over his snout, will look for all the world like a man in a fit. The cleverest doctor would be deceived. It'll only be left then to get him packed into a cab, and as it so happens, the cab we shall pop him into will belong to one of our pals . . . While I'm busy with him, you, Paulet must be telling the crowd helping us to get him in—you may be sure the crowd will help us—how grieved you are at the occurrence. You must cry in a big voice: 'Oh! my poor dear friend . . . what a calamity . . . such a nice fellow, too . . . to think he's always having these attacks . . . well, we'll soon get him home now'—and so on and so forth. Don't worry, my boy. Rest assured, the cutest won't suspect a thing! . . . I told you before, and I say so again, I have a notion in my head that's getting clearer and clearer . . . We're going to do great, great things, never you fear!"

4. An Epileptic Seizure

Towards five o'clock that afternoon a busy-looking individual was crossing the Tuileries gardens at a rapid pace. Without a moment's hesitation, like a man accustomed to follow the same route almost every day, he strode over the Pont Solférino, then turned to the left and hurried along the Boulevard Saint-Germain. It was a man of thirty-five, on whose powerful features could be read the signs of numerous cares and anxieties, quick-eyed, alert, evidently a person of distinction, and one well known by sight to many Parisians. Not a few passersby turned round to look after him, seeming to search their memories to find the name that belonged to the face they saw. Others again, better informed no doubt, gave a start of surprise, then bowed respectfully.

The pedestrian paid little heed to their salutations, pressing on, deeply absorbed in his own thoughts, and not so much as casting a careless glance when he happened to meet or overtake a young, pretty and well dressed woman. Nevertheless, on arriving opposite the Ministry of Public Works, he halted in his rapid progress to cordially shake the hand of an old man, wearing a decoration in his buttonhole, who, despite the difference of age, saluted the younger man with a profound bow.

"Good day, Monsieur le Ministre . . ." began the old gentleman, for the individual so addressed was in fact no less a person than the Minister of Justice, Monsieur Désiré Ferrand.

After thanking the latter warmly for an official appointment lately received through his instrumentality, the elder man, an Engineer-in-Chief, M. Vauquelin by name, expressed his surprise at meeting the Minister moving about the streets alone.

But Désiré Ferrand made light of his objections:

"My dear sir, my temperament is too energetic, my nature too exuberant, to endure a purely sedentary life. I must be up and about and on the move for some hours every day. Very often I go to see friends who live at the farthest extremity of the Boulevard Raspail, and one of my greatest pleasures is to find my way there afoot whenever my duties allow me the time . . . yes, on foot and quite alone," added the Minister, "like any ordinary citizen."

"Alone, quite alone?" protested the other. "However, I take it that is only in a way of speaking, Monsieur le Ministre, for I feel very sure the Prefecture of Police keep an eye on so exalted a functionary as yourself and that, according to custom, officers of the Criminal Investigation Department assure your personal safety."

"By no means," protested the Minister, "I am afraid of nobody, and will have no one accompany me."

The old engineer made no reply, but on taking leave of Désiré Ferrand, he shook his head skeptically, pointing to two men who appeared to be following the Minister, but keeping at a respectful distance behind.

"And those two?" he queried.

Presently, as the Minister was proceeding on his way, he took occasion to glance behind him and noticed that the two individuals pointed out were actually following the same road as himself and seemed to be dogging his steps.

The two men were of totally different appearance. The one, dressed in a long frock coat and an old silk hat, was of a common, vulgar type. His companion was a young man wearing a light, well-cut jacket, breeches and a cloth cap. He looked like a cyclist and might have been twenty at most.

Watching them more carefully, Désiré Ferrand felt convinced they were deliberately shadowing him. This was intolerable, and a few yards short of the intersection of the Rue de Rennes, the Minister came to a sudden halt and challenged the pair:

"What do you want, gentlemen," he demanded, "why do you follow me?"

"M. le Ministre," replied the elder of the two, "we are Inspectors from the Investigation Department. We are instructed by the Prefect of Police to safeguard your person."

Désiré Ferrand looked annoyed. "The Prefect," he said emphatically, "is excessively officious. I have no fears, all I want is to be left alone in peace. Be so good as to leave off following me. I will be responsible for the order I now give you to your superiors." The two bowed deferentially and made a show of turning back the way they had come.

Meantime Désiré Ferrand, cursing the Prefect's precautions, halted at the edge of the sidewalk, waiting for the traffic to slow down and grow less dense before crossing the Rue de Rennes. He was just opposite the exit from the North to South Underground as a numerous and compact crowd of passengers issued from the bowels of the earth. Taking advantage of the press, the two men whom the Minister of Justice had ordered to turn back, but who had only made a feint of doing so, approached their intended victim, whom they had not lost sight of.

Paulet, rather staggered by the Minister's rebuff, began questioning M. Moche, not without a note of anxiety in his voice:

"I never thought," he began, "we were going to meddle with a toff of this swell sort . . . such an important bloke as all this . . . a Minister's not just like everybody else."

"Silly boy," replied the old fellow, "Ministers are made of flesh and blood like the rest of us, and I can even assure you . . ."

Père Moche broke off suddenly, his face losing the look of indifference it had worn hitherto.

"Attention!" he muttered, "the play's beginning!"

A big man with huge hands and an evil face, standing a few yards away, had just signaled to M. Moche. This done, unintentionally it seemed, the fellow bumped violently against Désiré Ferrand, who staggered, taken unawares as he was, and uttered a furious: "Look out, sir, look where you're going, I say . . ."

But at the same instant Paulet, in accordance with the directions he had received, taking the Minister in the rear, violently tripped up his heels. What old Moche had foreseen happened. The Minister pitched over backwards, striking his head on the pavement and lay there half stunned. Then Paulet, quick as lightning, dropped on his knees beside the fallen man and dragging the jaws open with his sinewy hands, slipped the rubber ball into Désiré's mouth.

Instantly the choke-pear dilated to thrice its size, and try as he might, the unfortunate Minister could not call out a single word.

A crowd quickly collected. Moche for his part had prudently slipped away to one side, while his eyes searched anxiously among the vehicles prowling round in search of fares for a certain one whose driver was his confederate. Soon, this particular cab hove in sight; indeed it had never been very far from the scene of action. It was a taxi that had been following the little group ever since they left the Pont Solférino.

Paulet meanwhile was playing his part splendidly. With the help of the big fellow with the knotty hands who had butted into the Minister in the first instance, he was clearing a ring, pushing back the overcurious.

"I beseech you, ladies and gentlemen," he was shouting, "go away. It's a poor fellow, an invalid, who has just had an attack. Yes, he's in a fit . . . he's ill," he kept repeating, and everybody agreed the young man was perfectly right.

The Minister in fact, utterly at a loss as to what had befallen him, merely aware that he could not utter a word and that they would not let him get up, was writhing and wriggling like a man possessed. A frothy lather covered his cheeks and poured from between his lips.

The spectators were of one mind, all parroting the same words:

"It's a man been taken ill, an epileptic just had an attack!"

The taxi selected by old Moche drew up to the pavement. With the help of kindhearted assistants, Paulet and his accomplice hoisted the Minister into the cab, still vainly resisting!

The two brigands took their places inside with their victim. Then, just as the vehicle got underway, old Moche with surprising agility sprang on the step and took his seat beside the chauffeur.

The plot had succeeded—a triumph, indeed!

But, after all, with what object had they kidnapped the Minister of Justice? What did they expect to make of it?

In the Chamber at the Palais-Bourbon, excitement was at its height. There was a constant coming and going of Deputies, talking together eagerly without paying the smallest attention to the demand for silence from the President's chair, whose bell rang out unceasingly. Presently, however, quiet was restored when the President of the Council, the much respected M. Monnier, mounted the tribune to make the following announcement:

"Gentlemen, I regretted a while ago to have to inform you that our honorable colleague, M. Désiré Ferrand, Minister of Justice, had not returned to his house . . . I have this moment received an extraordinary letter, so extraordinary in fact that I am tempted to believe it to be the work of a practical joker. Nevertheless, under present circumstances, I consider it my duty to make you acquainted with its contents."

"Read, read!" rose a unanimous cry, and in a voice trembling with emotion, M. Monnier read out:

"—By my decree, Désiré Ferrand has been held prisoner since yesterday. Again by my decree, he will be released today at five o'clock.

"By seizing the Minister of Justice and holding him at my disposition, I have merely desired to afford an indication of my power to compel the House to negotiate with me. I want money, I must have a million francs. Let the Government decide to give me this sum, and I will disappear. If not, the direst consequences must be faced. I shall begin with the Minister of Justice; the entire Government will be dealt with in turn."

The reading of this monstrous document roused in the auditors divers feelings of the most opposite nature. While some members laughed uproariously, persuaded it was simply a grotesque joke, others looked perturbed, asking themselves if the President of the Council had not lost his head. But a vivid curiosity was universal. There could be no doubt something prodigious, phenomenal was involved! Supposing the defiance to be facetious, still the disappearance of the Minister was alarming.

What was this mysterious power that functioned thus in the dark, but whose existence could not be disputed? Instinctively, reason, logic, common sense urged one and all to seek to know the author of these atrocious pleasantries, and M. Monnier was exhorted to make known the name signed at the foot of the letter.

With a wave of the hand the President demanded silence, then he announced, in troubled tones, not knowing whether his words would provoke an outburst of mockery or of panic:

"It is signed," he said, "Fantômas!"

The Chamber was in an uproar. The name was too familiar, too notorious, too terrifying, not to sow distraction in the ranks of the people's representatives. In truth all were pretty well agreed that only Fantômas could have had the audacity to imagine such a scheme could succeed.

"Fantômas!" they declared, "yes, Fantômas is at the bottom of all this, that is certain, beyond dispute!"

But numerous objections were raised against any such conclusion: "Fantômas, why yes, he exists, that cannot be denied. But the police unearthed the fellow, the elusive brigand was none other than the Criminal Investigation Officer, Inspector Juve! Now, Juve had been in jail for the last six months! He was to be tried. Meantime the prisoner was under safe watch and ward at the prison of La Santé."

At the same time, Juve-Fantômas had accomplices no doubt, and the head of the gang being under lock and key, it was a justifiable supposition to allow that one of his subordinates had taken over the direction of his nefarious schemes. Already Deputies were busy suggesting names, and that of Jerome Fandor emerged conspicuous amongst the various conjectures tentatively advanced by Members. All were unanimous in loudly and furiously proclaiming the enormity of the scandal.

But suddenly a dead silence fell on the assembly. Five o'clock had just struck. Now everyone remembered the terms of Fantômas' letter, according to which the Minister of Justice was at five o'clock precisely to be at the Palais Bourbon. Anxiously the Deputies waited. Some minutes passed amid tense excitement . . . Then, suddenly, like a clap of thunder, broke out a storm of applause and heartfelt congratulation, in which all parties joined unanimously. Issuing from the corridor at the back of the hall Désiré Ferrand has appeared.

The Minister's powerful features wore a look of assumed indifference, but for all the man's command of his feelings, it was plain he had passed through appalling experiences. His face was drawn and pale, and the hair above the temples seemed to have whitened!

A mighty rush surged towards the Ministerial bench, each more eager than the other to express his cordial sympathy and to hear what had happened to the unfortunate Minister. The latter was explaining to those around him as much as he had been able to understand of the strange adventure, speaking hurriedly, in broken sentences.

"The thing is inconceivable, insane, mad! . . . An attack in broad daylight, in the center of Paris, in the middle of a crowd of people . . . Resistance was useless. . . . I was forced into a cab! Once inside the vehicle, brigands gagged me, blindfolded me, bound me hand and foot. The taxi drove on and on a long, long time . . . I had no notion where they were taking me. . . . I spent the night in a damp cellar, in cold and darkness, while a masked man, holding me all the time under threat of a revolver, tried to extort a promise of ransom from me. He talked about a million francs . . . I was dumbfounded!"

"Fantômas!" was the general cry, "it is Fantômas' work!"

The Minister went on: "This morning they brought me food, I was dying of hunger . . . I took what they offered. Then, about three o'clock, my jailer of the previous night, masked as before, returned after being away for some minutes. He blindfolded me again, bound me and once more led me to a waiting car, which drove off and only stopped at last after a long time . . . I was told to get out, and two men informed me I was now a free man, while each set to work to unloose my bonds . . . A few minutes after, my hands being now free, I tore away the bandage that covered my eyes and discovered I was in a wood bordering a high road. The car which had conveyed me was vanishing in the distance, carrying my captors with it. I walked straight before me till I came to the nearest house to be found, where I learned I was on the outskirts of the Bois de Viroflay. An hour ago I was there still . . . my first thought, gentlemen, was to come to the Palais-Bourbon . . ."

The Deputies, after listening to this extraordinary narrative, looked at one another in amazement as they exchanged ideas in excited tones. Meantime M. Monnier had drawn his colleague on one side and was showing him the letter bearing Fantômas' signature.

"What is to be done?" asked the perplexed President of the Council, a fine politician no doubt, but lacking in decision in times of crisis.

Désiré Ferrand, in no way unmanned by the tragic adventure whereof he had been the hero, was boiling with rage and indignation. Springing to the tribune:

"Gentlemen," he thundered, "the ludicrous outrage of which you have been informed affects not simply and solely a Member of the Cabinet, it affects the Government itself, the Chamber as a whole, it is a blow aimed at the entire Country, an insult you can never brook! More than ever Paris lies terror-stricken at the crimes of Fantômas and his accomplices. This is no time to mitigate stern measures—far from it, we must show an iron fist! As Minister of Justice, I give you my guarantee that the most peremptory orders shall be issued for the wretches guilty of these acts of violence, the last of which was directed especially at myself, to be energetically pursued and then punished with the utmost rigor of the law. The danger should not make us draw back, it should inspirit us to go forward! The Government will ask for your votes, pledging itself to respect the claims of Right, of Justice and of the Public Safety!"

A thunder of acclamation greeted the Minister's bold words, while from divers quarters came cries of:

"The names! . . . the names of the malefactors! . . . Juve! . . . Fantômas! . . . The police—to work, the police . . . Jerome Fandor . . . down with the Press! . . ."

Again and again cries were repeated and through the ever

swelling roar of this human flood, that tossed like a tempestu-
ous sea, pierced again and again the names of Juve, Fantômas,
and above all of Fandor:

"Fandor is at large! . . . Fandor has disappeared! . . . arrest
Fandor! . . . lock up Fandor! . . .

Standing like a statue in the tribune, arms crossed on his
breast, eyes aflame, as he looked down at his fellow members,
Désiré Ferrand signaled his assent and approval. But his authority must win a sanction, his power be reinforced, and as the
Minister left the tribune, not without reiterating his promise
that the sternest and most peremptory orders should be given
the whole police force for the arrest of the criminals, a member,
leader of one of the most important parties, laid on the table of
the House the draft of a motion. This was immediately read by
the Clerk of the Chamber, as follows:

*"The Chamber, justly indignant, but confidently relying on the
Government's declaration of its resolve energetically to pursue the
criminal or criminals guilty of the unspeakable outrage whereof
the Minister of Justice has been the victim, hereby offers the latter
its sincere and heartfelt sympathy, and proceeds to the order of
the day."*

The motion was received with unanimous shouts of approval. By show of hands the Chamber voted the order of the day, as
proposed, and when, for custom's sake, the President demanded if any were of the contrary way of thinking, not a hand was
raised, not a protest was heard.

"By 527 votes in a house of 527 members present, the order
of the day is approved!" announced the President triumphantly,
as he vacated the chair.

"The first time in history," declared the old hands of the Palais-Bourbon, "the Chamber has ever recorded a unanimous
vote!"

It was now seven o'clock in the evening, and as they emerged
on the Quai d'Orsay, greeted with acclamation by the throng
of idlers waiting outside, members jostled against newsboys
crying special editions of the evening papers, wherein were
already described in the minutest detail the extraordinary

events that had just taken place.

5. Disappointed Hopes

"So your birth certificate is an unknown quantity, eh? And there's no means of knowing what your name properly is?"

"What can that matter to you, Monsieur Moche?"

"Oh, it's nothing to me. I don't care a bit. You're a tremendous good fellow, that's all I want to know. Your patent of nobility you can leave with your 'uncle,' if that's where you've deposited it, eh, my lad?"

"That's where it is—or somewhere else, Monsieur Moche."

"Remember, prisons keep records, now, don't they?"

"Don't talk about that, sir!"

"Agreed, my boy! Now look, for the friends of the family, for Paulet, the wench Nini, and the rest of the pals, you shall be 'Little Tremendous,' that's settled. Then, if clients come to see me, well, I'll give you a title of ceremony—you go along with that?"

"I'm agreeable."

"I shall call you . . . let me see . . . I'll call you my 'Chief of Staff.' That'll put a stopper on their gab."

"No doubt it will, Monsieur Moche."

It was in a dull, depressed, specious, fawning voice that Jerome Fandor replied to his new "master."

In the garret where the dreadful old fellow stored his archives, huge masses of dusty paper, cheek by jowl with all sorts of miscellaneous rubbish, worthless bric-a-brac, old worn out furniture, clothes fit only for a hand-me-down shop, Fandor had passed a not too uncomfortable night.

Accordingly he had risen in a cheerful frame of mind. A hasty wash at a trickle of cold water that escaped with a nerve-racking noise from a leaky tap on the landing outside his door, had quite made him his own man again. Whistling a tune he had rejoined M. Moche.

"Now, sir," he had asked, "you have work for me to do, eh, in your place of business?"

M. Moche, already ensconced in a leather armchair, from which tags of the horsehair stuffing stuck out in all directions, but which formed a permanent seat of state behind his desk, loaded with multitudinous papers, had nodded assent.

"Work? Yes, my young friend, yes. At my place there's always work to do, only as there's not always cash, for times are hard, we must settle about conditions. I offer you board and lodging, and now and again a bit of money does that suit you?"

Jerome Fandor would have thought himself in heaven, had not the dubious looks of the unpleasant old man driven all celestial ideas clean out of his bead.

"That'll do me," was as much as he had cared to say.

Thereupon the worthy M. Moche had proceeded to put a number of leading questions.

What could Fandor do? Write? Yes? . . . Good. That was capital. He could draw, too? Then he could draw signatures? In fact, copy signatures, eh? Copy them, you know, eh? Yes, again? Better and better . . . The old man seemed delighted.

Fandor had judicially sized up his new employer by this time. Yes, there was no doubt he could be of great service to him on occasions.

Then M. Moche had asked the young man to tell him precisely who and what he was. But on that point, Fandor had proved reticent to the last degree.

"I've got pals," this was all he would say, "who have nicknamed me 'Little Tremendous,' because I'm pretty nimble with my fists and ain't afraid to use 'em."

The information was vague enough. But Moche was not the man to insist on any excessive precision of statement. He felt little doubt his new clerk must have had a somewhat checkered past. If it didn't suit him to let out exactly who he was, well, that was his business . . . And that was why Moche, after informing Fandor that he would be where clients were concerned the "Chief of Staff" in his office, addressed the young man familiarly by the name he had chosen to give himself.

"Look here, young Handy Man, I'm going to send you on an errand."

"Very good, M'sieu Moche."

"An errand to a pretty girl's. . . ."

"Better still, M'sieu Moche."

"But no nonsense, you know! It's a serious matter, and you must be serious. No larks with the girl, she's going to be my tenant."

"You're a house owner then, M'sieu Moche?"

"Yes, my boy, a house owner, but a poor, hard-up one at that. Don't you go and think I'm a millionaire . . . Anyhow, I've a bit of a place where the young lady in question has rented a flat."

"And that's where I'm to go, M'sieu Moche?"

"No, my 'Little Tremendous,' you're to go to the Rue des Couronnes . . . d'you hear? The Rue des Couronnes while my house stands in the Rue de l'Evangile."

"Now I can't quite follow you, M'sieu Moche."

"That's because you talk too much, my lad! Shut your trap a bit, and I'll explain."

"Shut it is, M'sieu Moche."

"Good! Well, here's how it is: The lady has hired my flat; only as I can't say if she'll fork out the tin regularly, I should like you to go and have a look what furniture she's got, to know if it's good to cover the quarter's rent."

"Good, M'sieu Moche."

"You twig—do what I tell you without seeming to, eh?"

"In that case, I'd want an excuse, eh?"

"I never said I couldn't provide one, did I? Look, my son, search under that green bookcase and you'll find some patterns of wallpapers . . . got 'em?"

"Yes."

"Well, take 'em with you, young sir! For the last six months I've found 'em useful for the same little game. You see, I send a pal, as it might be you, to call on the guy who wants to take my rooms. He comes under pretense of offering the new tenant a choice of wallpapers. As a matter of fact, I simply use him to inspect the furniture that must guarantee the rent. As you may suppose, I never do pay for the papering. Not much! The offer's made—and there it ends!"

Fandor showed no surprise. The business his strange employer was sending him on was of course perfectly straightforward and legitimate! Still keeping to his slangy way of speaking, Fandor merely asked:

"And what's the name, M'sieu Moche, your bird goes by? And what's her exact address in the Rue des Couronnes?"

M. Moche, while talking to his clerk, was busy changing his down-at-heel slippers for a pair of elastic-sided boots, obviously too small for him, the light brown cracks in which he masked by smearing them with ink. He was bending down behind his desk and could not see the other's face as he answered his last question:

"The bird, as you call her, lives, to be exact, at 142 *bis* Rue des Couronnes. As to her name, that's pretty well known. She's the sister of a man who was murdered. You can't help remembering about it. She's called Mademoiselle Elizabeth Dollon. You'll not forget?"

In a shaking voice it needed an almost superhuman effort to steady, Jerome Fandor promised he would not forget the name! A thousand thoughts were whirling madly through his brain, his heart was still beating high with excitement, when M. Moche went on:

"Well then, hook it, my boy. Here's a few sous for going, to pay your Underground. It's not far, you can walk back."

Yes, he could walk back quite well, Fandor agreed, hardly conscious of what he was saying.

Ten minutes later he was on his way to the Rue des Couronnes.

Elizabeth Dollon! He was going, he, Jerome Fandor, to see Elizabeth Dollon! As if the past had suddenly risen before his eyes as on the film of an imaginary cinematograph of dreams, Jerome Fandor lived again in pain and grief the torturing crises, the grim tragedies that name called back to memory, a woman's name, the name of Elizabeth Dollon. No, never had he forgotten the pathetic heroine of those terrible days.

Elizabeth Dollon, the unhappy sister of the painter, Jaques Dollon, Fantômas' victim, deemed by some to be himself Fantômas till the day when Juve and Fandor rehabilitated his good name, was she not the only being Fandor cherished with a fond affection? Since the first day he had learned to know her, to appreciate the girl's proud and tender character, Jerome Fandor had loved her! It was for her, to do her honor, to rescue her from the most odious entanglements, that he had in those days devoted himself, body and soul, to the task of clearing up the mysterious affair of the *Messenger of Death*. Twenty times over, in the course of that police investigation, Fandor and Juve had risked their lives. Juve for his part was acting more for the sake of unmasking Fantômas than for any other reason, but for Fandor, he was spurred on by the interest he felt in Elizabeth Dollon.

Once, for a moment, he had believed his dearest wishes would be fulfilled. Then, at that very instant of joyful satisfaction, an appalling catastrophe had destroyed his hopes. The prey he was tracking down escaped, and Fantômas, to crown his victory, in eluding the wiles of his two pursuers, Fandor and Juve, had the cruelty to add yet another triumph. He wrote to Elizabeth Dollon—already his victim—"Fandor is Charles Rambert; Charles Rambert is a criminal and a coward," with the result that, terrified by this false and treacherous calumny, she avoided the young man, vanished from his life, swore she would never see him anymore!

And now, now when he was poor, helpless, condemned to live in company of bandits, apaches, the dregs of society, Fate gave him this sublime recompense, sending him this day to see whom?whom but Elizabeth Dollon!

"To see her, heavens! to see her! to tell her who I am, what I am, what I live for, to win a half-hour of sweet, calm converse with her, wherein to convince her of the truth, to explain to her Fantômas' machinations, oh! it is too much happiness!" Jerome Fandor strove to regain his self-possession, to master his nerves, but his pace was headlong as he sped to the Rue des Couronnes, where he hoped to win at last an unfeigned declaration of renewed affection from Elizabeth Dollon.

"I shall know very well," he murmured to himself at intervals. "I shall know how to show her I love her truly. By the ardor of my words I shall gain her confidence, the confidence she must grant me, which I must have, that she may feel I speak the truth, that I am not what Fantômas has told her I was."

Arrived at 142 *bis* Rue des Couronnes, Fandor found the house a crowded nest of working people's flats. Along a narrow, fetid passage, its damp walls stained and scarred over with inscriptions indicating the names of the tenants and the different floors they occupied, Fandor penetrated to the concierge's lodge. He tried to push open the door, but it would not yield.

"So," thought the young man, "the woman is not within." He called: "Anyone there?" but his voice was drowned by a deafening noise proceeding from a tiny courtyard near by.

Turning his steps in that direction, he discovered a woman busy with two sticks beating clouds of dust out of an unstitched mattress.

"The concierge?" asked the visitor.

The woman broke off her work to demand in a grumbling voice:

"What do you want with her, eh?"

"To inquire for a tenant's rooms."

"What tenant?"

"Mlle. Dollon."

"Mlle. Dollon? And what may you want with her?" Surprised at this discouraging reception, Fandor, who was anything but patience personified, merely declared:

"That I propose to tell Mlle. Dollon herself in good time."

But the virago had picked up her sticks again, preparatory to resuming her work.

"To begin with," she announced, "you'll not say anything at all to her, because you're not going up to see her."

"Not going up to see her! And may I ask why?"

"That's the orders she's given me—that's why!"

"Then you are the concierge?"

"Yes, I am. What then?"

Jerome Fandor realized he would inevitably be shown the door unless he could secure the good graces of this vixen who was so conscientious in the matter of obeying orders.

"Madam," he now addressed her in his most winning voice, forgetting how strange it sounded for an apache, such as he looked in his disreputable clothes to be speaking in tones of perfect politeness. "Madam, you would oblige me very greatly by informing me why Mlle. Dollon cannot receive me. I have not come to trouble her unduly. I am here to offer her a choice of wallpapers for the rooms she is moving into."

The young man had found an excellent way to conciliate the good woman. He had called her "Madam," whereas in the *quartier* she was invariably addressed as "mother" so-and-so, by reason of her enormous bulk.

"Well, my good sir," replied the fat portress, suddenly disarmed, "I'll tell you something. Come along into my lodge and I'll have a look first at your patterns, and if there's any that look like they would suit her, I'll go up and show them to her, or you shall go up yourself. She and I have the same taste in wallpapers."

To be sure, Fandor took care to express no doubts on the latter point, albeit it struck him as highly improbable that the fat concierge should share the same tastes as the artist, Elizabeth Dollon. He readily enough agreed:

"After you, madam,"—and, preceded by the fat woman trotting along in front of him, this being her own way of moving rapidly, Fandor advanced into the concierge's lodge.

"First of all," began his hostess graciously, "so as our talk may go easier, I'll tell you my name— it's Mme. Doulenques. Now, you mustn't bear malice because I was a bit rough with you just at first. The fact is the young lady is still upset after her adventure."

Boiling with impatience, Fandor wished Mme. Doulenques to the devil. The all-important thing for him was to see Elizabeth. Precious little he cared to listen to the fat creature's babble. But there, to hustle her was impossible. He questioned:

"Her adventure? Mlle. Elizabeth Dollon? . . ."

"Why, yes, you haven't heard? Ah! true, they didn't put it in the papers. Well, just imagine, Mr. Paperer, the poor, gentle lamb, yesterday evening as she was coming home from her work, was attacked by apaches."

"Good heavens! Not seriously hurt, I trust?"

"No, not much the worse certainly, seeing as how she escaped in time, but it was touch and go. She got back here terribly upset, poor child! That's why she won't see anybody today."

Fandor seized the opportunity to cut short the conversation.

"I see, but she will see me, for sure, as I've come about decorating the rooms . . . What floor does she live on?"

"Fifth floor, left . . . bell with a green bell-pull . . . But just wait till I tell you all about it. Just think, it was on the Boulevard de Belleville it all happened."

"Boulevard de Belleville! . . . yesterday evening?"

"Yes, yesterday evening—"

The young man had asked the question in such a strange voice that Mme. Doulenques felt her earlier doubts more than justified.

"Now, whatever's the matter?" she demanded, "One would think you'd been taken ill."

Indeed, Fandor had turned deadly pale as he listened to the woman's story. The coincidence was so startling—Elizabeth Dollon, the very evening before, assailed by apaches on the Boulevard de Belleville. Then, on the same boulevard, not far away no doubt, he, Fandor, defending an unknown woman against police officers . . .

The concierge took up the tale again:

"And the worst part of the story you haven't heard yet, Mr. Paperer—she knows the villain who assaulted her! Seems it's one Fandor, a low fellow who once had to do with her, and who actually . . . Why, what's wrong with you now? . . . God bless my soul! Stop him!"

Spinning round on his heels, like a madman, Jerome Fandor had abruptly left fat Mme. Doulenques in the very middle of her narrative.

And truly it was a mad thing the journalist had been guilty of in so acting. Commonly so careful and deliberate, so much master of his feelings, for this once he had failed to govern an overmastering impulse. So Elizabeth Dollon was the working girl he had saved the night before from the pursuit of the street patrol! And Elizabeth believed that Jerome Fandor, whom she had had time to recognize, was one of her assailants! What cared he now for any further details Mme. Doulenques might have to give?

Elizabeth lived on the fifth floor, and there he rushed, panting, filled with a frantic eagerness to proclaim his innocence to the woman he loved, to clear up this new, this fatal misunderstanding. While the portress, in sheer terror of the man's strange behavior, in the very middle of a conversation bolting away like a thief to dash up to her tenant's rooms, was screaming hoarse, half-stifled cries for help, Jerome Fandor sprang up the stairs four steps at a time.

Yes, there on the fifth floor he saw to his left a door with a green bell-pull beside it. He rang a peal, so loud and peremptory he could hear someone on the other side of the door hurrying forward at a run. A voice, Elizabeth's voice, challenged:

"Who's there? What's wanted?"

Fandor had a gleam of common sense, enough to make him disguise his voice:

"Someone from M. Moche's to see Mlle. Elizabeth Dollon."

There was a sound of a key turning in the lock and the door fell ajar, while Jerome could faintly catch a confused clamor reaching him from the courtyard below.

"You want to see me, sir?" and cautiously the occupant of the flat—doubtless the young woman had been resting on her bed and had hurriedly thrown a peignoir round her—opened the door a little wider.

Alas! hardly had she cast eyes on the visitor before she turned livid and tried to pull the door to again, screaming: "Help! help! . . . you . . . you, Fantômas! . . . Fandor! . . . I am undone!"

Instinctively throwing his weight against the door, Fandor

endeavored to prevent the girl from shutting him out. "For heaven's sake," he begged her, "calm yourself—yes, it is I . . . I Fandor! . . . who loves you. . . . Listen to me, I beseech you!"

But with a sudden, desperate effort, Elizabeth Dollon had dragged the door shut again, not without giving vent to another cry of frantic terror: "Help! It is Fantômas . . . Fantômas!"

All this had occupied but a moment, and already Fandor was regaining his composure. That Elizabeth, terribly upset by last night's violence, in which she believed him to have been concerned, took him for Fantômas, was after all of small importance. He could easily convince her of the truth. What was more serious was the monstrous folly he had committed in bolting away in that unceremonious fashion from Mme. Doulenques a moment before. Now on the stairs a prodigious uproar was swelling louder and louder, while the shrill voice of the concierge rose high above the clamor:

"A scoundrelly brigand, I tell you! One of the same lot for sure who attacked the girl yesterday!" People were thronging upstairs, heavy footsteps sounded on the boards, a crowd of neighbors was hurrying up to the scene of action.

Instinctively Fandor stepped back on the landing. For nearly six months he had been living the life of a fugitive. For all those months the unfortunate young man had known the gnawing anxieties of a never-ending flight from all whose interest it might be to discover his identity. Now, finding himself pursued, trapped on this stairway, he lost his bead. Instead of quietly waiting till the concierge and her satellites came up to him and then explaining the misunderstanding, Fandor, realizing that Elizabeth would be long in recognizing her mistake, resolved to fly. Swiftly, noiselessly, nimbly, he mounted to the seventh story of the house, in the vague hope of finding a hiding place.

Fortune favored him. The house was an enormous block of worker's dwellings, made up of several separate buildings, connected together and served by several different staircases. Fandor, following the corridor running between the rooms on the topmost floor, had the luck to come upon the landing of a second flight of stairs. To make up his mind, to dart to the top, to scamper down the stairway, never stopping to know what had become of his pursuers, to dash into the street and reach the line of the outer boulevards at a run, was the work of a moment. Bathed in sweat and panting for breath, he reached the Boulevard de Belleville—and knew he was safe.

Safe, yes, but alas! atrociously disappointed. An hour ago he was on his way, in joyful anticipation, to visit Elizabeth Dollon, blessing the happy chance that was to bring him to the girl's presence. Now he had but caught a glimpse of her, had not so much as spoken with her. All he knew was that she believed him guilty of the most dreadful crimes, that she coupled his name with a name of horror, a name of blood, a name of terror, with the name of Fantômas! Exhausted, he sank on a bench. All day long, crushed by the hand of Fate that day by day accumulated ever-fresh calamities on his devoted head, he wandered miserably about the streets.

At nightfall he regained some degree of self-possession.

"I must think out a plan," he told himself. "I know now where she lives, I know where she is going to live, by the Lord, I can surely contrive to clear my character in her eyes." His aimless wanderings had led him to the neighborhood of Père-Lachaise, and he now set out slowly and sadly on his way back to the Rue Saint-Fargeau.

"I will tell Moche," he thought to himself, "that I waited for Elizabeth all day, and have not seen her . . . or else I will assure him her furniture is good enough . . . or, better still, as it's nine o'clock at night, I will slip up to my garret, of which I have a key, without seeing my worthy master at all. Tomorrow I shall be calmer, and can then see what's best to be done."

6. Prisoner of the Lantern

For nearly two hours, Jerome Fandor had been back in his garret, the storage room M. Moche had put at his disposal, albeit without making any further provision for his accommodation beyond supplying a tiny lamp to give him a glimmer of light. But the journalist was not yet asleep. Kneeling on the floor, his lamp in front of him, he was reading and re-reading the evening paper, *La Capitale,* which he had bought with the sacrifice of one of the three sous presented to him that morning by his generous master. What he read was of the deepest interest and importance to Fandor. The young man was trembling in every limb, his face wore an expression of horror and consternation. At intervals he punctuated his perusal with half-stifled exclamations and frantic shouts of dismay: "What does it mean? . . . the audacity of it! . . . the unspeakable effrontery! . . . Are we on the eve of a Reign of Terror? . . . After six months' truce, are we to behold once more this figure of ill-omen rise threatening, terrifying, on the horizon? . . . And to think of it, my name too, on all men's lips! . . . Confusion twice confounded! Once again the man succeeds in thrusting on another the responsibility for his crimes! . . . a Minister kidnapped! . . . the Chamber in consternation! . . . The whole country attacked in the person of its highest representatives! . . . Ah! Fantômas is indeed a genius, the genius of audacity, the king of frightfulness, the monster that assails everything, that fears nothing, for whom nothing is sacred!"

For the tenth time, Fandor re-read the article in *La Capitale.* On regaining the Rue Saint-Fargeau, worn out by the stress and strain of his visit to Elizabeth, he had heard the newsboys crying at the top of their voices the latest edition of *La Capitale.* People were fighting for the paper, passersby reading the news with looks of horror and feverish excitement. No sooner had

Fandor cast his eyes on the copy he had secured than he started violently. In enormous letters he read the headlines:

"*Fantômas at work again.—A Minister carried off by brigands.—Fantômas demands a million francs to disappear.—The Chamber votes defiance.*"

Now, back in his garret two hours ago, Fandor was reading, still incapable, in the mad whirl of his thoughts, of regaining anything like calmness, the amazing details of the extraordinary sitting of the Chamber, the Chamber wherein Fantômas had thrown defiance, a veritable ultimatum to France, the sitting that had been held that same afternoon at the moment he was on his way to Mlle. Dollon's.

That Fantômas should strike a sudden blow, he reflected, a blow so extraordinary as the one he has just delivered, is astounding, but it is not perhaps so crushing as I thought at first. In any case, what a fine argument it supplies in Juve's defense. If Fantômas manifests his activity abroad, in public, why, Juve can no longer be confounded with him, seeing Juve is a prisoner in the Santé!

Then, with ever increasing agitation, the journalist began to read the passage in the paper giving the shorthand report of the debate in the Chamber, which stated how his name, his, Jerome Fandor's name, had been uttered aloud as probably masking that of one of Fantômas' chief accomplices.

"By God!" soliloquized the young man, "it's plain enough. Everybody believes that Juve is Fantômas! Now Juve is in jail, debarred from action. The inevitable conclusion, therefore, is that one of his lieutenants, one of his accomplices, must be credited with the atrocity of today. As I am known to be Juve's friend, it is naturally on me the police fix their suspicions, it is against me the public launches its accusations. Yes, the game is up, my fate is sealed. No stone will be left unturned to hunt me down and arrest me."

Fandor's reflections might have lasted longer yet perhaps, he might perhaps have thought out a plan of escape, for he felt convinced the bloodhounds of the Prefecture of Police would find little difficulty in tracking him down to Père Moche's, if he had not suddenly had the impression of footsteps, stealthy footsteps, at his side. Springing instantly to his feet, the young man challenged: "Who goes there?" but there was no answer, the garret was absolutely silent.

"Yet surely I was not dreaming?" he muttered. Holding his breath, motionless as a statue, the journalist waited with ears straining. But no, he must have been mistaken; there was not a thing to attract his attention.

"I'm getting nervous," he muttered. "True, I've good reason to be just now."

He made a tour of inspection, but found nothing that seemed suspicious. This done, he returned and knelt down again in front of *La Capitale,* where the paper lay open on the floor. He was on the point of resuming reading when he had the same unaccountable impression again. This time it was certain, definite, unmistakable. He had felt a current of air pass like a breath over his face. It was no hallucination, for the journal he was reading had half lifted from the ground, the unshaded flame of the lamp had flickered. Once more he started up, again he made the tour of his attic.

"Nothing there!" he muttered, "nothing at all!"

But as he was returning slowly, hesitatingly, to the middle of the room, with pursed lips and frowning brow, suddenly, with a sharp pop, his lamp went out, while whirling before a powerful draft, *La Capitale* fluttered across the floor. It was stupefying! Instinctively, in the pale moonlight, Fandor stepped across the garret, meaning to set his back against the wall, in case of further eventualities. But he had not taken three steps before a choking cry escaped him. Thrown with horrid violence, a lasso had wound itself about his throat! He was dragged to the ground, his limbs paralyzed, half strangled, half dead!

Then, with horror unspeakable, he looked and saw . . . The window of the attic, a dormer window, had been opened noiselessly. Clinging to the crossbar of the casement a dim shape was silhouetted against the starlit sky. At a glance Fandor recognized the sinister apparition: It was a man clad in black, close-fitting tights, the face hidden in a deep cowl, the shoulders wrapped in a great black cloak! A figure of horror, at once clearly defined and indistinct, a shape that absorbed in the darkness, momentarily disappeared, only to reappear in dark outline on the whiter background of the wall: it was the figure of Fantômas!

In a single second Fandor had felt himself caught by the lasso, in one second he had been thrown to the ground, in one second he had noted the black, fantastic form of the bandit glide into the garret—and in that one second he recognized beyond possibility of doubt the Monarch of Crime, the Master of Terror!

It was Fantômas! Fantômas, and no other!

A grim apparition—this hooded man—this man who now held Fandor, his relentless pursuer, at his mercy. The journalist had fallen into the trap laid for him. He thought: "I am in Fantômas' power! I am a lost man!" To move a limb was impossible, to resist a wild dream. Yet no sooner had he gathered a clear idea of the danger threatening him than, calm again and confident, he awaited events.

Swift and silent, Fantômas stepped over the crossbar of the window, sprang down into the room, and to Fandor's side where he lay stretched helpless on the floor. In a turn of the hand he made fast the knots of his lasso, gagged the young man, then slackened the ligature that was almost strangling him, and this done, fell to taunting his victim with odious mockery. But what a strange voice, toneless, metallic, scarcely human, it was that Fantômas adopted!

"Monsieur Fandor, good day to you! Monsieur Jerome Fandor, Fantômas presents you his compliments."

Helpless, gagged, bound hand and foot, Fandor could make no reply whatsoever. Only the eyes were alive in the dead face, and in those eyes Jerome Fandor concentrated all his power of resolution. With calm intensity he fixed his gaze on his enemy's face, on the eyes that glittered luminous under the black folds of the impenetrable mask, staring back unflinching.

"He can kill me," thought the young man, "but he shall never think he can frighten me!"

But Fantômas had dropped his bantering tone, and it was in a serious voice he now spoke:

"You were reading *La Capitale,* so you know the latest news? Interesting, is it not? . . . Unfortunately, Monsieur Fandor, the fools have thought fit to lay to your account the claim formulated by me against Parliament. At this moment the police are looking for you, tracking you down, determined to arrest you. A pity, Fandor! No, I could never allow that. I like you too well. In ten minutes officers will be entering this room to arrest you. But never fear, have no anxiety! If I am here, it is simply and solely to help you escape their reach. Surely Fantômas owes this much to you, to protect you against your friends, the agents of the law!"

A peal of laughter emphasized the bandit's last words, and Fandor was still pondering what precisely these expressions signified when Fantômas turned his attention to a task the object of which seemed quite inexplicable. He proceeded to drag out into the middle of the floor a tall stool, and depositing it there, climbed on the top, a maneuver which brought him on a level with an enormous Chinese lantern, one of those huge lanterns of wrought iron and colored glass, of the kind to be seen in the streets of Peking, and which are sometimes imported from the East to be suspended in the vestibules of houses. By what strange chances the thing had come to be hanging from the ceiling of old Moche's garret, it would be hard to say. Anyway, Fantômas must long ago have noticed its being there. He leaned over towards it, opened the door, and this done, descended from his perch.

"There, Monsieur Fandor," he announced, "inside there, you'll be in the best boxes for seeing the play—I may say in the grated boxes, for I'm pretty confident nobody will see you. One can see outwards from within, but not the reverse."

With a catlike dexterity, the man slipped off the long, black coat enveloping him in its folds, and without seeming to make any special effort, took up Fandor on his shoulders, mounted the stool once more, and deposited the young man inside the lantern!

"Now, Mr. Journalist, I refasten the door, by way of precaution, but I give you full leave to look out of the window to see what happens. You'll see, no doubt, the way Fantômas fights for his friends, and even for you, his enemy!"

Yes, he would look, no fear of that—and Fandor, still bound and ensconced inside the Chinese lantern, into which Fantômas had forced him, his limbs cramped, his flesh bruised by the cords, half suffocating, glued his face to the painted panes of his extraordinary prison.

Jumping down again, Fantômas set to work with the utmost rapidity. He pushed back the stool against the wall. He hauled up against the door a huge trunk stuffed full of papers to reinforce the crazy panels. From his pocket he extracted a screwdriver, and in a very few minutes had taken off the lock. Then, kneeling against the trunk, he produced a revolver, the nickel-plated barrel of which glittered in the moonlight, and passing the muzzle through the loophole where the lock had been torn away, waited.

Minute after minute passed in deadly silence. Presently, as often happens in the most tragic situations, Fandor in the midst of all his poignant anxieties, began to be tormented by yet another apprehension—a fantastic fear that the lantern in which Fantômas had imprisoned him was not strong enough to bear his weight.

"I'm going to come tumbling down!" thought the journalist, "to come tumbling down directly, with a crash of broken glass and an appalling rattle. That's something Fantômas has failed to foresee. Pray God, it might upset his plans!"

But the lantern held firm, and by the time he had been a quarter of an hour shut up in his odd prison cell, Fandor had ceased to give a thought to the possibility of taking a fall. His whole attention was again concentrated on Fantômas, but the brigand remained perfectly still and seemed to have forgotten the other's very existence. On his knees, his revolver all the time pointed through the improvised loophole, he was evidently watching for the arrival of someone or something.

And it was in a flash, without his having so much as given

a start, or moved a muscle, or uttered an exclamation, that the sharp explosion of his weapon rang out, followed by the dull thud of a body dropping!

Instantly the whole house resounded with cries of pain, shouts and screams, and the din of tramping feet. "Go on! Break down the door!" Fandor heard a voice yelling. Next moment two more shots tore the air, two other voices bellowed in agony, two more wounded men sank heavily to the ground. Then a mighty thrust shook the door and overset the trunk.

With one bound, Fantômas was at the window, Fantômas had disappeared, yelling as he vanished: "Hurrah! Three officers brought down! Hurrah!" while into the garret, preceded by the blinding rays of electric torches, sprang a whole troop of men, shouting, swearing, revolvers in hand.

A prisoner in his lantern, still gagged, still tied hand and foot, Fandor seemed the victim of an atrocious nightmare. Scarce had the men entered the room before Fandor realized the full horror of his situation, guessed the whole secret of the villainous design. The men were police officers, they were shouting: "Jerome Fandor, hands up or you're a dead man!"

Then they began to search the garret, to turn everything upside down, *hunting for him!* The young man felt a cold sweat bead his temples. What had been in Fantômas' mind? He knew it only too well. The brigand had spared his life once more only to keep alive the man who he was planning should bear the whole weight of responsibility for his, Fantômas' acts. If he had tied up the journalist instead of killing him, it was because Fandor was now marked by public outrage as being Fantômas. He had hidden him in the lantern, he had taken post behind the door, he had three several times fired on the police and disappeared, all this only because he chose to make men think that Fandor—the man they were come to arrest—really was Fantômas, and that it was he, Fandor—not Fantômas—who had used his revolver to such deadly effect!

"Let the lantern give way," thought the prisoner, "and tumble me into the middle of the constables, and I'm done for! They will kill me—and they will be justified."

Meantime the empty garret was the scene of a frenzied search. The police, who had invaded the place like pillagers into a captured city, were now convinced that the man they sought for had escaped. "The scoundrel!" screamed one of them, who running to the window had discovered a rope hanging from it, the rope that doubtless had helped Fantômas to escape over the roofs, "the scoundrel!"

Fandor could not see the man well, but he had a better view of another officer who answered him. It was Michel, Inspector Michel, who had once served under Juve's orders! "My word," the Inspector was saying, "but the villain had planned it all perfectly. He was expecting us. While we were breaking in the door, he had plenty of time to get away. . . . Curse him! To think three of us have got themselves knocked out of time!"

But at this point a constable who was still busy turning out a corner of the garret, interrupted his chief with a sharp exclamation: "Look, sir, just look here!"—"What is it?"—It was a small, shiny object—Fandor could see it quite plainly from his eyrie in the lantern—which the man held out for his chief's inspection. The latter seemed prodigiously surprised at sight of it:

"God bless us! Where did you find that?"

"In the corner over there . . . It means something, that does."

"Means something? . . . It means everything!"

The other men had gathered round the two:

"What is it, sir?"

"Look! an astonishing find! Leon has just picked up a button of the uniform the collectors of the Comptoir National wear."

While this was going on, a series of ominous cracks had seriously alarmed the unfortunate young man who was still hunched up on his uncomfortable perch. Meantime, however, the police officers had disconsolately taken their departure. They had arrived a dozen men, they returned to headquarters only nine.

Hardly had the constables gone when, suddenly, in a moment, without further warning, the bottom of the Chinese lantern fell out. With a mighty crash Fandor tumbled out onto the floor. Luckily, the ceiling was low. The young man was not hurt, but he lay stunned on the ground, and for some seconds did not know where he was. Then, quickly, with his usual courage, he regained command of himself.

"Oh God!" he reflected, "I made a terrible noise in falling. Unless everybody is out of the house helping to remove the wounded men, they'll come here in a rush and find me." Then, straining his muscles, Jerome Fandor, in spite of the intolerable pain these efforts caused him, struggled to unloose his bonds. At all costs he must regain his liberty.

"Ah!" he muttered at last. "I think, down my legs . . ." the rope that tied his ankles together had, in fact, yielded a little to his strenuous exertions. A few seconds more, and the rope came loose, he could shake off the coils altogether. He was able to get on his feet, he could get an arm free, unbind his fastenings altogether. But so cramped were his limbs, so numbed by long confinement, that the first step he tried to take, he staggered and had to sit down again.

"If they come up and find me," he told himself again, "I am done for!"

But little by little the circulation was restored. He could stand on his feet, he could walk!

Then, with the swiftness of decision that was characteristic of him, Jerome Fandor, without an instant's hesitation, hurried to the window, and leaned out over the sill.

"That's it," he muttered, "the police have forgotten to remove the rope, or more likely they have left it there as a piece of evidence in view of the further inquiries they mean to institute, no doubt. Good! Where Fantômas found a way, I shall know how to follow his lead. But quick! There's not a moment to lose."

No sooner said than done. Following Fantômas' example he climbed over the sill, seized the rope and let himself slide down into the void below. The night had turned dark, and the moon was hidden. As the journalist descended, he could barely make out, some yards below him, the dim outline of the roof of a tall building, and beyond again an endless succession of other roofs, broken by a forest of chimneys rising like specters into the night sky.

7. Fantômas' Ultimatum

"Long live the Minister of Justice! Bravo, Ferrand! Bravo! Bravo!" These and other cordial acclamations were still echoing in Désiré Ferrand's ears as the Minister, in his elegant livery brougham, returned calmly and peaceably to the Place Vendôme about one o'clock in the morning, accompanied only by his Parliamentary Secretary, the Conseiller Navarret. Ferrand was on his way back from the grand amphitheater of the Sorbonne, where he had presided over an associated meeting of the students in law.

Désiré Ferrand was a man of boundless ambition. A General Practitioner in the provinces, and in no way interested in the science he practiced, he had found himself from earliest manhood attracted, fascinated by the allurements and difficulties of politics. His profession as a doctor, a profession he exercised with a calculated generosity, provided admirable opportunities for winning the votes of his fellow citizens. At thirty-four he had been elected Deputy.

Eighteen months later, having attracted the favorable notice of the Chamber by his wise common sense, and the maturity of his views, he was invited by Monnier to join his Cabinet in the position of an Under Secretary of State. Then, in course of time, as resignations or deaths opened the way, Ferrand secured the portfolio of the Minister of Justice, the highest functionary after the President of the Council!

From that moment, his career was one series of triumphs. Far from setting him back, the extraordinary adventure of a few days before had actually added to his popularity. Henceforth he felt persuaded he had only to steer his bark adroitly to arrive at the very highest honors the country could bestow.

On reaching his rooms, the young Minister cast a weary, worried look at the heap of documents, whose contents he must master. Smiling to himself: "All that stuff," he said, "is marked 'urgent,' and for several days now a whole pile of these documents has been lying here that I've not even looked at. I wonder what really happens in a Ministry to matters that are *not* 'urgent'?"

Thereupon the Minister set feverishly to work at the task of sorting the voluminous correspondence heaped up in front of him. Two or three times his brow contracted, he made a gesture of exasperation:

"Again!" he groaned, "again! it is really abominable!"

From time to time, in fact, lurking among letters and papers, hidden under bundles of documents, Désiré Ferrand kept coming upon a little memorandum, identical in every instance, but repeated in quite a number of copies. It was headed: *The Million*. Its text, which never varied, was a discreetly worded and anonymous reminder of the claim, rather say the order, formulated by the person calling himself Fantômas, who called upon the Chamber to pay the ransom fixed by himself.

The fourth time this happened, the Minister banged his fist heavily on the table: "It is past endurance," he vociferated. "If one of my attachés has ventured on this pleasantry, the first thing I do tomorrow will be to show my gentleman the door."

But it was getting very late. To snatch a few hours' sleep was imperative. Within a few minutes, Ferrand had put out the light and gone to bed. With closed eyes, he was trying to get to sleep, when, just as the pleasant drowsiness that precedes slumber was creeping over him, the Minister sprang half up in bed, listening intently.

He had heard footsteps. Then he leapt to the floor, convinced someone was coming into the room, though he knew he was alone, that he must be alone, in his private suite! Too much alone, perhaps, he thought, as he remembered that at night the Ministry was entirely deserted and that his man slept in a sep- arate building a long way off. "Perhaps I have been unwise," he reflected, but his reflections were suddenly cut short.

Just as Ferrand, alarmed by the noise he had heard, was making instinctively for the electric switch at the other end of the room, the light suddenly flashed out, dazzling his eyes, grown accustomed to the dark. Someone with the same intention as himself, but with greater quickness, had anticipated him.

Désiré Ferrand gave a cry of terror. A few yards away, a masked man stood confronting him, a grim, appalling figure. He was wrapped in a black cloak, and carried a cudgel in his hand.

"The man of last week—my assailant!" cried the Minister, turning pale.

Yes, before him stood the redoubtable outlaw, who, a week before, had, with the help of mysterious confederates, laid hands on the Minister of Justice, had kept him secluded from his fellow men, and only restored him to liberty conditionally, delivering, in a letter addressed to the President of the Council, an ultimatum couched in threatening language.

Désiré Ferrand waved a hand ordering the intruder to leave the room, but the latter strode forward unheeding.

"Désiré Ferrand," he proclaimed, "the hour is come to obey me, you must decide . . . you have five seconds."

The unhappy Minister recoiled, utterly confounded: unarmed, barefooted, in night attire, he felt himself at a manifest disadvantage facing the scoundrel confronting him.

But Désiré Ferrand was no coward. Reckoning up his chances of escape, he put between himself and his antagonist the great desk littered with endless documents, and again repeated his order:

"Go," he reiterated, "go! . . . I will have you arrested."

But the man in black broke into a sardonic laugh:

"Fantômas does not take orders," he declared, "it is for Fantômas to issue commands. For the last time, I repeat that I demand a million francs. Give it to me!"

"But," protested Ferrand, "where do you expect me to get the money from? It is odious, abominable, your effrontery is unparalleled!"

"Unparalleled is the word, sir. Fantômas has no equal—only despicable imitators."

The Minister resumed:

"Neither Government nor Ministers will ever consent to obey you. *I* will never consent. Why, then," he added gloomily, "we should have nothing left us but to retire discomfited, dishonored, the laughingstock of France!"

Fantômas advanced a step or two nearer, and in insinuating tones:

"All said and done," he hinted, "I understand your scruples, and I quite see it is difficult for you to agree, officially that is, under pain of risking your post. Well, so be it. I now propose a compromise. There is the Secret Service fund. My million will be charged on it without scandal or publicity. You will hand me over the sum I need; in return, I will disappear. Is it a bargain?"

Désiré Ferrand was boiling with rage and indignation:

"Atrocious monster!" he screamed, "begone! How have I borne to hear out your odious proposals! Be sure, this very day the whole police force shall receive the most stringent orders to seize you! I do not know who you are, but no matter for that, I will punish you."

Fantômas folded his arms across his chest. Through his black mask his eyes flashed lightning at his unfortunate victim.

"So it is war?" he asked. "War to the knife? War to the death? . . . I bid you reflect . . ."

Ferrand made no reply. Seizing the first thing he caught sight of on his writing-table, he grasped a silver paper-knife in his hand, ready to sell his life dearly.

Fantômas saw the Minister was incorruptible. "Be it death then!" he grinned his defiance.

With a sudden, swift movement, the brigand whirled his cudgel round like a sling and hurled it full in the other's face. But the Minister ducked his head, the weapon missed its aim and struck the wall with a dull thud.

"Help!" yelled Ferrand, dashing for the window. But Fantômas barred the way, and a grim chase, pursuer and pursued, began in Désiré Ferrand's chamber. The Minister, with the energy of despair, fled before his assailant, throwing down obstacle after obstacle in his way, oversetting chairs, tables, every piece of furniture he could lay hands on.

Thus, following and fleeing, the two men made the circuit of the room, but just as fast as the fugitive cast a stumbling-block in the other's way, it was cleared away and tossed into a corner.

So the mad race went on. The competitors were well matched. No doubt one was armed, he had a revolver, but equally without doubt, he dared not use it for fear of making a noise. The thickness of the carpet deadened the sound of the steps, the heavy curtains intercepted the Minister's frantic appeals for help.

But suddenly, the wretched man, running barefoot as he was, gave a cry of pain, followed by another and another. Next moment he staggered, fell to his knees, cried out again; then tried to rise, but could not struggle to his feet. Blood began to trickle from the soles of his feet, from his thighs, his wrists, the arm on which he had fallen.

A last despairing groan was succeeded by utter silence, the tortured man had fainted. Fantômas, taking advantage of his adversary's helplessness, had snatched up his cudgel again, and with a yell of triumph, dealt him a stunning blow on the head. Then, calmly walking up to his victim without a trace of compunction, he lifted him bodily by the shoulders and knees and carried him to his bed, where he laid him on his back.

Ferrand's nightshirt gaped open over the chest. Fantômas passed the palm of his hand lightly over the damp skin to verify the exact position of the heart that was still beating in hurried jerks. Then, drawing from beneath his cloak a long, fine needle, the cowardly victor plunged it into his victim's body below the left breast and pierced the heart.

Holding a mirror to the lips, Fantômas made doubly sure that Désiré Ferrand had ceased to breathe. Yes, he was dead, stone dead!

Thereupon, walking quietly over to the switch, he plunged the room in darkness, and in the darkness vanished.

It was now about three o'clock in the morning. The concierge at the door of the Ministry opening on the Rue Cambon was awakened from a sound sleep by someone tapping softly at his window.

"Open, please!" came the usual request, in calm, deliberate accents.

In a thick voice the porter, still half asleep, asked mechanically who it was asking to be let out.

After a moment's hesitation, the answer came:

"An *attaché*, special service in the Minister's secretariat."

The concierge drew the cord, and a second or two later heard the door close.

He had just opened, without a thought of suspicion, for the murderer of Désiré Ferrand! As he dropped off to sleep again, the man merely grumbled to himself:

"Pretty hours for working, I don't think . . . One of them bloodsuckers who hang about Ministers. That fellow who's just gone, no doubt he's been staying late to work so as he needn't turn out so early tomorrow morning."

8. A Wireless from Mid-Atlantic

"A nail . . . another nail! Monsieur Havard, where did you put the others?"

"In the little bowl on the side table," replied the Chief of the Criminal Investigation Department from where he knelt on the carpet, while Professor Ardell, who was holding between his thumb and forefinger the nail he had just found, stood up again, rubbing his back with his free hand.

"Extraordinary! Most extraordinary!" muttered the learned professor, while M. Casamajols, who was also present, questioned the doctor anxiously:

"Well, your diagnosis, Professor?"

"Well! Monsieur le Procureur, my diagnosis is perfectly plain and simple, and equally positive, M. Désiré is dead, and he has been dead several hours now."

At seven o'clock that morning, the discovery of the dead body of the Minister of Justice lying lifeless on his bed had thrown the personnel of the Ministry into the wildest commotion. The domestics, well trained servants, had immediately advised the police, and M. Havard, hurrying with all speed to the Ministry of Justice, had passed on the intelligence to M. Casamajol's private residence and sent an urgent summons to Professor Ardell. The three men, when they arrived almost simultaneously at the Place Vendôme, had been forced to abandon any false hopes they might have entertained the instant they set eyes on the unfortunate man. Désiré Ferrand was dead! For the tenth time the professor confirmed the fact to M. Casamajols, who could not believe his own eyes and ears.

M. Havard, pale and haggard, intervened:

"Dead!" he exclaimed, "you mean murdered, do you not, Professor?"

"Why, yes, I do mean murdered. The fact is obvious. M.

Désiré Ferrand, awakened suddenly in the night, was struck with an instrument which evidently stunned him without leaving any wound—perhaps one of those cudgels murderers sometimes use."

"I see what you mean," M. Havard broke in, "a sandbag, a sack, that is, filled with sand. It makes the most deadly weapon you can imagine when wielded like a sling."

The professor signified his agreement with the Chief's version of the affair, and went on:

"The victim, thus incapacitated, nothing easier than to pierce his heart with a needle. As a matter of fact, we have discovered one driven in under the left breast of the unfortunate man."

Noting the disordered state of the room, M. Casamajols observed:

"Before the end there was evidently a struggle, a desperate struggle," and the professor agreed.

But M. Havard now broke in again:

"A struggle, however, that was suddenly interrupted when the Minister, who was barefooted, stopped all of a sudden and fell to the floor. Evidently the aggressor, in order to handle his man more easily, and taking advantage of a favorable opportunity, emptied a bagful of nails over the carpet, the nails we have been picking up all this time."

"You are quite right," agreed the professor, "the little superficial punctures we noticed scarring the dead man's limbs were no doubt caused by the nails scattered about the floor."

"The scoundrel! He provided for everything, it appears—left nothing to chance."

M. Havard was profoundly agitated and perplexed. Striding up and down the room like a caged lion, casting furtive glances at the Minister's body, he pondered the tragic origins of the crime and strove to fathom the mystery of who the criminal was.

At seven in the morning he had been awakened by the telephone ringing him up from the Ministry of Justice. Summoned in all haste to the Place Vendôme, in a quarter of an hour he was at the scene of action, questioning the staff, examining the

Minister's bedroom, the adjoining apartments and the precincts generally of the mansion, but entirely, absolutely without result.

Subsequently, however, when he came to search among the papers littering the Minister's desk, he had been astonished, as had Ferrand himself, by the great number of holograph memoranda, all relating to Fantômas' million francs and no doubt intentionally intermingled with the "urgent" correspondence. It was deliberately done, it was evidently the sign manual once more of the criminal, it was Fantômas, who, in an ironic mood, anxious to rouse public opinion afresh, thus affirmed his presence and confirmed his impunity.

Fantômas?—no, it could not be Fantômas! For six months past, M. Havard had cherished the absolute conviction that the notorious criminal had been personated by his subordinate, Inspector Juve, of the Criminal Investigation Department, who under pretense of relentlessly tracking down the elusive ruffian, had carried out a whole series of thefts and other crimes under this sinister disguise. But Juve was in prison, there was no shadow of a doubt about that. Then what was one to think?

As time went on and the day lengthened, corridors and antechambers grew more and more crowded, hummed louder and louder with excited talk—magistrates having appointments to confer with the Chief, electors from Ferrand's constituency come to see their member, officials and employees coming and going unceasingly. Outside the very door of the death chamber eager voices were raised in discussion and dispute, regrets for the past mingled with hopes for the future.

So far, however, the tidings of Désiré Ferrand's death had hardly spread beyond official circles. The Elysée, the Ministries, were aware of the tragedy, the public knew little or nothing. But this was not to last long. Suddenly a swarm of newsboys, crying special editions, burst with strident shouts into the Place Vendôme, debouching from the Rue de la Paix, deploying under the windows of the Ministry, then tearing off like a whirlwind towards the Tuileries, red and breathless, their papers selling like hot cakes at a premium. The special edition of *La Capitale* penetrated to the private apartments of the Ministry, and M. Havard, impatient to know in what terms the tragic story was told and to read the criticisms of the police with which the Press was evidently supplementing the narrative of the murder, secured a copy of the paper. Looking over his shoulder, M. Casamajols read in huge capitals, immediately below the name of the journal:

"Assassination of the Minister of Justice."

Below this again, figured the cryptic headline:

"Will he arrest Fantômas?"

"That question, M. Havard," M. Casamajols slyly suggested, "is probably addressed to you." The head of the Criminal Investigation Department made no reply, but with pursed lips, ran his eye rapidly over the detailed account of Ferrand's death, though without learning anything he did not know already, and then went on to the article he believed, like M. Casamajols, to specially concern himself. But as he read on, M. Havard was lost in deeper and deeper wonderment. The article in question ran as follows:

"From mid-Atlantic, from aboard the liner 'La Lorraine,' which sailed the day before yesterday from New York, bound for Le Havre, comes the information by wireless that the American detective, Tom Bob, a passenger on the vessel in question, strongly and justly moved by the daring acts of violence committed of late in Paris, has announced his intention to devote all his time and all his energy, from the first moment of his arrival in Europe, to the discovery and arrest of Fantômas."

The writer concluded the article with the words: *"Let us wish Tom Bob every good luck, but will he arrest Fantômas?"*

M. Havard and M. Casamajols looked at each other completely at a loss.

"Do you suppose it is serious, this story?" asked the latter. "Surely it must be a newspaper canard . . . very American, too American . . . I don't believe it, do you?"

"Alas!" declared M. Havard, very much put out, "I am bound to allow that this Tom Bob exists, and even that he enjoys a certain reputation in the New York police force, but then, to advertise himself like that, really!"

M. Casamajols suggested with a smile of irony:

"Well, Havard, suppose Tom Bob *did* run down and arrest Fantômas?"

Lifting his hands to heaven, the Chief of the Investigation Department turned his back on the Procureur Général:

"God Almighty!" he swore, "hadn't we enough to worry us, enough to make us look ridiculous, without this Tom Bob shoving his finger in the pie. Upon my word, it's the last straw, that! . . ."

Havard stopped dead in the middle of his tirade; the door of the room had opened.

"Do you mean me by that, Monsieur Havard?" demanded the newcomer.

M. Havard curbed a gesture of annoyance. Decidedly he was in Fortune's bad books that day. He drew back, and bowing low to the President of the Council—it was no other than M. Monnier himself who asked the question.

"I do assure you, sir," he replied respectfully, "I should never allow myself to think such a thing of you."

9. The Blue Chestnut

"Get along then, that's no way to treat people! What's he want with me, anyway, the nasty fellow?"

Nini Guinon was furious. Turning sharply round, she thus apostrophized an individual who had just signaled his presence by tickling her ribs more roughly than agreeably. It was a Monday, and about two o'clock in the afternoon. Nini had just issued from the Poissonnière Gate. Mounting the bank overhanging the moat of the fortifications and turning to the left, she was making for Saint-Ouen. The young woman stared suspiciously at the man who was following her without a word, good, bad or indifferent, a smile of doubtful import on his face.

Presently, reassured more or less by her examination of the stranger, Nini added:

"I thought it was the cops."

The man shrugged his shoulders. "D'you think I belong to the police? Do I look like it?"

"No, you don't," Nini admitted, "but come, let's have a look at your face. What does this here masquerading mean, eh?"

Obeying the young woman's demand, the other turned his face towards her. The cheeks were muffled in a great yellow silk handkerchief.

"That's along of my dominoes," he said, "I've had toothache for the last three days!"

"Well, what then?" pursued Nini.

"Why, I'm in funds today, especially as how it's Monday, and I'm going on the spree . . . suppose we make the bust together, eh?"

Superciliously, Nini looked her interlocutor up and down. "Nothing doing today," she told him, "I've got my man."

"Where are you going?"

"You're awfully curious, ain't you? Still, as the gentleman

wants to know, we've arranged to meet at the *Blue Chestnut*—that's plain and simple enough, what?"

"Why, yes," the other agreed, "but as it happens, I'm going there, too."

"Then, march on in front," ordered the girl, "and I'll stick behind. I don't care to look as if I were making up to fellows around these parts."

The man was all docility and obeyed instantly. Walking a few steps ahead of the young harlot, but every now and then casting a furtive glance over his shoulder to make sure the girl was following on the same road as himself, he stumped off in the direction of the *Blue Chestnut*, seeming very well pleased with the beginning he had so far made. With a quick movement he swept the hair lower on his forehead and pulled out the handkerchief he had wrapped round his jaws under pretense of protecting his aching teeth against the cold.

"So much to the good," he thought to himself. "She hasn't recognized me—and I have good hopes it'll be the same with the others."

Who was this mysterious person who had made bold to squeeze Mlle. Nini's waist as she was peaceably leaving the city by the Porte de Poissonniere? It was none other than Jerome Fandor!

For some days past the young journalist had been leading an absolutely appalling existence. Events had followed quick on each other's heels, each more disconcerting, more overwhelming than the other. Chance and mischance had thrown him into adventures that grew more and more baffling, and seemed to him to leave no loophole for escape.

First his meeting with Elizabeth Dollon, then his connection with old Moche—a tricky scamp he felt he could not trust—then after being unjustly accused by Elizabeth, he had been odiously victimized through Fantômas' vile machinations, bringing him under the strongest suspicion of having caused the death of three policemen. And all this, just a few hours after Parliament had acclaimed him one of the authors of the violent attack on the Minister of Justice.

Escaped by a miracle from the clutches of the police, the journalist had ever since the tragic night in M. Moche's garret led an insufferable existence, hardly daring to go out at all, and then only at night in the most out-of-the-way districts, spending whole days hiding in slums, concealed in ragpickers' hovels, in constant terror of being caught. And now, to put the copestone on his misery had come the assassination of Désiré Ferrand, a mystery still unsolved, a crime without doubt the work of Fantômas, thought Fandor, but which no less surely would rouse the Criminal Investigation Department to renewed exertions, and render his continued evasion more than ever precarious.

Yet Fandor was full of courage; he must not give in, it was all important he should remain at liberty, for the journalist was now firmly convinced that he was embarked on the right track, and that it would not be long now before he would unmask Fantômas' accomplices, perhaps Fantômas himself into the bargain. Luck, good luck, had in fact brought him in touch with a crew of shady individuals, the instruments and intermediaries of old Moche's nefarious schemes. Now these folks made no concealment amongst themselves of the fact that they were in the habit of receiving orders anonymous but peremptory about the source of which, however, they did not trouble their heads. They served and were glad to serve as Fantômas' lieutenants, they were in the pay of that notorious brigand. To trace back events to their source would be the surest way to discover the head that set all these arms in motion.

"I'm going to the *Blue Chestnut*," Nini Guinon had told him—and Fandor had boldly replied that at that very moment he, too, was on his way to spend the afternoon at that notorious resort of the Paris criminal world. In fact the discovery that Paulet's mistress was bound for the *Blue Chestnut*—a suburban semi-rural resort just outside the fortifications, and a favorite rendezvous with crooks and demireps of all descriptions—to meet "her man" had given the journalist a lively glow of satisfaction. Days ago he had come to the resolution of shadowing the young streetwalker, getting to know her comings and goings, and through her getting into close touch with the band of her nefarious associates.

And lo! in a moment his hopes were to be realized. Nini was going to the very spot where all these good, or rather bad, people would be gathered. Decidedly Fandor's lucky star was in the ascendant, he was to enjoy the priceless advantage of meeting and making closer acquaintance with that questionable character, the mysterious apache Paulet, whom the journalist already suspected, not without good reason, perhaps, of having murdered the bank messenger.

Moreover, he was feeling no small satisfaction at the success of his makeup, which had proved so admirable a disguise. Nini Guinon, of course, knew him quite well. She had seen him only a few days before, he was one of the gang and the reputed murderer of the police officers, if not perhaps of the Minister himself. His face and personality could not have faded from the girl's memory. Yet for five minutes he had been talking with her, and she had not recognized him!

"All goes well," the journalist congratulated himself, as he made his way into the garden of the *Blue Chestnut*. Yes, he was certainly in luck. The place that Monday afternoon was crowded with customers, a large number seated about the scattered tables, each of which with its load of wine bottles formed the nucleus of a group of laughing, chattering men and girls.

Fandor took his seat unobtrusively at the foot of a table, endeavoring to pass unnoticed while he consumed a modest half-pint and listened to his neighbor's conversation. He was just asking himself how he could best join in the talk himself when circumstances afforded him the opportunity.

A wave of excitement swept the garden from end to end. A gay companion, a musician with an old guitar under his arm, had just appeared, a man Fandor knew of old. It was one Bougille, the vagabond Bougille, the man with the shaggy beard and clownish face, Bougille the honest tramp, the incorrigible wanderer. The old fellow was well known and well loved at the *Blue Chestnut,* where on fête days he would often come to reap the reward in small change of his talents as a music-maker.

"A dance, a dance! the *Sonneuse!*" the company demanded with one voice, while all eyes turned in the direction of "The Beadle" and all hands pointed to "Big Ernestine."

Slowly, hands in pockets, with an affected air and a look of satisfaction, which he tried to hide, the man addressed the crowd:

"So, it's us you want to get at . . . must have us dance it for you again, eh? . . . well, well, off we go."

Cigarette stuck between his lips, cap cocked over one ear, the apache gripped Ernestine by the nape of the neck, whirled the girl round, and round again, to bring her facing him, then ordered her roughly:

"Go ahead, wench, give it to 'em, I say!"

At this Bougille struck up the tune, and the couple began their evolutions.

At first it was a slow waltz, with no precise rhythm, but dubious attitudes, languishing poses, embraces suggestive of passionate abandonment. Then, with a sudden brutality, the man hurled his partner away from him, caught her by the shoulders, threw her to the ground, then passing his arm under her supple waist, raised her to her feet, then lifted her up against his breast. Then, three times in succession, while "Big Ernestine" lay passive, "The Beadle," striking an attitude half Hercules, half acrobat, whirled the woman about in his arms and beat her head on the earth.

A thunder of applause broke out on every side. For sure there was not another pair to match "The Beadle" and "Big Ernestine" at dancing the *Sonneuse*. And what a dance it was, where the cavalier had to mimic the act of breaking his partner's skull against the ground as apaches beat to death peaceable citizens against the curb of the sidewalk.

It was fine, it was magnificent, the crowd was thrilled, electrified, and a young blackguard, "Beauty Boy" by nickname, caught by the wave of hot enthusiasm that stirred the passions of them all, seized the opportunity to give a bite at the nape of Nini's neck, who cuffed him soundly for his pains.

"Look where you're going, you idiot!" roared a furious voice as "Beauty Boy" fell foul of a shabby individual in his flight to escape the offended Nini's vengeance. It was no other than M. Moche. What could the old fellow be doing there? He was dirtier, shabbier, and more bent than ever. At sight of him, Fandor was filled with alarm, but at the same time it struck him that Moche's presence might prove useful to him. Yes, undoubtedly, it was a piece of good luck to find the old man had come to the *Blue Chestnut*. Assuredly, under pretext of dancing and amusing themselves, the band must have gathered there to receive their secret instructions from the chief, who doubtless was no other than Fantômas. The moment Fandor set eyes on Père Moche, he told himself: "Ha! Won't be long now before something fresh turns up!"

Meantime the journalist took good care not to show himself to the dubious individual in whose service he had been engaged for twenty-four hours. He had far from pleasant recollections of his stay at Moche's, and it might well be the latter was equally out of conceit with him. Quite possibly the old advocate believed it was he had killed the police officers, very possibly again, by way of ingratiating himself with the force, he might not hesitate to deliver up the supposed murderer into their clutches, should opportunity offer.

At the same time the young man slipped surreptitiously behind Moche, while the latter was talking with the "Beauty Boy." He overheard all they said:

"Lend me a yellow boy," the young apache was asking his companion. "It's not just for larks, I tell you, it's for biz."

"Why, what are you up to, eh?" the other asked in his turn.

"Beauty Boy" explained: "Tomorrow's Monday, ain't it? Well, Tuesday's the day the swell Trans-Atlantic reaches Le Havre with all the rich American travelers aboard. So I'm going to make my little collection, as usual—you know my game, eh, M. Moche?"

"Lord! No, not over well," declared the old scamp, doubtless with the idea of extracting a more definite account of the other's plans.

"But it's as plain as can be," retorted the apache. "Day before the boat comes in, I hook it to Le Havre, dressed up to the nines, then I slip into the special train where the swagger dames are, and on the journey up I get to work. It's mostly purses I do, now and then a ring, a bit of jewelry, or pocketbook. All that lot, when they step ashore, are upset, bewildered, sick, tired, *they* never care to kick up a dust if they happen to find their pockets have been gone through."

Père Moche nodded approvingly.

"Not bad," he laughed, "not bad! You're a clever fellow, my boy, for all your silly looks and dandified airs."

"Only," pursued the apache, "one must anyway have one's return ticket, and as it happens, I'm cleaned out just now."

"Whew!" muttered the old miser.

But "Beauty Boy" returned to his charge:

"Come now, don't be a mean cuss, hand over four crowns, won't you?"

At last Père Moche yielded to the other's eager importunities and forked it over. But, like a good businessman, he struck a bargain with the borrower that the latter, on his return, that is to say on the day after next, should pay him back thirty francs.

The cash once in his pocket, the apache vanished. Fandor had overheard it all, besides catching other scraps of conversation from one and another of the band, from which he gathered only one thing clearly, and that was that at bottom every one of them was upset about the arrival of the redoubtable and mysterious Tom Bob, whose coming was announced with such a flourish of trumpets and noisy advertisement—a proceeding by-the-by he, Fandor, deemed highly injudicious.

The journalist noted the "Beauty Boy's" departure, and he could not help thinking that it would be greatly to *his* advantage, too, if only he could get to Le Havre. But alas! he hadn't a sou and could not borrow from Père Moche, as the apache had done, inasmuch as he could not very well urge the same reasons to justify the loan. Still the idea tormented him that he *must* go to Le Havre. It was all important for him to get to know Tom Bob at the earliest possible moment, so to say before everybody else. He was still cudgeling his brains to discover some way of realizing his project when suddenly he shuddered to hear a hoarse, angry voice growling in his ear:

"Scoundrel, brigand, murderer, aren't you ashamed to show your face? Why don't I have you run in on the spot? Will you rid me of the sight of you, now, this instant, you hellhound of calamity!"

Fandor wheeled round in consternation, dumbfounded by this avalanche of abuse, this maelstrom of words. His eyes opened wide in amazement. It was old Moche who was addressing him in these furious terms—Moche, his face working with passion, unable to contain himself for anger.

The old scoundrel went on with a hypocritical assumption of righteous indignation.

"When I think how I befriended you, how I saved you in your extremity, and then you came and murdered people in my house and committed atrocious crimes, I don't know, I really do not know, you villain, what hinders me . . ."

Fandor looked his man calmly in the face. For one moment he had entertained the notion of seizing his accuser by the throat and choking him, for instinctively his bile rose at the outrageous charge brought against him. But he quickly realized that, to begin with, old Moche's indignation was only pretense, and then, that the least display of violence on his part could only have consequences disastrous to his plans. The journalist had gathered the firm conviction in the course of the two hours he had spent among the dubious frequenters of the *Blue Chestnut* that Père Moche was possessed of a strange, but indubitable authority over these sinister personages. There was no question that, for some purpose or another, he was in the habit of aiding and abetting them, lending them money as needed, or that he possessed an astuteness that made him master of the rest of his associates—and was perhaps the mysterious intermediary who transmitted to them the orders of the elusive autocrat Fantômas.

Postponing all thought of reprisals for the present, Fandor obeyed the old ruffian's orders and sneaked away. A few moments more and he left the *Blue Chestnut* without his departure being remarked by anyone whatsoever, not even by the landlord, who troubled himself very little about his customer going away, as he invariably observed the excellent custom of making everybody pay in advance.

"That's it, that must be the train!" Issuing from the Saint-Lazare terminus, an engine, heralded by the glare of its two headlights, plunged beneath the dark arch of the Batignolles tunnel. Enveloped in a dense cloud of smoke, the locomotive rolled slowly on, with a rhythmical roar and rattle, towing behind it a long line of passenger coaches.

His feet in the thick mud, his back against the clammy stonework, Fandor stood motionless halfway through the tunnel waiting till the train reached him.

The journalist, on leaving the *Blue Chestnut,* left alone with his thoughts, and now firmly convinced he had at last come upon the gang among whom he must look to find not only the murderer of the bank collector, but likewise the authors of the attack on the Minister of Justice, not to mention, in all likelihood, the assassin of Désiré Ferrand, told himself it was above all things incumbent on him from this time on to dare any and every risk to secure a collaborator in his task. His mind was made up: Tom Bob must be his ally and coworker.

Who and what was this Tom Bob? he did not rightly know. Two or three times at most he had heard his friend Juve speak of the man. Juve, this much was certain, admired the American—albeit they were not personally known to one another—as a clever, capable officer, full of modern ideas. Fandor pictured Tom Bob as being in fact a sort of Juve of the New World— with this difference, that the one seemed as fond of self-advertisement and popular applause as the other was an admirer of modesty and reticence.

Summing up the situation Fandor told himself:

"It is impossible, at the present moment, to show myself at the headquarters of the Criminal Department. In their stupid way they would simply arrest me without listening to my story, or even arrest me after they had heard it, if only by way of making a concession to public opinion. Juve himself is in jail, the unfortunate man can do nothing to help me. Rather it is for me to save him, and to have the power I must be free. It may be Tom Bob will not be sorry to have me as a discreet and anonymous coworker. Let us go find Tom Bob!"

This decision taken, the question was to carry it into effect. Now Fandor, at eight o'clock in the evening, had still less money in his possession than at four o'clock in the afternoon. But the journalist, having noted the time of the last train that would take him to Le Havre before the arrival of the American packet, viz., the 9:45 slow train, had thought to himself that, if it was impossible for him to travel without a ticket, it was perhaps easy enough to jump the train as it went by, and so be carried to his destination—on condition, of course, of not attracting attention by entering a compartment, but instead riding unobtrusively on a step, or on some buffer or other, or else lying at full length on the roof of a carriage.

He had explored the neighborhood of the station and made out that by way of the Rue de Rome and utilizing a scaffolding erected by the workmen engaged in enlarging the tunnel, he could easily in the evening dusk climb down the scaffold poles on to the line. But on second thought Fandor had conceived a much simpler plan. At 9:20 for four sous he purchased a ticket for Batignolles and made his way on to the platform, then seizing his opportunity when nobody was looking, he stepped on to the permanent way and so, keeping along the confining walls, reached the entrance of the tunnel and waited there for the passing of the Le Havre train.

He had set his watch by the station clock, and the train being due to start at forty-three minutes past the hour, he was at his post in the tunnel at half a minute before that time. He arched his back against the wall, and in spite of the blinding smoke, watched the line of vehicles as they moved slowly past him.

"Engine, luggage van, another van, several third class coaches, a corridor carriage, a first, a second . . . now's my time!"

The young man sprang on the next coach that came opposite

him, it was a risky job, a false step and he would be thrown on to the rails, under the wheels, but the journalist had audacity and fearlessness on his side, and dexterity into the bargain, and he landed safely. In a few seconds, by help of the handholds running along the sides and the moldings of the woodwork, which luckily projected outwards, he succeeded in first hoisting himself between two carriages and then climbing on to the roof of one of them. He stretched himself flat on his face and threw his arms round the projecting top of a lamp, then with legs wide to help maintain his equilibrium, he lay perfectly still.

Hardly was he in position before the train quickened its pace and emerged from the tunnel. The journalist breathed the purer air with infinite gusto. But his satisfaction was short-lived; the engine now began to emit showers of sparks and clouds of greasy, blinding smoke. He could only shut his eyes tight and wait in stoical patience.

"Bah!" the young fellow said to himself, "it's merely a bad night to get through! I shall be a bit cold perhaps, and a bit dirty, but the great point is, I shall get there. Le Havre is not so far away as they make out. I think we must already be getting near the bridge of Asnières, for the train, I see, is beginning to slow down, as they always do."

But next moment he let fly an oath. The train, contrary to all precedent, was taking a big curve, the rails were steeply inclined inwards and the carriages tilted over in the same direction, so that Fandor, who was not expecting it, very nearly slipped off his perch. He would infallibly have tumbled off if he had not made a wild clutch at the top of his lamp. The brakes were applied sharply and a jolt ran from carriage to carriage, then the train stopped dead.

Fandor opened his eyes and looked about him. He was in the middle of a vast shed. On either side he saw the roofs of carriages stretching away into infinity. For a moment he was at a loss what to think, then the truth burst upon him.

"Damnation!" he cried, "was it worth my while to lay my plans so carefully, and make such a monstrous mistake after all!"

Instead of taking the train for Havre, he had got on to a line of empty coaches which a yard-engine was simply hauling out to its siding for the night.

Even as he realized the fact, in the distance, full steam ahead and brilliantly lighted up, he saw a main line train go by—undoubtedly the train to Le Havre!

10. Tom Bob on the Spot

The *Lorraine* had just entered the port of Le Havre after an excellent passage across the Atlantic. As usual, her passenger list was a full one, and bore many names well known in the worlds of fashion and high finance. The decks were crowded with pretty women in brilliant toilettes and clean-shaven, keen-faced men in check cloth caps, a typically American company, not to mention a minority of other nationalities—Frenchmen, Englishmen, heavily built Germans, with a sprinkling of Spaniards and Italians and even a half-dozen bronzed Asiatics, a cosmopolitan assemblage.

The great ship lay alongside the huge customs shed, at the further side of which was drawn up the special boat-train destined to convey the liner's first class passengers to Paris, and only waiting on the latter's release from the formalities of the customs house. Now all was ready, and the heavy train got into motion, threaded its way at a snail's pace through the vast labyrinth of docks and warehouses, made a brief halt at the Le Havre train station to pick up a few travelers having special permission to avail themselves of this express service, then little by little gathering speed, began the headlong race that was only to end 300 kilometers from the start at the Gare Saint-Lazare in the very heart of the capital.

Very soon *déjeuner* was served in the dining coach.

"How pretty the country is," said Mrs. Silas K. Bigelow, enthusiastically. She was a young and charming American, who sat with eyes never leaving the window, gazing with admiring curiosity at the fertile plains of Normandy whirling past. Her *vis-à-vis* at her table in the dining car, Mr. Van Buren, one of the most famous of New York's multimillionaires, less enamored of landscape than his poetical fellow-countrywoman, insisted on his companion devoting a less perfunctory attention to the meal.

The wine steward approached: "What wine will the ladies and gentlemen drink—Saint Emilion, Pommard, extra dry?"

Mrs. Bigelow's neighbor, a superb creature, with hair as black as ink and eyes of an opalescent green, shook her head in reply to the inquiring glance of her companion, a young Englishman, with smooth cheeks and close-cropped hair.

"No, my dear Ascott," she declared, "now we are ashore again, I want no more of those heady beverages. All very well at sea, but not good for my health now. Order me some mineral water, will you?"

Ascott looked round in search of the wine steward, but the man was already at the opposite end of the car, booking the orders of the other tables.

"Sorry, Princess," the young Englishman excused him self, "soon as the man comes back, I will give him your order. Is there any particular kind you prefer?"

But the Princess Sonia Danidoff answered the question only with a careless wave of the hand and a brief:

"Oh! I don't know, I hate having to choose."

Then turning with a gracious smile towards another traveler seated at a neighboring table, the princess thanked him for the slight service he had rendered her by passing her the menu card with a very polite bow.

Meantime Mr. Bigelow, seated not far from his wife, uttered a startled exclamation. He had just unfolded a French journal and rapidly cast his eye over it. Indeed a number of the passengers in the restaurant car were similarly engaged, eagerly scanning the news columns of the morning papers.

No doubt during the voyage the news sheet that appeared on board every morning had contained sundry important items of information supplied by wireless, but detailed particulars were lacking, and for this reason it was a boon to the newly-arrived travelers to be put in possession of numberless piquant details of international events, and especially of the activities of the fashionable world of Paris, in which they were more particularly interested.

During the six days' sea voyage, the world had not stood still: the usual incidents, the usual joys and sorrows, the usual anecdotes formed the staple of the record—and the usual crimes. But here was something of direst import: these tourists who for nearly a week had been more or less isolated on the high seas were startled to learn that on arrival they were to find Paris a prey to the most acute alarm, and that since leaving land a series of tragedies had occurred, the most mysterious and the most terrifying ever known. The newspapers of every shade of politics, of every sort and kind, were full of the dramatic incidents that so excited public opinion, and above all abounded in the latest particulars of the daring and dastardly assassination of the Minister of Justice that had happened a few days before.

But there was one item that more than any other roused the keenest curiosity among the occupants of the restaurant car. This was the announcement of the expected arrival in France of the American, Tom Bob, and the statement that the detective in question was on board the SS. *Lorraine,* due to reach Le Havre on the very morning of issue. This was naturally a highly exciting piece of news to the passengers who had traveled with him, many of whom, moreover, knew of the reputation the man enjoyed at police headquarters in New York.

"Is it possible?" laughed the Princess Sonia Danidoff, to whom her cavalier had just read the paragraph, "is it possible we have had Tom Bob with us on board?"

"But why not, Princess," replied the multimillionaire. "Surely Tom Bob might be aboard without the world being turned upside down or the *Lorraine* dressing ship in his honor."

"But is it not strange," Mrs. Bigelow asked the question, "that he never made himself known to us?"

"A detective," observed Ascott, "is hardly likely to have his coming announced by ambassadors, and as a rule prefers his presence to be unremarked."

The same traveler who a minute or two before had courteously passed the list enumerating all the various sorts of mineral waters to the Princess Danidoff now joined in with a word of approval of Ascott's remark:

"The gentleman," he declared, "is perfectly right, and I entirely agree with him in thinking that a detective, were it Tom Bob himself, is bound under certain circumstances to keep the secret of his identity. In other cases, however, it is best he should make himself known, and that explains why Tom Bob, without therefore laying himself open to a charge of inconsistency, has chosen on the one hand to preserve an incognito on board ship while on the other informing the French press by wireless of his speedy arrival in Paris."

All eyes were turned on the speaker, who was evidently one of the *Lorraine's* passengers. He was a man of about forty, whose brick-red complexion was the more noticeable as his hair was deeply tinged with silver. Like many Americans, he carried in his buttonhole a miniature American flag in enameled porcelain. Two heavy gold rings adorned his finger, and he wore coat and trousers of light gray cloth. The inspection continued for some seconds after its object had quietly resumed his meal, for none of the first class passengers could recollect having ever seen this particular individual during the passage over.

At this moment a Frenchman who sat facing him, quite a young man, who had joined the train at Le Havre, addressed the stranger:

"Excuse me, sir, but they say Tom Bob proposes to take measures in this country to arrest Fantômas, that elusive brigand who always baffles the best efforts of the police . . . it is a bold venture!"

The man of the silvery locks looked up at the youth, then fixing his eyes on the other's face, answered calmly after a pause:

"It is very American, sir. What need to say more?"

"Well said, sir," exclaimed a stout, ruddy-faced man, known to all on the ship as being Hamilton Gould, an enormously wealthy Californian, who had been round the world three or four times already, "in America we are all like that."

Mr. Van Buren smiled, but said nothing, while Mrs. Bigelow, entering into the spirit of the conversation, suggested:

"Perhaps Tom Bob was just one of the bartenders or maybe that old lady with the white wig who by her own account travels for a Paris dressmaker."

The Princess Danidoff added yet another guess with a glance of irony at the last speaker:

"Or the Captain? . . . why not, while you're at it, dear Mrs. Bigelow?"

Presently cigars were lighted and the majority of the ladies left the restaurant car to return to their several compartments. Ascott, Van Buren and Hamilton Gould, however, had followed Mrs. Bigelow and the Princess Danidoff as they left the carriage, while behind them the man with the silvery hair had risen from his seat. The conversation was resumed in the corridor. A window stood open, and Mr. Van Buren begged permission to smoke a cigarette. Then observing that Sonia Danidoff was about to do the same:

"May I give you a light?" he asked the princess, who thanked him for the offer.

"Oh!" exclaimed the millionaire next moment, "what a nuisance! I thought I had my lighter in my vest pocket, and now I can't find it. I must have left it in my portmanteau."

A bantering voice was heard behind him:

"Or rather, haven't you perhaps had it stolen, sir?"

Van Buren wheeled round. It was the man with the silvery hair who had spoken. Without appearing to pay any heed to the astonishment he provoked, the man went on:

"You must know that these luxury trains, such as the one we are in, are often worked by pickpockets, and that these gentry find a malicious satisfaction in robbing passengers even of articles of little value, simply with the object of keeping their hand in."

Van Buren did not know what to say, Mrs. Bigelow smiled nervously, while not without a touch of anxiety, the Princess Sonia Danidoff, whose lips were trembling a little, murmured with a forced laugh:

"Bah! We ought not to be afraid, surely, seeing the renowned Tom Bob is with us . . . but is he really with us?"

"Why, yes!" cried Hamilton Gould. "I'm ready to wager he is."

"Will you show us the man?" demanded Mrs. Bigelow.

"Perhaps I may, who knows?"

Then all burst out laughing. Ascott had just drawn their attention to the smoking compartment at the far end of the car, where a passenger lay fast asleep, adding the suggestion:

"Perhaps it's that gentleman."

First the men, then the ladies, all equally amused and curious, stole one by one to peep in at the traveler who was still fast asleep, little dreaming of the interest he aroused.

But the man of the silvery hair again drew attention to himself by his criticism of Ascott's identification.

"It shows a want of perspicacity, sir," he declared, "to take the gentleman sleeping there for Tom Bob. In the first place a detective does not sleep. Besides which, one has only to look at your man in the smoking carriage to be quite sure, first, that he is a Frenchman, that is plain from the cut of his clothes, and second, that he is an officer, in fact I should say an officer actually serving with the colors."

Much impressed, Sonia Danidoff drew nearer to the speaker: "And what tells you that, sir?"

The man bowed gravely.

"Nothing simpler, madam! To begin with, look at that bundle of sticks and umbrellas in the net above his head. Amongst them don't you see something long in a green baize case?—a sword, an officer's sword, obviously! Then notice his temples: the hair lies flat to the head all round a circular line, while it sticks out like other people's just below at the level of the top of the ear—that means our gentleman usually wears a kepi. Then, consider, apart from the mustache, the only hair he wears on his face, the bronze of the skin, stopping short at the neck—there you have a man used to living in the open air. I believe I am pretty accurate in my diagnosis . . . what do you think of it?"

Hamilton Gould's big hand fell familiarly on the silver-haired individual's shoulder.

"I think, sir," he declared emphatically, "that to follow up a train of reasoning like that, to draw a conclusion with such clearness and precision, there's only one man in all the world, above all only one American—and I think you are that man, Tom Bob in person!"

The man addressed smiled as he looked with sparkling eyes in the face of the genial globetrotter.

"You are right," he said simply, "I am Tom Bob."

It was the signal for an outburst of enthusiasm and curiosity that soon spread to every passenger in the carriage. All crowded round the famous detective, each more eager than the other to speak to the great man.

"I beg and pray," Mrs. Bigelow urged her husband, "you will introduce me. How delightful, how amusing to know a detective!"

But already Tom Bob, like the perfect man of the world he was, was paying his respects to the Princess Danidoff.

"We possess some good friends in common, Princess," he was saying, "the Count and Countess Karenisky. I knew them well when I was staying at St. Petersburg. In fact, I had an opportunity of doing them a small service."

"At the time of the Nihilists, was it not?" interrupted the Princess Sonia.

"Yes, indeed, during that critical period . . ."

But the princess shuddered at the mournful recollections the words recalled, and stopped any further reference to the past: "Do not, I beg you, sir, revive these dreadful memories!"

However, Hamilton Gould broke in at this point, very opportunely changing the conversation.

"Then," he asked, "as you know us all, you were actually on board the *Lorraine?*"

"Why, certainly, sir," replied Tom Bob. "Do you want proofs? You occupied the state room No. 127, the Princess Sonia Danidoff had a cabin port side. We enjoyed a first-rate passage, though on the evening of the second day, a bit of a gale blew up about six o'clock, and we feared bad weather for next day. Is that correct?"

"Absolutely correct!" declared Mr. Van Buren. After that the conversation turned on a more enticing and more serious subject. Tom Bob had been announced by the Parisian Press as the declared antagonist of Fantômas. It was natural to question him as to the attitude he proposed to adopt towards the notorious brigand. But the American detective was not to be drawn, entrenching himself behind what he called "professional secrecy."

Mrs. Bigelow gave a groan of terror.

"Great heavens!" she cried, "supposing Fantômas were in this train and knew that you were here, too, Mr. Tom Bob, and chose to blow us all up, it would be appalling!"

"It would be a very natural thing for Fantômas to do, madam," the detective replied, "but for certain reasons I am well assured we have nothing to fear on that count."

The young Frenchman, who some while before had accosted Tom Bob, was just returning from the breakfast car, a fat cigar in his mouth, eyes shining, and hat cocked rakishly over one ear.

"First place," he began in a quizzical voice, "Mister detective, you have an easy job before you, for you must know Fantômas is in jail."

"Why, yes, that's true enough," admitted Mr. Van Buren. "Still, as Mr. Tom Bob is so clever, it's to be hoped he'll meet him all the same and finish by arresting his man."

. . . "Ah! It's extraordinary," Ascott suddenly exclaimed. "Here's a go, I can't find my pocketbook."

Tom Bob gave a start.

"Look carefully, sir, look again. What you say is really serious, you must make sure."

With a pale face Ascott searched through all his pockets—everywhere.

"No, there's no doubt whatever, my pocketbook has disappeared. It's not that I had a great deal of money in it, but the thing is very unpleasant."

Tom Bob lit a cigarette with a nonchalant air.

"Now that it's known for sure your pocketbook has disappeared, the only thing left to do is to get it back. That's not very difficult perhaps."

All eyes turned in astonishment at Tom Bob, who went on:

"A detective, and above all an American detective, owes it to himself to discover in any assemblage of people, no matter what, any pickpockets therein, and this at the first glance."

The young Frenchman started poking merciless fun at the sententious and dogmatic language used by the American detective:

"And pray, sir, by what do you know them?"

Tom Bob looked the youth up and down from head to foot, and said nothing for a moment or two. Then he replied: "By their boots."

His audience held their sides. Decidedly Mr. Tom Bob was an original and entertaining traveling companion, and everybody crowded to the far end of the corridor where he stood ensconced in a corner. The American detective proceeded to harangue his listeners.

"The pickpockets on luxury trains," he declared, "have this much in common with the officers of the Criminal Investigation Department, that they are usually ill-shod. With one class as with the other, there is nothing, speaking generally, to find fault with in the getup. Hat from the best maker, clothes of an irreproachable cut, tasteful necktie, well-kept hands, everything proclaims the man of the world. But there is a small detail, a grain of sand, the proverbial grain of sand that throws the best adjusted machine out of gear, and that grain of sand is nothing more nor less than the footwear . . ."

Tom Bob broke off, and turning to the young Frenchman who was listening with a highly quizzical smile:

"Sir," he asked, "will you allow me to ask you a question—what is your profession?"

At this direct and almost peremptory demand, the youth blushed in some embarrassment. The answer came in a dull, heavy voice:

"Why, sir, if I chose not to answer, I should be within my rights and would tell you nothing . . . But there, I have nothing to hide—I am a student, a medical student, sir."

The young man was evidently annoyed and turning his back

on his questioner, he left the corridor.

Suddenly, a few moments after this, the train was plunged into utter darkness. The track, after running for some distance alongside the Seine near Bonnieres, had entered a tunnel. The Princess Danidoff's anxious voice was heard complaining: "Why isn't the carriage lighted? How very extraordinary!"

Tom Bob gave a sharp order:

"Have a care, ladies. Look out, gentlemen. This darkness is altogether abnormal. It is due to no negligence on the part of the Company, but undoubtedly to the act of some miscreant. Guard your jewelry, watch your pockets."

A few moments passed, seeming like hours, and then, issuing suddenly from the bowels of the earth, the train regained the light of day and sped on across the open country. Mrs. Bigelow gave a cry: her reticule had vanished. "My bag," she groaned, "what has become of my little bag? Why, it's appalling, verily this land of France is nothing but a den of thieves."

Mr. Van Buren remarked: "I thought just now Mr. Bob was joking, but I am beginning to think he was perfectly serious."

"By God!" exclaimed Ascott, who could *not* believe his pocketbook had really vanished and had just finished turning his portmanteau upside down, "by God! I think I ought to know something about it."

The American detective was biting his lips with annoyance. Mechanically he lit a cigarette, then tossed it away, only to light another.

A ticket collector passed along the train, shouting "tickets! tickets, please!" But two passengers found themselves unable to produce theirs—Ascott and Mrs. Bigelow.

The group in the corridor, already aware of the strange disappearance of the Englishman's pocketbook and the American lady's reticule, attacked the Company's official, complaining of the thefts, claiming the protection of French law, threatening the most terrible reprisals. The unhappy collector knew nothing about it and grasped only one fact, to wit, that two passengers were traveling without tickets. The discussion was growing acrimonious when Tom Bob intervened.

"My good man," he said, "will you be so good as not to press this lady and gentleman for a few minutes. Their tickets are not lost, only mislaid—mislaid in somebody else's pocket. It will be all right, will it not, if the tickets are handed to you before reaching Paris? I guarantee this will be the case." Bob's specific undertaking reassured the man. "Very good!" he said, "we'll see about it at Asnières."

Ascott was about to pester the detective with a string of questions, but the latter stopped him with a shake of the head.

"Wait a bit," he said, "I think we're slowing down."

The train in fact was slackening speed, though no station was in sight. On the contrary it had just run into the Forest of Saint-Germain. Great trees bordered the line on either side.

Tom Bob dashed hurriedly down the corridor, the train going slower and slower all the time. Suddenly the detective sprang forward. The door opening from the corridor onto the permanent way had been unfastened from the inside by someone proposing to get out, presumably intending to take advantage of the diminishing speed of the train to jump down on to the ballast without fear of accident.

Quick as this suspicious movement had been, Tom Bob had forestalled it, seizing the individual by the collar.

"So! my young friend," he cried, without relaxing his hold, but on the contrary twisting his wrist hard, so as to paralyze all resistance, "so you wanted to give your friends the slip, did you? That's not pretty behavior, upon my word!"

Pale as death, with a look of fear on his face, the other growled in a savage voice:

"Let go, by God, let go, or I'll kill you."

But Tom Bob only smiled: "Kill me, eh?" he laughed, "with what—your revolver? Just feel in your pocket with your free hand, my fine little man, you'll find your gun's not there anymore."

The startled thief gave a choking cry of terror. Mechanically he did as he was bid and searched his pocket. The detective was right, his revolver had vanished.

"I confiscated it, my boy," the detective informed him, "you are too young to use such weapons handily. A student like you can't expect to have the dexterity of a master like me. Besides, we have this little difference between us, I'm on the job for honest reasons, while you . . ."

The arrested fugitive threw himself on the ground, hoping in this way to slip out of the detective's grasp. The latter went on calmly twisting the fellow's arm, who swore savagely, glaring like a trapped wild beast at his captor.

Attracted by the noise of the struggle a number of people had run to the spot. Among the first to arrive were Van Buren and Ascott. In a moment they had realized what had occurred, and with a mighty cheer acknowledged the wonderful perspicacity of their compatriot, who had picked out among the throng of passengers the individual who was undoubtedly the culprit and had arrested him so cleverly. All recognized the man, it was the young Frenchman, the same who had given himself out as a medical student.

Mrs. Bigelow had come to take a look at Tom Bob's prisoner, and now rejoined Sonia Danidoff: "It is quite true, my dear," she confided to the princess, "Mr. Bob was quite right, one must beware of people who are ill shod. That man wore horrid boots." The princess was very pale and still quite unstrung: "It's frightful, these things, appalling. It has made me quite ill!"

Meantime the compartment into which, finding it by chance unoccupied, the American detective had unceremoniously pushed his prisoner, resounded with a chorus of indignant outcries against the pseudo-student. As quick as lightning the police officer had secured the fellow's wrists with a miniature pair of handcuffs, so small as to be hardly visible, but strong enough to bear any strain.

The Superintendent now appeared on the scene much harassed by all these varied incidents, on which he would have to make a circumstantial report, a task made the more difficult by the fact that the worthy official, having no actual knowledge of the details, was asking himself which of the two parties was actually in the right and which in the wrong, these foreign fashionables traveling without tickets or the young Parisian whom an American police officer had taken upon himself to handcuff.

"I don't want to hear a word," declared the Superintendent, "I'm not going to decide between you, you will make your explanations to the Special Constabulary at the terminus."

"Nothing could be fairer," Tom Bob agreed, adding with characteristic phlegm: "At the same time, sir, if you wish here and now to have the two missing tickets, all you have to do is to search that young gentleman's pockets, I have no doubt they are in his possession."

"I prefer to do nothing," insisted the official, shaking his head in a puzzled way, "I shall do nothing, you will explain yourselves, as I said before, to the Constabulary Office at Saint-Lazare."

A quarter of an hour later, still in a state of breathless excitement, the first class passengers of the Trans-Atlantic express arrived at their journey's end. Instead of leaving the station, they all waited in silence on the platform where the train had pulled up, formed up in two lines, between which marched Tom Bob and his captive. They had been the last to leave the train, but not unaccompanied: four police officers, to whom the Superintendent had beckoned as the train ran in, escorted the pair, equally determined that neither one nor the other, detective or culprit, should escape.

Who was right and who was wrong? This was what nobody knew. However, a few minutes later, before the Special Commissary, light began to dawn. The individual whom Tom Bob had accused of theft was searched. On him was found Ascott's pocketbook, Mrs. Bigelow's reticule—*and* a leather purse, absolutely empty!

"Where have you put the money that was in this purse?" asked the Commissary sternly.

But Tom Bob burst out laughing: "That purse was empty to begin with, sir," he declared, "I can assure you of that much, for it is my own. It's what I call my decoy purse. When I'm bent on looking after matters in a crowd, I put it well in sight, hanging out of my vest pocket, and wait. The expected result never fails to arrive, the pickpockets take me for a fool, come after me and rob me with all the more ease, as I help them all I can. It doesn't bring them in a lot, for I can't afford to be generous with them, but it has this great advantage, it enables me to make the gentleman's acquaintance. That, Mr. Commissary, is how we do things in America, or at any rate how Tom Bob, the American detective, does 'em!"

The Special Commissary looked at the American in bewilderment, not without a touch of jealousy. It could not be denied the man was very clever and he had just done a pretty stroke of business, in which unfortunately the French police could find little to boast about. Still the Commissary thanked the detective, and added:

"We shall perhaps require you to give evidence, sir. Where shall I be able to find you?"

Tom Bob penciled a few words on his card, saying at the same time: "I have engaged rooms at the Hotel Terminus. The police will always find me there at their disposal."

A minute or two more and Ascott recovered possession of his pocketbook, and Mrs. Bigelow's reticule returned to its lawful owner. The Americans were one and all delighted, and wished that very evening to celebrate their fellow-countryman's splendid triumph. Tom Bob, however, asked modestly to be excused, declaring he was worn out, and quickly disappeared in the crowd.

In the Commissary's office, the requisite papers were in preparation for the committal of the pickpocket when a superior official entered.

"What is it, sir?" asked the Commissary.

"Why, this, sir. The individual in your charge is known to the police."

"Well, what about him?"

"That man is an old jailbird. We don't know his proper name, but among the crooks he goes by the nickname of 'Beauty Boy.'"

11. Mad as a Hatter

All was bustle and movement in the great entrance-hall of the Hotel Terminus, the imposing edifice that rears its bulk immediately outside the Gare Saint-Lazare. There was a never-ending coming and going of travelers, new customers continually arriving from the trains reaching Paris from all parts, others departing for a hundred different destinations in all quarters of the globe. The throng was especially dense round a small office of a severe and dignified aspect worthy of a public Ministry, but more elegant in its furniture and appointments, where three active young women were busy quickly and methodically answering countless questions in a dozen different languages, entering the names of the various newcomers in a great ledger and indicating the rooms assigned them.

Among other applicants was the American Tom Bob, cool and collected as always. In two minutes he had completed the necessary formalities, and, under the guidance of a servant of the hotel carrying his baggage, was crossing the hall towards the lift. But turning suddenly on the man, the traveler shook his head emphatically and announced his intention of mounting by the stairs to the suite he had previously engaged by wireless on the third floor.

"I don't like elevators," he said peremptorily, and heedless of the look of surprise on the servant's face at so unusual a preference, insisted on adopting the slower and more fatiguing route.

Before reaching the foot of the grand staircase, however, he was very unexpectedly—to the best of his knowledge the American did not know a soul in all Paris—accosted by a shabbily dressed young man, a total stranger to him, who earnestly craved the favor of a few minutes' conversation.

"I am a friend," he urged eagerly and ingratiatingly, "of someone who knows you, who has often had occasion to describe some of your exploits to me, and who, I have no doubt whatever, would authorize me to use his name to secure the interview I have the honor to beg of you, of your kindness, to accord."

Short and sharp, Tom Bob stopped him in mid career. "I have not a friend in France," he declared.

The young man smiled, not at all disconcerted, only saying, in a very low whisper:

"Oh, yes, you have—one at any rate—Juve!"

Not a muscle of Tom Bob's face moved. Nevertheless the great American detective must have been well acquainted with the name of the king of police officers, nor indeed could he well fail to know something of Juve's famous doings, for he replied at once:

"Follow me, sir"—and putting an abrupt end to the dialogue, he turned his back on the young man, and marching on in front without a word of apology, started to mount the stairs.

"No. 142, here you are, sir! your luggage will be up in ten minutes, sir."

Tom Bob and the unknown stranger who followed him had just been ushered into the room the detective had engaged several days ago by wireless from mid-Atlantic. Now, laying his hand on the waiter's shoulder, he ordered him:

"Have my luggage here in one hour from now, and not before! I particularly wish not to be disturbed."

The man looked at him in astonishment. This traveler had tastes exactly the opposite of the ordinary run of customers. However, the well-trained servant, without a word indicating his surprise, went on:

"Here is the bell, sir—one ring for the waiter who attends to your room, two for the chambermaid. This is the cold water tap and there's the hot. The electric switch is by the head of the bed."

Tom Bob was standing in the middle of the room and gazing steadfastly at the ceiling while the man was speaking. Then he put an odd question:

"How long ago was it the gentleman who has the bedroom

immediately over mine first came to the hotel?"

The waiter stared, more surprised than ever. "I haven't any idea, sir," he admitted, "but why?"

Tom Bob took the man by the shoulders and pushed him gently out of the room:

"It interests me enormously. It is now twenty past seven, you will find means to give me this information at twenty past eight, in sixty minutes, when they bring up my luggage. Now go!"

And now, when the servant was gone and the door shut behind him, Tom Bob at last turned to the stranger, who was, no less than the other, staring at him, bewildered by his queer behavior.

"You will excuse me, won't you," he asked, "but before I give you my attention, I have a little piece of work to do."

The other bowed, saying only by way of remonstrance:

"I must mention again, Mr. Bob, that what I have to say is pretty urgent . . ."

But the detective only smiled and cutting short his protest: "There's something else," he declared, "that's very much more urgent, Monsieur Jerome Fandor."

Then as the journalist gave a start of amazement at hearing his name spoken—it was as a matter of fact Jerome Fandor who had just now accosted the detective in the entrance-hall and asked leave to speak with him—Tom Bob, calm as ever, signified with an imperative gesture that he was not to interrupt:

"Something very much more urgent, I repeat. Will you be so kind as to help me in my little piece of work?"

More and more surprised, but confounded by his host's phlegm, Fandor nodded "yes," without so much as opening his lips.

"Then," Tom Bob went on, "here's how I start the job. Look! I take off my hat . . . like so. Then I plant my chair against the wall . . . like so. I take my seat on the chair . . . Have you a pencil on you, Monsieur Fandor?"

"I have, sir."

"Very good! Will you be so very obliging as to take it and draw a line on—on the door. See here, exactly on a level with the top of my head."

Fandor carried out the order, lost in astonishment.

"He's mad," he thought to himself. "The good man's as mad as a hatter! What does it all mean?"

His reflections were cut short by the detective, who announced in his deliberate voice:

"The fact is, you see, I have a horror of high chairs." And as he uttered these extraordinary words, Tom Bob got up and, kneeling down on the floor, turned the chair he had been sitting on the minute before upside down, then drew from his pocket a hunting-knife.

"Don't be afraid, Monsieur Fandor, I'm not going to open the blade. It is the saw I want to use."

So saying, he extracted from the handle a little saw of the kind often found in such knives.

"Go on, sir, go on!" Fandor protested. "Can I help you?"

"Oh! no, it's done in a moment," and as if he were performing the most natural action in the world, Tom Bob, still on his knees, began to saw off the legs of the chair in front of him.

"I have a horror of high chairs," he repeated, "that's why I saw off the legs, as you see, and convert it into a low one. It'll cost me a trifle to pay for the damage, but what of that? . . . Ah! that's done!"

The detective had in fact abbreviated the chair legs by eight or nine inches. He set the chair on its feet again, and after making sure it stood firm, sat down. Then springing up again, still without uttering a word, he went over to the bed standing on one side of the room, and picked up a pillow and bolster, which he threw down near the wall.

"You are a young man, Monsieur Fandor," he remarked. "You are not just come off a journey. you are not tired like me. Besides, I don't want to demolish all the hotel furniture . . . in a word, will you be so kind as to seat yourself on these improvised cushions? . . . yes? cross-legged, if you like."

This time Fandor showed such a comic face of astonishment that even the phlegmatic American could not help smiling.

"I am not mad," he observed simply by way of explanation,

"but I have a horror of seeing people sitting in high chairs when I am myself seated in a low one—a whim, Monsieur Fandor, a monomania, if you like, of no importance. . . . Now, what can I do for you?"

Jerome Fandor squatted on the ground in obedience to the detective's strange invitation, while the latter took *his* place on the seat so oddly truncated.

"Sir," declared the journalist, "the name I have mentioned, the name of Juve, must have informed you of the object of my visit. You can guess . . ."

But Tom Bob uttered a sharp protest: "No, I know nothing, I cannot *guess*. Besides, I never guess. I infer, that's all."

"Nevertheless you guessed my name, Monsieur Tom Bob?"

"Not at all! I only inferred you were Fandor from the fact that you invoked Juve's name by way of introduction to me and that, as I look at it, there can hardly be another individual but you, Jerome Fandor, to act so imprudently as to name Juve as guarantee, when Juve is generally taken to be Fantômas!"

On hearing the American's words, Fandor sprang up instinctively to grasp his hand.

"Oh, sir," he cried, "thank you for what you say, I thank you from the bottom of my heart! At the first word, I guessed you were to be an ally. *You* do not think, do you, that Juve is Fantômas?"

Tom Bob interrupted sharply again:

"I think I told you to sit on the floor! You get up instead. You are in the wrong, you must do what I ask. If you mean to jump up and down like this, I prefer to put off the interview you desire till tomorrow."

"But, sir . . . but!" Fandor stammered, again bemused with surprise, as he sat down again, while the other insisted:

"There's no 'but' about it, it is so! However, let's leave that. You did not come to see me, I presume, for the mere pleasure of annoying me by standing? You came to tell me something. What have you to tell me?"

Fandor called up all his coolness, shut his eyes a second, pulled himself together, and now, in a calm voice, assented, without troubling further about his interlocutor's eccentricities:

"You are right, sir: I *have* come to tell you something, to tell you this—I am indeed Jerome Fandor."

"Excuse me," broke in Tom Bob, "but how came you to recognize me?"

"Ah! sir," confessed Fandor, smiling innocently, "the newspapers, announcing your sensational arrival the other day, published your portrait, which no doubt they had among their stock of blocks. I knew, moreover, that you would land from the *Lorraine,* saw the Trans-Atlantic special come in, I followed you from the Commissary's office which you visited, I don't know for what reason, to this hotel, and . . ."

"Very good! . . . Now, you came to tell me?"

"Sir," replied Fandor, "you have challenged Fantômas to mortal combat. Fantômas, as you know, has set himself to terrorize Paris, to make war on France, on civilization itself . . ."

Tom Bob interrupted again: "I have heard of his challenge to the Chamber. Proceed!"

"Good!" Fandor agreed. "But Fantômas has committed crimes you have not heard of. Yesterday a Minister was killed . . ."

"I know," again affirmed the detective.

"Already?"

"Already? . . . the papers I bought at Rouen!"

"Then you also know that the day before yesterday, Mr. Bob, Fantômas murdered three police officers, so arranging it as to make it believed I was the criminal?"

"No, I did not know that."

"In that case I well tell you about it"—and Fandor proceeded to relate clearly and succinctly his extraordinary adventure, concluding his narrative with the words:

"Which comes to this, Mr. Tom Bob, that at this present moment not only does the fear of Fantômas paralyze all Paris, but further, public opinion accuses me of being Fantômas' accomplice, or even Fantômas himself!"

All the time the young man was speaking, Tom Bob kept nodding his approval at intervals. Now he broke in on the other's remarks.

"If you please," he said, "better lie down, don't you think, on the floor instead of just crouching, as you are now?" And as Fandor gazed at him in a sort of panic, the detective added in an explanatory tone:

"My monomania, you know! Don't be alarmed . . . You were saying, Monsieur Fandor, that people took you for Fantômas? But Fantômas is in prison. He is generally thought to be Juve, I understand?"

"People don't know what to think, sir. Certainly, two weeks ago, everybody accepted this monstrous improbability. Now, in face of the new facts, they are doubtful. As for me, as you may well suppose, I have never varied in my belief. I know that Juve is Juve. You, sir, know it, too."

Again the detective nodded approval: "Certainly I do! By reputation I know Juve well. Nay more, I have had occasion to pursue certain inquiries in conjunction with him. So I know he is not Fantômas. Besides which, like public opinion, Monsieur Fandor, I am for believing that if Juve was Fantômas, the present crimes could not be committed . . . But, after all, in what you tell me, even, in your story of the strange attack of which you were the victim, I see nothing particularly novel. What would you propose to do?"

Fandor's face paled: "It is something more than a proposal, sir, that I am here to make you. When I read the announcement of your arrival, and recalled all Juve had told me in praise of Tom Bob, I congratulated myself, I say again, on the noble ally you would be for me, on the fine opportunity I had of obtaining by you, and thanks to you, Juve's release from jail—and that is the reason I resolved to come to you and give you the means, at the first moment after your arrival, to make a grand impression on the French police."

"I fail to understand you."

"I will explain. Succeed in effecting an arrest, Monsieur Bob, a difficult arrest, within twenty-four hours of your arrival in Paris, and you will instantly be the hero of the day! They cannot any longer then affect in high places the same indifference the

French police will certainly show towards you, chagrined as they are that you should come to help them out of their difficulty. A sensational arrest, loudly proclaimed and commended by the Press, will give you prestige, add weight to your declaration, when you come to declare, as I hope you will, that Juve is not Fantômas."

"And this arrest, Monsieur Fandor?"

"This arrest, Monsieur Bob, I am going to tell you of."

Carried away by the importance of his statement, Fandor again rose to his feet. But barely a second did he retain that attitude! Quick as thought, Tom Bob sprang from his chair, fell on his knees, seized the journalist round the waist and forced him back on the floor!

"Stay lying down, I tell you!" he ordered in a furious voice. "Have you no nose?"

"No nose?" stammered Fandor, really alarmed by the detective's conduct.

Already the latter had resumed his seat on his abbreviated chair: "Forgive me," he said with a smile—"my monomania! only my monomania again! . . . You were saying?"

Fandor resolved to show no more surprise at anything, and above all not to move again.

"This arrest," he went on, "this sensational arrest that is needed to give you prestige, I am going to supply you with the means of carrying out. Some days ago an unfortunate bank messenger was murdered in M. Moche's house, the same house where, as I described just now, I was myself the victim of mysterious violence. The police at this present time have proved unable to discover either the body of the victim or his murderer. His murderer, I know, I denounce him here and now: it is, it must be, it cannot be any other than M. Moche!"

"M. Moche?"

"Yes!"—and Fandor began a detailed account of how he had come to know that dubious man of business. He said how he associated with notorious apaches, how he was habitually engaged in shady transactions with those gentry, that in particular he was the intimate and friend of a bully, one Paulet.

He concluded: "There is besides a damning piece of evidence against him. While I was in the Chinese lantern, where Fantômas had imprisoned me, I saw the officers find in the garret a button from the uniform of the bank collector who has disappeared. This garret belongs to M. Moche, it was in this garret the crime was committed. Moche must be the criminal. You will understand, Mr. Bob, that after I had crept away along the rooftops after my extraordinary adventure, I could not, under pain of being immediately arrested, return to make investigations at M. Moche's. Nor have the police, for their part, being convinced that Fantômas is responsible for the murder of the collector and that I am Fantômas, troubled M. Moche. *You* are free to act: I beseech *you* to move heaven and earth to clear up with all speed the mystery of the bank employee's death."

The detective nodded his comprehension.

"What you tell me is interesting, very inter—"

But, cutting him short, with a dull roar that was unmistakable, an explosion shook the room. It came from above the two men's heads, like a hurricane sweeping by. Facing them, fragments of plaster, bits of the woodwork, broke away, and the wall was pitted with little holes. A thick, acrid smoke, smelling like gunpowder, rolled through the room in heavy blue-gray wreaths.

Tom Bob did not so much as start. Fandor stammered a terrific oath. Then after a moment's silence, the detective in the calmest way completed his interrupted sentence: ". . . Very interesting what you are telling me . . . but what has just happened is interesting, too. And now, Monsieur Fandor, you can stand up."

But a loud knocking was heard at the door. A waiter was asking:

"What is the matter—an accident?"

"No," Tom Bob assured him, without opening, "an incident. I was shaving and my water-heater burst . . . only tell them to bring up my luggage in an hour and a half's time, not before."

The detective's voice was so calm the man seemed satisfied, while amid the never-ending turmoil of the great hotel the violent explosion in the room had apparently passed almost unnoticed.

When the waiter was gone, Tom Bob got up from his chair, remarking:

"So now, Monsieur Fandor, you understand why I made such a point of our both being seated as close to the ground as possible."

But Fandor shook his head. "I don't understand anything at all," he protested.

"Well, go and look at the pencil line you drew just now, on a level with my head."

Fandor ran to the wall and could not restrain an exclamation:

"My God! the line is exactly in the zone riddled by the explosion of the bomb!"

"It was not a bomb."

"Not a bomb? What was it then?"

"A shot fired by Fantômas."

"By Fantômas?"

"Precisely, by Fantômas."

The other's calm was so wonderful, his imperturbability so complete, that Fandor felt almost ashamed of himself to be so profoundly agitated. Once again he called upon his strength of will power and mastered his feelings. In a quiet voice he asked:

"Well then, sir, what *has* happened? Why did you ask me to mark just that height on the wall? You guessed? . . ."

Tom Bob, hands in pockets, was looking up at the top of a tall wardrobe.

"I did not guess anything," he said. "I never guess, I infer."

"But what have you inferred then?"

"Why, I observe . . ."

"But, good lord, what do you observe?"

"What occurs, Monsieur Fandor! Now look here, is it, yes or no, a logical conclusion that Fantômas was put out by my arrival? Was it, yes or no, logical to conclude that knowing, as everybody knows, thanks to my wireless messages, that I am setting to work to arrest him, while *he* proposes to terrify Paris and force the Chambers to satisfy his demands, was it, I ask again, logical to suppose that he was going to try to murder me?"

"Logical, why yes, but how did you guess?"

"I argued, Monsieur Fandor, I argued that Fantômas, wishing to murder me, would do it as swiftly as possible. Consequently, if I wished to escape his criminal maneuvers, it was advisable to lay a trap for him. The trap consisted in engaging a room here. Fantômas knew of this. How, I cannot say, but Fantômas knows everything. For my part, *I* knew—knowledge is power—I knew that, on my coming to the Terminus, an attempt was going to be made on my life. What sort of an attempt? I felt uncertain. I suspected the lift—that risk avoided, in revenge I was pretty well convinced, when I entered this room, the room I had engaged in advance, that something was going to happen here. But what? I thought of a poisonous gas infiltrated during the night, and that is why I questioned the waiter about the occupant of the room above. Monsieur Fandor, I told you you had no nose, did I not? The fact is I am astonished that you didn't, like me, detect in the room a faint smell of burning, of burning tinder."

Fandor, lost in admiration at the precision of the American detective's discoveries, the nature of which he was beginning to fathom, declared: "I noticed the smell of burning perfectly well, but . . ."

"But you drew no inference from it. *I* inferred that a slow-match was burning—but where? To search for it was running a risk, an incautious movement might precipitate the crisis. Instead, I said to myself, Monsieur Fandor—the natural thing for a traveler to do when he enters a bedroom is to sit down. Therefore it is more than probable, if a shot is to be fired, from a revolver say, or from a gun, that the weapon will be leveled at the height of a person's head seated on a chair. I cut down my chair so as to be below the line of fire! I made you sit on the floor to save you from being hit!"

One thing, and one thing only, could Fandor find to say to express his admiration adequately: "Juve could not have done better!"

"Truly, it was not so bad. Now, if you would like to get to the bottom of things, we will take a look on top of that wardrobe . . . There, what did I say?"

From the top of the wardrobe Tom Bob, mounted on a chair, proceeded to unship a sort of gatling-gun, consisting of six barrels fixed side by side, the muzzles of which, arranged fanwise, commanded the whole room.

"Don't you see," the detective concluded, "it's all as plain as daylight. Here's how Fantômas set to work. He hired this room, up to seven or eight o'clock this morning, I imagine. Seeing it was taken for tonight by me, it was evident no one would occupy it between us two. On top of the wardrobe he lashed an extraordinary contrivance loaded up with grapeshot, which swept the whole place with a hurricane of lead. To touch off the charge, he laid down a slow-match of tinder."

Fandor shook his head: "No," he objected, so enthralled in spite of himself by the interest of the investigation as to have completely recovered his clearness of mind. "You seem to forget one detail: if he lit the slow-match before leaving, it's ten to one the smoke would have been noticed by the hotel waiter. Then besides, it would have needed a great length of slow-match, and that meant risking a conflagration . . ."

But Tom Bob indulged in another meaningful smile, as he said:

"Fantômas left, I suppose, about eight in the morning, quite early anyway. But his match was not lit till two or three o'clock in the afternoon. You needn't be surprised, Fandor, the trick is quite elementary! Look there, on the carpet, near the wardrobe. You see those little shards of glass? The fragments of a burning-glass! The tinder was set alight by means of that lens, scientifically adjusted for the precise moment when the sun had reached the altitude chosen by Fantômas. It's really very ingenious, after all!"

And as Fandor remained silent, struck dumb with admiration for the coolness displayed by the American, who had thus escaped by a hair's breadth the terrible machinations of a murderer, and at the same time saved his companion from a hideous death, Tom Bob resumed:

"The present business being now cleared up, and Fantômas responsible for yet another attempted murder, let us pass on to serious matters. *This* is not really important, as it only concerns two of his individual enemies, you and me . . . You were telling me just now, that M. Moche was guilty of the bank messenger's murder? . . . Hmm, that's not so sure. Come, Monsieur Fandor, just give me a little information about the man's associates."

At the detective's invitation Fandor had at last installed himself comfortably in a big armchair. "Moche's associates," he said, "are a deplorably bad lot. To begin with, among other notorious ruffians, I can give you the names, or rather the nicknames, of several: "Beardy," "the Beadle," "the Cellarman,"—women too, "Big Ernestine," little Nini, who, I told you before, has for her fancy-man, the bully Paulet—calls himself a stone mason, even works at his trade in his spare moments, for I know Moche has lately given him several jobs to do. Then there is "Beauty Boy," another choice blackguard, and . . ."

But Tom Bob suddenly interrupted his informant.

"I am dog tired," he declared, "and half dropping asleep. Listen here, Monsieur Fandor, my own opinion is, an investigation is advisable before deciding on anything. I give you my word I will investigate . . ."

12. A Stroke of Genius

The American detective Tom Bob was no ordinary man. The very first day after his arrival he had signalized his presence and drawn public attention to himself in a manner at once original and redounding greatly to his credit. Within a few hours of landing on French soil he had shown his mettle by the arrest of a dangerous malefactor, a professional criminal, "Beauty Boy," the apache. The same day he had adroitly escaped an abominable attempt on his life, and, to crown it all, in the course of a series of interviews accorded to the reporters of the different newspapers, he had, in direct contradiction to the generally received opinion, stoutly maintained that the ex-journalist Fandor, the friend of the man Juve, now incarcerated in the prison of *La Santé,* was a very honest man, the last person to have committed the crimes imputed to him.

For several days, in fact up to the time Tom Bob had come to divert the public curiosity, the Inspectors of the Criminal Investigation Bureau had carried out the most minute investigations at the house where the bank messenger's murder was supposed, if not to have been committed, at any rate to have been planned and prepared. For whole days together police officers in plain clothes pursued careful inquiries, questioning the inmates, even going so far as to collect evidence as to the past life and antecedents of each of the tenants.

True, no actual trace had been found of the unfortunate employee of the Comptoir National, but the uniform button discovered in the garret where M. Moche had with such misplaced generosity, as he said himself, given a charitable asylum to Fandor made it reasonable to conclude, without any undue pressing of the evidence, that the collector had disappeared not of his own free will and initiative, but simply because he had been first robbed and then murdered. Was the same assassin also responsible for the death of the police officers? Was Fandor the author of both crimes? Many members of the Department were inclined to think he was, though others hesitated to commit themselves to any definite opinion.

At any rate, there was one certainty, one sure fact, that delighted the inmates of No. 125 Rue Saint-Fargeau, to wit, that the police, diverted from the old line of scent and henceforth mainly preoccupied to discover the assassin of Désiré Ferrand, were more or less relaxing in their embarrassing attentions, and no longer exercised the same constant and careful surveillance over the scene of the first tragedy.

At an early hour one morning, three or four days after Tom Bob's arrival in Paris, old Moche, looking just as dubious and dirty as usual, reached his office in the Rue Saint-Fargeau, where he had not been for several days not that this was a matter to cause the concierge any surprise, M. Moche being habitually a decidedly intermittent occupier of his rooms. The old man seemed in jovial spirits. With little, quick steps he mounted the stairs, whistling a tune. Then inserting a key in the lock, he entered his flat. But the old brigand, a cautious man ever since his adventure with Paulet and Nini, took good care to double lock the door again behind him. Changing his long frock coat for a short jacket, and planting on top of the wig that covered his bald pate a velvet skullcap in place of his silk hat, the old fellow set to work to sort out the numerous letters that had arrived by post. To tell the truth, he did not take the trouble to open them, for he knew by merely glancing at the address what each contained, to wit, nothing whatever—a sheet of blank paper or a cutting from an old newspaper. The fact is, Moche was in a better position than anyone to know beforehand the contents of each of his letters, inasmuch as, being desirous of putting the concierge off the scent and impressing him by the voluminous correspondence intended for him, the old man had the habit of every day addressing a dozen letters and prospectuses to himself! It was a dodge to make people believe he really followed the profession of a business agent and could boast a numerous clientele.

This time, however, in sorting his letters, Moche put one aside. This particular one he did *not* recognize, and discontinuing his scrutiny, he tore open the envelope in feverish haste. It was written on good paper—evidently from a correspondent of importance. M. Moche read:

"Sir—I have to inform you that I have just arrived in Paris and propose to call on Wednesday morning at your office. You obliged me some time ago by a loan of money; I now intend to discharge the debt. I am therefore coming to repay you . . ."

"Ha, ha!" laughed Père Moche, "a pleasant surprise! For once a debtor writes to say he is going to pay up without any need to twist his tail. Well, the exception proves the rule. All the same I rather doubt what it all means."

Then he jumped to the fourth page and examined the signature.

"By the Lord," he exclaimed, "it's my young friend Ascott . . . Ascott, that feeble-minded Englishman I have heard nothing of for a very long time—though I never felt any anxiety about the man. Oh! I knew very well he'd been in Paris the last forty-eight hours! Is there anything that happens Père Moche *doesn't* know? Let's see what else the young gentleman has to say? . . . He wants to settle up with me, a very laudable intention, coming from a very honest man. Now how much does the chap owe me?"

Leaving the letter on his desk, the old man trotted over to his safe, opened it, and hauling out a ledger began turning over the leaves eagerly.

"*Ascott,* here we are! Yes, eighteen months ago I lent him 15,000 francs; unless my calculations are all wrong, at the rate of interest agreed upon, he ought to pay me back today 22,000. Ha! not a bad bit of business! If only a man could have windfalls like that every day, he would be a millionaire in no time!"

So saying, M. Moche locked up the book again in the strongbox, and came back to his desk, rubbing his hands.

"I've only read the first few lines of his letter," he said to himself, "and there's four pages of the stuff. Can it by any chance be that Ascott at the end of his epistle has modified the good intentions expressed at the beginning?"

Moche took up the letter again and skimmed through it eagerly. "No," he said, his face brightening, "no, he really means to pay me back."

But a look of chagrin suddenly darkened his ugly face.

"Why, this is vexing," he muttered. "Now he doesn't need me anymore, he scorns me, he wishes us to break off all relations, he intends never to see me again. Oh, ho! none of that, my fine fellow! Just when the goose is fatted, I'm to part with it, eh? No fear, I'm not such a fool! It's up to you, my good Monsieur Moche, to arrange things so as to creep up Mister Ascott's sleeve from now on—and now more than ever."

The old advocate was at this point in his lucubrations, more and more convinced that at all hazards he must remain the rich young Englishman's friend, when he was startled by a loud knock at the door.

"That's Ascott," thought Moche, "let's be quick and let him in." The old fellow darted to the entrance of his modest dwelling, rapidly turned the key in the lock and threw the door wide open.

To his profound surprise he found the newcomer was not the elegantly dressed gentleman he expected to see, but a little woman in a flowered peignoir, her hair down her back and her feet crammed into an old pair of sandals. It was Nini Guinon, who had come down from the floor above to pay a neighborly visit to Père Moche.

"Hallo!" cried the child, who, without waiting for an invitation, had slipped into M. Moche's office behind the barred partition, "why, you're a regular bird of passage! never at home, always out! Every time I pass your door, I knock, I ring a peal, I stand there waiting—nothing! nobody! the bird's flown, the old fox is not in his earth."

Nini was both angry and excited, as she stood before the old man, passing a feverish hand over her pale brow and ruffling her black locks, while the other looked at her without moving a muscle or saying a word.

"I'm in a hole," went on the young baggage, "and I've got to get out of it, Père Moche. I'm fed up with the whole business, I am! Anyway, here's straight talking—if you don't go the way I want, I'll just be off and blow the gaff to the police."

"You'll never do that, Nini," the old man expostulated in cajoling tones, "you're much too nice a girl."

But Nini declined to be softened by compliments: "I shall do what I say," she insisted.

"But come, out with it! what's it all about?" Moche demanded.

"What's it all about, eh?" returned the girl, "why, it's as clear as mud. I'm in a tight place, and other folks are going to be there too if things go on as they are. To begin with, I've had enough of living with Paulet. He frightens me, the man frightens me! Ever since I saw him do in the bank fellow, I'm terrified all the time he'll do my business for me, too. He's no spunk at all. It's not blood he has in his veins, it's water. I sleep with him and I know what I'm talking about. Every night he lies and sweats. It's fear, that's what it is! He dreams of the police, he dreams about the dead man, he yells out in his sleep. The man's all broke to pieces, he'll come to a bad end. If the dicks ever come questioning, he'll never have savvy enough to sweet talk his way out of it, and then, by God! we'll all be in the soup!"

"Alas! my dear child," murmured the old fellow hypocritically, "what do you want me to do? All that business has nothing to do with me. You have killed a man, the stolen money has disappeared, you understand, disappeared, nobody can say where it is. Now suppose they accused me, the thing wouldn't hold water for a moment. Why? because I'm well known as an honest, respectable businessman. So get out of your own difficulties!"

As a matter of fact Nini had from the first understood perfectly well what attitude old Moche would adopt under the circumstances. Not a doubt of it, if things turned out badly, the old business agent was clever enough to pull his iron safely out of the fire, and certainly cynical enough to leave his confederates in the lurch. But Nini had no notion of things going like that. She strode up to M. Moche, and shaking her little fist in the old man's wrinkled face:

"As sure as my name's Nini," she swore, "if ever we get run in for this job, I give you my oath, Père Moche, you'll leave every feather of your dirty plumage behind, but if we come to an agreement. . . ."

"If we come to an agreement . . ." the advocate repeated the phrase with newly aroused interest.

"Well, then," Nini went on, assuming the soft, coaxing, wheedling voice every woman can use on occasion, "if we come to some agreement in case of trouble arising, we shall be two, you and I, to say we have nothing whatever to do with the affair of the bank messenger, and that it was Paulet who did the trick all by himself, and got all there was to be got out of it . . . There!"

The offer of partnership thus formulated by the young slut was just the sort of thing to appeal to the old usurer. Nodding his head approvingly:

"Your notion's really not such a bad one, my little girl," he said. "Only, what's to become of you?"

Nini, encouraged by the way the interview was shaping, had dropped nonchalantly into the one and only armchair the room contained. Now, with eyes fixed on the ceiling, the girl sat in a daydream, a prophetic dream.

"I have a sort of a notion," she murmured, "that with all these new complications, Paulet is going to get nabbed. First, there's that journalist Fandor drawing attention to the house, then they find the button off the poor devil's uniform in your garret. Fandor disappears, on the other hand Tom Bob arrives. What does the fellow count for? I don't know, but I have my doubts. He must be pretty smart, he nabbed "Beauty Boy" in less time than it takes to tell the story! So then, it all comes to this—little Nini's had enough, thank you, she's got to bolt, and that at sixty miles an hour, and Papa Moche, who's no fool neither, has got to find her a place with the well-heeled, to save her from any future worries. Does that suit you, Père Moche? Is it settled, eh? . . . You'll clearly understand this, I didn't leave the bosom of my family to go and rot on Devil's Island or be eaten up by the mosquitoes at New Caledonia."

Père Moche was prodigiously diverted by this announcement of her principles of action on the part of Paulet's girl mistress. Undoubtedly there was something to be made of this little minx with the wide-awake look and bright eyes, so vicious and so astute. He was about to reply, when suddenly a peal of the door bell was heard.

"Who's that coming?" Nini asked anxiously, as she instinctively laid a hand on her bosom to restrain the excited beating of her heart.

But Moche reassured her: "It's nine o'clock," he said. "No doubt it's a client who has an appointment. Hide yourself. I'm going to take him into the salon, then you'll take off while I'm receiving him." Moche was right: on opening the door he found himself face to face with the young Englishman, Mr. Ascott, whose abusive letter he had been reading half an hour before. Moche with the supple servility that belonged to his mean, cautious nature, was lavish in bowing and scraping, bending to the ground before the wealthy foreigner, while the latter, with an icy dignity, barely acknowledged his creditor's courtesies with a curt nod:

"If milord will condescend to step into my reception room? . . ." suggested M. Moche . . .

Ascott obeyed mechanically, but disclaimed the rank his host had given him.

"I am not Lord Ascott, Monsieur Moche. I am plain Mr. Ascott. The title of lord belongs to my honored father."

"Ho, ho!" suggested the old man with a tactless grin, "a father—a father may die one fine day, and if I'm not mistaken, the sons inherit both the money and all the privileges and prerogatives."

The young man shrugged his shoulders:

"I forbid you to speak of my honored father, sir, and besides that, you must know that in no case shall I bear the title. I am a younger son of the family, my older brother will be My Lord."

But Moche was incorrigible and went on to insinuate: "The elder brother no doubt . . . but suppose he should happen to die, too."

Ascott stamped his foot angrily and cast a furious look at the old moneylender.

"That is enough, sir," he declared in an indignant voice quivering with restrained anger, "that is enough! Let us settle up our accounts. That done, we will break off all relations."

But Moche was for slipping away: "Forgive me, dear sir, noble gentleman, honorable signor, if I trouble you to wait a few moments, but there is a lady in my office, a very important client. I must conclude my business with her. By your leave . . ." Moche, with another low bow, awaited the reply. "Get done, and be quick about it!" was the rough answer.

The old brigand went back immediately to the office, where Nini was still waiting. She had never budged. Moche approached her with an air of triumph, calling softly:

"Come here, little girl!" and on her obeying, drew her to the window, setting her with her face to the full light. With his coarse, hairy hands the old usurer lifted the child's tousled locks, parted them on her forehead and imprisoned the tangled curls in his palm. Nini let him do as he liked, puzzled and uncomprehending.

"You know," declared the old man, "with your hair down like a little girlie, you look ever so young."

"But," protested Nini, "I'm not old. I'm barely sixteen and a half."

"I daresay," resumed the other, "and when you don't put on your naughty look and haven't been drinking, you might verily be taken for a little saint. Now let's see your hands."

Again Nini did as she was bid, and Moche spreading out the fingers on his forearm, examined the nails. "Quite good, again," he announced, "carefully enough kept for a poor man's child, and not too well kept neither, to make them think it's a harlot's hand."

Next moment, taking the girl by the shoulders, he gazed fixedly into her face with the air of one inspired.

"Nini," he cried, "I have a brilliant idea, and if only you're not too clumsy, we're going, you and I, to do something mighty smart. Nini, next door there I've got a ripe pear, it's up to you to pluck it. Only, listen to me, I give you ten minutes to rig yourself out—not, mind you, like a street wench, but like an innocent little maid. Leave your hair down, don't wear a hat, put on your plainest frock, drop your eyes, look sweet and modest, and think of what you were a year ago, a good little virtuous girl, living with her mother and just done learning up her catechism. Presently, that is to say, soon as you're ready, come and pay me a visit. . . . I'm good for the rest!"

Nini did not need telling twice: "I'm fly," she declared, slapping the old fellow shrewdly on the back. Then, lightly and airily, she darted off.

"She's a jewel!" thought Père Moche, as he noted the tricksy grace of the young harlot, "with a bit of training, and if she'll but listen to me, I'll make something of the girl!"

But this was no time for daydreams.

Reassuming an air of gravity and importance, Moche went in search of his client, whom he invited to return with him to the office.

Such was the geniality displayed by the old usurer that the phlegmatic Englishman, who had come to see him with the clear and definite intention of exchanging simply and solely the words absolutely necessary to effect the repayment he wished to make, allowed himself little by little to be drawn into conversation.

"Moche," declared Ascott, "here are your twenty-five notes of a thousand francs. You will give me a receipt."

"Why certainly, most noble sir, with the greatest pleasure."

But the old scamp feigned forgetfulness: "You owed me twenty-five thousand francs you say, *was* that the sum?" he asked innocently.

"Twenty-five thousand, yes," Ascott repeated.

In reality it was three thousand less, but the old thief took good care not to recall the fact! Wishing to complete the formalities with a certain solemnity, he went over to his strong-box—there was actually next to nothing in it—and drew out the one and only article it contained, the big ledger to wit. After turning over a number of blank leaves, he opened at the page showing Ascott's name. For a long time the businessman hung over the columns of figures as if making a series of complicated calculations. At last he looked up:

"My excellent client," he said gravely, "you will excuse my contradicting you, but it is not twenty-five thousand francs you owe me, it is merely twenty-four thousand, five hundred. I am nothing if not honest. I wouldn't wrong you by a single centime."

The effect of this declaration was to make the young Englishman laugh: "Lord! Monsieur Moche," he declared, "they've changed you surely, the thing's impossible!"

But the usurer put on his grandest air: "My dear sir, strict probity in business is my maxim! I assure you it pays, the future is to the men of honor, and it's just because I am conscientious that I benefit by the fidelity of my clients. You yourself, Monsieur Ascott, will certainly require my services again some day, and you may rely on always finding me devoted to your interests."

"That," Ascott broke in drily, "I cannot promise. I don't care, I tell you frankly, to have relations with men of your stamp. In the last eighteen months I've been traveling up and down the world, I have changed very much, I have money now. I am going to make a home in Paris, where I propose to live as a good citizen, spending no more than my income."

"I've been told," M. Moche interrupted, "that you have just bought a delightful little house in the Rue Fortuny."

"How came you to know that?" demanded Ascott, not denying the fact.

"Ha!" said Moche, "in the great world of business and finance to which I belong, we know pretty well everything that happens."

"Really?" said Ascott incredulously, amazed to think that so insignificant a person as Moche, a moneylender of a low type, could be in any way connected with the big and highly respected bankers of the Place de Paris through whom he had negotiated the purchase of the house in the Rue Fortuny. But Moche was well posted without a doubt. By a fresh question he more than ever surprised the rich Englishman. He now suggested, speaking without any reticence or beating around the bush:

"Doubtless it's to build a pretty nest for a grand mistress you've bought that exquisite house. I have heard say that a certain Monsieur Ascott, here present, is head over heels in love with a certain Russian princess named Sonia Danidoff, with whom he crossed the Atlantic on board the *Lorraine*."

Ascott sprang up in extreme agitation.

"Moche," he cried, "you think you are a wonderful man who knows everything, but you are behind the curve this time, my friend. Yes, I admit, I *was* deeply in love with the Princess Danidoff, and I confess I was in hopes that in France, after the persevering court I paid her, she would at last consent to grant me her favors—but events have decided otherwise."

"Poor Monsieur Ascott!" murmured M. Moche. Then he added, casting a side glance at his companion to judge of the effect of his words:

"To think that fool princess prefers a common detective to you!"

Ascott literally flew at the old villain's throat, and shaking him by the shoulder:

"So then," he vociferated, "so then, you know everything?"

Moche smiled quietly:

"No, not everything," he protested, "but some little matters! . . . I take it the Princess Danidoff has no more brains than a sparrow, she must be out of her wits to like this low-class police spy better than you . . ."

But Moche suddenly stopped dead: "I beg your pardon, but there's someone knocking," he exclaimed, and went to open the door, pretending to be greatly surprised.

Throwing out his arms and speaking loud enough for Ascott to hear him, he greeted the visitor warmly:

"Oh! Little Nini, it's you, is it? What a stroke of luck! How is my dear sister, your good mother? Do you bring me good news?"

Like a finished actress, Nini stood up on tiptoe, threw her arms round the old scamp's neck and kissed him on the brow tenderly, but respectfully. Paulet's mistress had perfectly well understood Père Moche's instructions. With her modest, decent getup, she had all the appearance, all the charm of youth, freshness and purity, of an honest little Paris working girl, one of those pretty flowers that bloom in many a happy home of good, respectable, industrious working people. The girl was entirely charming with her virginal air of innocence and chastity.

Père Moche was all smiles as he looked at her. Such was the old scamp's artfulness in disguising his true feelings that as he stood beside the young girl he offered the very picture of a kind, good uncle, proud and happy in the beauty of his little niece! The man seemed to forget his sordid trade amid these tokens of family affection. Like a father proud of his child, he turned to Ascott, who had been the interested witness of this intimate and touching little scene.

"Allow me, my dear sir," he said, "to introduce my young niece Eugenie Guinon, a good little working girl, who makes at this present time her three francs a day. She's barely sixteen, but a tall girl, don't you think for her age?" Ascott bowed to the young girl, muttering to himself: "She's charming, charming!" But Moche, seeming not to hear the remark, went on, addressing himself to Nini:

"Come, don't be frightened, show you know your manners, say good day to the gentleman, offer him your hand!" Nini dropped her eyes, shyly extended her arm, let Ascott imprison her little hand in his nervous fingers, which held it a moment or two—perhaps longer than was quite necessary.

But old Moche was anxious, as a good uncle should be, not to make his niece waste her time.

"My dear child," he declared, smacking a big kiss on her blushing cheek, "I'm so pleased to have seen you, but you must run away now, for I suppose you've work to do, eh?"

"Yes," replied Nini in a little soft, childish voice, "I must be off to deliver a bodice for the lady on the third floor, and then I'm to match some things at the shops near the Bourse. But I came to ask you, dear uncle, to come to dinner with us this evening. Mama will be so pleased." Moche never moved a muscle as he listened to the little speech Nini Guinon reeled off, looking her straight in the eyes and preserving an imperturbable gravity. The old brigand was lost in wonder. Ah! how well the child played her part, so cutely, so cleverly—with her way of never looking at Ascott, but all the same contriving to attract the Englishman's admiration. Most certainly he would make something of little Nini, never fear!

The bogus uncle and the pseudo-niece took leave of each other prettily. Nini dropped a curtsy as she withdrew, while Ascott, with shining eyes, bowed to the ground before her.

Hardly had the charming vision disappeared before Ascott, hitherto so frigid and impassive in demeanor, showed a complete change of attitude, marching up and down M. Moche's office in the throes of a feverish excitement. But the old scamp pretended not to notice anything, busily occupied it seemed in sorting his papers. Suddenly he started round. The Englishman was addressing him. "Monsieur Moche, Monsieur Moche!" he called. Then in hesitating accents Ascott went on:

"Monsieur Moche, you have a niece, sir . . . and a devilish pretty girl she is!"

"Well, yes," the old brigand observed, feigning not to understand the young man's drift, "it's true she has fine eyes, but she's quite a child yet . . . the 'awkward age,' you know . . . later on, I believe, when she's developed a bit, then her good mother and I will find the girl a good husband."

"Moche," broke in Ascott, "I want to know your niece."

"But," returned the villain, still with the same affectation of naïveté, "you do know her, didn't I introduce you?"

"You are a trifle obtuse, Monsieur Moche, or else a bit too clever. It's not in that sense I wish to know her, not I. Your niece is to my taste. At the present moment I have no mistress . . ."

The old "advocate" sprang back, feigning the most extravagant indignation:

"Oh, sir, sir," he cried, "my dear sir, no, upon my word, I could never have believed that of you. Do you dare to come to me to make such a proposal? Certainly I'm not a rich man, and little Nini's sole and only capital is her virtue and her beauty—it is something, it is a great deal even—but by the Lord God, I give you my oath, I will never, never agree to such a bargain. What do you take me for?"

But Ascott still persisted:

"I take you, Monsieur Moche, for a man of common sense . . . come now, I or another, what harm can it do you? . . . while, seeing it is I—"

"But, my dear sir, my dear client," stammered Moche, who was acting to perfection despair, embarrassment and perplexity, "but, sir, not you any more than another. My little niece is still a child, and then, she is an honest girl and good and virtuous. I wouldn't for anything in all the world . . . Besides, just think of it—I, her uncle!"

Ascott interrupted the indignant speaker:

"Come now, how much?"

M. Moche seemed overwhelmed by the insult. He sank into his armchair and took his head between his hands, vociferating in heartbroken tones and a voice choked with sobs:

"Why, what sin have I committed that God lets me be treated in this fashion! I am only a poor advocate, and my niece just a humble work-girl, but we are both of us—I should say, all three of us, for I mustn't forget her sainted mother—we are all honest folk, worthy of the highest respect . . . and we're expected to . . . God in heaven . . . we're expected to . . ."

Moche left his sentence unfinished, broke off his peroration in mid career, for it had become entirely unnecessary. Peeping through his parted fingers, the old rascal had not missed a single one of Ascott's movements. Now the latter, leaving the old man to finish out his litany of lamentations by himself, had suddenly left the room, slamming the door behind him. This was just what Moche was hoping for; he calculated that the Englishman, seeing nothing could be made of the uncle, was going to try and catch up with the niece before she had left the house. Treading softly, he crept to the door opening on the landing outside, the same one Ascott had shut a moment before, and set it ajar. There he stood listening, his face beaming, and rubbing his hands.

Ascott, who had caught sight of Nini Guinon on the floor below as he was going downstairs, was leaning over the bannister and calling in a voice shaking with excitement:

"Mademoiselle! Psst! Mademoiselle, I say! Mademoiselle Eugenie! Listen!"

Then it was Nini's clear, flute-like voice, pitched in a tone of perfect innocence, that answered:

"Who's calling me? Is it you, dear uncle?"

Ascott, lowering his voice, and now flying three steps at a time down the stairs to join the girl below, went on: "Why, no, mademoiselle, so to speak, it's not exactly your uncle, but it is I, his friend, the gentleman who was in his office just now. Listen, I've something to tell you. Will you let me walk with you?"

Then the two voices mingled in an indistinct murmur, and the pair could be heard leaving the house.

Moche went back into his rooms with every sign of profound satisfaction, skipping about clumsily like a dancing bear in a merry mood.

"Taken! The bait's taken fine!" he chuckled. "Without a doubt, here's another stroke of genius to good old Père Moche's credit!"

13. The Wall That Bled

Elizabeth Dollon was busily engaged installing her belongings in the new flat in the Rue de l'Evangile, into which she had moved the previous evening. The girl possessed a modest stock of furniture of the simplest possible sort, but on the upkeep of which she lavished the most fastidious care. For her every piece of furniture, every article in the rooms, was replete with fond associations. Since the sinister events that had saddened her life, since the tragedies of which she had been the heroine, here were the only things she loved, the only objects that appealed at once to her memory and her affection. Today she was settling in, bent on arranging an interior that should be to her taste.

It was a Sunday. The weather promised to be magnificent, and though her windows looked out on the not very attractive spectacle of the city gasometers, they yet possessed the enormous advantage of facing no buildings from which inquisitive or offensive neighbors could overlook her. The day was bright and cheerful, the air pure and balmy, and from time to time Elizabeth, choking with the dust raised by her domestic operations, would go and lean out of the casement to breathe its freshness. She was thoroughly enjoying her day of rest. All week she was engaged over the books of a big business house in the gloomy district of Aubervilliers.

Her new home in the Rue de l'Evangile suited her well, not only because the rooms were pleasant, but also for the fact of its nearness to the scene of her labors. At the same time, she had heard within the last few days of a chance of finding another post that would suit her still better—a position as cashier in a large restaurant in the Bois de Boulogne. The girl hoped with all her heart that this possibility might become a reality.

But presently the girl's thoughts turned to graver matters,

and her smooth brow was furrowed with lines of care and anxiety. Her eyes, usually so bright and clear, darkened in melancholy reverie. It was the look, at once angry and regretful, that appeared on the girl's face every time she remembered Jerome Fandor. Whenever she thought of the journalist, a sense of disquiet and perplexity filled her mind. Was she still in love with him? Could it be that she still felt a mysterious passion for the man who was the author—at least so the unhappy girl was convinced—of all her misfortunes, the source of the fatal events that had cast a gloom over all her youth? Was it really possible that so amiable a young man was the accomplice of Fantômas, if not Fantômas himself? For long she had refused to believe it, but henceforth it was impossible to doubt the fact. The latest developments, the events that had just befallen, the violence offered her on the Boulevard de Belleville, confirmed the suspicion beyond all question.

Dreading further persecutions by the monster that seemed relentlessly bent on her undoing, Elizabeth Dollon had experienced a deep sense of satisfaction after her change of abode, persuaded that an era of peace and tranquility was now before her. Nevertheless, in excess of caution, she had charged Mme. Doulenques, the concierge of the house in the Rue des Couronnes, not to give her new address to anyone whatsoever. Moreover, having been only forty-eight hours installed in her new apartments, she was not expecting anyone to call.

It was therefore not without considerable perturbation that suddenly, about two o'clock that afternoon, the girl heard a violent ring at the bell. Who was it? Who could be coming to pay her a visit? However, she was somewhat reassured on recognizing the concierge's voice calling to her through the door.

"Mam'zelle, I say, mam'zelle! Are you asleep then, or are you gone deaf? It's five minutes we've been tugging at your bell!"

On opening the door, Elizabeth Dollon found herself confronted not only by the portress, but by a man as well, a man of forty or thereabouts, with a pleasant, jovial-looking face. He was dressed in a long-skirted white blouse, and carried under one arm a half-dozen rolls of paper, while the other hand held a deep paste-pot with a big brush with a wooden handle sticking up in it. The workman greeted the young girl with an almost imperceptible nod of the head, as she unclosed the door.

"Excuse me, mam'zelle," he said, "but I'm the painter and paper-hanger and I'm come from the landlord to paper your place. Seemingly you want it done?"

"Certainly I do," the girl answered him, "there's the whole of one room wants fresh papering. But," she added, "I'm not entitled, am I, to choose the paper?"

The man smiled and nodded.

"Oh, yes, you are, mam'zelle, and I've brought patterns!"— adding, with a big laugh. "Do you suppose I'm going to paper your walls straight away like that, in less time than it takes to say 'knife'. You've got to choose, then we'll see how the thing looks, and then, when you've made up your mind, we'll see about fixing up the stuff."

The concierge, seeing her presence was no longer required and the introductions being duly made, took her departure, with a word of excuse.

"I'll leave you now," the good woman said, "and get back to my lodge. The fact is, I've got company this afternoon."

Elizabeth Dollon led the way into her flat and took the paper-hanger straight to the room that was to be decorated. It was the furthest from the entrance-door, the one in which M. Moche, the landlord, had had the partition re-established that had been removed by the previous tenant to make the two sets into one. The workman displayed no great hurry to set to work, and began to ferret about everywhere and examine the young woman's furniture in a rather inquisitorial fashion.

"A sweet, pretty place, this!" he observed. "Quite a little nest for turtledoves!"

Elizabeth Dollon forced a smile: "Oh!" she protested, "you are mistaken, sir. Love is not a happiness I can ever hope for."

The workman looked at her with a flattering smile: "It won't be your fault, then," he declared. "A pretty girl like you can't fail . . ."

But Elizabeth Dollon was not in a mood to listen to the silly speeches the forward fellow might choose to make her. Not wishing, however, to seem too prim and prudish, she adroitly turned the conversation:

"How comes it," she asked, "you're working on a Sunday?"

"Lord! mam'zelle," replied the workman, "because I go on the spree Mondays, but that's neither here nor there, we've gassed enough, eh? and it's high time to get to work."

The man laid the rolls of paper he had brought with him on the floor, and opened them out one by one, asking the young lady to make her choice. "Do you prefer the sky-blue ones, or the pink, or the light green? There's some of all sorts—gay and bright and fresh—like your color, mam'zelle!"

But "mam'zelle" took no notice of the compliment, and fixed her choice on a light blue paper. Then, as the paper-hanger seemed more inclined to gossip than do his work, she announced:

"I'm going into the next room to put various things in order. You'll call me if you want me presently."

Then something occurred to her suddenly. "Sir," she asked the man, "I have a large picture there, too heavy for me to manage. If it's not troubling you, will you be so kind as to fix it up on the wall?"—to which the workman agreed readily enough: "With all the pleasure in life," he assured her, "you know all I ask is to make myself agreeable."

Elizabeth thanked him drily, almost regretting she had ever asked the favor. The man's advances rather frightened her. Without quite knowing why, the young girl felt suspicious and began to wish the fellow gone as soon as could be. Meantime the workman began to make hay in the room where he was, a sure sign he was going to do something at last. Mademoiselle Dollon withdrew into the adjoining room, shutting the door of communication behind her.

But barely a moment or two had passed since the girl had left the workman to his own devices when she heard a heavy crash followed by a terrific oath from the man's lips! She dashed to the door and was on the point of re-entering the room where the paper-hanger was at work, when the latter sprang forward and prevented her.

"What now, sir!" she cried, "open the door, I say!"

But from the other side the workman still barred her entrance: "Don't come in, mademoiselle, don't come in!"

"But, after all, what's happening?" she demanded.

"Nothing to do with you, don't come in!"

"But I insist. This is ridiculous, I'm in my own house, let me in!"

Then she heard the strange occupant of the room whence the mysterious noise had come turn the key in the lock, making any further attempt to force an entrance impossible. Elizabeth was more and more terrified.

"Sir," she ordered, "I must, I *will* have this door opened, I wish to know what is the matter, what that noise was."

But the more excited the poor girl grew, the calmer the workman's voice became. He announced composedly: "I will not open the door, I told you so before, do what you will!"

In vain the frightened girl shook the locked door, it would not yield. Clearly, a mere waste of strength! What *could* be happening within? What was the secret, the tragedy perhaps, this man of mystery was resolved at all hazards to conceal?

Driven beyond all patience, Elizabeth Dollon hurried on to the landing outside and leaning over the balustrade of the stairs, at the top of her voice, that rose shrill in panic and fear, called for: "Help! help! help!!"

Neighbors came running up, surprised and alarmed, and presently, the girl's frantic cries still continuing, the concierge, attracted by the uproar, appeared on the scene.

"Whatever is the matter, my dear?" she demanded—and in broken accents Mademoiselle Dollon told the good woman her story. The portress was astounded at the workman's extraordinary behavior. She boldly advanced in her turn, to beat with her heavy fist on the closely guarded door.

"Open," she shouted, "open the door! or there'll be mischief doing."

But the calm, slightly sarcastic voice of the individual who had locked himself within, replied as before: "I will not open."

Meantime an impromptu council of war was being held among the neighbors gathered on the landing:

"Go for the police, that's the only thing to be done. It's a criminal or a madman has locked himself up in there! We can't have that poor young girl left alone at his mercy."

The concierge, firing her last round of ammunition, threatened the man:

"If you don't open the door, they'll go and fetch the police!"

And the mysterious intruder, in the calmest way, without so much as raising his voice, replied:

"Yes, go and fetch the police!"

Some minutes passed, during which this last proposal was being put into effect.

Presently the heavy footsteps of a police sergeant and a constable made themselves heard on the stairs, and the two representatives of law and order effected a cautious entry into Mademoiselle Dollon's rooms:

"It is the police," they announced themselves. "Will you open the door, yes or no?"

They waited a few seconds, then the key turned in the lock and the door opened softly a little way. The paper-hanger's face appeared in the aperture and the man, addressing the sergeant:

"I will trouble you to step inside, sir," he said. "Queer things are happening here, your presence is required," then added, pointing to the constable: "The other gentleman as well, perhaps, but no, he might prefer the duty of getting the ladies out of the way. It is no sight for women."

The calm, authoritative manner of the workman impressed the two officers, and the sergeant mechanically ordered his subordinate:

"Make them move on, please!"

Then the sergeant followed the man into the empty room with its four blank walls. The latter led the officer straight to the party-wall that had lately been reconstructed by the landlord's orders.

"What do you see there?" he demanded, pointing a finger

at the white surface. The sergeant looked long and curiously at the spot indicated.

"I see a stain," he announced at last, "a brown, or is it a red stain. What does that mean? . . . Are you poking fun at me? Might you be wishing to pull my leg, I wonder. Now, to start with, I call upon you to explain yourself, why did you refuse to open that door to the young lady when she asked you?"

The workman shrugged his shoulders: "That's not the question in hand," he said quietly. "What do you think of that stain? I ought to tell you it made its appearance immediately after I had made a hole by driving in a nail."

"I think nothing," retorted the sergeant, "except that all this is nonsensical and incomprehensible balderdash. . . . Yes, and that I am going to take you to the station for having put the authorities to unnecessary trouble!"

The workman went on smiling: "Unnecessary!" he remarked, "don't you think?"

To disabuse the sergeant of such an idea, the other picked up a hammer and started hammering the wall round the little brown patch. The plaster broke away in little flakes that crumbled and fell in dust on the floor, and presently, under the rain of blows, the wall itself showed a crack. Suddenly a brick tumbled out, and the officer, who was watching the operation with eyes of amazement, sprang back with a cry of horror, while even the paper-hanger himself gave a little start of surprise.

Behind the plaster, inside the wall, which was of considerable thickness, appeared an appalling sight! It was a human head, wan and livid, a man's head with features streaked and spotted by the discolorations of death!

The sergeant gazed at the workman in indescribable agitation. "What is it?" he asked, "what is it? I call upon you to tell me what it is?"

"It is a dead man, no doubt about that—a dead man they've walled up in there, there can be no doubt of that either!"

"But in that case," exclaimed the sergeant, "it must be a question of crime, murder! It is a most grave and serious matter. The Commissary must be advised!"

The mysterious workman bowed: "I am entirely of your opinion," he said, "the presence of the Commissary appears to me to be indispensable."

The sergeant, quite beside himself, ran to the outer door, where his subordinate was keeping good guard.

"Japuzot!" he ordered, "run quick to the station and bring the chief. I have discovered a crime. I have just found it is a question of murder!"

Meantime a confused clamor came from the crowd still thronging the landing, at the top of the stairs. Elizabeth Dollon, who had remained transfixed with terror in the outer room, wanted to see what was happening. Opportunely enough the sergeant stopped her.

"Stay where you are, mademoiselle," he ordered. "It is not a sight for a young lady. The concierge will keep you company."

Then, as the gallant officer did not wish the place to be invaded by the curious crowd, nor yet to lose sight of the dubious individual within, he shut to the outer door of the flat. Leaving the people on the landing to their various conjectures, he returned to the gruesome room, where the paper-hanger still remained. The latter was seated quietly on the floor, for there were no chairs in the room, and had lit a cigarette, and now, with the utmost composure, offered one to the sergeant.

"There's a bad smell," he remarked. "It's the corpse. Will you smoke?"

The sergeant, dumbfounded by the man's calmness in presence of such tragic happenings, could not manage to light his cigarette. His lips were as tremulous as his hands. At last, at the third or fourth attempt, he succeeded, but he had not taken half a dozen puffs when his sense of discipline made him suddenly toss his cigarette out of the window. A peremptory ring had just sounded at the outer door, and the sergeant at once inferred it was the "chief" demanding admittance.

He was right. The Commissary, a little, fat man, with an imposing paunch, dashed forward out of breath, hustling everybody to right and left, and hurried into the ill-omened room. His eyes fell first on the grim head that looked out, an image of horror, from the wall where it was embedded. Then he turned to stare at the paper-hanger, who without the smallest show of respect towards the magistrate, remained sitting on the floor, still smoking with imperturbable aplomb.

The magistrate demanded: "What's to do here? Who are you? Who is the man? How does he come there? What have you to say for yourself?"

"There!"

"What do you mean by *'there'*?"

"There," the paper-hanger concluded his sentence: "there's what you want to know about, before your eyes."

The Commissary was boiling with impatience.

"Why, of course I want to know. What's been happening? How was this extraordinary discovery made?"

The workman, getting to his feet at last: "I would point out to you, Monsieur le Commissaire," he protested, "that it is not my business, but rather yours, to find out all this! Nonetheless, I am very willing to help you and give you my cooperation."

Going up to the wall, the workman began, with little measured taps, to break away the plaster round the dead man's head. As he worked, he explained:

"Driving a nail just now into the wall here, I saw drops of blood ooze out—a wall that bleeds is not a common sight—and before pushing my investigations further, I had the police sent for. Directly on your sergeant's arrival, I brought to light the unfortunate man's head. We have waited out of respect for your authority before carrying the investigation further. But, now you are come, Monsieur le Commissaire, I don't think there's anything need prevent our bringing to light the rest of the poor fellow's body."

The magistrate gave a twist to his mustache and acquiesced. "Proceed with your work," he directed, and the workman took up his hammer again. With a few rapid blows, he brought down the rest of the party-wall, and the unhappy victim's body was revealed in its entirety. It was a gruesome spectacle! A human being had been walled up there. The body had previously been coated with quicklime, and the extremities were already burned away. Still, the general aspect of the corpse was more or less intact. At the nape of the neck the dead man had a huge bruise, now quite black, and forming, at the top of the vertebrae, a great ball full of extravasated blood.

The victim wore a uniform, easily recognized, the familiar long, blue frock coat with silver buttons of the collectors in the service of the big credit houses. While the Commissary stood motionless, rooted to the spot, the workman had gone closer, and had cast a rapid glance at the inscription engraved on the buttons of the uniform. Next moment he announced the result of his scrutiny:

"*Comptoir National!* . . . There can be no doubt about it, Monsieur le Commissaire; the man is the collector of the Comptoir National who was murdered, hardly ten days ago, in the house in the Rue Saint-Fargeau!"

"But—but," stammered the Commissary, "how does the body come to be here?"

The paper-hanger urged suggestively:

"The house in the Rue Saint-Fargeau where the crime was committed and the house in the Rue de l'Evangile where we discover the corpse, belong to the same landlord, the business agent trading under the name of M. Moche."

The Commissary started violently: "M. Moche! I will have him arrested . ."

"You would be making a mistake!" the paper-hanger interrupted the magistrate.

"Why?"

"Because, if M. Moche was the murderer, he would never have been so imprudent as to hide his victim's body in a house belonging to himself. Besides, there are other people to suspect . . ."

"Why? Who?"

"God, sir!" declared the workman, "perhaps the individual from whom the bank messenger took up his last payment—one Paulet by name. Perhaps, again, the working mason who built that wall?"

"Who was the man?" questioned the Commissary.

"It is not for me to tell you, but for you to find him!"

The Commissary stood puzzling his brains, while the workman went on:

"Then, again, there's an individual open to suspicion on several counts, the man M. Moche lodged for forty-eight hours in his garret in the Rue Saint-Fargeau, who seized the opportunity to kill two police-officers who were coming to arrest him!"

"You accuse the journalist, Jerome Fandor, of the bank employee's murder?"

The workman shrugged his shoulders: "I accuse nobody," he protested, "I form hypotheses, and that's all. I . . . my part, in fact, is not to bring accusations, but simply . . ."

The Commissary, exasperated by these repeated suppressions, this reticence on the part of his interlocutor, suddenly came up to the workman and clapping both hands on his shoulder:

"This is all awfully mysterious," he complained, "now, for a start, you are going to tell me what you are doing here?"

"You can see for yourself I am a painter and paper-hanger, I came to put up papers."

"Put up papers! On a Sunday?"

"Yes, Monsieur le Commissaire."

"On a Sunday!—that won't wash! And besides, you strike me as a mighty hard-headed fellow. This crime is out of all ordinary—you show no surprise. This discovery is appalling—you never turn a hair! My lad, you make out too well . . ."

"Must a man be an imbecile because he's a working man?"

The Commissaire checked himself, vexed at his own want of tact: "I don't mean to say that, but still I find you a puzzle. You make your appearance here a short hour ago, you knock in a nail, the wall bleeds, you knock away the plaster covering the masonry and the corpse comes to light! You wait for the police to come to explain the crime. What have you to say for yourself?"

"Nothing!" the workman shook his head.

The Commissary was getting more and more annoyed: "I really do not know," he blustered, "what stops me from arresting you."

At this, the workman, suddenly assuming a sly look, looked his companion up and down:

"What stops you from arresting me? Why, nothing! But what will stop your doing it, I'm going to tell you . . ."

"Tell me then!"

"This . . ." and the mysterious workman with a quick movement, stripped off his blouse, and, beneath his working garment, he appeared elegantly attired in a dark blue suit. He wore a silk neckerchief of a quiet, gentlemanly cut and color, a collar of immaculate whiteness. Removing his cap, which till then had been pulled well down over his ears, he displayed a broad, intellectual forehead. His hair was of a light blonde, sprinkled with silvery threads at the temples.

Without giving a thought to the intense surprise he had created, the self-proclaimed workman looked the Commissary hard in the eyes, as he declared gravely:

"I am Tom Bob, American detective. A week ago I arrived in Paris, having crossed the Atlantic with the express purpose of tracking down Fantômas and effecting his arrest!"—adding courteously: "Monsieur le Commissaire, I am grateful to circumstances that have afforded me the pleasure of making your acquaintance."

So saying, the detective—for it was no other—made slowly for the door and was about to leave the room, when the Commissary called him back:

"Sir, what is this you tell me? You are Tom Bob?"

"Do you require proofs of the fact, sir?"

The magistrate begged pardon: "No, no, certainly not! I have no doubt whatever of your identity. Indeed I have seen portraits of you, I recognize you perfectly well. But I wanted to ask you one thing—you think this is a crime of Fantômas?"

Tom Bob threw out his arms in a wide gesture: "With Fantômas, can one ever tell? But to be quite frank with you, I do *not* think so, and you may rest assured I have my reasons for holding that opinion . . . Monsieur le Commissaire, your servant!"

"Monsieur Bob!"

"Well, sir? You have something else to say to me?"

The Commissary, growing more and more embarrassed, stammered out:

"Yes . . . no . . . in fact . . . at any rate. . . . You are going off like that? and leaving me alone? . . . But the corpse? . . . and suppose I wanted you?"

The American drew a card from his pocketbook and offered it to the Commissary:

"I have told you my name, it is Tom Bob. I am staying at the Hotel Terminus. If ever French justice has need of me, it will always find me at its disposition."

The Commissary had not recovered from his general state of bewilderment when Tom Bob disappeared.

14. In the Bois de Boulogne

"You appear to me, my dear fellow, to be enjoying yourself just like the fashionable folk, and you are the most ungrateful man on earth to go on talking about 'the cruelty of Fate' and 'the stings of Fortune' and a heap of other unpleasant things. After all said and done, what is your present outlook? It is the month of May, surely, it is ten in the evening, the scene is as pretty as a picture, the night warm and fragrant, in one word it is the hour when the restaurants in the Bois are crammed with merry customers, the hour when it is exquisite to sup beneath the budding foliage, to roam the deserted walks, to saunter in this magnificent Bois de Boulogne, a park such as no other capital in the world possesses. Now, what have you been doing? What are you going to do? Hallo, my friend, I feel something in your pocket, hard and crumbly at the same time, that gives me the impression of a crust of bread. So you've been dining in the Bois, my lad! And now what do you propose to do? Walk round the lake? Evidently you've forgotten your carriage and you're going on foot. Evidently again there's every chance that, an hour from now, it won't be a little, stuffy hotel you go back to, but the vast caravansary that is lit by the stars of heaven. Still, you're beginning your evening the same as the fashionables—dinner, promenade! And what's to stop you dreaming, like any other innocent, that you are destined tonight to wed the fairest princess in all the world."

The person holding this discourse, so full of a philosophic optimism, was none other than Jerome Fandor. The journalist was talking to himself, having indeed nobody near him to whom he could address his moralizing. As he had observed, it was about ten o'clock. It was a superb night, and taking everything together, the young man would not have been greatly to be pitied for finding himself in the Bois de Boulogne and about to take an agreeable stroll, if, as again he had remarked, the walk in question had not been bound to end in his passing this night in the vagabond style in some thicket or other of the park, at the imminent risk of being taken up by the police, who are invariably very strict with poor devils guilty of the heinous crime of not being rich and sleeping out of doors! As a matter of fact, the journalist's condition showed no improvement. Since his interview with Tom Bob, he had had no occasion to renew acquaintance with the American detective, who, as the object of a hundred flattering attentions on the part of the Parisian population, seemed to him, all things considered, a decidedly dangerous personage to see much of, in view of the close relations maintained between him and the authorities. Fandor was now making a living by all sorts of queer odd jobs—risking his life opening carriage doors on the occasion of grand weddings at fashionable churches, of selling evening papers on the boulevards, picking up a few sous by casual labour at Les Halles, just enough to keep body and soul together. Nevertheless, he would not have been over and above disquieted by his precarious situation but for the fact that public opinion had little by little come round to the preposterous belief that he, Fandor, was, if not Fantômas, at any rate one of the chief accomplices of that dangerous criminal, now a prisoner in the Santé. This easy, blockhead theory the whole police force had adopted, and every journal was proclaiming.

At a time when Fantômas, with unheard-of effrontery, was committing crime after crime, when the most appalling murders had grown so common that the public, seriously alarmed, were asking themselves if it was not best to pay Fantômas the tithes he claimed, at such a time Fandor told himself that the view which represented him as the guilty party had every chance of finding favor, just because it possessed the merit of being simple to the last degree!

"Once let them catch me," he thought, "and it'll be short shrift and no mercy for me!"

Accordingly, every night, while waiting events and looking confidently for the result of Tom Bob's inquiries, Fandor would betake himself to the Bois, and there spend the night, if not in comfort, at any rate, so at least he hoped, safe from the searches of the Criminal Investigation officers.

But what precisely was Tom Bob doing? On what lines was he pursuing his investigations against Fantômas? As to this, Fandor was very much in the dark. Like the general public, he had read in the newspapers of the sensational discovery of the bank collector's body which the American detective had succeeded in making in Elizabeth Dollon's flat. Fandor, like everybody else, more perhaps than most, for he knew the difficulties that beset police researches, had felt a profound admiration for the astuteness the American had given proof of on that occasion.

"No doubt," Fandor said to himself, "I put him on the scent when I told him about Moche, but all said and done, I had no information to give him of a sort to lead him to the discovery of the victim. The line of reasoning that took him to Elizabeth's, that brought about the finding of the 'wall that bleeds,' after rousing his suspicions of Paulet, this reasoning was purely his own and it is marvelous in all respects."

He had even added in his soliloquizing:

"If my fine fellow goes on as he has begun, I verily believe Fantômas will have found his match!"

It was the sole gleam of hope still left to Jerome Fandor.

"Ho there! my man."

"M'sieu?"

"What d'ya mean, strolling about like that? You're a gentleman of means, eh?"

"No, m'sieu, I'm strolling because . . ."

"Right oh! D'ya care to earn six sous an hour? you know how to hold a shovel?"

"Yes, m'sieu, yes, I'm willing."

"Come with me then!"

The man who had hailed Fandor, as the journalist was finishing his circuit of the lake and had now reached the Racing Club enclosure, was evidently a roadman of the city of Paris.

He wore the flat, silver-laced cap of the roads department, he had the heavy gait of an employee in that service, and the same good-natured look:

"If I take you on," he explained, leading Fandor towards the further end of the lake, near the Rond Royal, "it's on account of pressing job, for tomorrow's fête. I want hands."

"There's a fête tomorrow?" Fandor asked.

"And a smart one, I can tell you, my boy! A fête on the lake in honor of I don't know what good Dutch folks, who are paying an official visit to Paris. Seems they're going to take 'em on the water. It's the municipality gives the show. Now I got my notice only just in time, so I've not been able to get my men together, and I'm glad enough to find outsiders like you to give a hand."

"What is it you want done?" queried Fandor, delighted at the opportunity that offered of earning a few sous.

"You'll soon see," the other replied with a shrug. "It's not difficult and it's not fatiguing. At this end of the road coming from the Pré Catalan—you know, the road that joins the one round the lake yonder—we're removing the wire fencing that divides the avenue from the grass lawns that border the lake all round. We're taking up the curb of the roadway, too. The turf's to be dug up and laid down again at the sides. In fact, we're making a road, so to say, going straight down to the water's edge, so as the grandees may get out of their carriages at the very same spot where they're to get into the boats. You see, don't you, we couldn't begin the works yesterday evening, nor yet this morning, nor even this afternoon, because that would block the regular road."

What cared Jerome Fandor for these details? He followed the head roadman and soon reached the roadway that was to be carried on right up to the very edge of the lake. There, by the light of acetylene lamps fixed on tall standards, a whole crew of laborers was busily engaged.

"Stand to!" shouted the foreman, "I'm bringing you a new chum, find him some easy work." A second foreman came running up, and looked Fandor up and down, then:

"You're not a roadman? No? You don't understand gardening, neither? So much the worse! I am going to use you for digging up the road then. Come this way." He led Fandor to the middle of the causeway that goes round the lake.

"Look here," he explained, "so's to lengthen out the roadway, we take up the turf of the lawn, using a spade—very carefully so's not to spoil it. We're going to sand over and beat flat and so make a bit of road down to the lake. But as the carriages will arrive from the Pré Catalan, where tea's to be served at five o'clock, it's not worthwhile, you see, to leave the road that circles the lake still practicable. Accordingly, we take the turf lifted from over there and lay it down all across the lake road. As the sods are lifted carefully one by one, it's only a question of laying 'em one beside the other, a drop of water and the grass'll look quite green. That'll give the impression, not that a new way has been specially opened down to the lake, but rather that the regular road from the Pré Catalan continues straight on to the water's edge, passing through a grass plot, the ordinary grass plot, the one we are now after extending."

Fandor nodded his comprehension and waiting till the other had finished, asked:

"Then *my* job is to pick up the sods and lay 'em down side by side across the road round the lake? so as to extend the grass lawn?"

"That's the ticket, lad! and try to work lively, won't you?"

Fandor had been at work ten minutes when another man, an engineer most likely, appeared from behind a clump of trees. He was elegantly, yet quietly dressed. Hailing one of the foremen:

"You've got enough men now?" he asked.

The other looked doubtful: "Hmm, it's a close call, especially as we've got to be finished by midnight! I've had to enlist casual labor—fellows that were getting ready for a night under the trees. There's nothing wrong about that, I suppose?"

"Let me have a look at them!"

A second or two later the foreman who had enlisted Fandor came up to the journalist, who was working away very hard and conscientiously, all alone, away from the other roadmen.

He stared at him for a minute without a word. "You don't know how to work, my man," he said at last, "it's not worth two cents, what you're doing!"

"But, sir," protested Fandor, very much surprised, "I'm doing my best."

"Well, then, your best's not good enough. You're not getting on!" Then, as if coming to a sudden decision:

"No, you're no good at all and now the chief has been jawing me for taking on outsiders. Here, here's forty sous. Clear out!"

There was nothing to be said. Moreover, the instant he had fingered his forty sous, a fortune in his present plight, Fandor lost all interest in the work at hand, good, bad or indifferent.

"Right you are, sir!" was all he said, "I'm off. Many thanks all the same"—and slipping the two franc piece in his pocket, he walked away, pursued by the foreman's scrutinizing and suspicious gaze.

Scarcely had he disappeared before the engineer—it was evidently he who had ordered his dismissal—again appeared from among the shadows. He advanced to the shore of the lake, nodding familiarly to the men working there, and on reaching the water's edge, gave a shrill, short, sharp whistle, then stood quite still, waiting. The night was dark, without moon or stars. In a few seconds after he had blown his whistle, there showed up on the dark waters of the lake a shadowy, fantastic shape. It was indistinctly seen at first, but it approached so rapidly that very soon it became easy to make out what it was—a boat of rubber, a collapsible boat such as explorers use. A man was on board, rowing silently and soundlessly. Soon the figure grew plainer and its outline could be vaguely discerned, the boat was entering the zone illuminated by the acetylene flares.

Then the mysterious rower rose to his feet. What would Fandor's feelings have been, had he been there to see? The man who stood in this mysterious craft, who was approaching this scene of impromptu road-making, issuing from the impenetrable shadows of the lake, was clad from head to foot in a suit of black-close-fitting tights. His shoulders were draped in a dark cloak, the face was invisible behind a cowl, a black mask!

A figure of horror, a very incarnation of crime, a form of terror without a name! It was the form of Fantômas, come in the night to inspect the work of the roadmen engaged in preparations for tomorrow's fête!

The hour was divine, the scene fascinating in its charm and seduction, at once sumptuous and refined. Nor was the setting less delightful, this elegant restaurant, this favorite haunt of fashion, where the invited guests one and all belonged to the wealthy aristocracy of Paris. Supper was drawing to an end, the talk grew more brilliant than ever, the music was ravishing, the women lovely, the perfumes intoxicating, the flowers a feast for the eyes! No less than everything else the mysterious hues of the foliage, a weird tint of blue painted by the gleam of the electric lights, contributed to lend this corner of the Bois a look of unreality, a fairylike aspect like some fantastic scene on the stage, charming, delicious, entrancing!

This evening the place was even more brilliantly lighted than usual. The papers had made much of the coming festivity. In celebration of a treaty of Commerce signed the previous week, the English Ambassador was paying this compliment to his colleague the Ambassador of Russia. Dinner was served at separate little tables. It was past midnight, the meal was almost over and conversation was more animated than ever.

Apart from the other guests, at a table set at a distance from the others, sat dining quite alone a very beautiful woman, of an irreproachable elegance and one who, better still than Sonia Danidoff, could claim the rank of Royal Highness. The waiters named her to each other with baited breath: "Her Highness the Grand Duchess Alexandra." It was in fact the haughty great lady, friend of Frederick Christian IV, King of Hesse-Weimar, the proud lady whom Juve and Fandor, and they alone, knew to be in reality the enigmatic Lady Beltham, the mistress of Fantômas!

And truly, if some observer had chosen to watch the pretty woman in question, he would have shuddered to note with what a look, at once tragic and distraught, full of hate and violent animosity, she gazed at her gay and laughing neighbors, the guests of the Ambassadors of England and of Russia. It would seem indeed that the grand duchess had some secret motive for wishing to remain unseen by these members of Parisian society. Not content with choosing a remote table enveloped in deep shadow, she had likewise extinguished the little electric table lamp in front of her. The light thrown by the surrounding lamps was sufficient for her to see by. All through her meal the grand duchess sat pale and mute, barely answering the *maître d'hôtel* who hovered near, eager to supply her wants, her eyes fixed on the other diners, from whose tables came burst after burst of merry laughter.

Already the grand duchess was thinking of taking her departure when suddenly, as if drawn by some surprising vision, she half sprang up, then with a quick recoil threw herself back into the shadows, as though terrified and yet more anxious than before to shun observation. Bowing low in courteous greeting to one and another acquaintance, a man of slim, well-knit figure and elegant bearing had joined the circle formed by the official guests. His name passed from lip to lip, and he was welcomed with a chorus of friendly and admiring exclamations, sometimes marked by just a touch of raillery:

"Tom Bob! why how late you are. What, have you been hunting till this hour of the night for your strange enemy, the ever evasive Fantômas?"

But while the sound of that dreaded name still broke the stillness of the summer evening, while the Grand Duchess Alexandra, Lady Beltham in reality, still shuddered to hear her lover's name pronounced, gaiety quickly resumed its sway among the other guests.

"My dear," remarked a tall young woman, a trifle eccentric in appearance and manner, a Russian who, report said, had been involved in a highly diverting scandal, "My dear, you are sad?" But the Princess Sonia Danidoff, to whom the words were spoken, shook her head with a smile:

"No, you are mistaken, I am not sad, but I am thinking."

"Thinking of what?"

At the little table where the two pretty women were conversing, there sat, among several attachés of the Embassies, the wealthy young Englishman, Mr. Ascott, who now followed up the question addressed to the beautiful princess.

"Princess," he said, "we cannot long allow you to remain so self-absorbed, so serious, on so lovely a night as this and at so delightful a fête."

A smile of raillery curled Sonia Danidoff's lips. With a touch of impatience, a suspicion of mockery, she replied:

"So, sir, if you can prevent my being sad, for it appears I am sad, I gladly give you my permission to try. But I am very much afraid you will find it difficult to make me merry."

"That depends," returned the Englishman. "Tell us, if it may be, the wish you have in your mind. All here, I make bold to say, are gallant gentlemen. At the risk of attempting the impossible, we will use every effort to give it satisfaction. I even notice by the smile on my friend Tom Bob's face, and you know a police officer rarely smiles, he admits that to please you nothing is impossible. It is a guarantee that, if we fail in our desire to banish your depression, it will be no fault of ours."

The Princess Danidoff was opening her lips to reply when her friend stopped her.

"Gentlemen," she said, "I think Sonia will forgive me for my indiscretion, if I betray the secret of her melancholy. Sonia Danidoff, kinswoman of the Tsar, enormously rich, pretty enough to make all the women on this earth jealous, Sonia Danidoff, good sirs, is preoccupied simply and solely because she is . . . bored! Nay, do not protest. It is not that your society has displeased her! But Sonia, I know, finds life flat, stale and unprofitable. Sonia dreams of a great passion, of romantic love, such love as is hardly to be found in our times, such as she has hardly a chance of inspiring. And so Sonia is profoundly homesick. Now you are fairly warned!" With a wave of her slim, white hand: "Never believe that scatterbrain," the princess protested. "I am not so . . . romantic."

A burst of laughter had greeted the statements of the young Russian. Now all were listening to a charming, an exquisite Neapolitan boat-song:

But Tom Bob's attention was not with the music. Leaving his seat—it was nearly two in the morning and the men were trifling with Egyptian cigarettes—he had come to lean over the back of the fair princess's chair.

"Princess," he was saying, "why do you refuse to seek a love a little more original, which means a little more real, than that commonly met with? *I* do not think that so absurd a quest.

In an instant those wondrous eyes of the Princess Sonia Danidoff's lit up, shining with a deep, soft radiance. She half turned round to look at the speaker, that amazing Tom Bob whose doughty deeds filled the Press, that wily detective, that hero.

"Sir," she made answer, "you speak strangely. So you believe in love?"

"I do, madam," replied the American, "and the more profoundly, and it may be the more sadly, as this very evening I have been a witness to the birth of two sentiments, one a half indifferent attraction, the other a genuine passion."

"What reason for sadness in that, sir?"

"Every reason, for I am much afraid that these two sentiments will end in sadness and disillusionment."

For a moment the princess sat silent, puzzled, hesitating. At last she spoke with an affectation of haughtiness such as every woman knows how to assume:

"I do not understand you very well, sir. You speak in riddles. I am a Russian, you an American. I beg you use some other dialect than Parisian nonsense. Be more explicit."

With a quick glance, Tom Bob made sure there was no listener to pay heed to his talk with the fascinating princess. The Neapolitan singers had been succeeded by a bevy of quaint step-dancers, whom all the company was attentively watching.

Reassured on this point, Tom Bob, intoxicated perhaps by the beauty of the night, perhaps crazed by Sonia Danidoff's loveliness, charmed no doubt by the sympathy she had never ceased to lavish on him throughout this after-dinner talk, resolved to burn his boats:

"You do not understand, madam," he resumed, "you surprise me! I imagine you have not failed to notice the marked attentions, to say no more, paid you by our common friend, M. Ascott? Oh! never deny it, madam! Tonight, as indeed he does habitually, M. Ascott has made the most determined efforts to win your favor."

There was almost a touch of mockery in the words, and Sonia Danidoff was too quick-witted not to catch the other's drift.

"It would seem," she said, "these efforts do not strike you, sir, as having been crowned with success! You think my conquest is not an accomplished fact yet?"

"I do not think, madam . . . I *hope*."

And with these two little words which meant so much, which were equivalent to the most formal of declarations, Tom Bob, like a well-advised suitor, aware that a man must never demand an answer but always wait till it is offered, made his bow to the princess and walked away.

"I am going to call your carriage," he said.

The company was, in fact, rising from table. It was growing very chilly and the time was come to think of quitting the Bois for the city. Everywhere the guests were exchanging farewells, then the women of fashion, escorted by their *cavaliere servente*, made for their elegant broughams or sumptuous automobiles. All were leaving, and leaving all at the same time, to return together as far as the barrier of the Porte Dauphine, when the final adieux would be exchanged.

All together? No, not so. There was one fair lady, at any rate, who did not intend to make one of the merry crowd. Indeed, the Grand Duchess Alexandra showed not the slightest desire to quit the table at which she had sat from the very beginning of the evening, isolated, sullen almost! She had never ceased her watch of the official guests, and above all had not failed to mark the flattering attentions and manifestations of sympathy lavished everywhere on Tom Bob. Now her eyes were fixed askance on the Princess Sonia Danidoff, the acknowledged queen of the festivity, as she took the arm the detective offered. The white teeth of the Grand Duchess Alexandra were nervously biting her lip. The noble lady was doubtless thinking with acute agitation how she was the mistress of Fantômas and that this hero of the hour was the very same man who had sworn to bring her lover to the scaffold!

But it was high time to be gone, and the grand duchess summoned her *chasseur*.

"Call up my car," she ordered, "but tell my chauffeur he is carefully to avoid returning with the rest of the company. He is to drive by the less frequented roads. I do not care to be compelled to greet all these folks, who, luckily, have so far neither seen nor recognized me."

The menial bowed and went his way, but he was back again the next minute.

"Your Highness's chauffeur," he said, "has to inform your Highness that an accident has happened to the car. He is busy repairing the damage, but it will take a good half-hour. Your Highness does not wish me to go for a hired carriage?"

The Grand Duchess Alexandra, or rather Lady Beltham, seemed to hesitate a few moments. She cast a dark and venomous look of suddenly awakened anger in the direction of the last lingering guests mounting their vehicles, then quickly:

"No, I am in no hurry. Tell the chauffeur to do the repairs, and come and tell me when all's ready"—and the footman vanished once more.

"You are infinitely obliging, madam, to offer to drive me back to Paris. Instead of sitting sad and solitary in a hired conveyance, it is no small happiness for me to journey a few minutes in your company and enjoy, with no unbearable third party present, the favor you are so amiable as to show me."

In fact, as Sonia Danidoff was on the way to her limousine, hanging on Tom Bob's arm, the princess had observed that the latter, having no conveyance of his own, would be obliged to get back to Paris alone as best he might, and there and then she had made the offer: "Come, won't you get into my car? You can drive with me to the house, then they'll set you down at your destination."

Tom Bob, needless to say, jumped at the offer, delighted to seize the opportunity of so charming a tête-à-tête. And soon the princess and he were talking amicably together, while their car sped through the deserted Bois along the road, lit up for a dozen yards ahead by the glare of the acetylene lamps on the hood. They talked, let it be said, of indifferent subjects, the American carefully avoiding any reference, however casual, to the declaration of love he had ventured to make a moment before, and Sonia feigning not to have understood his meaning.

"You have a wonderfully fine car, madam," observed Tom Bob, as the princess's chauffeur, making a clever turn and taking advantage of the exceptional speed of the car, took the head of the procession formed by the different cars. We shall be there in a few seconds. I shall be sorry for that, madam."

"You . . ."

But at the very instant Sonia Danidoff was about to reply, a cry of horror and anguished fear escaped her lips, while for his part, Tom Bob could hardly restrain a startled oath.

What had happened? Impossible for the occupants of the cars to perceive in the bewilderment of the moment! What blunder had the chauffeur made to provoke the accident? Suddenly, without any diminution of speed, without even any application of the brakes to slow up the pace, the four first cars following the road from the Pré Catalan had plunged into the lake of the Bois de Boulogne!

Fortunately the lake is not very deep. Still, the danger was serious that confronted those who found themselves thus involved in so sudden a shipwreck. The women were muffled in their cloaks, the men hampered with their great coats. Moreover, the cars had been pitched almost one on top of the other, and cries of terrified bewilderment rose on all sides.

Inside Sonia's limousine events followed each other with dramatic swiftness. Tom Bob, a marvel of presence of mind, a miracle of coolness, had not lost his head for an instant. The moment the princess broke off to scream, the moment he felt the ground slip from under the wheels, he realized what was happening. In a flash he concluded at first that the princess's driver, deceived by the darkness, had misjudged his turn, and cried out instinctively:

"We are over."

But the limousine itself was struck heavily by the car behind, and the detective and the princess were thrown forward and bruised against the sides. Then the whole horror of the situation was revealed. Sonia had fainted, and the dark, surging waters of the lake were pouring into the vehicle in icy torrents through the broken windows. The limousine was sinking!

"Damnation!" roared Tom Bob. Then, quick as lightning, gripping the princess by one arm, he forced open the door in spite of the weight of water and struck out. He was a powerful swimmer, and in a few seconds more he and his precious burden had reached the bank of the lake.

There, the wildest confusion reigned. The first four cars had plunged in one on top of the other. Fortunately those following, being a short distance behind, had been able to brake and pull up in time. At the cries of the drivers all with one accord had sprung to the ground, and were now asking names, counting numbers, uttering exclamations of surprise and fear. The panic was indescribable.

It was indeed a most lucky chance there was no fatality to deplore. Sonia's car, the first in the line, was as a matter of fact the only one that, by reason of its speed, had rolled far enough into the lake to be half submerged. The drivers of the vehicles behind, seeing the accident, had sheered off to one side, had more or less jammed down their brakes and, thanks to their reduced speed, had been able, not indeed to avoid the disaster altogether, but at any rate to diminish its ill consequences. The cars had come to a stand on the very verge of the water.

Help was soon organized, and brave men sprang into the lake to the rescue. Half an hour after the catastrophe, it could be said for certain that it would have no very serious sequel, apart of course, from any effects that might ensue on the violent agitation all had experienced, and the painful bruises some of these "shipwrecked mariners" had received. Only the Princess

Sonia Danidoff, imprisoned in a vehicle that had actually sunk, was ever in positive danger of death. And so, when the first bewilderment was over, it was round the young Russian lady that the crowd gathered thickest, questioning and congratulating.

Meanwhile Tom Bob, his brow knit in anxious thought, had drawn some of the men apart and was demonstrating to them the causes of the accident.

"It is beyond belief!" he declared, "... just look over there! ... the thing was a criminal attempt! They have masked the turn in the road by laying down the bogus grass lawn over a length of ten yards, and extended the road itself in a straight line right up to the waterside. The footway is cut through! the wire fencing removed! Why, they have even chalked over the rammed earth to make it look as white as the road! For sure, no blame attaches to the chauffeur. In the glare thrown forward by the lamps he was bound to make a mistake. He could not possibly see the trap laid for him, and so, quite naturally, he drove straight on till the final crash came."

Tom Bob was going to say more when suddenly a cry burst on the silence of the night, a cry of stupefaction, of tearful distress. The detective flew to a group standing round the Princess Danidoff, who still lay on the ground inhaling a restorative.

"What ... what is it? what is happening now?"

The English Ambassador replied to the American detective's question.

"It is atrocious," he cried, "the Princess Sonia Danidoff has just discovered she has been robbed of articles of very considerable value."

For the moment the American stood stock still, as if paralyzed with amazement.

"What," he exclaimed, "what is that you say?"

"I say, my good sir," returned the Ambassador, "that the Princess Sonia has been stripped of all her jewels, all her jewels—do you hear what I say?—rings, bracelets, necklaces, hair ornaments. Some hundreds of thousands of francs gone!"

In his bewilderment Tom Bob could only repeat himself: "But the thing's beyond belief. It's impossible! When did it happen? and how?"

He darted to the princess's side, while the Ambassador, turning to a young attaché, finished what he was saying for his benefit.

"For my part," he declared, "I consider the whole catastrophe had but one object—this theft! It must have been done while the princess lay in a faint and Tom Bob had left her to help in saving life. Tom Bob, police detective as he is, never saw the wood for the trees!"

The attache nodded: "You are undoubtedly right, sir, but who can have organized this daring, this audacious plot?"

It was in a hushed voice, almost in a whisper, that the Ambassador made answer:

"Who? My God! I think there is only one man in all the world . . . and you know his name!"

"Fantômas?"

"Yes, Fantômas."

Already on every lip the dread name was being repeated, the name of horror and of blood, the name that alone could make credible the incredible reality, that could make it seem possible, that could account for it.

"Fantômas! Fantômas! He and no other must have planned all this!"

And through the night, more grim than ever the three tragic syllables re-echoed, spreading consternation—Fantômas!

15. In a Private Room

M. Moche was in a generous mood that morning. He now beckoned to the waiter of the drinking shop where he sat with a companion, the apache known by the nickname of the "Gasman," and ordered a bottle of wine and glasses to be set on the table. But the old man had certainly not summoned this "Gasman" to meet him merely for the pleasure of standing the young ruffian a drink. For a good quarter of an hour they had been hobnobbing together, and the old business agent had been engaged in explaining to his man the particular service he required of him. To start with, indeed, and by way of preliminary to ensure the confidence and goodwill of his ally, Père Moche, as he shook hands on saying good-morning, had slipped between the "Gasman's" gnarled fingers a nice little bank note for fifty francs, which the apache, nothing if not practical, had instantly pocketed, prepared to learn later on what he would have to do in return, or even to refuse to take on the job if he did not fancy it.

When the bottle was half empty, Moche came back to the business at hand.

"Then it's settled," he asked, "we may count on you?"

The apache pushed his chair back, leaned his great body far across the table, rested his head between the palms of his hands and looking hard at the old business man:

"That depends," he announced in a decided tone.

"What d'ya mean?" asked Moche in surprise.

The "Gasman" repeated: "That depends. Question is who're we working for? For my part, since all these here to-dos, you'll understand, I'm beginning to be a bit off. Fantômas' gang and me being in the know with 'em, that's all very fine and large; but sure as I'm here drinking at your expense, the thing can't go on, and it's bound to end badly."

"Don't you worry about that, my man; this business is my little game and nobody else's. Fantômas has nothing to do with it. And what's more, let me tell you, Fantômas don't like folks prying into his business, whoever they may be. Swell guy as you are, Mr. 'Gasman,' you'll be getting yourself into trouble, if you poke your nose in there."

"Right oh!" agreed the apache. "Let's talk about, *your* business then instead!"

"Well then," resumed Père Moche, "you quite understand I count on you implicitly for tonight. Now there must be two of you for the job, so stir your stumps this afternoon and find a bully boy at a loose. end. Who are you going to take, eh?"

The apache thought a moment, twisting his long mustache, then suggested:

"I don't see anyone hardly but 'Bull's-eye,' you know who I mean, who'd just do . . ."

Moche approved the selection: "That's the ticket, go and fix it up with your friend. He's a good cuss and no white liver," he grinned.

But Moche grew grave again: "Don't forget to bring along all the properties—some good strong rope, and of course a handkerchief, you know, to make a gag—part of your stock in trade all that, eh, 'Gasman'?"

Then, discovering it was half past eleven, and he was behind time, M. Moche shook the apache hurriedly by the hand and vanished. With rapid strides the old usurer made his way down the Rue de Belleville and so to the line of the exterior boulevards, where he hailed a cab, telling the man to drive him to the *Silver Goblet*, a restaurant on the Place de la Bastille.

What new scheme could the dubious advocate of the Rue Saint-Fargeau be meditating now? What was the shady enterprise he was planning, for which he needed the cooperation of two notorious apaches from Ménilmontant like the "Gasman" and "Bull's-eye"? On arriving at his destination, M. Moche took the landlord on one side. The latter seemed an old acquaintance.

"I want you to keep me for tonight," he whispered in his ear, "the little pink room. I shall be coming to dine there about eight o'clock with some swell clients. Put on a man who can hold his tongue to wait."

The restaurant keeper bowed respectfully.

"You can trust to me, Monsieur Moche, you shall have what you want, and you shan't be disturbed. Anyway, the season's drawing to a close and we're hardly serving anymore dinners in private rooms. You may count on having the whole floor practically to yourselves."

The old fellow was entirely satisfied by what he heard, and at once took his departure, striding fast along the streets and whistling a cheerful march tune.

"Dress coat, smoking jacket? What is monsieur going to wear this evening?"

"Neither, John. Lay out my lounge coat."

"You are not going out then, sir, and you have not anybody asked to dinner?"

Mr. Ascott stopped in the middle of arranging his tie, and turning to his man, said sharply:

"I am not dining at home, and I ask you for my lounge coat, that's all."

John, while obeying orders, still wore a scandalized air:

"Excuse my speaking like this, sir, but I cannot help telling you, sir, that for some days now you have been neglecting your personal appearance, sir. What, you are going abroad, sir, in a lounge suit and dining out in such a costume? In New York or in London, you would never think of such a breach of etiquette."

Ascott interrupted his manservant's flow of words with a look of weary discouragement:

"I shall do just what I choose, John, and let me tell you, it's only out of consideration for your age and the years you have been with my family I don't reprimand you severely for the liberties you take."

The man dropped his eyes and with a chagrined air:

"I beg pardon, sir, it was only the interest I take in you, sir, made me say what I did."

Ascott let the matter drop. Presently, his hands very busy

adjusting a carnation in the buttonhole of his coat, he asked:

"The Princess Danidoff did not ring up on the phone this afternoon."

"No, sir, in fact it is several days now we have had no news of the princess."

"Well, John," grunted Ascott, turning stiffly and facing the man, "I am pleased to think it will go on so for a long time. I've had enough of the Princess Sonia Danidoff, she's an ungrateful coquette. God knows how ready I was to love her, how gladly I would have devoted my life to her service, but she is crazy, crazy for another man. . . . So much the worse for me! But there, that's her look out . . ."

John looked his approval.

"Quite right, sir, these great ladies always give more trouble than they're worth, and if I might offer you a piece of advice, sir . . ."

"Well, out with it."

"Well, it would be just to take for mistress one of those pretty actresses there's so many of in Paris and who would ask nothing better, or else get to know a nice, good little girl, a gentle and modest young thing who would love you tenderly . . ."

Ascott burst into a loud laugh.

"Upon my word, John, you're in a prophetic vein today, ha ha! Who tells you I'm not going to follow your advice to the letter?"

"Why, sir, do you know some young girl in society?"

"In society, hmm! Not high society certainly . . . but one that is honest and peaceable and sincere. Yes, perhaps I do, and I'm beginning to think even I'm pretty deep in love."

John rubbed his hands in naive satisfaction. He ventured: "You must tell me about it, sir."

But next minute Ascott checked himself and his face resumed a stern look full of haughty reserve.

He was ready to go. "John, hand me my hat."—"Very good, Sir."—"My stick."—"Here it is, sir!"

"John, I shall not be back perhaps till late at night perhaps not at all. No need to wait up for me."

"Very good, sir . . . goodnight, sir!"
"Goodnight, John."

Seated at the back of the omnibus office in the Place de la Bastille, two persons were conversing in low voices. They were Père Moche, wearing, as always, his everlasting top hat with the mangy nap and draped solely in his long frock coat, and little Nini Guinon, modestly clad in a navy blue skirt barely reaching to the ankles and a straw hat trimmed with wildflowers. To look at the pair you would have taken them for people of the small shopkeeper class—the father a worthy business employee, the daughter a schoolgirl, hardly out of the Convent. No one would ever have dreamt he had before him the old usurer of the Rue Saint-Fargeau, comrade and accomplice of the worst apaches of the district, and least of all that the modest maiden he saw there was a vulgar streetwalker, a common murderer's mistress, seduced and ruined long ago, for all her tender years.

Père Moche was grumbling sourly:

"The thing's disgusting. Since they did away with the *correspondance* tickets, the omnibus offices are getting fewer and fewer and less and less used. I had the devil's own job to find just this one here to arrange to meet you at."

"But why," demanded Nini, teasing the old man, "why couldn't you let me join you at the pub on the corner there? We could have swigged a half-pint or so then in the mug's honor."

M. Moche started, and putting on a grieved look, began to scold the too-outspoken Nini—albeit he felt a strong inclination to laugh all the while.

"You slut, will you never be serious? You spend your time humbugging, trying to frighten me, you do. I'm all the while in a stew you'll let out a *big 'un* before him . . ."

Nini completed the old advocate's sentence for him:

". . . A *big 'un* that'll make him see I'm not exactly an angel come down from heaven with her crown of orange blossom on her head, all ready to fall into his arms, eh, Père Moche, isn't that what makes you sweat?"

But Moche knew better. He gave the child a friendly tap on

her rosy cheek: "No, not really, mind you. I'm not a bit afraid, you're a deal too artful to give yourself away," and looking admiringly at the girl, he added:

"It wouldn't take much more to take me in, too, with your modest, virtuous air, and those great innocent eyes of yours!"

"Attention!" he cried. "Steady! Here comes the pigeon. Stand by to blush, niece!"

"Never you fear, dear uncle," replied Nini, biting her lips not to burst out laughing.

Thereupon Ascott appeared at the door of the omnibus office. The young Englishman might have stepped out of a bandbox, smart, elegant, freshly shaved, and carrying in his arms an enormous bunch of flowers!

The complicated plot arranged some days beforehand by old Moche seemed to be working out under the most favorable auspices. He had introduced his bogus niece to the rich young Englishman at a highly opportune moment, just when Ascott, chagrined at having paid assiduous court to the Princess Sonia Danidoff, only to see the latter prefer to himself the latest recruit to her band of admirers, the American stranger, the detective, Tom Bob, who, from the first moment of his arrival in France, had worn in all men's eyes an aureole of glory and success. Moved less by love than by a sort of obstinacy, Ascott had indeed striven to contend against this adversary, but events had occurred so rapidly and so much in favor of his rival that the wealthy Englishman, in spite of being the first in the field and the first accredited suitor for the princess's hand, had been forced to take second place. For was it not, in fact, this same Tom Bob again who, forty-eight hours earlier, had rescued the unfortunate Sonia Danidoff from a terrible and almost certain death? Evidently the detective had not succeeded in saving the princess's jewels, but he had saved her life, and swore to protect her against the mysterious and terrible attacks of the ever elusive and enigmatic scoundrel, who seemed especially bent on her destruction.

Wounded in his self-love and balked in his passion, the young Englishman had quickly come to his senses, and this the more readily from the fact that, as his love for Sonia Danidoff cooled more and more, he felt his heart more and more stirred and charmed by a youthful passion for the pretty child he supposed to be niece of the old moneylender, the grotesque M. Moche. Moreover, startled by the indignant refusal his first audacious proposal had provoked, Ascott had immediately realized that this was not the right way to deal with the old business man. In fact, when he accompanied Nini on her leaving the house in the Rue Saint-Fargeau, he had also seen pretty clearly that the latter, good, obedient girl as she was, must needs entertain the highest respect for her uncle. So he had wisely told himself how desirable it was in the first place to win the old man's favor in order to secure the child's good graces.

The young Englishman accordingly invited M. Moche to lunch, lunch for two, tête-à-tête. Moreover, despite the instinctive repulsion he felt for the fellow, he found himself forced to admit, before the meal was over, that he was after all a cheerful boon-companion, not lacking in wit and possessed of a store of racy anecdotes well calculated to dispel his melancholy. Adroitly enough, Ascott brought the conversation round to the subject of M. Moche's little niece, displaying an interest in the child's future, and he deemed himself more than clever when, after endless beating around the bush, he finally succeeded in persuading Père Moche to dine with him and bring little Nini with him one evening soon.

Poor fellow, he little dreamt he had to do with a man far cleverer than himself, and that the favor he had obtained at the cost of so many difficulties was really and truly but the consummation of the plot conceived by the Machiavellian business agent and his abominable little accomplice.

. . . Thus Ascott arrived to the minute at the rendezvous, in the omnibus office in the Place de la Bastille at 7:30, his heart in his mouth, his mind in a joyous tumult, his arms full of flowers, all for the woman towards whom he now began to feel a genuine and sincere affection!

The merry little dinner was drawing to an end. Old Moche

had positively sparkled with wit throughout the meal, but most of the time it was simply trouble wasted, for Ascott hardly listened to a word. Moche sat facing the two young people, who, as if by inadvertence, had taken their places on a narrow divan, so that as the festivity proceeded they were perpetually coming into casual contact with each other. At first the young man had discreetly kept his distance, but little by little, growing bolder under his senior's indulgent eye—the old man seemed to be getting tipsy—the lover drew nearer to his charmer. From time to time he would squeeze her hand under the table or throw an arm around her waist. The child looked demure and a trifle startled, affecting to be embarrassed, sometimes even shocked, but at the same time casting occasional sideways glances at the rich Englishman that were full of encouragement and spoke of passion only held in check by maiden modesty.

Ascott, entering more and more into the spirit of the thing, kept on replenishing his guests' glasses with champagne, hoping to intoxicate old Moche altogether and make the girl sufficiently tipsy to prove less obdurate in repelling the caresses he lavished on her. He himself, too, by way of stimulating his courage, was drinking pretty hard, and, all things considered, was very likely consuming on his own sole account a great deal more than his two companions both together.

Once, as he was bending down behind Nini, pretending to pick something up from the floor, in reality in order to put his burning lips to the cool, inviting surface of the girl's neck behind, Ascott failed to see how Père Moche, with the lightning quickness of a conjuring trick, sprinkled a whitish-gray powder over the frothing liquor in his champagne glass. Dessert was on the table. But while Nini, nibbling at the strawberries on her plate, refused to drink any more wine, Ascott, who was tormented with a thirst that grew momentarily more intense, had a fourth bottle of champagne uncorked, of which he poured a good third into a glass for himself and drained it off in one draft.

The Englishman was rapidly getting drunk, and now threw discretion to the winds in his plaguing of Nini, who more than once, playing her part to perfection, administered some shrewd slaps on the young man's over-enterprising hands. She even sprang up from her seat, as if to fly for refuge to her uncle and demand his protection.

Old Moche followed the whole scene with a very wide awake glance, humming a tune at intervals and mimicking the ways of a man excited by the fumes of a heady wine and viewing life under the most roseate aspect. At a given moment, however, the old fellow, after looking surreptitiously at his watch, noted that it was half past eleven. He rose from the table staggering. Ascott burst out laughing. "By the Lord! my dear Moche," he cried out in a thick voice, "I verily believe you're jolly well drunk!"

Moche swayed more unsteadily than ever on his feet.

"Drunk!" he replied, with a fine imitation of a drunkard's hoarse tones, "never such a thing! I'm merry, just merry—as we all are. Here, just look here if I'm drunk; my hand don't shake."

Moche picked up a full glass, solemnly lifted it from the table, rounding his elbow in a majestic gesture. Doubtless his condition balked his praiseworthy efforts, for the glass after some frantic oscillations suddenly turned topsy turvy, spilling the wine over the carpet.

The accident provoked an uproarious fit of wild mirth from Ascott: "Oh! there is no doubt about it, the old man is awfully drunk." And now the young Englishman's cup of happiness was filled to the brim, as he heard the other declare:

"Why, yes, I don't feel very well, my head's going round a bit. With your leave, I'll go out and breathe the fresh air a minute. But none of your nonsense now while I'm away! Ascott, I count on your good behavior, I entrust that dear, good, virtuous child to your care"—and Père Moche disappeared.

Scarcely was he out of the room before Ascott shook off his intoxication and managed to rise from the divan on which he sprawled. Stepping to the door of the private room, he shot the bolt with an unsteady hand. Then, regardless of Nini's hypocritical prayers and protests, he went to the switch and turned off the electric current.

"Oh! sir, sir!" shrilled the girl in a terrified voice, "what are you doing? . . . oh! . . . for God's sake, let me be . . . mother!"

Meantime, no sooner was Moche out in the passage leading to the private rooms than he recovered all his coolness and self-possession, as if by a miracle. The old scamp was much too astute to have let himself get tipsy. It was simply a piece of play-acting he had been at for the benefit of his host, a comedy that did not in the least take in his confidante and accomplice, Nini Guinon, though it completely bamboozled the young Englishman. With no small satisfaction Moche noted—as indeed the landlord had led him to expect when he came that morning to order the little dinner—that the adjoining rooms were unoccupied. After that he made sure that no one could spy on them from the floor below.

Everything was as it should be. The host of the *Silver Goblet* was used to these little private entertainments and knew it was not the proper thing to disturb those attending them under any circumstances. No doubt, somewhere about one o'clock in the morning, a waiter would come up to announce that it was time to be leaving, as the house was going to be closed, but till that hour guests could count implicitly on the most absolute peace and quietness.

Next, slipping down the back stairs leading directly from the entresol into the street, Moche was quickly in the open air. Advancing a few paces along the sidewalk, he whistled and then stood listening. A second later a succession of notes became audible, similar to those formed by the old man's lips. Again advancing, he came upon two fellows lurking in a doorway. It was the "Gasman" and "Bull's-eye," and not far off stood an automobile, to which the old man pointed with the question: "It's yours, that contraption over there?"

"Yes," replied the "Gasman," "that's to say it's a pal's machine. We chose him because he's as silent as the tomb, and don't have no eyes in the back of his head. He'll do what he's told—asks three louis for his night."

"All serene!" declared Moche, rubbing his hands. "Now listen to me, men. Keep an eye on the shanty I've come out of, and when I show my hat out of the window, you must come along softly, the pigeon'll be asleep. The pigeon's mate'll go with you and no fuss, you may rely on that. As you drive on, best clap on the cords and the gag. You might be interrupted, and it must all be shipshape, just to avoid accidents. Got it?"

"Right oh!" sang out "Bull's-eye" and the "Gasman" in chorus.

Moche, in generous mood, handed over to each of them a fifty franc note: "You see," he pointed out, "I always pay well."

"Yes," growled "Bull's-eye," "that ain't like Fantômas, that ain't! Didn't I give him a hand in that there lake business, when he cleared off with the princess's jewelry. Well, if I've made a brown or two out of it, that's about all—just because he didn't see me at work. I'm thinking if Fantômas don't fork out . . ."

"All serene," Père Moche interrupted his grumblings, "there's no question of Fantômas for the moment. Be smart, be ready . . . I'm going up there again."

At the door of the private room, the old man, resuming his former role, gave a discreet tap, saying with a laugh:

"Why, what now? . . . so you've locked yourself in, eh? a little joke, for sure? . . . but no more nonsense now! Come, come, open the door. Do be serious a bit . . . and then you know, I'm still thirsty, I want to finish out the bottle!"

Then he stopped talking to listen. Not a sound came from inside and the old fellow was growing impatient. He knocked twice, sharply and peremptorily.

At last the door opened, and Nini appeared, her hair flying loose and her clothes in disorder.

"What a time he's been giving me!" she whispered grinning, "a devil of a fellow, my dear man!"

But Moche was in no joking mood. He demanded: "And now?"

"Now," Nini proceeded, still speaking under her breath, but opening the door a little wider, so that Moche could slip into the room, which was still in darkness, "now he's snoring like a good 'un! Suppose it's the powder you tipped into his champagne. I bet he's good to sleep on till tomorrow morning, come what may."

Moche looked down at Ascott, who lay stretched on the divan, and saw that Nini was speaking the truth. The young man was sleeping like a top. The old usurer shook him by the arm, twitched his hair, but the Englishman, as drunk as a lord and bowled over into the bargain by the soporific he had swallowed, was beyond rousing.

Without relighting the lights, Moche ran to the window and waved his hat out of it. Then coming back into the room, he laughed delightedly.

"First rate, my gal, it's going first rate," he assured Nini. "To my mind the job's as good as done!"

The two accomplices fell silent a moment, then with one impulse both stood listening. On the stairs communicating directly with the street the sound of stealthy footsteps could be heard. It was "Bull's-eye" and the "Gasman" coming up.

16. Next Morning!

Heavy-eyed, with a smarting brow and a raging headache, Ascott awoke late the following morning. It was about ten o'clock when the young man in the big four-poster, whose twisted Renaissance pillars almost touched the ceiling, stretched his cramped limbs and slowly came back to a consciousness of his surroundings. His throat was parched with an insatiable thirst. Mechanically and without opening his eyes, for he knew precisely the position of the various articles that stood near his bed, he extended a faltering arm towards a little table at the bedside, reaching for the water bottle his carefully trained servant used to put there every night full of water. His hand felt over the marble top of the table, but failed to find what he sought. He was so weary, his head was throbbing so painfully he could not at first summon up courage enough to rise. Again lazily stretching, he turned over between the sheets and tried to get to sleep again, setting his face to the wall to guard his smarting eyes against the light of day that penetrated the heavy curtains drawn across the window.

Not a sound was audible. The mansion the wealthy Englishman had purchased some weeks ago was as silent as the grave, the domestics far away in the basement where the offices and kitchen were situated going about their business softly so as not to disturb their master's slumber. Nor did the latter feel the smallest desire to get up, though out of doors the weather was magnificent, the sky of Paris as blue as on an Italian summer's day and the temperature, genial even at this morning hour, promising an afternoon of almost tropical heat.

But sleep refused to come at the young man's call. His throat was burning, his mouth dry as a bone. Drink he must at all costs to quench the fire that consumed him, to mitigate these painful and inevitable consequences of his overindulgence in the generous wines of the night before. Screwing up his courage to the needful effort, slowly, painfully, moving like an automaton, Ascott sat up in bed, clasped his damp brow, then slipped one leg from between the sheets. The other followed, his naked feet shivering as they touched the bedside mat. Catching a glimpse of a dressing gown lying within reach on a chair, he put it on with the cross and sulky looks of an ill-used martyr.

"That beast of a John," he was thinking, "by forgetting to put my water ready last night will have made me ill for the rest of the day!"

Stumbling across the room, his eyes still only half open, Ascott made for the dressing room adjoining his bedroom, in which he felt sure—at least he hoped so—of finding a supply of clear, fresh water that should revive his energies depressed by the consumption of unlimited alcoholic liquors and liqueurs. He opened the door of his bathroom, but on the point of entering, he stopped dead on the threshold, dumbfounded by what he saw, albeit with a very vague and confused comprehension of the apparition that met his gaze! The room, generally so neat and tidy and meticulously ordered, every crystal phial and pomade pot and toilet article in its appointed place on the dressing table, was this morning in the wildest disorder. There were bottles without stoppers giving out heady perfumes, brushes scattered about the floor, towels tossed at random over the backs of chairs.

But what above all else surprised the young man and filled him with the most intense amazement was to see on the Louis Seize settee, where he often threw himself after his bath to be massaged by his servant man to restore his numbed limbs to their proper suppleness, a woman lying there, half undressed and her hair undone, curled up on the couch buried in heavy, but restless slumbers. Her clothes, her skirt, her bodice lay about the floor, her shoes lay one in a corner next to a copper kettle, the other precariously perched on the shelf of a what-not!

Ascott had no need to look twice to recognize the sleeper. It was Nini Guinon, old Moche's niece, the girl he had dined with yesterday evening in the private room . . . who at the close of the entertainment when her uncle went away, had been left alone with him . . . whom he had made his mistress!

Ascott gazed long at the sleeping figure in utter bewilderment. He was still very tired and his mind was slow to understand, while an atrocious neuralgic headache tortured him. What had happened then, following the moment when he had found himself alone with Nini Guinon in the private room at the restaurant in the Place de la Bastille? He could remember nothing, he had forgotten everything. All the same his conscience told him that the history of subsequent events should not be very difficult to reconstruct. At the same time he was suffering atrociously, his head, his forehead, the nape of his neck were all seats of horrid pain. It felt as though every hair that bristled on his skull was a needle point painfully pricking the scalp. Putting off till later all thought of seriously considering his plight, Ascott, on tiptoe, moving carefully to avoid making the slightest noise, but as a first preliminary having drained at a draft half the contents of a water jug, crept across the room, resolved to regain his bed and sleep off the last vestiges of his fatigue.

But hardly had he taken a couple of steps when he started and swore. A soft knock had sounded on the door. The tired man deemed no reply needful. No one surely would venture to come in without his permission, and that he was not disposed to give. But evidently it was ordained that the unfortunate young man should not be left in peace that morning to sleep off the effects of his last night's indulgence. In defiance of the established customs of the house, hitherto invariably respected, the door, without leave given, was half opened. A head appeared, a face of consternation, the head and face of his servant John. Ascott, who, at the moment was making for the bed, turned sharply round and sitting down on the coverlet, addressed the domestic in angry tones:

"Whatever has come over you, John what do you want? I haven't rung, that I know of."

For all that the man pushed into the room and advanced some steps nearer his master.

"Forgive me, sir," he murmured, "I should never have dared to come into your bedroom, sir, without being summoned, but there's someone wishing to . . ."

Ascott stifled a yawn, signifying by a peremptory wave of the hand his refusal to hear another word.

"You are mad, John. You know perfectly well I never receive visitors at this hour of the day."

"Excuse me, sir, but it seems it is important."

"Nothing is important enough to wake me up for," declared Ascott.

But the servant went on with extraordinary and unprecedented persistence.

"It is the old fellow who sometimes comes to see you, sir, the business agent, your lawyer, sir, old M. Moche. I explained you could not see him, sir, but he insisted all the same, he almost forced me to come up here . . . please excuse me, sir, but . . ."

His master was furious. Calling up, not without difficulty, all the will power he possessed, all the energy he was capable of that morning, he vociferated passionately:

"I will not see him and if the old man insists, chuck him out of the house!"

Ascott had hardly uttered the words before a grave and dignified voice was heard in the anteroom adjoining the bedchamber, and at the same moment there issued from the shadows, pushing his way into the room, someone whose identity could admit of no mistake even to the Englishman's sleepy eyes. It was in fact M. Moche coming in, in defiance of all prohibition. Dressed, as always, in his long, black frock coat, holding in his hand his tall hat with the dulled, dented surface, M. Moche showed dirtier and still more repulsive-looking in the broad light of day than by candlelight, but also more solemn and more majestic.

The old man bowed slightly to Ascott, who sat silent and impassive on his bed.

"I have to speak to you, sir, to speak to you, alone," he announced, casting a thunderous glance at the old servant, but the latter never budged, waiting for his master's orders.

Ascott resigned himself to the inevitable: "Go, John," he ordered, "we wish to be alone."

Hardly had the door closed behind the servant before Moche, throwing his calm and majestic manner to the winds, rushed up to the young Englishman and in a beseeching voice half choked with emotion, but nevertheless showing just a shade of menace, demanded:

"Sir, where is my niece, my child? What have you done with my sister's child?"

Ascott shook in his shoes. Just what he was fearing had occurred, and that at a time, at an hour in the morning, when he would have given all he possessed to be left in peace. He made a slight, nonchalant, evasive gesture, feigning he had never an inkling of the meaning of Père Moche's question.

"Your niece," he protested, "I know nothing of what has become of her. Am I her keeper?"

But Moche broke in again. With rising passion the old business man shouted:

"You lie, sir. You have odiously abused my trust in you, abused the friendship I felt for you. Do not try to deny your guilt, I know all. To begin with, taking advantage of a moment's negligence on my part, you locked yourself in alone with Nini in the private room where we all three dined, and like a satyr, a perfect monster of vice, you were dastard enough to seduce my niece, poor child!"

Playing his odious comedy to perfection, the old fellow sank into a chair, and dropping his head between his hands, pretended to sob. In a piteous voice, he whined:

"Poor child! Poor darling Nini, so gentle, so pure, so virtuous, what a hideous awakening must this have been for her. Oh! I can picture her despair and horror. It is frightful, maddening!"

Moche sprang up and again approached Ascott, who, vexed beyond measure, was gazing on the scene with a dazed expression in his haggard eyes.

"What has become of her? We have spent a dreadful night, sir, I tortured with fear and anxiety, her poor mother in terrible suspense, for Nini has never returned home. Where is she? You alone can say, and you must and shall."

Meanwhile, as he spoke, Moche had gone over to the window and half-drawn back the curtains, admitting daylight into the darkened room. Seeing that the bed was empty, that the bedroom showed no signs of disorder and held no one else save the young Englishman, the old brigand appeared surprised, not to say disconcerted. For some moments he stood hesitating, at fault, thinking to himself:

"So! then the business can't have turned out quite as I expected! That imbecile of a little Nini must have misunderstood. Can she have been such a fool as to go before I got here?"

Moche stood biting his lips in perplexity, hesitating what course to follow, and to gain time began shouting at Ascott again:

"What has become of Nini? What have you done with her? Answer me, sir, answer me!"

But the young man was trembling with apprehension. He had been listening and in spite of the rumpus old Moche was kicking up, he caught the sound of faint, furtive noises coming from the adjoining room. For a little while the Englishman had been congratulating himself on his success in feigning ignorance and seeming to attach no meaning to the questions addressed to him by the unspeakable uncle of the pretty child he had made his mistress the evening before. He hoped that, wearying of the contest, old Moche would go away, and firm in his original intention, he swore to himself he would then double lock his door and at any cost go on sleeping for at least another two hours!

But now the noise in the dressing room was upsetting his plans, for he felt convinced that Nini was certainly awake. What would the girl decide to do? Infuriated by the attitude adopted by the man who, taking her by surprise and defenseless, had become her lover, would she spring forth and demand vengeance, or else, dumb with despair, covered with shame at her dishonor, would she be afraid to show herself in the disorder of her morning toilet before the eyes of the old uncle she loved and seemed to esteem so highly?

Ascott had no time left him to weigh probabilities at length, for the first of these two hypotheses was promptly realized. Besides which, M. Moche had also, like Ascott, heard noises in the adjoining room, and instinctively the old fellow was making for the door of the dressing room when Nini appeared.

The girl was pale as death, her eyes glittered with a strange brilliance, her lips quivered in a nervous spasm. At the sight of her uncle and as if surprised to find him there, she made a show of hesitation, first advancing, then drawing back. Finally, she darted to the old man's side, threw her self into his arms and hiding her face on his shoulder, broke into loud sobs, crying:

"Oh, uncle, uncle! dear uncle!"

The scene the two base accomplices were playing with such noteworthy spirit to cajole the rich Englishman was assuredly touching, and it was interpreted with a consummate art worthy of professional actors. But the play was only beginning! Nini now tore herself from the arms of her supposed relative and turning to Ascott, gazed long at her lover with a look at once tender and aggrieved. Then, very softly, she murmured:

"Oh, sir! sir! what have you done?"

Next old Moche took the cue: "You have dishonored her, sir. You have committed an irreparable crime. It is shameful, abominable!"

While her uncle was speaking, Nini, overwhelmed by the intensity of her emotion, fell to the floor and lay sobbing in the cleverly calculated pose of a beautiful statue of Grief!

Ascott was dreadfully upset by the unpleasant incident. The young man cursed the mad fit that had come over him the night before, while he experienced a very genuine regret at the thought that he had ruined this pretty child, who through his fault had lost her good name for ever.

Meantime a fresh witness of the lamentable scene suddenly arrived. John burst into the room like a whirlwind. Running to his master:

"Sir, sir," he cried, "the world is corning to an end!"

The Englishman, whose raging headache, so far from getting better, was growing more agonizing every minute, nevertheless preserved an imperturbable calm.

"What is the matter, John, what d'you want?"

"Sir," continued the domestic, who with blanched face and eyes unnaturally dilated, was staring at his master and Père Moche, and above all at the young woman lying on the floor, "Sir, it is the law!"

"The law!" cried Ascott. "You are mad, John!"

"No, sir, no, I am not mad. It is a Judge, a Court of Law, I don't know what all!"

His master was soon to be enlightened. Just as a little before M. Moche had pushed into the bedroom without being announced, with a like lack of ceremony three individuals had made their way along the corridor to the door of the room, and now stepped across the threshold. One of them advanced in front of the other two, a man of forty or so, short, with a jovial-looking face and a heavy, black mustache. He pulled from his pocket a tricolor scarf, which he displayed before Ascott's astonished eyes.

"I am the Commissary of Police, sir," he announced. "Is it to Monsieur Ascott I have the honor to speak?"

"To the same," replied the young man, turning pale, while drops of cold sweat gathered on his brow.

"You sent for me, sir," pursued the Commissary.

"I!" exclaimed Ascott. "Never such a thing! It wasn't I!"

M. Moche broke into the dialogue: "It was I, Monsieur le Commissaire, who took the liberty of asking you to come, and also, you will remember, the two gentlemen who are with you."

"I'm utterly lost," muttered Ascott, in a wearied voice. "I don't understand . . ."

"You will soon understand!" declared Moche, truculently.

After that Ascott began to scrutinize in sick bewilderment not only the Police Commissary, but also the two men who stood behind him, a pair of white-faced loafers of dubious aspect and repulsive countenance. They stood twisting about in evident embarrassment, jumping from one foot to the other and mechanically turning about their greasy caps between their fingers.

Presently the Commissary addressed the two apaches, pointing to M. Ascott.

"Do you recognize that gentleman?" he asked.

"Why, yes, it's as you might say, the party that engaged us last evening, about midnight, at the restaurant of the *Silver Goblet* . . ."

The Commissary questioned Ascott: "You were dining, were you not, at a restaurant in the Place de la Bastille, with the gentleman here present and mademoiselle?"—and the magistrate, to avoid any possibility of mistake, pointed in succession to M. Moche and Nini Guinon.

"Yes," admitted Ascott, not understanding what his questioner would be at.

"Good," continued the Commissary, and put another question:

"Are you ready to let us hear the proposals you made to these two gentlemen?"—this time pointing to "Bull's-eye" and the "Gasman."

But the Englishman could only stare in bewilderment at the two ruffians. He racked his brains in vain, and despite the strain he imposed on his addled wits, he could not remember having made any proposal whatsoever to the individuals before him.

"But I don't know those persons," he articulated with difficulty.

The Commissary gave a skeptical smile.

"Speak!" he ordered, addressing the "Gasman." "Repeat to the gentleman the deposition you came to my office to make."

"Here goes then!" the apache spoke with some show of embarrassment at telling his story before everybody. "It was like this—the two of us, 'Bull's-eye' and I, we were just on the saunter last evening, as you might say, near by the Bastille, when all of a minute we saw a toff a-coming down the stairs of the swell pub. It was the gentleman you say, the Englishman here present. He seemed a bit squiffy as he talked. He said to us like this: 'There's a brace of quid to be made, my lads, if you'll lend a hand to help a lady who's seemingly ill upstairs, and take her back to her home. Only, case she should kick up a bit of a rumpus, mustn't let her talk.' We chaps, we ain't no million-aires, you know, sir, and two quid's not to be refused. 'Right oh!' we told the Englishman, and there we were a-going up the stairs of the house. The Englishman, he took us into a private ken, where there was a wench, who set up a devil of a screech-ing when she saw us, but the Englishman claps a napkin over her mug, seemingly to make a gag. Then says he to us: 'Off you go, hook it, stir your stumps! There's another two quid if you do it sharp!' That made four quid, so you may bet your life we were on, sir. Then we get the baggage downstairs, clap her in a motorcar, and the four of us drive off here, all serene like. The wench never moved. By the Englishman's orders she'd been tied up hand and foot. He paid fair and square and went straight in.

"But look, sir, getting back to the Bastille, we two, 'Bull's-eye' and myself, we began to feel a bit squeamish, telling ourselves maybe we'd been lending a hand at a dirty job. Then just as we came out on the Place from the last Underground and were harking back to the *Silver Goblet* to see what had been doing since, blessed if we didn't come upon the stout gentleman who's sitting in the armchair there, and who we've found out since is called M. Moche—the old bird was singing out a good 'un, tearing his hair, he was! His niece, he kept bawling, had disap-peared, had been carried off by a satyr! He was in despair, he said, he didn't know where she was. Then 'Bull's-eye' made up to him:

"'Wasn't she a little, dark girl, the wench you're howling about?' he asks him.

"'Yes, yes . . . Might you, maybe, know where she is?'

"'Maybe we might, and maybe we might not.'

"'Bull's-eye,' he was getting to feel funny-like, and I wasn't too happy, we'd gone and done a nasty trick. But there was a way, perhaps, to make up for our foolishness, and we made up our minds to do the right thing. Old Moche, he stuck to us all night. Back we trotted to the district we'd taken the wench to, hunted round to recognize the house and found it at last.

"'And then Père Moche, he out with it:

"'Must come along with me to the Commissary, men, and

tell him the truth, the whole truth, and nothing but the truth, or else you may be certain you're in for a hatful of trouble! So there you are, sir, that's what we did!"

The apache broke off, then suddenly, with a superb gesture, drawing four gold louis from his pocket, he spread them out in the hollow of his hand, and marching up to Ascott, he made a proposal to the rich Englishman that astounded the latter more than ever.

"Would it hurt you, sir, to take back your money? The tin was not honestly earned, and it burns our fingers!"

With a look of disgust the apache tossed onto the young man's knees the four gold coins, which rolled under the bed.

Père Moche broke in: "Such, Monsieur le Commissaire, are the facts as they occurred—you know them yourself, sir. Indeed, M. Ascott does not deny them. Besides which, the presence in his house of my unhappy niece, a mere child, sir, barely sixteen years of age, whom he has odiously wronged, is surely the best proof of guilt . . ."

But Moche never finished his sentence. At last Ascott was master of the situation. A grim passion of indignation was rising in his breast, the blazing anger only men of a cold, calm temperament are capable of. With never a thought of the dignity of the functionary he addressed, he pointed to the door, and: "Out of the room, sir!" he ordered the Commissary. With majestic mien, the magistrate turned on his heel, still holding, however, his tricolor scarf in his hand.

"Moderate your language, sir!" he protested, in haughty accents. "Do not forget you are speaking to the representative of law and order. However, I obey your wish, deeming my duty to be completed in this house." Then, turning to the two apaches:

"I will likewise ask the witnesses to withdraw, in an orderly way and in silence."

Finally he addressed himself to M. Moche:

"If the young lady, your niece, sir, wishes to go, she will find a conveyance at the door."

Moche overwhelmed the Commissary with his thanks, while Nini, who had a little before retired into the dressing room, was hastily completing her toilet to quit the house of the man who had become her lover in so strange a fashion. Some minutes passed in silence, during which the several actors in this amazing scene were busy with the most varied reflections. Père Moche remained impassive to all outward seeming, but in his heart he was overjoyed at the happy turn events were taking. Once or twice he threw a meaning glance at his two confederates of the previous evening, who had carried out his instructions so well.

In telling his story, invented for the occasion, the "Gasman" had actually spoken in the very tones of one convinced of the truth of what he was relating. The fellow had made no mistakes, he had narrated the adventure exactly in the way agreed upon, and above all, Père Moche admired the apache's final act, one that had not been arranged beforehand, the act of giving back to Ascott the accursed gold wherewith he had, as he thought, bought the complicity of the two wretches, an act calculated to remove all doubt from the Commissary's mind, if by any chance he should have been dubious of the witnesses' good faith.

"By God! though," Moche muttered to himself by way of conclusion. "Ascott makes eighty francs by the transaction—eighty francs I shall have to make good to the two scamps!"

As for Ascott, he was asking himself in ever-increasing bewilderment, if he were not the victim of a delusion, a nightmare, a hideous dream. Yes, he had a perfect recollection of the evening's dinner that began so gaily, and he was bound to confess that at the end of the meal, taking advantage of old Moche's absence, he had indeed wronged little Nini—though all the same, he could not help thinking the girl had not offered any very determined resistance. But of what might have happened afterwards, he could recall nothing whatever. He seemed to remember falling fast asleep, and he could not for an instant believe he had gone out to look for a pair of apaches to have Nini Guinon forcibly carried off to his house . . . Yet, it *might* be so, for on the one hand they said it was, while on the other, on awakening he had actually found Nini fast asleep on the couch in his dressing room.

But presently the young Englishman began to ask himself what, after all, was the vast importance of all these incidents, and why such a mighty disturbance was being made over the adventure. He had not to wait long for the explanation!

Meanwhile, Nini was ready to go. The girl looked prettier than ever with her modest mien and assumed look of shamefacedness, as she made slowly for the door, by which "Bull's-eye" and the "Gasman" had already taken their departure some while ago. After casting a long look of affection and reproach at her rich lover, she preceded her uncle and the magistrate as they left the room.

But before actually crossing the threshold, the magistrate called a halt, to point out to Ascott the consequences implied by his visit.

"All this, sir, makes it my duty," he announced sternly, "to draw up an official report. You must be aware that the position in which you have placed yourself is a very serious one. It is a matter for the Criminal Assize, involving as it does, abduction of a minor, further aggravated by violation and rape. I ought, properly speaking, to arrest you. Be very grateful I do not do so, and hold yourself at the disposition of the Court."

"What is that you say, sir?" cried Ascott, in sudden alarm. But the magistrate merely bowed to the Englishman without another word and made his exit.

For a moment the young man was left alone in the room, but presently, plucking up his spirits, he sprang hurriedly to the door of the anteroom:

"Moche, Monsieur Moche!" he called the old man back in a voice choked with agitation. Moche was already halfway down the stairs, but he turned back and re-entered the room:

"What do you want with me, sir?" he asked, eyeing the Englishman haughtily up and down.

"Moche, come here," said the latter, and hurriedly catching the other by the sleeve of his coat, he led him into an adjoining room, his library and study. In feverish haste he pulled open a drawer and took out a checkbook. Dipping a pen in the ink, he paused before writing to ask:

"Monsieur Moche, how much?"

"Beg pardon!" said the old brigand.

Ascott, mastering his nerves, repeated once more:

"I ask you, how much do you want? This is a check I have here, which I am ready to sign in your favor. Fix the amount yourself, and let us be done with this nonsense."

A gleam of cupidity flashed in the usurer's eyes, but that astute personage did not yield to the temptation. It was not in that fashion he hoped to bleed the Englishman. His project was more pretentious, his plan more complicated than that. The old man feigned the greatest indignation:

"It is shameful, sir. You insult me! After your villainous treatment of my niece, you offer me money. Sir, you mistake my character altogether! No, sir, I do not take that bait, the affair must follow its course!"

Ascott turned livid. "Moche," he supplicated, "we are friends . . ."

"We *were* friends, sir."

"Moche! . . . Monsieur Moche! I cannot have a scandal!"

"Nini Guinon, my niece, sir, is dishonored."

"But, Moche, how can this be arranged?"

"There is but one way, sir, to right the wrong done, religion and society offer you the means."

Ascott hesitated a moment, then he replied with a shudder.

"Marriage, you mean?" he cried. "You would have me marry Nini Guinon . . . you forget that I am a great nobleman!"

Moche corrected: "Lord Ascott, yes, but that's not you, that is your father."

"I am his son . . ."

"His younger son, sir, which is by no means the same thing. There is nothing should hinder your marrying an honest girl whom you have led astray from the paths of duty."

Ascott was obviously wavering. "Moche, my good friend, Moche!" he besought the old scamp, "there must be other ways of settling the question. I am rich, I care nothing for the money . . ."

"Enough!" Père Moche cut him short peremptorily, "I have told you, sir, what a true-hearted gentleman, what a man of honor, would not for one instant hesitate to do. On the basis of repairing the wrong by marriage, you will find us always ready to listen to you, to facilitate matters. Otherwise, it is of no use attempting to see me again"—and the old man marched majestically for the door, leaving Ascott absolutely dumbfounded, the pen trembling between his fingers, his checkbook lying open before his eyes.

However, before finally going, M. Moche came to a halt on the threshold, and in a ringing voice, threw down a final challenge, a supreme work of menace and defiance:

"We shall meet again, sir . . . in the Court of Assize."

17. Fantômas Meets Fantômas

In the drives of the Parc des Princes, as a rule deserted in the evening, the somber ways that start from the fortifications and unite Paris with Boulogne-sur-Seine, ways bordered by sumptuous private mansions, elegant villas and blocks of luxurious flats, there was tonight an unaccustomed coming and going of motorcars, broughams, and even democratic taxis. All these vehicles were going in the same direction, and all were swallowed up by the great gates that stood wide open before a private dwelling standing just halfway down the grand avenue that runs between the city conservatories and the Bois.

There for some months had been living the Grand Duchess Alexandra, bosom friend of the King of Hesse-Weimar, one of the most noted personalities of the foreign colony in Paris. No one, in fact, making any pretense to belong to society, could fail to be acquainted with the elegant and enterprising grand duchess. All knew her as a pretty woman, a wealthy woman, and report said a good and charitable one. Many a time her witty sayings had raised a laugh in fashionable drawing rooms, while she enjoyed a reputation for Parisian chic that was certainly not unjustified.

Great lady as she was, there was something mysterious, possibly equivocal, about her personality, and, if life in Paris were not so stirring, so exacting, so absorbing, many who frequented her receptions might well have asked who precisely she was, and have searched curiously through the pages of the Almanach de Gotha to find the credentials for her ducal blazon. The high rank she held at the Court of Frederick Christian II was indeed a matter of common knowledge, further, that she was honored by the very special friendship of the Prince Gudulfin was whispered in private conclave, but this pretty well summed up the total of what society in general did know about her. But it is never the custom, so long as a woman is rich, beautiful and witty, so long as no open scandal attaches to her name, to be over-exacting as to details. At any rate, each time the grand duchess threw open her drawing rooms for one of the superb and sumptuous entertainments she was in the habit of giving, no eagerness was too shameless to secure an invitation, and all were only too proud and happy to be numbered among her guests.

Though it was already May, the Grand Duchess Alexandra was tonight giving a fancy-dress ball. This had long been promised, but having been postponed in consequence of the great lady's being indisposed, was at last fixed for this belated period of the season.

It was eleven o'clock, and guests were beginning to arrive, carriages driving up in rapid succession to the steps of the villa, one after another depositing masked figures, some baffling, some charming, in costumes borrowed from legend, history, in some cases even recalling contemporary politics. Dancing had not yet commenced, all were devoting their energies to applauding, enthusiastically applauding, the most becoming dresses, the most ingenious disguises, as they appeared. The evening was delicious, the mild spring weather perfect, so that the masquers could gather under the wide awning that sheltered the steps and there welcome each new arrival.

The general attention was beginning to flag, and the duchess herself, abandoning the attempt to shake every new arrival by the hand—their number made the task impossible—was about to return to the reception rooms, where the Gypsy orchestra had just struck up one of their softest and most melodious waltz tunes, when a magnificent automobile pulled up to the steps. The car roused no little curiosity by the fact that its blinds were drawn down so as to make it impossible to see who was inside. Instinctively almost, as sometimes happens, the talk grew hushed. Heads were turned and necks craned to see. Staying momentarily the play of her ever-moving fan, the grand duchess herself seemed to be puzzled as she eagerly awaited the newcomer, whose very sex was still a secret.

Then the door of the car opened at last, and suddenly through the crowd, till then so gay, ran a shudder of distress and terror. "Ah, ahs!" of amazement could be heard, while even the hostess's cheek paled. A striking, an extraordinary figure it was that alighted from the mysterious equipage. The costume, to be sure, was recognized by one and all—but who, who had had the boldness to don it?

In the dazzling illumination shed by the lights scattered everywhere about the front of the mansion, the newcomer's figure stood out with extraordinary clearness. It was that of a man, still young. He was clad from head to foot in a complete suit of closely fitting black tights. His shoulders were wrapped in a long cloak, also black, even his face was hidden beneath a black cowl that prevented so much as a guess at the color of his hair.

A dreadful costume! a tragic figure! an emblem of fear! The name of this mysterious masquer passed quickly from lip to lip, set every heart beating fast and furiously, sounded a grim refrain to every sentence spoken:

"Fantômas! . . . it is Fantômas!"

But while his arrival was causing so great a sensation, while the company, taken by surprise, showed itself afraid, almost panic-stricken, the unknown himself was advancing to greet the Grand Duchess Alexandra. Bowing low before his hostess with the manner of a finished gentleman, in a grave, but agreeable voice:

"I was told, Madame la Duchesse," he said, "that Fantômas attended every festivity. No sooner had I landed in France than they swore to me he was afraid of nothing. That is why I did not think it needful to warn you of my coming to your fête. That is why I believed myself justified in visiting you under this . . . disguise."

The Grand Duchess's voice trembled a little as she questioned him:

"But to whom have I the pleasure to be speaking?" The masquer replied:

"To Fantômas, madam!"

"To Fantômas, of course! . . . but besides?"

Clearly it would have been discourteous to carry on the secret further. Indeed, the unknown had not failed to note the half concealed fear, the very real distress, his arrival had produced among the grand duchess's guests. To prolong this constraint would not have been becoming. The "Fantômas" therefore answered:

"Very good, madam, as it is your pleasure to unmask me, I cannot deny your wish, and I pull off my cowl . . ."—and he lifted the silken folds concealing his features. Next instant a tempest of applause, a whirlwind of acclamation, from all present, greeted the hero of the hour. It was indeed a fine piece of daring, a splendid stroke of defiance, something quite Parisian and cynical, this grim disguise adopted by the man who wore it. In the half minute he stood there unmasked, he had been recognized. The masquer who had put on the outward semblance of Fantômas was none other than Fantômas' declared enemy, none other than Tom Bob!

Meantime the latter was bowing right and left, then glided swiftly among the groups of his acquaintance, grasping the men's hands, kissing the ladies', a very gallant gentleman. A curious thing, too, to observe that, while these fashionable men and women would never have condescended to clasp hands with a common inspector of the French Investigation Bureau, they were making much of Tom Bob, just because he was a foreigner. True, he had originally joined the police as an amateur, out of curiosity and for the sake of amusement, and it was only by degrees, after a series of notable successes, that he had become a professional detective—and the fact was not forgotten.

But the mystery was dissipated. After the inevitable panic created by this apparition of the terrible figure of Fantômas, a very real satisfaction, a genuine feeling of relief had been experienced in learning that beneath this horrid disguise was hidden the man who had pledged himself to deliver Parisian society from Fantômas! In fact there was not one of all the grand duchess's guests but entertained in his heart a secret dread of the desperate criminal. Ever since the brigand had sworn to the Parliament to spread terror far and wide, every man felt himself more or less menaced. The American detective, by taking up the challenge thrown down by the Minister, had to some extent relieved these apprehensions, and society was grateful to him.

For half an hour the Grand Duchess Alexandra, like an accomplished hostess, had been moving through the different rooms, declining to dance herself, but finding for each an agreeable word, a gracious phrase of greeting, when in a doorway by chance she came face to face with the "Fantômas."

"Monsieur Bob," she was beginning, when next moment she broke off in startled surprise. And truly the great lady had good reason to be amazed. The masquer, whom she was about to congratulate once more on his clever disguise, had just committed a grave breach of etiquette. Bowing, he had, without a word, while pretending to kiss her hand, slipped a note inside her glove. Then, turning on his heels, not giving the grand duchess time to protest or answer, he had glided off among the dancers, putting between them the effective barrier of the whirling couples.

More than surprised, the grand duchess said and did what any woman would have said and done under the circumstances.

"Tom Bob dares to slip a *billet-doux* into my hand! What insolence! Most certainly I will go and throw it down at his feet, this execrable token of bad taste!" Then she reflected that, before getting rid of the scrap of paper she could feel under her glove, it would perhaps be amusing to cast a glance at it, and, her lips curling in a disdainful smile, the grand duchess, leaving the dancing rooms for a moment, went up to her private apartment. There, hastily turning on the electric light, she hurriedly glanced at the extraordinary letter.

At first she thought she must be dreaming. The writing was not Tom Bob's, nor was it the detective, that was certain, who had written on a corner of the paper by way of address, and there was no other, the five words, "For pity's sake, read this!" Who was it then? Whose messenger had Tom Bob constituted himself? The grand duchess did not hesitate a second longer. Unfolding the note, she read, and the contents instantly blanched her cheeks:

> Madam, you will pardon the means I take to bring myself to your notice in consideration of the feelings that prompt me. In the name of all you hold dear, in the name of whatever pity your woman's heart may know for an unhappy lover, I beseech you to grant me your attention for a few minutes this very evening. It is no enemy who writes to you, albeit my name may make you shudder. It is an unhappy man, an unhappy being who loves a young girl whom you know, one who cherishes no hope save in the influence you can exert over her, one who, amidst these merry-makers, under the black mask that veils his features, will be impatiently waiting the moment when you shall accord him the brief interview he asks, the brief minutes of confidence he craves.   JEROME FANDOR.

Jerome Fandor! The grand duchess thought she was dreaming. Was it indeed possible it could be Jerome Fandor who had written to her? . . . Jerome Fandor, the ally of Juve? Jerome Fandor, the implacable enemy of Fantômas? Jerome Fandor whom all the world accused of the vilest crimes, but whom she well knew to be innocent! Jerome Fandor, how that name evoked at once fear and pity in the breast of that beautiful and mysterious personage, the Grand Duchess Alexandra. What memories did it not call up of the saddest tragedies of her life?

Jerome Fandor, perhaps the only living being who could possibly share with Juve the knowledge that she, the Grand Duchess Alexandra, was in reality named Lady Beltham, was in reality the mistress of Fantômas! And now it was this same Jerome Fandor, today her lover's implacable foe, tomorrow no doubt his accuser, who came asking the favor of an interview! who asked the boon in the name of love!

Lady Beltham stood trembling, her breath coming quick and fast as she read and re-read the brief note just passed to her. Then suddenly, shaking off all doubts, she made her decision. Yes, seeing it was in the name of love that Jerome Fandor wrote, seeing he besought her pity, she would not refuse his prayer.

"My life, my unhappy life," thought Lady Beltham, "has but one excuse—love. Whensoever I hear that name invoked, I shall be found ready to recognize the only sentiment I feel some little respect for!"

But a bewildering, a terrible problem still confronted the great lady. With what surprise, with what agitation she realized that Fandor was in her house, and must be there, the very terms of his letter showed it, disguised as Fantômas—in the same disguise as Tom Bob? There were two "Fantômas" then among the dancers, the American detective and Jerome Fandor.

It was quite possible, quite probable indeed, as she soon came to see. The costumes the detective and the journalist had donned must obviously be alike, if they were correct: was it not therefore allowable to suppose there were two "Fantômas" in the room without anyone having so far noted the fact: naturally people would conclude it was the same masquer they saw each time. Why, she herself was deceived just now, believing herself in the presence of Fantômas-Tom Bob, when she was actually standing before Fantômas-Fandor!

Eventually Lady Beltham returned to the dancing rooms, thinking to herself:

"I will go presently into the conservatory. He is sure to be watching me and will join me there."

While the grand duchess in the retirement of her private apartments was reading the strange note slipped into her hand by Fandor, who had likewise come, as she had guessed, disguised as Fantômas, a diverting scene occurred in the dancing rooms below! The fact is Fantômas-Fandor had caught sight of another Fantômas.

"Hallo!" the young man told himself, "someone has had the same idea as myself, it's really capital!"

Then he disappeared in the crush, ready to keep a watchful eye on Lady Beltham. But now the second Fantômas, Fantômas-Tom Bob, had also noted his double, and the news was flying fast from mouth to mouth:

"You know, there are two Fantômas! . . . a highly original

idea, don't you think?"

"Why yes, highly original!" all agreed.

Yet no one observed that not merely two Fantômas were at the dance, but perhaps three or four, or even more! A few minutes afterwards, the lovely Sonia Danidoff was waltzing with one of the men wearing the grim black cowl when the second masquer clad in the same tragic garb knocked against the couple. A dialogue verging on the ludicrous ensued.

"Sir!" the first Fantômas, Sonia's partner, was saying, "I think it a very bold proceeding to have adopted my costume!"

"And why so, sir?" retorted the other Fantômas in the same emphatic tone.

"Because, sir, it is a heavy costume, and a dangerous one, to wear! No brigand, save myself, had ever dreamt of adopting it till you."

To this the second masquer replied in a tone of raillery: "You are in the wrong to complain, sir. It would more become *me* to protest against *your* audacity. You are an impostor, you carry a disguise. I am the genuine Fantômas!"

"Easy talking, sir!"

"Easier still to prove, sir!"

"So it's a quarrel, is it? We must settle between us, arms in hand?"

"As you please, sir!"

"Now, at once?"

"At once!"

A laughing group had gathered round, finding a new and piquant diversion in this altercation between the two masquers, each defending with apparent seriousness his title to be the true Fantômas.

"The vanquished," cried Sonia, merrily, "shall take off his cowl for the rest of the evening."

At this one of the disputants wheeled round, and in answer to the gibe:

"No, madam," he said, "the vanquished will not appear again, for one good reason—he will be dead."

"Madam, I will use no empty words of compliment to thank you for granting me this interview. Words are incapable of translating my feelings, and between us they would be yet more vain than with others."

The "Fantômas" who uttered the words bowed low with infinite respect before the Grand Duchess Alexandra, whom he had just come upon in one of the little nooks of greenery, so quiet and retired, so convenient for flirtations or confidential talks, which the great lady had contrived in the superb winter garden, opening out of her drawing rooms. The masquer went on:

"I will not thank you, madam, for on us, alas! weighs a past too heavy to allow soft words to do aught but call up sad memories in our hearts. That past you do not disown any more than I do, but I ask your permission to remember in speaking to you two facts, that you, you, the Grand Duchess Alexandra, are Lady Beltham, and that I, under this travesty of Fantômas, am Jerome Fandor."

In a weak, trembling voice, Lady Beltham questioned: "Speak, sir! But first, why this disguise? why, why do you, you of all men, wear that cowl?"

"Because, that mask, madam," returned Fandor, in a broken voice, "that mask lets me remain nameless among your guests. Probably you forget, Lady Beltham, that at this present moment Jerome Fandor is held by general consent to be a criminal. And, besides this, madam, yet another reason—you will forgive my naming it—led me to adopt this disguise. Was I not certain you would accord a few minutes' talk to the man wearing this costume. I could not tell if it would be possible for me to give you the letter, but I felt convinced if as Fantômas I asked to speak with you, you would not refuse your lover three minutes' conversation."

Lady Beltham, pale and trembling, made no reply—what answer could the unhappy lady find to give Fandor, the man who at that very time was suffering the direst torments at the hands of the real Fantômas, her lover? She could only repeat again: "Speak, sir, what do you want of me?"

"A small thing, madam," returned Fandor, "a small thing, and yet of infinite moment—*happiness*. I am going to beg you to say three words—three words that will assure me the chiefest joy of my life."

Almost on the defensive, in a voice of fear, Lady Beltham said for the third time: "Speak, sir, speak!"

"Madam," Fandor resumed in trembling accents, "I love deeply, with all my heart and all my soul, an unhappy young girl whose name you know, for it bears a melancholy renown. Elizabeth Dollon, I mean. Madam, by your lover's doing—nay, never protest, all denial is in vain between us—by your lover's doing, I, I Jerome Fandor, am deemed by Elizabeth Dollon, as by all men, to be Fantômas. She would love me if she knew me innocent, now she hates me, fears me, flies from me! Madam, I have always been to you, and even to him who is dear to you, an honorable foe, the dreadful penalty I suffer today as the result of the war I wage is the more cruel as it is undeserved. What hurt can it do you, Lady Beltham, what hurt can it do Fantômas, even should I enjoy a little happiness, should I win Elizabeth's love? . . . This is the prayer I would make to you. She is single-hearted, she is enthusiastic, she sacrifices my life to you. Madam, I beg you, I beseech you, go to Elizabeth and tell her I am not Fantômas, and that she can love me!"

Such profound feeling inspired Jerome Fandor's words, his voice vibrated with such deep emotion as he spoke, that Lady Beltham herself could not help being greatly moved. Yes, Jerome Fandor was surely right, he had always been an honorable enemy. Surely he was right again in describing his position with Elizabeth as horrible. Surely again, what harm could it do Fantômas for him to enjoy a little happiness?

Lady Beltham was touched, won over. She burst out suddenly:

"I know you are Jerome Fandor, sir. I know it, and I need only know that! I decline to understand the allusions you have made. But if you beseech the Grand Duchess Alexandra to go to Elizabeth Dollon, the grand duchess is verily too much your friend, too well persuaded of the depth of your love for Mlle. Dollon, to refuse the boon you ask of her."

"Oh! madam,"—and Fandor, with a quick almost instinctive movement, seized Lady Beltham's white, ungloved hand. But the great lady drew back, manifestly she could not prolong forever her talk with this masquer, this "Fantômas." None had come to disturb them, but their conversation was bound to have attracted notice. The place was lined with mirrors, they were at the mercy of every chance reflection.

"Where can I see Elizabeth Dollon?" asked the grand duchess.

"The poor girl," replied the other, "in spite of her enemies, still lives an honest, hard-working life. I know—I learned this only a day or two ago—she is engaged as cashier, I think at one of the restaurants in the Bois, the restaurant on the island in the lake."

Lady Beltham had already risen and was moving away when she threw these words by way of adieu to the young man:

"By all I hold most sacred, sir, I swear that Elizabeth Dollon, no later than tomorrow evening, shall know that Jerome Fandor is worthy of her love."

"I beg your pardon, Monsieur Fantômas!"

"You mean?"

"I mean to say that costume is heavy for your shoulders."

After Lady Beltham's departure, Jerome Fandor had stayed behind in the conservatory, motionless, rapt in absorption. The great lady's promise had given him the wildest hopes. If the grand duchess saw fit to convince Elizabeth Dollon of his innocence, it was easy enough for her to do so. If she kept her promise, and Jerome Fandor never doubted she would, a happy future, a future of love lay before him! But as he was thinking these rosy thoughts, plunged in an ecstasy of anticipation, a disquieting incident befell.

The young man was standing in the center of the winter garden, on the very spot where he had talked with Lady Beltham. On every side of him, on the walls, between the interlacing boughs of palms, araucarias and kentias, hung mirrors reflecting his own image and that of his surroundings. Now, amid these reflections, appeared one, a second "Fantômas," that moved and gesticulated and presently advanced, while the same mocking words, spoken now for the second time in the course of the evening, struck Fandor's ear:

"That cloak is heavy for your shoulders, sir!"

The journalist felt a cold sweat bedew his temples. Who was this other "Fantômas"? for it was in truth, a second "Fantômas" advancing to meet him! the same perhaps he had observed among the dancers just now? or else, perhaps, another, or else . . . or else. . . . In a supercilious, defiant tone, Jerome Fandor retorted:

"If the cloak is heavy for my shoulders, sir, is it, tell me, any lighter for yours?"

"They are, at least better used to wearing it."

Fandor started at the words, but before he had time to answer, suddenly, in an instant, with an unparalleled swiftness and violence that disarmed all power of resistance, a savage dagger thrust caught him immediately, over the heart. A red mist blinded the young man's eyes, as he staggered under the force of the blow. A buzzing filled his ears, and a curse, a cry of fury, escaped his quivering lips. Then slowly the place began to turn round and round, darkening and taking on fantastic shapes. Jerome Fandor was fainting.

But he was too energetic, too brave a man, to lose consciousness for long. Three seconds after the blow was struck, his senses were returning to him. "Fantômas! Fantômas!" he stammered. "It was the real Fantômas stood there before me!" He struggled painfully to his knees, then rose to his feet in spite of the sharp pain, and forced himself to look round—the conservatory was empty! Stumbling forward, he took two or three steps, his hand pressed to his breast, then sank into a rocking chair, muttering in a weak and still bewildered voice:

"Lucky for me, all the same, the coat of mail I took the precaution to wear under my disguise withstood the stab! I knew, when I put on this Fantômas costume, I was risking the brigand's anger. I was well advised to guard against it as I did. Verily, I believe this time I have looked death close in the face!"

Meantime in the ballrooms the festivities were still in full swing while these untoward events were happening in the winter garden, but at last the dance was now drawing to a close. Four o'clock was striking, and the wan, pallid light of day peeped in at the doors half open into the park: the loveliest faces began to look faded, the smoothest locks ruffled, it was time for pretty women to beat a retreat, under pain of seeming positively plain.

Then suddenly, no one knowing whence the news came, all stood frozen in rigid horror at a dreadful report that circulated from group to group. There was a general rush for the park, while broken phrases passed between the hurrying guests.

"Wounded?"

"Dead!"

"You are sure, madam?"

"It was a chauffeur found the body."

"Yes, a dagger was still stuck in the heart."

"Appalling!"

"So it wasn't Tom Bob, then?"

"Who *was* the victim?"

"It is not known."

"Where are the 'Fantômas'?"

"One of them has just gone."

"Who? Which?"

"The cloakroom attendant recognized him. It was Tom Bob."

"It seems he was wounded?"

"Yes, the attendant said he had blood on his sleeve. He had actually turned back the sleeve and looked at his arm. There was a long, red gash there."

"But Tom Bob is no assassin!"

"Ah! but was it really Tom Bob? that is just the question, my dear sir."

Fandor still lay exhausted in the conservatory, still dazed from the attempt on his life he had only just escaped. But in a moment he sprang up with a start, the Grand Duchess Alexandra, Lady Beltham, stood before him. She looked agitated, she was panting and frightfully pale.

"Run! run!" she cried distractedly.

Jerome Fandor looked at the great lady in wide-eyed astonishment.

"Run! run!" she could only repeat. "Oh! for pity's sake, begone! It is horrible, appalling. They have just found in the park a man dressed as Fantômas lying dead, stabbed in the heart—an officer of the Criminal Investigation Bureau!"

Fandor listened without a word, while Lady Beltham went on again, wringing her hands:

"But flee, I tell you, flee! Don't you understand they will accuse you? You were seen just now, dressed as Fantômas, leaving the rooms with another 'Fantômas', they will make sure the first masquer was the murderer, that is you!"

Still dazed as he followed Lady Beltham, who was leading him towards a hidden door, Fandor asked:

"But then there were three 'Fantômas'?—Tom Bob, myself, this officer?"

"There were four or five," replied Lady Beltham. "I cannot tell how many: there was you, there was Tom Bob, there was an officer of the Bureau . . . there was. . ."

Fandor finished the sentence the grand duchess dared not complete. "There was . . . there was," he hesitated, "there must have been the true Fantômas!"

A malediction rose to Jerome Fandor's lips, but all ready to make his escape as Lady Beltham urged him, he yet stayed his flight an instant. He had heard, like a blessing the unhappy woman murmur a parting word.

"Tomorrow, tomorrow! I have promised you Elizabeth shall know you are innocent!"

18. "Fantômas Speaking!"

M. Havard was almost apologetic, almost polite, a fact which in his case was proof positive of the deepest respect. Habitually plain-spoken, accustomed to give orders in clear, precise terms, and to ask questions in a more downright fashion, still, M. Havard appeared for once to be making heroic efforts to preserve a respectful, deferential attitude.

"My carriage is not over and above luxurious" he was saying, pointing to the inside of the brougham in which he had just taken his seat in company with a personage of a keen, anxious-looking countenance, but you must know that, to make up, it is one of the safest."

"What does that mean?"

"It means that, copying the Emperor of Germany, I have taken the precaution, Monsieur le Ministre, to have the woodwork lined with steel plates. In my carriage one is secure against the latest and most approved revolvers, the sharpest daggers."

The Minister smiled approvingly. "And that is always something!" he laughed.

"Yes, it is indeed something," M. Havard proceeded, "when, like me, a man is continually exposed to acts of vengeance, of reprisal, the object of ill-will and hatred."

But it was pretty plain the Minister was paying but a divided attention to M. Havard's remarks.

"Quite right," he said, in an indifferent voice. "Yes, I admire your precautions. You were certainly well inspired to fortify your carriage in this way. . . . But come now, tell me what line you propose to adopt with this individual?"

"The individual we are going to see?"

"Precisely, this man Tom Bob . . . this Tom Bob who would seem to be Fantômas—ridiculous as the supposition may appear at first sight."

On hearing this remark, M. Havard was suddenly afflicted with a very convenient tickling in the throat. He said nothing—the Head of the Investigation Department would, under no circumstances, have taken upon himself to contradict a Minister of State, but . . . well, he coughed. And to cough, in all the languages of the world, has always indicated that a man would not be disinclined to prove his interlocutor mistaken in the opinions he is enunciating in his presence.

Observing the police official's hesitation, the Minister insisted:

"Why, yes, Tom Bob must be Fantômas! The thing is self-evident, obvious. Don't *you* think so, too, Havard?"

For, impossible as it seemed to admit that Tom Bob was really Fantômas, the Minister had almost come to believe it—to wish to believe it at any rate, since the tragic events of the previous night! On the other hand, M. Havard, more accustomed to think things out coldly and impartially, to weigh the arguments for and against a proposition, was less convinced. "Events," he reflected, "do certainly seem to show Tom Bob to be Fantômas. But there are so many facts on the other side that go to prove the contrary that we must not rush to so extravagant a conclusion. Devil take it, Tom Bob is a police officer—an officer of repute in America. He has already, here in Paris, since his arrival, effected some telling arrests. . . . No, he cannot be Fantômas! If appearances are against him, they are, after all, only appearances, probably contrived by the real Fantômas. It is true. . . ."

M. Havard broke off his reflections to answer the Minister's question:

"Alas! sir, in all these baffling difficulties, I really do not know what I think."

"A very canny answer."

"But a sincere one, sir."

"Sincere, why, yes, I grant you. But surely not very frank. However, I will force you to give a plain reply—yes or no, do you believe Tom Bob is the murderer?"

M. Havard coughed again. It was evidently a chronic complaint, this cough of his! Finally, sinking back in discouragement on the cushions and nervously cracking his finger joints, he confessed in a dubious voice:

"Believe! What do I believe? . . . well, I just make guesses, Monsieur le Ministre."

"But, my dear man, you told me yourself . . ." then breaking off again, the Minister started afresh.

"Come, tell me the exact particulars—I have so much business on my mind there are times when I cannot trust my own memory—tell me the precise results of your investigations. You were saying that yesterday . . ."

This time, when it became a question of setting out the results of a police investigation, without deducing the consequences, without drawing any compromising conclusion, M. Havard recovered all his usual coolness, all the peremptory tone of authority that was habitual with him. So it was with perfect lucidity, with the strictest logical precision, he now answered the Minister.

"My investigation has established nothing absolutely definite. All it justifies us in doing is to specify certain facts, relevant facts I admit, but in no way conclusive."

"And these facts are? . . ."

"These facts are as follows: Yesterday, the Grand Duchess Alexandra gave a ball, a costume ball. At this costume ball were several 'Fantômas.' How many, precisely, it is impossible, sir, for me to inform you. I have not been able to ascertain the number. On more than one occasion, this is certain, two masked figures, two 'Fantômas' were seen talking together, which would go to prove there were two 'Fantômas.' But after all, this is not positively certain, for because two men in black cowls have been seen, it obviously does not follow there were no others elsewhere in the rooms. . . ."

"But why this hypothesis?"

"Why? Hmm! because. . . . Anyhow, sir, let us remember this fact, this primary fact—two 'Fantômas,' exactly alike, two disguises of identical shape and make, attended the Grand Duchess Alexandra's fête. Very good, but who and what were they? Here we enter the domain at once of certainties and hypotheses. One certainly we have—one of these masquers was Tom Bob. He was seen, recognized, identified by name. The second of these masked men, and here we have another, a melancholy, certainty, was an agent of the Criminal Bureau, one of our excellent officers, indeed, Inspector Joffre—he was the man they found subsequently, you know, under the trees in the garden, stabbed to the heart."

"And he was the man," affirmed the Minister, "who was seen to go off with Tom Bob, with the other 'Fantômas,' after a laughing colloquy, in which our agent, like Tom Bob, had claimed to be actually and indeed the ever-elusive brigand. From which I infer . . ."

But M. Havard made a gesture of dissent:

"Yes, you infer, sir, but you go too fast in your inferences. What precisely occurred between the moment when Tom Bob as 'Fantômas' arrived at the grand duchess's, a little before our agent Joffre, also disguised as a 'Fantômas,' and that when the unfortunate officer was found dead, murdered? It would be hard to say. You remember the laughing dispute that took place between the two 'Fantômas'? That dispute actually took place. My investigation has enabled me to find many who can vouch for it, amongst other witnesses the Princess Sonia Danidoff. I do not dispute it, but you miss one point, Monsieur le Ministre, and that is that when the two men made a pretense of going into the park to settle their difference arms in hand, both wore the sinister black cowl, and could not therefore be recognized, and that in consequence there is nothing to justify our alleging that the man who was with the unfortunate Joffre was really Tom Bob."

"Why, yes, there *is* one thing. . . ."

"Namely, sir?"

"Why, think, the incident in the cloakroom."

M. Havard smiled.

"I do not forget it!" he cried, "yes, the cloakroom incident does constitute a serious impeachment against Tom Bob, a terribly serious impeachment. But you remember the exact details, sir?"

"I think so! Come, now, events happened thus. . . ."

"I will detail them precisely as they did happen. At the very moment at which the chauffeur found the murdered Joffre's body in the gardens, the rumor was circulating among the dancers, a well-founded rumor, that Tom Bob, Tom Bob, still wearing his 'Fantômas' costume, had just left. If we are to credit the cloakroom attendant, he had come in a few minutes before to claim the black mantle that covered his shoulders on his first arrival, and which he had entrusted to the man's care in the course of the evening. Now, as he put on the garment, Tom Bob would appear to have mentioned that he was wounded in the arm, and on the man expressing surprise, he would seem to have gone on to say: 'It's the penalty for having chosen to play up a bit too hard against the real Fantômas.' Then, still going by what the attendant says, he seems to have pulled up his sleeve, unbuttoned his cuff, and—the cloakroom was empty at the moment—examined a deep cut on his arm, halfway between shoulder and elbow, to be precise, a cut apparently made by a knife, and which, moreover, was still bleeding freely. Tom Bob seems after that to have pulled down the sleeve again, declaring it was a trifle, and so taken his departure."

M. Havard fell silent, the Minister seemed to be thinking, then suddenly he asked:

"Monsieur Havard, why do you speak in the conditional mood? . . . Tom Bob *would appear* to have done such and such a thing, said such and such a thing: *seems* to have taken his departure I So you don't believe the witness to be trustworthy?"

This time, M. Havard's habit of plain speaking took the upper band, and it was in a tone by no means over and above respectful that he replied:

"Oh, yes, I do! The witness is telling the truth, the story is quite correct. But if I do speak in the conditional, the real fact is all these happenings, all this evidence about the wound, is so . . . so odd, so improbable, that . . ."

"How improbable?" protested the Minister. "Why, sir, if Joffre *was* murdered, I take it he was not killed without defending himself. Even if he received a mortal blow quite unexpectedly, he could have struck back, wounded Tom Bob, wounded his assailant. . . ."

In a tone of raillery, M. Havard finished the other's sentence:

". . . And Fantômas could have committed the imprudence of boasting of it in the cloak room? But, my dear sir, that is foolishness, utter foolishness! I won't so much as think of it! If Tom Bob was Joffre's murderer, he would be Fantômas. If he was Fantômas, he would never have been guilty of the mad inconsistency of showing his wound to a witness."

M. Havard's objection was evidently well founded, the whole story was undoubtedly baffling. But the Minister still refused to confess himself beaten. *He* believed in Tom Bob's guilt. Had the detective not been seen in the "Fantômas" costume? Was he not known to have had an altercation with Joffre, to have gone off in his company into the gardens, where Joffre had been killed? Nothing if not logical, the Minister drew the conclusion: "Tom Bob is the murderer."

Then another point struck him, and he added triumphantly:

"Besides, Havard, if Tom Bob were not guilty, why should he not have come in answer to your invitation this morning?"

M. Havard shook his head doubtfully, and made no answer. This point, raised by the Minister's last question, was precisely what most exercised the head of the Investigation Department. When at an early hour he had been awakened by a ring on the telephone and a message from the Commissary's office at the Parc des Princes, telling him that a new and appalling crime had just been committed by Fantômas, a crime that was spreading frantic terror among the members of Parisian society, a crime that it seemed must be set down to Tom Bob, M. Havard had come to several important decisions. He telephoned immediately to the Prefecture to send officers of the Department to shadow the Hotel Terminus, where Tom Bob was still in residence. For himself, he set off at once to the Grand Duchess Alexandra's. There he had, with his usual ability and acumen, held a rapid investigation, in the course of which he had discovered certain facts, facts if not directly relevant, at least suggestive.

On leaving the villa in the Parc des Princes, M. Havard hurried to the Ministry of Justice. It was eight o'clock when the head of the Criminal Bureau reached the Minister's private apartments. By dint of eager representations to the ushers on duty and a like insistence with the ministerial attachés, he obtained immediate audience of M. Désiré Ferrand's successor. A few moments more and he was closeted with the Minister of Justice, and was rapidly narrating, almost without drawing breath, the extraordinary events of the previous evening.

"Monsieur le Ministre," M. Havard concluded, "I deemed it expedient to put you in possession of the facts at once, in order to save myself from incurring too heavy a load of responsibility. At this present moment a man is suspected, and reasonably suspected. This man is Tom Bob, the American detective. Unless we arrest him, public opinion, alarmed, agitated, terror-stricken, is going to cause us the most troublesome embarrassments. Questions will be asked in the House, for certain! On the other hand, to arrest Tom Bob is a serious step. He is an American citizen, a foreigner, and will no doubt claim the protection of his consul and involve us in diplomatic difficulties. In fact, to arrest the man seems a monstrous thing to do."

The Minister, after a few minutes' thought, advised M. Havard to dispatch a special messenger to see Tom Bob and beg him to come at once to the Ministry of Justice where the Minister wished to speak to him. But the messenger had been to the Hotel Terminus, had seen Tom Bob, and had brought back the answer:

"Mr. Bob directs me to say he is very tired, almost ill, and cannot be disturbed."

Neither Havard nor the Minister could make anything of it, and while the former was still marveling at the amazing attitude the American detective had chosen to adopt in refusing to obey the personal invitation of a Minister of State, under the flimsy excuse of fatigue, the Minister insisted:

"You must admit, M. Havard, that this refusal to come and see me is, to say the least, extraordinary. Why, devil take it, if Tom Bob was not wounded, that is to say, was not guilty, that is to say, had not pressing reasons for not showing himself just now, he would have come along here post haste. How did he know I was not meaning to decorate him?"

M. Havard laughed frankly at the great man's little joke. He was still laughing when the brougham stopped at the door of the Hotel Terminus.

"Whatever you do," the Minister observed, as they got out, "whatever you do, address me as 'my dear fellow,' from now on. I don't at all like the idea of that American being able to boast of having put out a Minister of France. I mean to preserve the strictest incognito."

M. Havard handed his card to a waiter, bidding him go and inform Mr. Tom Bob that he desired a few minutes' conversation with him. Then, after the man had gone, he assured his companion:

"Do not be afraid, Monsieur le Ministre . . . beg pardon! . . . do not be afraid, my dear fellow: nobody shall guess who you are."

"Monsieur Havard, I was expecting you"—smiling, cheerful, debonair, not the very least like a sick or tired man, Tom Bob welcomed M. Havard in one of the small sitting rooms of the hotel.

"You were expecting me, my dear colleague?"

"Certainly!"

Then, as Tom Bob was drawing up seats, and his eyes fell on the Minister, M. Havard thought it needful to add: "Allow me to introduce my senior secretary."

The American vouchsafed a little supercilious smile for this subordinate. "Delighted, sir, delighted to meet you!" and he turned again to M. Havard, resuming:

"I was expecting you, because I supposed the Minister, having sent for me this morning and finding I did not come, would send someone to see me."

The opportunity was too good a one for verifying an important point for M. Havard to neglect:

"You were right, quite right in your supposition. But, by-the-by, why did you not come to the Ministry?"

A smile appeared on Tom Bob's lips. With his usual phlegm he answered M. Havard:

"And pray, why should I have gone?"

The reply was so startling in its quiet unconcern that the Head of the Criminal Bureau was struck dumb for a moment. However, he quickly recovered his self-possession and answered back:

"Why, my dear sir, because . . . because when a Minister sends for one, surely one ought to take the trouble to obey."

But Tom Bob, quite unruffled, only shrugged his shoulders. Taking a cigarette from his case, he lit it without a sign of embarrassment, then:

"You think so?" he said. "Well, I think the opposite! If we differ in our ideas, it is probably because you, M. Havard, are purely French, and I, Tom Bob, equally American."

"Which means?"

"Which means," concluded the detective, with his Yankee bluntness, "that having nothing to say to the Minister, I did not feel any need to go and see him, and I considered if he wanted to speak to me, that he might very well take the trouble to come as far as the Hotel Terminus."

Listening to this speech of the phlegmatic American, M. Havard turned first pale, then green, sorely embarrassed as he remembered they were spoken actually before the Minister's very face. The interview was taking an unpleasant complexion and it was best to push into other matters: "Tell me, my dear Bob," he asked by way of turning the conversation, and getting back to serious affairs, "you can guess, I take it, why I have come this morning?"

Immediately Tom Bob's face lost its look of calm unconcern. It was evident a genuine curiosity pricked the detective as he replied:

"Upon my word, I don't, Monsieur Havard! I know nothing at all about it, though I must confess it interests me very greatly . . . Could I be of any use to you, I wonder?"

The Head of the Criminal Bureau, after a moment's pause, and speaking sharply and incisively in a way to throw the other off his guard:

"Useful?" he exclaimed, "yes, you can be very useful to me"—and, almost showing his cards, he demanded:

"I expect you to give me an explanation of last night's events."

"Last night's events?"

"Yes, the tragedy that happened at the Grand Duchess Alexandra's."

"A tragedy happened?"

"In a word, I want you to tell me how your wound is."

"My wound? . . . why, you are gone crazy, Monsieur Havard!"

"Crazy indeed! But, now . . ."

"What on earth are you talking about now?" Tom Bob's face wore such an expression of amazement, stupefaction, utter lack of comprehension, that with one accord M. Havard and the Minister, who had to hold himself in hand hard to keep his lips shut, sprang up and faced the detective.

"But," screamed M. Havard, boiling over with exasperation, "but you are not, I presume, going to deny that yesterday evening you were at the Grand Duchess Alexandra's ball?"

Tom Bob struck his breast in perfectly unaffected surprise.

"I?" he stammered, "I was at the Grand Duchess Alexandra's ball!"

"Good God! Yes, as Fantômas, come now!"

"And as Fantômas! But, really, Monsieur Havard, I don't understand one word you are saying. I have never been in the Grand Duchess Alexandra's house, neither at her dance, nor at any other time: neither yesterday, nor ever before!"

"And you are not wounded?"

"Wounded where?"

"In the arm."

Tom Bob took off his coat and pulled up both his shirtsleeves.

"There, look!" he cried, "where can you see a wound?"—and he passed his hand across his forehead, exclaiming:

"Why, whatever do you mean, in God's name! I think I must be dreaming!"

This time, M. Havard and the Minister gazed at each other in doubt and bewilderment. Tom Bob was not wounded! Tom

Bob had not been at the grand duchess's ball! Tom Bob was dumbfounded at the mere mention of their suspicions. It was beyond everything.

Then the Minister took up his parable. "Listen, Monsieur Bob," he said "we are not crazy. This is what occurred, this is what we believed . . ."

At great length, with details confirmed by M. Havard, with endless comments, the Minister narrated the whole incomprehensible imbroglio of the preceding evening, and at the end waited anxiously for the detective to speak.

"Come now," he demanded, "do you understand anything about it all?"

Tom Bob shook his head. "No!" he declared, in a preoccupied tone of voice and with a meditative air, "no, I know nothing—or rather, from what you tell me, M. Havard, and you, Monsieur le Ministre . . ."

But at this mention of his rank, the Minister started violently. "What!" he exclaimed, "then you know?"

"Yes, sir! yes, I know. Pardon me, but I know perfectly well I have the honor to address the Minister of Justice. Well, with Tom Bob, I assure you, there is no incognito can last long. But enough of that—I was going to tell you there is only one thing I do understand in all these tragic and bloody accidents that befell at the grand duchess's ball . . ."

"And that is?"

"Just this," declared the detective, "that Fantômas was present at the ball and that Fantômas made himself out to be me, Tom Bob: that it was actually Fantômas who was wounded, that he boasted of it out of a criminal's vanity who takes his impunity as a matter of course. And, that he committed a blunder, after all, for this wound in the arm will help us to identify him the more easily."

But now, as Tom Bob finished speaking, the Minister and M. Havard exchanged a meaning look. Both had been struck by the same idea.

"Well!" M. Havard spoke in a low voice, almost as if talking to himself, "if Mr. Bob is right, we shall have the means, once and for all, of clearing up all these matters. Fantômas is in prison, Fantômas is Juve . . . if Juve is wounded!"

But the Minister broke in: "Yes, Havard, you are right. Juve is Fantômas, then it is Juve must be wounded. But inasmuch as Juve is in the Santé prison, inasmuch as Juve is in jail, he was not, he could not be, at the Grand Duchess Alexandra's ball yesterday!"—and as if the better to strengthen his conviction, the Minister repeated in a loud, emphatic voice:

"Fantômas is in jail! What the devil, Fantômas is in jail!"

Tom Bob was going to reply, when the door opened, and a manservant put in his head to announce:

"If you please, Monsieur Bob, you are wanted at the phone— someone who declines to give his name."

The detective got up, took two or three steps as if to leave the room, then observing there was a telephone standing on a side-table near at hand, he told the servant: "Very good, my man, put me through here, will you?"—and turning to the Minister and M. Havard, who sat buried in their own thoughts: "Excuse me," he said, as he unhooked the receiver.

But he had hardly put the receiver to his ear before Tom Bob started violently.

"One second!" he cried. "Hello, just a second! Will you hold the line? I'm shutting a door so as to hear you better."

The detective laid down the receiver and turning quickly to the Minister and M. Harvard, he said in a mocking voice:

"Fantômas is in jail, you say? What a mistake! Do you know who is telephoning me at this moment?"

"Not I!" said the Minister, looking up.

Tom Bob answered in half-a-dozen words, spoken with all his usual phlegm, without so much as raising his voice: "Well, the person now speaking to me is just simply the man—just Fantômas!"

And as the Minister and M. Havard looked at one another incredulously, the detective, turning the instrument round, politely offered one of the two receivers to the Minister, keeping the other himself, and proceeded with the conversation over the wires:

"Hello! Yes, I'm back again now. It is I, Tom Bob, speaking. You say—will I excuse you for having borrowed my personality? Why, certainly. It would be very poor taste not to forgive you, Fantômas, for I must own it was a stroke of genius! Hello! Yes—you want to make it up to me for the liberty you took? Yes, thank you. Hello! What say? D'you mind repeating. Oh! You tell me, in order to let me win a score off you in the eyes of the Criminal Department, that tonight, this very evening, something will be doing at the Restaurant Azaïs . . . what time? . . . seven! . . . very good, thank you again!—I'll make a careful note of it . . . I shall be there . . . hello! hello! are you there?"

But a blunder of the telephone girl had cut off connection, and henceforth it was in vain Tom Bob repeated his hello! hello! There was no answer. So he put down the receiver, while the Minister also hung up his.

"Well!" remarked the detective, "you see, sir, we are on the best of terms."

The Minister seemed to be living in a nightmare. He thought he was dreaming, perhaps going demented, and it was in a weak voice he answered:

"But it's a joke, all this, eh, Mr. Bob? It is not Fantômas phoning you, come now!"

The detective shrugged: "Not Fantômas?" he said. "Then who is it? . . . who do you think it is?"

"Fantômas would never tell you beforehand he was going to commit a crime at this restaurant in the Bois."

"Pah! If he's sure, once more, of not being arrested?"

"No matter that! It would be too audacious. Come now, Mr. Bob, you won't go?"

"Oh, yes! I shall, sir! I shall be there."

The Minister was thinking. Suddenly he went on:

"Well, if you go, by all I hold most sacred, I will go too! Yes, I will go! It shall never be said . . ."

Tom Bob turned to M. Havard: "And you, my dear colleague, will you come? You seem pensive for the moment?"

M. Havard indeed—from Tom Bob's answers he had quite well gathered, or at any rate guessed, what Fantômas probably said—was thinking deeply.

"Oh!" he declared at last, "yes, I shall certainly go, but it will be without too much belief in the thing."

"Why so?"

"Because . . . because it was a practical joker telephoned you."

"A practical joker? No, I don't think that."

"I do!" declared M. Havard, who was getting annoyed. "Yes, a practical joker! a practical joker, I repeat, for, look, there is one thing you are forgetting, that we are all forgetting at present, a fact that is certain, indisputable . . ."

"To wit?"

"Why, that Fantômas is in prison, that Fantômas is in the Santé, and that consequently he could not have done murder yesterday, he cannot be telephoning you now, it will be impossible for him to be at the Azaïs tomorrow!"

The Minister, who for the last few minutes had been getting more and more impatient, laid his hand on M. Havard's shoulder.

"Listen to me!" he said, "all this is very bewildering, so bewildering in fact, that we are forgetting our logic. There is one step we must take instantly. Monsieur Havard, in coming to see your colleague, to see Mr. Tom Bob, we have made a blunder. It is elsewhere we must go now. By the Lord, we shall soon see if Juve is wounded, we shall soon find out whether he telephoned this morning, whether he can go this evening!"

Before the great man had done speaking, M. Havard had clapped on his hat again and slipped on his topcoat.

"You are right, Monsieur le Ministre," he declared, "let us go there at once."

19. The Prisoner of the Santé

It was the hour of general reveille at the prison of La Santé. Along the corridors, still in semi-darkness, tramped the warders, jangling their ponderous bunches of keys, on their way to wake the prisoners for the morning meal. Before the door of the cell where Juve was confined, Hervé, the jailer, usually entrusted with the surveillance of the ex-detective, stood hesitating, only finally making up his mind to go in on hearing the step of a chief warder at the far end of the paved passage.

The door turned slowly on its hinges. As a rule the sound of the key turning in the lock was the signal for Juve to start wide awake and sit up in his bed, in eager expectation of . . . what? Perhaps his release! But alas! morning after morning the apparition of the jailer's sullen countenance only brought bitter disappointment with it.

But this morning the prisoner did not wake. He was sleeping heavily and, if appearances were to be trusted, very uneasily. He kept groaning and crying out peevishly, muttering incoherently, twisting and turning in his bed. Waving about his arms, one of which showed stains of blood, blood that had run down in two red rivulets over his torn shirt and marked the white sheet with little brown spots.

Hervé approached the bed and stood looking down at the sleeper. The jailer showed no particular signs of surprise at seeing the condition his prisoner was in, but wore rather the preoccupied look of a man who cannot make up his mind to one course of action more than another. Eventually, he shook the sleeper roughly, hauled him up by the shoulder into a sitting posture, and when the prisoner, though still looking dazed and rubbing his eyes sleepily, seemed more or less awake, berated him:

"What's wrong with you? Where does that blood come from?"

"Blood? Where do you see any blood?"

"There, on your arm, on your shirt, on your bed sheet. How came you to hurt yourself?"

"I don't know. I hadn't noticed it before. It must have been in the night, I must have torn the skin tossing about."

"Come, come, that's an impossible story! What could you have done it with?"

"There, look at the corner of the bed, there's a blood stain there: that's where I hurt myself, no doubt. I've had a shocking night—bad dreams, nightmare: my head aches, I feel worn out, I must have kicked about in my bed, it's no wonder I knocked the skin off banging my arm against one of the iron bars."

"Hmm! It don't seem to me just as clear as daylight, somehow. Anyway be quick and get dressed, I must report to the Governor, and he'll see what's best to do."

M. Chaigniste, the able and well-known Governor of the Santé prison was in his working room, engaged in reading through again a report he had drawn up the night before on the general condition of his establishment. He was rubbing his hands in token of satisfaction, equally pleased with the elegance of his own composition and his skill as an administrator that had enabled him up to the present to avoid any, even the most trifling, of those "affairs" that are the *bête noire* of persons in authority, when the warder appeared: "I've come, sir, to let you know I found Number 55 wounded in his cell when I went there this morning."

"Number 55! Why, that's Juve, is it not, the ex-police-officer?"

"Yes sir."

"Is it serious?"

"No, sir, only a bit of a cut on the arm."

"Take him to the infirmary. I will go there myself, as soon as the doctor arrives."

At that very moment a bell tinkled in the Governor's study. It was the house porter phoning M. Chaigniste that Doctor

Du Marvier was come for his daily visit. The Governor and the practitioner found Juve in the waiting room, sitting on a stool, holding his head between his hands and puzzling over his wound, which struck him as, after all, hard to account for. The doctor tapped him lightly on the shoulder. He was a little round man, with a merry face, a smile forever on his lips, the very spirit of gaiety, a man to heal his patients by the mere sight of his beaming face! "My standing panacea," he was in the habit of saying, "is a funny story."

Accordingly it was with a pleasantry he greeted the ex-police-officer, with whom he had already come in contact previously to his imprisonment.

"Well, what's the matter now? We're not satisfied with the Governor's treatment of us, eh? so we go and try to kill ourselves, is that it?"

"Doctor," Juve replied in the same vein. "I could very readily dispense with the privilege of being Monsieur Chaigniste's guest, but all the same I can assure you I have not the smallest wish in the world to escape his hospitality by committing suicide. I am just as much surprised as anybody else at the wound in my arm. I can only account for it by the supposition that in my sleep I knocked up against a corner of my iron bedstead." While speaking, Juve had removed his jacket and turned up his shirt sleeve. The wound was plainly visible, a clear cut an inch or a trifle over in length on the upper part of the arm pointing downwards. The trifling nature of the wound indeed made the doctor's whimsical suggestion seem utterly absurd—a man wanting to kill himself would set about the job in quite another fashion.

But was Juve's own hypothesis any more probable? Was it against the corner of his bed the police officer had hurt himself while asleep? Evidently such was not the view taken by the doctor, who after a rapid examination, turned to the Governor, saying:

"The wound is quite superficial, the skin is only slightly broken, and if the hurt has bled rather copiously, that is only because one or two small veins have been divided. With every confidence I can assure you the prisoner's bed has nothing whatever to do with the accident. It is a cut that is in question, and a cut that cannot have been made by anything except an implement with a cutting edge. A blow, as violent as is assumed, would have produced a bruise, a swelling, the blood would have collected under the epidermis, might indeed have spurted out, but we should never have seen an incision so clean-cut as that."

But while the doctor was speaking, Juve had turned as pale as death. He seemed to have lost all power in his limbs and sank down exhausted on a stool. Doctor Du Marvier was quick to notice the prisoner's condition. Taking his hand he felt his pulse carefully.

"Tell me," he said, "is your pulse so slow usually?"

"No, doctor, I have always supposed myself to have a normally rapid pulse, but today I don't feel quite well, I slept very badly last night and I have a violent headache."

"Let me see your tongue!" It was quite white, like a man's after a high fever. Then the doctor put his ear to the prisoner's heart. When he raised his head after a long auscultation, he had apparently found the solution of the problem, for a look of conviction illuminated his face. Drawing the Governor on one side, he spoke to him in a low voice. What he said must have been of the very gravest import for, when he had done, the Governor was as pale as Juve himself and seemed to be profoundly agitated. M. Chaigniste was turning to the prisoner, no doubt intending to question him further, when one of his private servants came in to tell him:

"M. Havard, sir, is waiting in your room to speak to you on some very urgent business."

"I will go to him," replied the Governor, and beckoning to the warders:

"Take the man back to his cell," he ordered, "and keep him under observation."

M. Havard was much excited. His idea had been to follow up his researches regarding the crime committed at the grand duchess's by satisfying himself as to Juve's condition. Inasmuch as it was a proven fact that Fantômas had been wounded in the arm, if Juve was really and truly Fantômas, he argued, Juve must be wounded. Accordingly, M. Havard had betaken himself to the Santé prison. Well, scarcely had he arrived there before he learned that the Governor and the doctor were with Juve, who had been wounded in the night! It was the confirmation of all his hypotheses. It was the new and unexpected fact that should bring daylight into a laborious investigation, hitherto anything but fruitful in results! Juve was verily and indeed Fantômas! the ex-detective was the most redoubtable of all malefactors! If he showed such acuteness and sagacity in unraveling the most tangled affairs, it was because the very crimes he brought to light he had himself committed!

Easy to imagine with what impatience the Head of the Criminal Bureau awaited M. Chaigniste's arrival! The latter was hardly in the room before he sprang to meet him:

"Juve! What ails him! He is wounded? wounded where?"

The Governor was barely recovered from the agitation caused him by the doctor's startling announcement. So it was in a rather shaky voice, and after a moment's pause to recover his self-possession, that he answered:

"He has given himself a slight, quite a slight wound."

"How?"

"With an implement, knife or penknife, we do not yet know which."

"Whereabouts is the wound?"

"In the arm."

"Why, the man's a demon, nothing less!"

The Governor had no knowledge of the events that had occurred the night before at the grand duchess's, so he was quite at a loss as to the meaning of M. Havard's exclamation. In amazement he watched the latter as he strode up and down the length of the great room, lost apparently in the deepest thought. But his amazement grew to stupefaction when M. Havard went on to say:

"What, can a prisoner contrive to leave your prison of an evening and return again before daylight?"

The question was, indeed, of a sort to rouse M. Chaigniste's indignation. He, the model administrator, he who since he first came to the Santé had never had an "affair"; he, who was so proud of his staff that he looked upon himself as the father of his subordinates; he, who, only yesterday, had written a masterly report declaring in no uncertain terms that everything was for the best in this best of all possible prisons; *he* was suspected of having allowed prisoners the possibility of taking their walks abroad in the night! "His" prison, it seemed, was a hotel which people might leave at will, to go about their private affairs and come back again when they had enjoyed their liberty long enough!

He was on the point of returning M. Havard a cutting and dignified answer when the latter, guessing his thoughts, broke in:

"Monsieur Chaigniste, I feel convinced all duties are performed to perfection in your establishment. But still, answer me this question: Does Juve's cell contain any implement capable of making the wound you have noted?"

The Governor was nonplussed. Shaking his head emphatically, he declared:

"I can confidently say no! There are numbers of prisoners who, when they are locked up, try to do away with themselves, so not only do we search everyone, but every article that might be dangerous is removed and the cells hold no single thing that could cause a wound, even the most trifling."

"Then," M. Havard went on, "if Juve did not hurt himself in his cell, he must have left his cell. You see that, surely! Now listen, Monsieur Chaigniste, I came here this morning to inquire into Juve's condition. But long before your warder opened the prisoner's cell door and saw his bleeding arm, *I* knew that Juve must be wounded, and all I came for was to have my suspicions corroborated. A horrible crime was committed last night. Its author was wounded in the arm. I suspected Juve, and Juve is wounded in the arm! Then, I say, Juve did that crime! Juve escaped from your prison last night, committed a cowardly murder in the middle of a ball, killing one of my inspectors, who no doubt had managed to penetrate his disguise. Then he came back and voluntarily put himself under lock and key, in order to provide himself an alibi . . ."

"Horrible! horrible!" stammered the Governor, quite overcome.

"Yes, it *is* horrible, but the culprit shall pay dearly for his misdeeds, for we have him now safe and sure!"

"Horrible!" again groaned M. Chaigniste.

"Yes, indeed . . . and yet there's something strikes me as strange about the business and makes me hesitate. Let us reason it out calmly and quietly. There is one quality we cannot deny Juve possesses, and that is intelligence. He must have felt pretty sure the murderer's wounded arm had been noticed at the grand duchess's. He must have seen that it would be proof positive, irrefutable proof of his crime. He was not pursued, he had time enough to leave Paris and gain the frontier. That, to my eyes, constitutes a problem it is necessary to solve in order to hold the key to the mystery, and it seems to me difficult to solve it except in favor of my old subordinate."

Little by little, M. Chaigniste had succeeded in gathering his wits together and reducing his thoughts to some sort of order after all the successive shocks he had undergone in so short a space of time. He now recalled the startling confidence Dr. Du Marvier had whispered in his ear and felt it was incumbent on him to share his knowledge with M. Havard.

"I am going to tell you one thing," he began, after some hesitation, "a thing that will possibly help you to clear up this mystery. Dr. Du Marvier, after examining Juve's wound, noticed that the prisoner looked pale and appeared greatly exhausted. He questioned him, listened to his heart, and observed that its action was considerably retarded. By what he told me in confidence, all this would seem to point to his having been poisoned, very probably with chloral hydrate. But that is, after all, only a hypothesis, and besides, I don't quite see how one could establish a connection between this kind of poisoning and the wound we are talking about."

But at the words, M. Havard sprang up from the chair in which he had at last seated himself.

"What!" he cried, "you don't see the connection? Why, don't you know that chloral is not only a poison, but also a soporific? Juve would seem to have taken a soporific? But why? With what object? Not only does this not throw light on the mystery, but it makes it still more obscure . . . Monsieur Chaigniste, are you sure your staff are to be trusted?"

The Governor threw up his head like a man deeply offended, and replied in a grave voice:

"I can answer for them as surely as I can for myself. I have carefully studied the characters of all my warders, and I can assure you there is not a single one of them on whom the fullest and most implicit reliance may not be placed."

"And since Juve's incarceration there have been no changes? Which is the warder specially in charge of him?"

"A man called Hervé, a man employed here ten years or more, and of whose conduct I have never had any but excellent reports."

"Then, sir, I have one favor left to ask you, to be authorized to visit the prisoner in his cell. After that I need only thank you for the information you have been so good as to give me this morning."

The Governor was hardly out of the Infirmary before Juve's wound was summarily attended to, and he was then handed over to the warders' tender mercies. Not without the accompaniment of some hearty cuffs, the straitjacket was put on and the prisoner was taken back to his cell. Juve made no protest. The same state of weakness and prostration still continued and reduced him to a condition of unresisting and silent passivity. It was only by degrees that he recovered his self-composure and could look the new situation in which he found himself in the face. His first impulse was to give way to the utter abandonment of despair. Alas! even in prison he was not secure from his adversary's machinations! He had thought that, after thus depriving him of all power to act, Fantômas would be satisfied with the freedom so secured him to pursue at his ease the series of his crimes, and would forget the existence of his foe.

But lo! he now found himself once more the prey of his savage adversary! For Juve felt no doubt the wound in his arm, the distress that tormented his whole body, were Fantômas' work. Fantômas had accomplices inside the prison, and it was these confederates who had come at night to make a cut on his arm as if he had been wounded, after first sending him to sleep by means of the drug the debilitating effects of which he still experienced. With what object had they so acted? He did not know and he could not guess, ponder the matter as he might. But at least the fact was certain, undeniable, and it put the crown on his calamity! Fantômas had accomplices in his prison! The thought never ceased tormenting the unhappy man with ever increasing intensity, when suddenly a new idea struck him that made him spring up joyfully from his chair and stride up and down his narrow cell.

"If Fantômas has accomplices in the prison, I am bound to know them, these same accomplices, they must come in contact with me every day," thought Juve. "But if I know them, it will be possible for me to detect them and confound their plans. What was the saddest feature of my position was that I was powerless, and could expect the discovery of the truth only from the efforts of others. Now I am going to work for myself, and deep as the mystery may be, I shall clear it up, just because I am so resolved to do so."

Juve was at this point in his reflections when M. Havard entered his cell. At sight of his old Chief the prisoner made a movement of recoil. The Head of the Criminal Bureau pretended not to see this and took a seat on a stool. Then he signed to the two warders, who since morning had been permanently stationed in the cell, to withdraw, and when they had shut the door behind them, he began in these terms:

"Juve, since this morning, a grave suspicion rests upon you. The wound you have on your arm is a very damning proof of your guilt."

Juve was persuaded that M. Havard was the prime mover in his ruin, so that the friendship and devotion he bore his Chief previously to his imprisonment had been succeeded by something of rancor.

"Sir," he replied, "you think you have been clever enough already to discover many indications of my guilt. I make no doubt you will be ingenious enough to discover many more. What I am afraid of is that you are not clever enough ever to find the proofs of my innocence."

"Juve, you are in error in supposing I nourish any fixed prejudice against you. You know in what esteem I have held you and what friendship I have felt for you? I have deplored more than anybody the combination of circumstances that led to your arrest, and ever since then I have conducted my investigation loyally and without preconceptions. It is highly important in your own interest to answer frankly the questions I am going to ask you about your wound and your illness in the night . . . now . . ."

It was plain from the tone of studied moderation exhibited by M. Havard that the Head of the Criminal Bureau desired but one thing, to throw some light on the mystery that so distressed them both, and that the information M. Chaigniste had given him with regard to the prisoner's having swallowed a strong dose of chloral hydrate had very considerably shaken the conviction he at first professed as to Juve's culpability. It followed that the way he put the questions he had indicated was such as little by little to bring about in the prisoner's breast a return to feelings of trust and friendliness. Without making any definite confidences to his former Chief, Juve gave the latter a glimpse of the hopes he entertained of succeeding by way of the inside of the prison in unveiling a corner of the mystery.

The conversation was a long and evidently a satisfactory one, for on parting, M. Havard extended his hand cordially to his erstwhile coworker, while Juve's face beamed with glad relief, and reawakened hope.

20. A Woman's Self-Sacrifice

The ferry-boat that plies between the bank of the lake and the Ile de Beauté on which the Restaurant Azaïs stands had not actually touched the landing stage before M. Havard, standing up on one of the thwarts of the boat, in which indeed he was the only passenger, leapt ashore, in a paroxysm of nervous excitement.

"What am I going to find here?" thought the Chief of the Criminal Bureau. "What fresh difficulties am I to be faced with, agitated as I am, and really not knowing what to do? Then how simply grotesque the visit I paid along with the Minister of Justice to that impossible person Tom Bob—grotesque to the uttermost degree! I arrive with a companion who is to be incognito; before I have been there three minutes the man addresses him by his name! I come to charge him with crimes committed at the Grand Duchess Alexandra's house; he has never set foot inside the place! Then, to crown all, he is rung up by Fantômas, offering him contemptuously a petty piece of revenge—by way of annoying the Department! Then presently, when we reach the prison, it is to find Juve wounded and declaring he knows no more about it than we do!"

M. Havard, so formal and precise a man, so staid and deliberate as a rule, was for the moment so enraged he entirely forgot his dignity and dashed helter-skelter, running like a schoolboy, across the little terrace separating the Restaurant Azaïs from the lakeside. There were only a few diners that evening occupying the tables, and already the majority were hurrying for the ferry-boat, that was making ready, after landing the Chief on the island, to re-cross to the mainland. Only one man remained seated at a table at the farthest end of the restaurant, where he was finishing his meal. M. Havard recognized this solitary diner at once and ran up to him.

"Well?" he panted.

Tom Bob lifted his head and recognized the newcomer. Speaking in his quietest tones: "Oh! so there you are, M. Havard?" he observed.

"Yes . . . well?" again asked the Chief.

"Take a chair, Monsieur Havard. You'll help me drink my coffee? No?"

M. Havard was boiling over. "The devil take your coffee!" he shouted. "Have you seen anything?"

Still quite unmoved, Tom Bob shrugged.

"I have seen," he said, "that the cooking here is quite decently good and that it's an excellent place for eating a quiet dinner."

"Devil take you and your dinner! Come now, answer me seriously . . . Fantômas?"

"Fantômas has not come yet."

M. Havard heaved a sigh of relief, and at last allowed himself to sink into the chair Tom Bob had pushed forward for him.

"Not come yet!" he exclaimed. "Ah, well, I'm rather relieved after all. It was just a joker then?"

"A joker! Whom d'you mean?"

"Oh God! why, the man who phoned you!"

"I don't think so."

"Still—as nothing has happened."

Tom Bob called the waiter. "Bring the cigars," he ordered. Then, turning again to the Head of the Criminal Bureau:

"Well, Monsieur Havard," he said, "if nothing has happened, I fancy that's because the time hasn't come yet for anything to happen, that's all."

M. Havard growled out: "You think the . . ."

"I think . . . upon my word! Monsieur Havard, I think the wisest thing to do is to wait patiently. Anyway, Fantômas strikes me as being quite a man of the world. If he really means to destroy the charming surroundings where he has brought me for this little dinner, I think he has had the politeness to wait till I have finished. It was the least he could do."

But M. Havard failed to appreciate the American detective's irony. Interrupting him in the middle of his sentence, he sprang from his chair, and slapping his forehead:

"And my men?" he cried. "I must make sure they are there."

"What men?"

"The officers."

"You've sent police officers here?"

"Ten inspectors from the Bureau, yes!"

An amused smile flitted over the detective's lips as he looked at M. Havard whimsically.

"By the Lord!" he cried, "if I was Fantômas, I should be flattered. At a telephone ring from him, you set a little army in motion, Monsieur Havard! It's a pretty compliment, d'you know, on your part."

But M. Havard would hear no more.

"It's a compliment, or it's not a compliment," he struck in in a dry tone that, he hoped, would cut short the American's irony. "Anyhow, this is the way it is: you, if by any chance you succeeded in catching one glimpse of Fantômas, they'd all be shouting *wonderful! miraculous!* If *I* were to arrest him, why, they'd just say it was all in the day's work. Now, as I don't arrest him, they throw stones at me! . . . See you again soon, I'm off to see if my men are posted."

M. Havard took three steps to go, then thinking better of it and coming up to Tom Bob again:

"Look here," he excused himself, "I was a bit blunt with you, but you mustn't be angry, for some while back I've had good cause to be irritable, you'll admit that?"

"I do," Tom Bob agreed.

"Then forgive me! Now tell me—you've done some smart things since your arrival in this country, I can't deny you're clever— tell me, have you any idea what Fantômas may try to do this evening?"

Tom Bob was evidently too good-hearted and too nice a fellow not to commiserate the bad temper M. Havard suffered from, for it was in a very cordial tone this time that he answered the Chief of the Criminal Bureau:

"I can form no supposition on that point—nay, I will go further, and admit there's something that worries me . . ."

"What is it?"

"This: if Fantômas has invited us here, it is because he is quite confident we are not likely either to guess or parry the blow he is preparing. Moreover, I've been engaged since I got here, in making a cursory investigation, and having learned nothing . . ."

But M. Havard, to the last degree perplexed, had become deeply buried in his own thoughts.

"For my own part," he admitted, "do you know what it is worries me?"

"No! What does?"

"I keep asking myself whether Fantômas has not enticed us here, has not enticed you here in particular, you, Tom Bob, on purpose to have a free hand at some other spot in the city which it was his pleasure perhaps to visit."

Tom Bob too, debated the supposition M. Havard had just formulated.

"No, that would not be playing fair," he said at last, "and Fantômas has never been dishonorable. No, I can't believe he would do that."

M. Havard shrugged his shoulders by way of answer. He distrusted the American's psychological acumen.

After a short silence, M. Havard resumed:

"Well, as you please, Monsieur Bob, but my opinion is that for tonight, either we are the victims of some practical joker, or in any case the affair is off. Fantômas must have seen that my officers were here in force. For my part, I am going to take a turn to look after my men. I know where they are, hidden about the island. Then I shall take the ferry again and so back to the Prefecture. Will you join me?"

Tom Bob shook his head.

"No," he declared, "I shall spend the night here. I make it a point to keep my tryst with Fantômas. However, M. Havard, I will go with you in the boat as far as the other bank. That will give me the pleasure of another row on this pretty lake, a perfect jewel at this time of an evening, the finest thing of its kind, surely, in Paris."

Still in a hurry, M. Havard did not stop to listen to the American's praises of the Bois de Boulogne. He crossed the little wooden bridge joining the two parts of the island, made sure that the officers he had sent there in the afternoon were at their posts, ordered them to keep a most careful watch all night on the lake and its approaches, then made his way back to Tom Bob.

"You are coming?"

"I am quite ready."

The detective got up, paid the bill for his dinner, and took another cigar, while M. Havard, faithful to his usual habits, refused the Havana Tom Bob offered him and drew a cigarette from his case. The two police officials left the restaurant and made for the landing, where the ferry-boat was again putting in.

"Get in," M. Havard urged the American.

"After you!" protested the Head of the Criminal Bureau. "Hallo, have you a light about you? Will you pass me a match, I haven't got one."

Tom Bob looked at his cigar. "I'm not well alight myself," he said, and pulling a box of vestas from his pocket, he lit one, handed it to M. Havard, then took it back and applied it to his own cigar. Then, as the match was beginning to burn his fingers, he tossed it into the lake.

But then, suddenly, with terrifying intensity, with an incredible rapidity, a fantastic, unheard-of, appalling thing happened. The very instant the burning match touched the water, the lake caught fire and blazed up fiercely, giving off dense clouds of smoke and sending up huge flickering flames of red and blue that instantly covered the whole surface with a sheet of fire.

Fortunately Tom Bob had managed to grip M. Havard by the arm and drag him back from the boat he was just getting into, and both started running breathlessly for the middle of the island, accompanied as they went by the various employees of the Azaïs, the manager and a few customers who were still on the premises, all flying headlong before the flames. The sight was fairylike, unforgettable, but tragic to the last degree.

The whole lake indeed was a veritable sea of fire, which the eye could not pierce. From this gigantic brazier a sooty smoke went up in swirling eddies, instantly veiling the sky with thick, heavy clouds. The heat was terrific, so intense that the sweat rolled in torrents down the faces of the unfortunates imprisoned on the island. The air indeed was almost unbreathable. All round the party branches kept breaking off the trees and the smaller boughs beginning to flare up, while the shrubs dipping in the water were in turn taking fire.

"We are done for!" groaned M. Havard. But Tom Bob preserved his presence of mind.

"To the middle of the island!" he shouted. "Come this way,"—and he led all his companions to the center of the little island. Once there, he proceeded to calm their apprehensions.

"Keep cool!" he said, "keep cool! If the lake is on fire, there can be only one explanation, that they've emptied over the surface barrels of naphtha or petroleum. Oh God! Fantômas can't be far. It's a miracle we have escaped, Monsieur Havard. I imagine he was only waiting for both of us to be in the boat between the bank and the island to put a light to his naphtha and roast us to death."

"Yes, indeed," M. Havard agreed, "a minute more and we were dead men."

Tom Bob shook his head gravely. "If only there are no fatalities," he said. "Look, it strikes me the flames are not so fierce now? Evidently the layer of naphtha cannot have been very thick. Yes, the flames are dropping, but ... but ..."—as he spoke, fearful screams broke out coming from a little further away. M. Havard and the detective looked at each other in consternation. The cries grew louder and louder, and with one impulse the two men dashed to the rescue. They had distinctly heard the words:

"Help! help! ... Fantômas! Fantômas! Fantômas is here!"

While M. Havard and the unlucky Tom Bob were in such imminent peril from the monstrous audacity of the ever elusive brigand, while the lake was taking fire with alarming rapidity, a tragedy had been enacting on its banks.

It was the day after the Grand Duchess Alexandra's ball, and that very evening Lady Beltham, in fulfillment of her promise to Fandor, was to go and see Elizabeth Dollon to assure her of the journalist's innocence. Fandor never doubted that the great lady would keep her engagement and find some way of meeting the girl. After the furious dagger thrust, against which his coat of mail had so fortunately protected him, after his flight from the grand duchess's, a flight that lady had in fact facilitated, the journalist could no longer doubt that Fantômas had been really present at that festivity. And from that moment the death of the unfortunate police officer was no riddle to him—Joffre had fallen by the hand of Fantômas. This fresh murder in no way surprised him.

Accordingly Jerome Fandor, anxious above all things to meet Elizabeth Dollon and secure a renewal of the girl's favor, had all the afternoon been watching for Lady Beltham's arrival at the lake in the Bois. But it was only at nine in the evening that she arrived, and Fandor had of course taken care not to reveal his presence just then. When Lady Beltham should be returning and re-crossing the lake, then he would go to her and thank her and ask her if he might now go to Elizabeth to find her convinced of his innocence. For the moment it was very necessary to keep concealed.

But just as the boat reached the landing place of the Restaurant Azaïs, Fandor, who was still prowling on the road beside the lake, caught sight of M. Havard's figure, and Tom Bob with him, both evidently intending to take the ferry on their way back to Paris.

Then in an instant came a flash, a blaze, an impassable wall of fire separating the journalist from the island and the restaurant. Like a madman, the unhappy man ran along the bank, wringing his hands in despair. But what could he do? what could he do? In an agony he pictured the terrible position, perhaps the fatal position . . . in which the wretches now on the island might find themselves.

"Elizabeth!" he cried, "Elizabeth, oh! We are under a curse!"

Fandor in fact was asking himself if the fire was not going to reach the island, if indeed the island itself, drenched with petroleum, was not blazing too. If Elizabeth were not doomed to die by that awful death, the death that is worse than a thousand deaths, death by fire!

Fandor could divine the whole villainous plot. No, it was no mere coincidence that the lake should take fire at the very moment Elizabeth learned that he was innocent. Not a doubt of it this was another of the horrid acts of cruelty Fantômas loved. Fantômas had willed Elizabeth should die at that precise moment. Yes, for he knew all, he had learned the rendezvous arranged with the grand duchess, for had he not been present at the whole conversation between Fandor and the great lady, when Fandor merely supposed he was looking at one of the many reflections in the mirrors ornamenting the walls of the winter garden.

The lake had been burning for nearly three minutes. Suddenly Fandor made up his mind. Throwing off his coat, the brave young man ran to the bank of the lake, whose waters were still blazing. His face was pale, but a look of determination flashed in his eyes as he plunged into the torrent of fire!

"I will swim underwater," the daring fellow told himself. "No, I cannot let Elizabeth perish so; if she is to die, I will die near her, with her!"

It was a heroic but a mad venture. The channel separating the mainland from the island was broad, and halfway across, he had no breath left and must at any cost come to the surface, magnificent swimmer though he was. The water was still blazing. Barely had he time to snatch a mouthful of mephitic, scarce breathable air, when he must dive under again on pain of being burned alive.

"Ten strokes more! . . . five more . . . three more!"—his knees grazed the bottom, he had reached the shore!

Panting, breathless, Fandor climbed on the bank, grievously hurt, bleeding, half dead; but he was near his goal. He cried, "Elizabeth!"—and in the distance, his eyes still dazzled with the glare of the fire, the journalist seemed to see a woman's form. He staggered towards her, a haggard terrifying figure. But no sooner was he near the girl, for it was really she, flying with

Lady Beltham before the advancing flames—she had taken refuge there—than he started back, struck with consternation.

Lady Beltham had not yet had time to speak to Elizabeth Dollon, and the girl, seeing this dreadful apparition rise before her, Fandor, pale and bleeding, had screamed out in frantic terror:

"Fantômas! Fantômas! It is Fantômas!"

"Where is he gone!" Lady Beltham eagerly questioned M. Havard and Tom Bob, who had run up on hearing the cries. She had not recognized Fandor, but on the other hand she knew it was not Fantômas who had shown himself. Instinctively she pointed in the direction in which the journalist had taken to flight.

Thereupon followed a veritable manhunt, duly organized. Blowing a shrill whistle, M. Havard called up his men, scattered more or less everywhere about the island.

"Fantômas is there," he yelled, "he has just swum over. . . . Dead or alive he must be taken, dead or alive!"

Every clump of trees was searched. The waters of the lake, no longer aflame, looked dark and gloomy as before, clouds of soot made the air oppressive to breathe, the only light to help the officers in their frantic search came from some trees that were still burning on the bank of the lake. From all sides sounded cries, shouts, exclamations. For Fandor was now in full flight before the pursuing myrmidons of the law.

What did it all mean? He was far from having any clear conception of this. Once more Fantômas had laid his plans marvelously well. Once more Fortune had favored him. He it was, Fandor could surely guess, who had contrived that Tom Bob and M. Havard were on the island at the very moment the lake was to burst into flame. Fantômas had of course felt no doubt that Fandor, prowling about the neighborhood waiting to know the result of Lady Beltham's visit, would be one of the first to make a dash for the island. In this way he would tumble into a regular trap.

Fandor was in full flight, seeing everywhere men hunting for him, revolver in hand, for the scattered conflagrations, dying down one by one, still afforded some light.

"By God!" he thought to himself, "I have no choice. I must take to the water, stay as long as possible out in the middle of the lake. It'll be the devil's own luck if I don't manage to put them off the scent." But at that moment a ball whistled past his ear. He had imprudently come too close, an officer had caught sight of him and fired.

"Damnation!" muttered the young man, springing back sharply, "it seems a price is set on my head."

"There! there, I tell you! God Almighty, give me a revolver!" The pursuit was still hot, when suddenly a splash was heard in the water. The police officers gathered in a crowd. "He'll get away! and never a boat!"

But one of the men was equal to the occasion: "'Dead or alive!' M. Havard told us we were to capture Fantômas dead or alive! By God! it was childish to spare his life when we had him at our mercy. A volley!" cried the man, "Fire, all together!"

His advice was followed, the officers fired off their revolvers at a venture in the direction of the splash. And next instant, drowning the sound of the shots, a sharp cry rang through the night:

"Help! . . . oh! . . . help!"

"Hit! Fantômas is hit!"

But Tom Bob was already making for the restaurant at a run. A boat lay high and dry on the bank. Swiftly he dragged it to the water's edge, sprang in, and in a few strokes of the oars was at the spot the cries had come from.

"Fantômas" he yelled—he could be clearly heard from the shore—"Fantômas! surrender!"

Other boats came up. Each second seemed an eternity. But now M. Havard, leaning over the side of his boat, gripped a dark shape struggling in the water. "I've got him!" Then in triumph, he shouted an order to the officer who was at the oars:

"Row, my man, bring us to the shore! . . . there, beside that tree, it is still burning, so we shall see plain, anyhow! . . . he must be seriously wounded, he has stopped struggling."

But as the boat entered the zone illuminated by the blazing

tree, M. Havard, still holding the mysterious human body he had gripped in the darkness, could not check an exclamation of dismay.

"Oh! curses on it! curses on it! It is not Fantômas! It is not the man! it is a woman!"

Others helped, and the inert form was soon carried ashore. Then suddenly, Lady Beltham, who had looked on in frenzied distress at all this scene of horror, came forward, a tragic figure, her eyes wide with terror.

"Oh! It is horrible," she groaned, falling on her knees beside the half-drowned woman's body. "It is horrible, she tried to save him, to put them off the scent! They have killed an innocent woman! They have killed Elizabeth Dollon!"

21. Joy Can Kill

"You are good and kind, madam."

"No, no! Don't say that."

"But you are! You are exquisitely good, exquisitely kind."

A spasm of pain crossed the Grand Duchess Alexandra's face, and it was in almost a harsh tone that she protested again:

"You are mistaken. Then, to begin with, the doctor forbids you to talk. You must obey his orders so as to get well, and you know very well you have to get well quickly."

Moving soundlessly over the thick carpets of the sickroom, the grand duchess stepped up to the bed on which lay the young girl she addressed. With a light, skillful touch she shook up the pillows, re-arranged the bedclothes and settled the patient in the most comfortable position.

"Try to get to sleep, won't you?"

"I am not sleepy. I am burning with fever and I feel thirsty—oh! so thirsty."

The grand duchess carefully measured out a few drops of champagne into a glass, added a little water, and held out the cool, refreshing beverage:

"Drink, my poor darling. The doctor did not forbid this."

A wan smile hovered on the patient's lips, as she eagerly quenched her raging thirst.

"The doctor!" she murmured, "why does the doctor worry me with his prescriptions? He knows I shall not get well."

But in a severe voice now, a tinge of bitterness even in its tones, the grand duchess replied:

"I do not wish you, Elizabeth, to talk like that. You have no right not to get well . . . Think of him!"

By what series of strange events came Elizabeth Dollon, for the injured woman was indeed Elizabeth Dollon, to be in this house, the house of the Grand Duchess Alexandra, to have that enigmatic personage for a nurse?

The pursuit of Fandor among the underwood of the Ile de Beauté, while the blazing lake was burning itself out, had ended in a startling tragedy, the discovery of Elizabeth wounded, shot by the police officers, who had fired on her in the belief they were shooting at Fantômas. How had the mistake come about.? Alas! it found its explanation in a terrible scene that had just passed between the Grand Duchess Alexandra and the unhappy girl the young journalist loved. When the first moments of stupefaction were over, and the officers of justice were hotly pursuing the fugitive, Elizabeth Dollon had confessed to the grand duchess in the stammering accents of terror, that it was really and truly the journalist Fandor she had seen and denounced under the name of Fantômas.

Then the grand duchess had hesitated no more. She had come there to undeceive Elizabeth Dollon, to convince her of Fandor's innocence, and now she carried out her intention with a vigor and emphasis born of her sympathy with the pair, and even as she spoke, she could see the girl turn pale and almost faint in her excitement. It was true then, Fandor was innocent? Fandor was worthy of her love! Fandor was the victim of a cruel Fate!—and it was she who had set the policemen on his track, the men who at that moment were ransacking the island to seize him, dead or alive!

In an instant the brave girl had resolved on a sublime act of self-sacrifice. Realizing that Fandor was done for if the pursuit continued, she made up her mind to interrupt this dreadful manhunt. But how? By a terrible, a tragic ruse. In the darkness she ran to the waterside, threw herself into the lake, where she swam about vigorously, splashing with might and main so as to attract attention.

The hoped for result followed. The men heard the noise, they thought it was their quarry escaping, confusion grew worse confounded.

All this she had expected, but, alas! one grim consequence of her act she had not foreseen. In the fierce eagerness of their pursuit, the officers did not rest content merely to dash off on the fugitive's traces. Fully believing it was Fantômas trying to escape, they fired off their revolvers, hardly stopping to take aim. A bullet struck Elizabeth, she gave one despairing shriek, and it was a wounded, half-drowned woman M. Havard brought ashore.

All crowded round the unfortunate girl, who still lay unconscious, and presently she was carried to the restaurant, where the Grand Duchess Alexandra was the first to kneel beside her, exhausting every means to recall her to life. She alone had seen all, and had guessed the true explanation of the terrible adventure. Her own love story a tragedy, herself a heroine in her day, the grand duchess could not fail to understand the motives that had guided Elizabeth, while the young girl's noble self-sacrifice, her marvelous courage, had won the great lady's highest respect and admiration.

Waiting till the police had completed their inquiries, the grand duchess herself organized the transport of the injured woman. She was determined to take her home with her and had her carried to her house in the Parc des Princes. There she summoned to her bedside the highest medical talent to be found in Paris. Doubtless she hoped by thus devoting herself to Elizabeth Dollon, by soothing away so far as was possible the girl's dreadful anxieties, to repair, as much as in her lay, the cruelties of her lover, of Fantômas, the man she loved in spite of everything.

Two days had passed, and during that time Elizabeth Dollon's condition, far from improving, had actually grown worse. The surgeons, called in one after the other, had departed, shaking their heads ominously. The bullet had struck Elizabeth full in the chest and grazed the lungs. "She may be saved. It is possible she may recover!" such had been. Professor Ardel's pronouncement. He had prescribed absolute quiet, rest, a light diet, but alas! had not concealed the serious apprehensions he felt for the patient's life.

It was in a feeble, breathless, almost inaudible voice, that Elizabeth appealed to the Grand Duchess Alexandra.

"You have had no news of him yet?" she asked.

The grand duchess, seeing the girl was awake, had drawn up a chair to the bedside and was holding between her slim, aristocratic fingers, Elizabeth's little hands.

"No, I have no tidings of him yet. But, as I told you, he has escaped. No doubt he finds it difficult to come here, my house is perhaps watched. How can we tell! But do not agitate yourself, Elizabeth, I repeat, Fandor is bound to find out that you are here, and knowing you are here, he also knows that I must have convinced you of his innocence. I am persuaded he will not be long before he comes to see you. . . ."

But suddenly the grand duchess broke off. Framed in the doorway the figure of a man had appeared. His face was worn with suffering, and he had pushed his way in frantic haste to the bedchamber, throwing aside the footman who was for showing him into an adjoining sitting room. It was Jerome Fandor! The unhappy young man strode across the room and fell to his knees beside Elizabeth's bed. With a passionate, yet restrained ardor he took the girl's hand and covered it with burning kisses.

"Elizabeth! Elizabeth!" he murmured, "oh! what misery, and yet what bliss! to find you here, wounded, wounded for me! For I understand your noble self-sacrifice. What happiness to find you again, to have the right to love you!"

At sight of him, Elizabeth had instinctively sprung up in bed as if to rise and meet him. Then, exhausted by the effort, pale as a dead woman, she had sunk back on the pillows. The hand Fandor held lay cold and lifeless in his, and it was in a weak whisper the girl asked:

"You forgive me, dear, for my suspicions, my distrust of you?"

The tears stood in Fandor's eyes as he asked:

"But you do not distrust me any more?"

Elizabeth answered with a wan smile, and the young man sprang up impulsively and with outstretched hands, approached the grand duchess.

"Madam!" he cried, "never, madam, can I forget that it is thanks to you . . ."

No less moved herself, the grand duchess returned Fandor's

hand clasp.

"Sir," she began, "when, in the name of love, you came to beseech me, me, Lady Beltham. . . ."

But there she stopped. With a cry, a groan, Elizabeth Dollon had repeated the name, "Lady Beltham?"

Without intending it, the grand duchess had revealed to Elizabeth her real title, her tragic identity. To be sure, Elizabeth had heard of Fantômas' ill-omened mistress! Many times had she read the tragic name of Lady Beltham in the public prints coupled with that of the notorious brigand. "Lady Beltham!" So it was Lady Beltham, this Grand Duchess Alexandra, who was nursing her with such devoted kindness!

But already, Jerome Fandor was on his knees again beside Elizabeth's bed.

"For pity's sake," he besought her, "be brave, my darling! be calm! be courageous!"

Alas! even as he spoke, the young man felt the sick woman's hand grow heavier, more deathlike in his. Like a flower that has borne the buffets of the storm and fades at the outburst of too fierce a sun, the unhappy child, after the grievous hours, the tragic, the dreadful times she had lived through, could not endure the too overpowering delight she felt at seeing Fandor again, and knowing him innocent, the too overwhelming shock of discovering that Lady Beltham stood before her!

"Elizabeth! Elizabeth!" Jerome Fandor cried in tones of sudden terror. Oh! how pale she was now, lying there with closed eyes, her head thrown back on the pillows, her golden hair disheveled!

Lady Beltham, like Fandor, was seized with a sudden misgiving. The minutes seemed hours in the slow agony of suspense. At last the girl opened her eyes. She threw a grateful look at the grand duchess, this mysterious Lady Beltham, who had taken pity on her. Then, with a superhuman effort, she whispered faintly: "Jerome Fandor!"

But as she lifted her hand to meet the journalist's clasp, a faint sigh breathed from her lips, a sigh so light, so calm, it was a full minute yet before Jerome Fandor, before Lady Beltham, realized the dreadful truth, the dire calamity, the fell catastrophe—Elizabeth Dollon was dead!

In the darkened chamber Jerome Fandor's long-drawn sobs proclaimed the unfortunate young man's infinite distress! Vaguely and indistinctly, as in a dream, the young man, still on his knees by the dead girl's bed, draining to the dregs his grief and despair, had heard a footman come in a few minutes before, seeking the Grand Duchess Alexandra. Absorbed in his grief, dazed with suffering, Fandor had not so much as raised his head. But the death chamber communicated by double doors, at present wide open, with an adjoining sitting room, and from this room voices could be heard.

The grand duchess, mastering her very sincere grief, had consented to see a visitor, who was now with her. Jerome Fandor, in the automatic way people's attention is fixed by external trifles at times of the most poignant emotions, in the midst of the deepest sorrows, found himself listening to the conversation.

"Madam," a voice was saying, a voice Fandor recognized with a startled exclamation to be that of M. Havard, "madam, the step I am taking today, believe me, is official, but in any case I think you will be ready to do as I desire."

"Speak, sir."

"You have recently, madam, taken the initiative in organizing a public subscription with the object of collecting the sum demanded by Fantômas as the condition of his disappearance, and refused him by the Chamber. That is so, is it not? you admit the fact?"

Haughtily the grand duchess assented.

"Yes, sir, that is so. I will even add that the money is beginning to come in."

"Madam," resumed M. Havard, "I do not know what motive prompted you . . ."

The grand duchess did not let the Head of the Criminal Bureau finish his sentence.

"The motives that prompted me are quite simple," she said.

"The Chamber has refused to accept Fantômas' ultimatum. That brigand, recoiling at nothing, now that Parliament has refused his demands, is adding crime to crime, piling atrocity on atrocity. What the Government declines to approve, it struck me as incumbent on private initiative to carry out. Fantômas the murderer promises he will kill no more if he is paid a million francs. What more natural, Monsieur Havard, than to open a general subscription to provide this million? to put Fantômas in a position to fulfill his undertaking? to induce him to halt in his bloody and deadly career?"

M. Havard did not answer at once. After some moments thought, however, he took up the word:

"Natural it may have been, madam, I have no wish to gauge the morality of the motives that may have led you to start this subscription, but I am bound to note the consequences of your action."

"And they are, Monsieur Havard?"

"Deplorable, madam, deplorable!"

"But, sir! . . . It is a reign of terror. The vilest abominations are of daily occurrence. Crime follows crime, each more terrifying than the last, more monstrous, assuming even the character of crimes against the state. I believe my subscription will quickly prove a success, that I shall soon raise the sum of money required, that soon Fantômas will disappear. That is no deplorable result, is it?"

M. Havard had one of the little coughing fits he so frequently suffered from and which commonly served to disguise his embarrassments.

"What is deplorable," he said at last, in a peevish tone, "is the fact that this subscription of yours, madam, makes my duties a farce, renders the French police ridiculous. How can we consent to Fantômas being paid to do us the favor to leave off murdering? He is an assassin! He should be arrested, that's all there is to it."

In a tone almost of mockery, certainly of irony, the grand duchess protested:

"But, Monsieur Havard, you don't arrest him!"

"No," confessed the Head of the Bureau, "no, not yet! But we shall arrest him."

A silence followed, which Lady Beltham at last broke, to say: "So that, according to you . . ."

"According to me," declared M. Havard—"and again I tell you this officially—it would be well, Madame la Grande Duchesse, to put an end to your subscription. It is, I repeat, really an insult to my office."

M. Havard paused, then proceeded:

"However, you are free to act as you deem fit. . . . It is evident that after all. . . . In a word, madam, my visit had another object. I may disapprove of your subscription, I have no right to misappropriate its funds. The fact is I have received . . . from an anonymous contributor a sum of ten thousand francs with the request to hand it to you. Here is the money."

All the time the grand duchess and M. Havard were thus conversing, Jerome could not help shuddering. He was barely a few yards from the man who was tracking him down with such determination! Lady Beltham was talking to M. Havard in an adjoining room, but hidden by the curtains, while he, Jerome Fandor, who was supposed to be Fantômas' accomplice, with the whole Criminal Bureau in pursuit of him, was only a few yards away! Was Lady Beltham going to betray him? She had adored Fantômas madly, she undoubtedly adored him still. Did she not intend to help in her lover's work, to deliver him, Fandor, to the Bureau? After all, she knew quite well that Jerome Fandor was the only man—Juve being in jail—capable of checkmating the brigand. How she must be tempted to denounce him to M. Havard! But no, no! He must, he ought to trust to her good faith. Lady Beltham was an enemy, but she was an honorable enemy!

Then Fandor weighed the value to be attached to what M. Havard had said. He could well understand the annoyance the Head of the Criminal Department might reasonably feel about the subscription opened by Lady Beltham. But then, what was the meaning of this gift from an anonymous well-wisher transmitted through M. Havard's hands? Must one not, in fact, gather that the Head of the Criminal Bureau, anxious above all measure to be rid of Fantômas, was equally desirous, while concealing his *modus operandi,* to contribute to the fund and so hasten the time when the grand duchess would have the million francs in hand and be in a position to secure the brigand's disappearance?

But Jerome Fandor's reflections were suddenly interrupted. He had heard Lady Beltham speaking again:

"M. Havard, you may, as a police officer, regret the opening of my subscription, which I can well understand hurts your professional interests, but as a woman, I confess I am afraid of Fantômas, I shudder at the thought of the atrocious crimes this brigand is still committing, and may go on committing. That is why I shall continue to accept all the sums of money given me with this object."

M. Havard in turn replied:

"You are free to act, madam! Still, I hope we shall have laid hands, not on Fantômas, who the public is too apt to forget, is in prison, but on Jerome Fandor, his redoubtable accomplice, before you have had time to deal with the funds you are collecting for him . . . and, consequently. . . ."

Lady Beltham did not reply at once, causing Fandor a moment's suspense that seemed an eternity. He threw a rapid glance round the room. He was too ill acquainted with the grand duchess's mansion to be able to make good his escape if she told the police officer he was there. If she was for betraying him, she could deliver him up without his having the power to stir a finger to save himself.

But just as the journalist was feeling himself to be caught in a trap without an issue, he heard Lady Beltham's voice saying:

"I wish you every success, Monsieur Havard, in effecting your arrest of Jerome Fandor—seeing you believe that Jerome Fandor is Fantômas' accomplice."

22. A Volunteer Waiter

Tom Bob had been waiting some while in a small room reserved for the use of callers on the ground floor of the house. The detective seemed extremely impatient, again and again he looked at his watch.

"Half past nine," he muttered, "I cannot afford to waste time, yet I must make sure Ascott will not fail. . . ." The man was frowning in evident anxiety, as he asked himself what sort of a reception the wealthy Englishman would accord him. Since the strange affair of the Pré Catalan, which had culminated so extraordinarily in the capsizing of the automobiles into the lake, Tom Bob had not seen Ascott again, save on very rare occasions. For this there were several reasons. In the first place the detective had been very much taken up—at any rate he said so—with the events that had occurred since his arrival in Paris, since he had officially declared his intention to devote himself to the pursuit and discovery of Fantômas. Moreover, the intrigue between Tom Bob and the Princess Sonia Danidoff was not, could not be, unknown to the members of the intimate little group of fellow-travelers that had come together on board the *Lorraine* on her passage across the Atlantic. Better than anyone, indeed, Ascott, who had been deeply smitten by the Princess, must be aware that in Tom Bob he had a fortunate rival, who had quickly won his lady's favors. In truth, it required all the American's calm effrontery thus, without any preliminary testing of his footing, to come calling on the young Englishman, who might very well be proposing to give him a highly unpleasant reception.

"True it is," Tom Bob told himself, "that since he abandoned his unsuccessful wooing of the Princess Sonia, Ascott has had other amorous adventures that should surely at this time of day prevent his being jealous of me." The affair at the *Silver Goblet* had, in fact, become a matter of general gossip, albeit not specially spoken about among the detective's own circle of friends, and the American appeared to be perfectly well posted as to what was happening, as well as what was likely to come of it eventually.

At last Ascott's manservant, John, appeared, and invited the detective to follow him upstairs to his master's study, where he found the Englishman seated at his desk, writing.

"Up already!" exclaimed the visitor cheerfully, "and ready for anything! Upon my word, my dear fellow, Paris has quite changed your habits. How are you this morning?"

Ascott turned half round in his chair, extending a careless hand to his visitor:

"Not so bad, and you, Tom Bob? To what do I owe the pleasure of your visit? Take a seat, please!"

"Good!" thought the detective, "he is not over and above angry with me!" At the same time, remembering that time was flying with alarming swiftness, he announced:

"I have merely come to shake you by the hand, as I was passing your way."

But Ascott, who appeared to guess the object of his visit, began to hunt through his pocketbook, from which he presently extracted a bank note. Holding this out to the detective:

"Here is my subscription," he said, "will you be so obliging as to hand this thousand francs to the Grand Duchess Alexandra when you have an opportunity of seeing her."

Tom Bob expressed his willingness with an almost imperceptible smile.

"Just fancy, my dear sir," he remarked, "how timorous Parisian society is. To think that it is now a perfect mania, a fashionable craze, quite the correct thing in fact, to subscribe to this fund. They want to see Fantômas waxing fat! . . . Upon my word! it is excruciatingly funny. Henceforth, I take it the light-fingered gentry will have an easy time of it when they want to make their fortunes. Instead of wearing themselves out committing crimes, they will only have to make it known through the newspapers that they are short of cash for the moment, and the money will come tumbling in straightaway! Why, sir," continued the detective, "it will be the ruin of the police. I ask you, what are we to do, my colleagues and I, when there are no longer any culprits to hunt down, any criminals to arrest?"

Tom Bob had uttered his little speech in a tone of laughing irony well calculated to divert his host, but the latter declined to be amused.

"What do you think about it?" the detective insisted. "What impression does all this Fantômas business make on you?"

Ascott, rousing himself from a prolonged reverie, shrugged his shoulders.

"I don't care a fig about it," he declared, "I am bored to death. . . ."

The other feigned no little surprise.

"Well, that is just what struck me, my dear sir. You look tired, altered, you never go into society nowadays. Have you had worries perhaps?"

Ascott nodded and was about to speak when the American broke in, making his question more definite:

"I've heard vaguely of some untoward adventure you were the hero of a while ago. . . ."

"Rather say the victim," put in Ascott.

The detective caught him up:

"The victim! Come, that's a big word. What *did* happen to you?"

The young Englishman seemed unwilling to explain his words.

"Oh! nothing," he said, "or nothing much!"

Then, after a pause, and as if he had just come to a supreme decision, he got up, strode two or three times up and down the room, then standing before the detective with folded arms, he declared:

"Tom Bob, I should by rights be more angry with you than in fact I am, for you have played me a trick, a damnable trick, involuntarily, I am sure of that, but the fact remains, you have played me one of those tricks men find it hard to forgive, you have supplanted me in the affections of a woman I loved."

The detective gave a gesture of protestation.

"Pah! My good sir," he said, "women and their ways! These things are never to be taken seriously."

"That depends. No doubt, you will tell me I had for ages been courting the princess without winning the smallest favor from her, while it was enough for you to arrive on the scene to become instantly the darling of her heart . . . well, so be it! I do not press the point, and you may have noticed this, that I never tried to compete with you. No, luck or ill luck decreed that at that very moment my affections took the field elsewhere. . . ."

Tom Bob heaved a sigh of relief.

"I am delighted to hear it, I should have been grieved to give you pain."

"Man!" pursued the young man, "you cannot imagine what happened next."

Throwing off his indifference more and more, Ascott, glad of the opportunity to tell his troubles to another, confided to the detective his extraordinary adventure with Nini Guinon and the threats addressed to him. The consequences of a passing caprice had come to a head.

Tom Bob preserved his calm as he listened to the story.

"And then?" he asked, when Ascott stopped to take breath.

"Then," declared the latter, "it is my duty to give you a piece of news, a great piece of news—I am getting married, I am marrying Nini Guinon!"

"Good luck!" cried the detective, "and when is it to be?"

"This morning, almost at once."

"Bad luck!" exclaimed Tom Bob—"and I was just wanting to ask you to breakfast!"

"Yes," went on Ascott, with an air of dejection, "in two hours' time I shall be the lawful husband of an old usurer's niece, Père Moche's niece. Oh! It is a fine kettle of fish!"

"Ascott," put in Tom Bob, trying to console him, "you are marrying under French law. You know, don't you? that divorce is allowed."

Ascott shrugged his shoulders: "That would make things no

better!"

"But why?"

The young man assumed a still more despairing look as he looked in the other's face and announced:

"My dear Bob, I must tell you all. Nini Guinon is pregnant."

Ascott looked so crestfallen that, for all his phlegm, Tom Bob all but burst out laughing. However, he dissembled his feelings with wonderful self-restraint. Rising, he stepped up to the young Englishman with an air of heartfelt sympathy and pressed his hand.

"My dear sir," he declared, "you are a good and honest man!"

But Ascott had no illusions. "Or an idiot!" he groaned. A silence followed, which the detective broke to say: "You will please excuse me, I must be going," adding with a spice of irony:

"I won't press you to have breakfast with me. I take it that after the wedding, a reception . . ."

"No!" Ascott interrupted, "don't make fun of me, Tom Bob. The ceremony will be strictly private. Naturally it does not call for any festivities. The mother, who has to signify her consent, only comes to the Mairie and to church, and I have definitely refused to invite to the breakfast anyone whatsoever besides the witnesses."

"And you start, no doubt, on your wedding trip afterwards?"

"That is to say," returned the young man, "I take to my heels, I go away to hide myself, also I go in order to try and get my wife away from the deplorable associations connected with her family and relations."

As he reached the door Tom Bob turned for a last goodbye to his host: "As a matter of fact," he questioned, "do you love her?"

"No!" replied the rich Englishman gloomily.

But, modifying his statement and blushing to the roots of his hair, he added:

"Still, I am bound to confess, there is something makes her not indifferent to me."

Tom Bob raised his hand as if to invoke heaven, and in a thrilling voice:

"The child, perhaps . . ." he suggested.

"Yes, that is it," Ascott agreed, and hurrying over the good-byes, he returned to his working table, while the detective took his departure.

*   *   *   *   *

At the far end of the Bois de Vincennes, near the Saint-Mandé boundary of the park, is to be found, standing among trees, a restaurant of quite a rural aspect, and bearing the significant name of *The Orange Blossom*. Within are a number of vast rooms and outside in the gardens arbors of likewise ample proportions. It is here in fact that the democracy resorts to make merry on the occasion of weddings after the religious or civil ceremonies, sometimes one, sometimes the other, occasionally both, have have been rapidly dispatched.

This morning evidently the landlord of *The Orange Blossom* was not expecting any great number of customers, for he had thrown open only the smallest of his salons. In the middle of the room he was laying the table for a very limited number of guests:

"Scurvy devils!" he was grumbling to himself, "what's the good of folks who ask only the marriage witnesses to the break-fast—skinflints surely! True they've paid in advance without any bargaining much, still in my humble opinion we'd best keep a sharp eye lifting to see they don't pocket the spoons. Mostly indeed I keep the silver locked up. A breakfast for six at six francs a head, that don't come to a couple of louis. However, let's hope we'll make it up on the drinks and cigars."

The good man stopped in his work. Someone had entered the room and was coming towards him.

"Excuse me, sir," he said, "but are you the landlord of *The Orange Blossom?*"

The innkeeper turned to his questioner and looked him up and down disdainfully. The newcomer was not of a distinguished appearance—middle-class evidently, soberly dressed in black, a man of thirty or thereabouts, wearing a very heavy beard.

"What do you want?" he asked him.

"Sir," asked the stranger in return, "are you by way of engaging waiters?"

"Certainly not," was the uncompromising answer, "and least of all today. Why, there's nothing to do—a meal for six at six francs a head—I and the maidservant will be amply sufficient to wait."

"Still I should be very wishful. . . ."

"Nothing doing!"

"Not even if I paid?"

The innkeeper looked wonderingly at the man, surprised at such persistency.

"What d'you mean by that?"

"Look here," the would-be waiter explained. "I'm very anxious to wait at table, to wait at this table, it's a business I'm keen on. If you'd let me have the tips for myself, I'll pay you twenty francs to make it up to you."

The landlord of *The Orange Blossom* hesitated. The man's offer was a good one for him, too good indeed. That was more or less what made him suspicious, for neither of the two could fail to know that the tips would never in the long run reach any such amount. To tell the truth, it was this very fact that inclined the innkeeper to look upon the unknown's application in a favorable light. But he was still suspicious. Perhaps the fine fellow had some cute idea at the back of his head, or perhaps he wanted to kick up a disturbance. Was he a rejected lover, the bride's fancy man, or possibly the brother or kinsman of a former mistress discarded by the bridegroom? One never knows, such queer things happen! Once more the innkeeper looked hard at this fellow who was so monstrously eager to take service with him. He saw the man was calm and composed enough and had not a bad face of his own.

"Look here," the landlord of *The Orange Blossom* began again, "you're not pulling a fast one? you want to pay a louis to wait at table, and you don't mean to play any tricks?"

The unknown laughed frankly in the other's face:

"Why, not a bit of it, sir, that I swear. I tell you, it amuses me to wait on these people, it's as you might say, it's . . . it's a wager I made with my pals."

"The tips won't be heavy," the innkeeper was charitable enough to warn him.

"That's all one to me."

"Well, my fine fellow," thought the landlord of *The Orange Blossom,* "you strike me as a mighty queer sort, but there don't seem to be any harm in you. After all, what risk do I run?"

He accepted, and held out his hand to clinch the bargain. "Agreed," he cried, "hand over your louis."

"Here you are, sir!"

"Now, my lad," continued the boniface, getting on very familiar terms, "go and fetch an apron and a jacket, I suppose you have a clean shirt-front. The meal's ordered for half past twelve, but I don't expect our customers before one o'clock. Look, here's where we put the plates. About the glasses, you'd better polish 'em up a bit. As you've time to spare, that'll give you something to do, my boy. By the way, what do they call you?"

After a moment's hesitation, the new waiter named himself Daniel.

"Well, Daniel, get to work. Work's the cure for boredom, you know."

No sooner was he left alone in the salon where the breakfast was to be served than this volunteer who had got himself taken on in so odd a fashion dropped into a chair and gave a long-drawn sigh!

"Ah!" he exclaimed, "here I am, but it's an expensive treat—a louis! No doubt my poor watch, thanks to 'my uncle's' generosity, raised me the money without too much difficulty—but when shall I ever get my dear ticker back?" Then: "Oh God!" he groaned, "how this false beard does tickle. If only it don't come unglued while I'm waiting at table!"

He got up and went over to a mirror to make sure his disguise was holding firm. He gazed long at his reflection in the glass, his eyes full of melancholy.

"I did well to adopt this travesty," he told himself, "I am absolutely unrecognizable"—and he was right. The new waiter of *The Orange Blossom* was, in fact, none other than Jerome Fandor.

Ever since the dreadful trial he had gone through, since the day of Elizabeth Dollon's death, the journalist had been plunged in a state of terrible prostration. Wild with grief, he had felt his sanity leaving him. All his high courage, his generous ardor, had departed, and again and again the thought of suicide had haunted his mind. It had called for all the energy that formed the basis of his character to stay him from proceeding to such dread extremities.

Little by little, however, as his will power mastered his dejection, a deep, fierce anger seized him and grew stronger every day. He had a mission to fulfill, this he realized, and his purposes grew clear and definite. Henceforth it was not solely his friend Juve he must rescue from his unhappy plight, but there was Elizabeth's fearful death he was called upon to avenge. And as he considered these two duties, one as dear to his heart as the other, Fandor recognized that in reality he was pursuing one and the same object, for indeed the own author of all these calamities, the responsible agent, the being who by his sorceries had sown mourning and desolation round about him, was still and always the mysterious, the ever elusive Fantômas! Oh! to unmask the monster, to come face to face with him, to discover in which of the group among whom he worked and maneuvered was really and truly incarnate the mysterious malefactor, this was what the journalist swore to himself to achieve! At all costs he must get done with it. To make an end was necessary, indispensable, and that with the briefest possible delay.

Fandor was filled with a new hope. Though still in hiding from the police and living the life of a pariah, he was yet able to glean occasional information from casual conversations and newspapers, and he noted a certain veering round of public opinion in favor of his friend. It was impossible, people were saying, that Juve, a prisoner in the Santé, could be guilty of all the murders and robberies ascribed to the agency of Fantômas. To this was added Fandor's definite and undoubted discovery of certain activities of the gang at whose head old Moche figured. Though kept somewhat at arm's length by the members of this gang, the journalist did nevertheless succeed in learning a number of facts that enabled him to prosecute his investigations on clear and precise lines. Now he had lately acquired the certainty that Père Moche counted for much in the profitable enterprises engineered by Fantômas.

But where was Fantômas? Not far off, for certain! Yet, with equal certainty, more difficult to track down, more elusive than ever. Nor was it only Fandor who was at fault. The American detective Tom Bob was in the same predicament. In fact, the latter, despite his fine audacity and his first triumphs, had not continued his successes. For quite a long time now people had ceased to talk about him. He seemed to have lost interest in the war he had declared against Fantômas.

Furthermore Fandor had observed that the American, who on his first arrival had promised him his protection and support, had suddenly left off seeing him, indeed made little or no concealment of the fact that he no longer desired to be in touch with him. Why this change? with what object in view? Was Tom Bob ashamed to avow himself beaten? or was he hoping, alone, by himself, to run Fantômas to earth?

Such were the young man's thoughts when the landlord of *The Orange Blossom* suddenly burst into the eating room.

"Daniel," he cried, "you must make haste, my lad! Here's the wedding party coming, they're not late after all. Quick, put on your apron and jacket, breakfast will be served instanter!"

Two landaus had just pulled up to the entrance of the gardens, two simple, unpretending vehicles, with none of your wide plate-glass windows, none of your big carriage lamps at the four corners of the coach.

23. The Wedding Breakfast

As Ascott desired the wedding was carried out in the strictest privacy. The party reached the Mairie at an early hour. Ascott had for witnesses his manservant John, and a casual secretary from the Consulate, bound over to the closest secrecy. Moreover, the young man in question, a person of much discretion who saw how things were with half an eye, had vanished immediately after the ceremony, saying he did not care to attend the breakfast, understanding in fact that his absence would not be taken in ill part, but very much the reverse. Nini Guinon's witnesses were her uncle, Père Moche, recruited again for the purpose, and the vagabond Bouzille, who had been fetched from a drinking shop at Ménilmontant, and dressed up for the occasion in a second-hand frock coat. The formalities at the Mairie were quickly completed, the party adjourned to hear a mass at the nearest church, and then set off for the Bois de Vincennes.

The last act of the grotesque adventure, the wedding breakfast, remained to be staged. Ascott, to Mme. Guinon's bitter chagrin, had emphatically refused to make her acquaintance, thereby making the good woman desperately unhappy. Thus she had barely caught a glimpse of her son-in-law, when at the Mairie she authorized her daughter as a minor to pronounce a definitive and binding "Yes." Ascott, in fact, had shown himself quite uncompromising all morning. For this marriage, this hole and corner marriage, so to speak, in which he had systematically avoided all publicity, he had not chosen that his bride should wear the orthodox white gown sacred to such occasions. In a word, the ceremony was a gloomy, funereal function, depressing to the last degree.

It was abundantly clear the bridegroom was fulfilling a duty, carrying out an irksome obligation. Indeed, the whole thing wore so lugubrious an aspect that Nini Guinon began to feel anxious, asking herself if really and truly she had acted wisely in following old Moche's advice, for at the bottom of her heart she was far from convinced of the advantages to accrue for her from her union with the rich Englishman. On the drive to the restaurant, sitting silent in her corner of the carriage, Nini was thinking all the while:

"If I'm in for a bad time, if old Moche has got me in a hole, I'll make him pay for it."

However, Bouzille, who had kept quiet enough during the morning, began to liven up on arriving at *The Orange Blossom.* He smiled broadly at the regiment of bottles drawn up on a sideboard, and, like the good-natured ninny he was, having never an inkling of the preposterous situation of the bridal pair and those about them, he clapped his hands gaily, suggesting:

"Well, good folks, about time for a bit of a spree, eh? What if we cracked a bottle now before going any further?"

Ascott, for all his preoccupation, could not help smiling. In fact, if there was any one person in the whole crew that revolted him less profoundly than the rest, it was certainly this merry-hearted tramp. The fellow was rough and brutal, but he seemed to be an honest man. On the contrary, Ascott felt greatly embarrassed at the idea of sitting down to table with his servant. In his own mind he decided there was only one thing to be done—to send the man about his business that very evening. Besides, *The Orange Blossom* itself was little to his taste. What a place! What a vulgar show!

Still, he must make the best of things, and taking Bouzille's hint, Ascott called the waiter and demanded drinks. And it was none other than Fandor who stepped forward to take the rich Englishman's order.

Without further ado, Ascott took his seat, putting Nini on his right and old Moche on his left. This done, he kept his eyes fixed on the tablecloth, not knowing in the least which way to look or what to do. Bouzille's fine enthusiasm had suddenly quieted down, while the rest of the company were not "playing up" one bit: there they sat, each more stockish than the other.

If anybody had come in hopes of diversion, he was finding himself singularly disappointed. John, sitting facing his master, dared not utter a word, Moche never opened his lips, Nini was cross and angry, Ascott pale and silent as the grave!

Fandor, with the landlord's help—for the journalist had proved himself from the very start a most indifferent waiter—served the first course, during which not half-dozen words were spoken. The landlord, when he found himself in the kitchen again, alone with Fandor, could not hide his surprise.

"For the last twenty years," he declared, "I've had wedding parties here, I've known customers of every sort and kind, but anything like those folks there—never! They couldn't be more dismal if it was a funeral they'd been at!"

Meanwhile, Ascott sat deep in thought. He was realizing the appalling folly he had been guilty of in marrying Nini Guinon.

"How could I ever for one single instant have entertained such an idea . . . and put it into execution?"

But the unfortunate young man quickly called to mind that, if he had not followed the injunctions of Père Moche, the plaint lodged by the Guinon family would have taken its course, and that would have equally involved disgrace, disgrace more terrible still, more irremediable even than the grotesque marriage he had just contracted. Ascott saw clear now—he was the victim of an odious piece of blackmailing, an abominable plot. He was so worked up he felt himself prepared to do the maddest things, he meditated going straight to the Procureur de la République to denounce the whole business. . . . But the unhappy man, when he looked closer into this last desperate resource, realized that the situation was past cure, that no one could help him, that he was simply a victim, and a ridiculous victim at that, and that, in fact, there was something else, something more serious, which after all tied his hands and gave him pause. Nini Guinon was pregnant. He must not, he could not forget that fact. Ascott could stand no more of it. Still controlling his feelings, he leaned over to his wife, sitting next him, and whispered:

"I am a little unwell, so I am going to withdraw into some

room nearby. I count on being left to myself, and shall expect you to join me there when you have finished breakfast." Nini had scarcely gathered the sense of her husband's words before the latter had disappeared.

In a moment, as if by enchantment, all recovered their spirits. They clinked glasses, they drained bumpers, they ate with a better appetite, gaiety reigned on every face: decidedly, the English milord had done well to leave them to themselves. They would be more of a family party, more at their ease.

"Say, Père Moche," observed Bouzille, "he don't strike me as being much of a gallant, your niece's husband! How's she going to hit it off, little Nini, with a lump of wood like that, eh?"

"Don't you trouble your head," broke in the girl, "I know what I've got to do."

Then, as everybody stopped talking to listen:

"Jabber away amongst yourselves," she growled, "I'm going to have a talk with Père Moche."

The talk became general, while a very animated discussion began between Nini and her reputed uncle.

"If you think it's any fun," began the young woman, "this marriage you've brought about, I tell you I'm about fed up with it already. I don't give myself forty-eight hours before I book it from my husband."

Moche shrugged his shoulders:

"Nini, you're a born fool. A bit of patience, my lass, and you'll see Père Moche was in the right." Then, in a lower tone: "You're far too pretty and too clever to spend all your young days among this crowd, a parcel of rotters who're good for nothing but talking loud and getting drunk. I've told you, haven't I, I'd make you rich, I'd make a great lady of you, more than that, a queen of beauty, a queen of Paris, a queen of society! Play your cards, Nini, listen to me. . . ."

A gleam of covetousness flashed in the girl's eyes.

"I shall be rich?" she questioned, "I shall have the nibs?"

Moche went on:

"Rich, and better than rich, my girl, but for that don't go and play the fool. Just keep yourself in hand for another nine months. Your brat must come into the world strong and healthy. After that there'll be something new to think about, you can trust Père Moche for that!"

While the young Englishman's queer helpmate and the enigmatical personage who had passed himself off as her uncle for his own ends were thus debating future projects, Jerome Fandor, under pretense of paying every attention to the customers' wants, was never far from the table, picking up scraps of talk as he hovered near. And in spite of himself, Fandor could not keep his eyes off M. Moche's face. As he stood over him, he could, for the first time, observe otherwise than through the glass of his spectacles the mysterious old fellow's eyes. And they disconcerted the journalist extremely, their clear, cold, steely glance perplexed him beyond measure. Most certainly Fandor could trace no likeness there, he had no recollection of having seen that expression before, yet it seemed to him that a person like the old business agent of the Rue SaintFargeau, whose caricature of a face betrayed the man's commonness of type, *could* not have such a look of the eyes as he actually had.

And, as a fact, who and what was this man who—Fandor saw it all—had conceived so Machiavellian a scheme as that of marrying the street wench Nini Guinon to Ascott, the wealthy Englishman of the Rue Fortuny, and who, having conceived, had carried it out!

Père Moche . . . Fantômas? . . . ? . . . ?

Fandor, as the result of a series of logical deductions, possibly also through giving a certain weight to the presentiments that rarely deceived him, had come to ask himself if the man of the Rue Saint-Fargeau, really too mysterious a personage, was not one of the incarnations of Fantômas himself. Since he had been watching his man, and particularly since he had seen his eyes and their expression, Fandor clung more and more closely to this opinion.

Ah! if only he were right! if he had discovered the villain? That would be an extraordinarily fine trump card for him in the grim game he was playing with Fantômas as adversary! And now, many hitherto unexplained details recurred to his memory. Notably he recalled the strange apparition of the man in the black mask on that terrible night he had spent in M. Moche's garret. He did not forget how on that occasion Fantômas, under pretense of safeguarding him from harm, had involved him in the direst peril, evidently in the hope that the police would discover him hidden in the Chinese lantern.

"Why," he thought presently, "but why did not Fantômas kill me when he had the chance? that is what I cannot understand."

But, when he examined the question more deeply, Fandor realized the fact that Fantômas' crimes invariably had a double object—to get rid of an obnoxious adversary and at the same time to throw suspicions on the dead man that went to prove by their very nature the innocence of some accomplice of Fantômas or of Fantômas himself. Thus he pondered, all the while carrying on with the utmost awkwardness his duties as a waiter, under the wary and ever watchful eye of the landlord of *The Orange Blossom*.

At the same time Fandor did not allow his attention to be absorbed solely by the conversation between Moche and Nini. A short while before Ascott had left the rest of the party—it was an incident which had, in fact, contributed not a little to the rising nausea that had driven the young Englishman from the table—two of the apache gang, the same two, "Bull's-eye" and the "Gasman" who had signalized themselves in the *Silver Goblet* affair and at the unpleasant interview with the Police Commissary, appearing unexpectedly within sight of the window, had been invited to join the wedding feast by the irrepressible Bouzille. The two intruders were now seated at the table, and the *soi-disant* waiter made a point of plying them with drink and incidentally catching up any fragments of their talk that struck him as being to the point. The apaches, in ambiguous terms, but in a fashion explicit enough for Fandor's comprehension, were discussing recent enterprises in which the gang had been mixed up. It became very evident that a unanimous and general feeling of suspicion and ill-will towards Fantômas was growing up among the criminal confraternity. Fantômas, they muttered, used everybody for his own purposes, forced each man to risk his skin and in the end compensated nobody. In covert phrases, too, they spoke of Père Moche, who, they hinted, must know all about Fantômas, and whose task was always to pour oil on the troubled waters, who was forever putting off till tomorrow payments that should have been made yesterday, in a word playing a double game.

"Oh!" grumbled the "Gasman," while Fandor was refilling his glass, "things can't go on no longer like this, tomorrow night and the hour sounds for definite and final explanations. We want our money, Fantômas will have to answer our questions."

"Bull's-eye" bent over to his comrade, and in his hoarse voice asked:

"So the rendezvous still holds good at the same place, eh?"

At that moment Fandor was obliged to go away, M. Moche was calling him. Nevertheless the journalist had gathered from a remark of the "Gasman's" that the following night there was to be a meeting of the gang on the outskirts of the city, near the banks of the Seine at the far end of Alfort.

A superb limousine had pulled up at the back of the restaurant of *The Orange Blossom*. It was about four in the afternoon. The breakfast had resolved itself into a drunken debauch. A horrid uproar of ribald songs disturbed the quiet of the establishment. Bouzille was the noisiest of them all. The wine bottles had been left on the table at the end of the meal; in an hour's time they had to be replaced. Ascott, heedless of the whole riot, had paid without a murmur.

Ten minutes ago Nini Guinon, at Moche's urgent suggestion, had gone to join her husband, who had spent a strange afternoon for a bridegroom, shut up alone in a room on the first floor, anxiously awaiting, not so much the return of his wife, as the arrival of the motorcar he had ordered, eager to escape from Paris with all speed and hide himself and his intolerable situation in some remote corner of the provinces. Hardly had Nini appeared, all flushed and excited, before Ascott, looking her coldly up and down, ordered her:

"Put on your hat, we are going."

Furious at bottom to be so treated, but scared by her husband's manner, and also remembering old Moche's counsels, she obeyed, muttering curses under her breath. "He shall pay me for this, come the day I can bring him to heel."

Hastily she put on a long dust cloak, settled her hat in place and followed her husband, and the two, without a word of goodbye to anyone, got into the car, which started away at once. Père Moche, however, had run up hastily to see the last of them. With a wave of the hand he bade farewell to the newlywed pair, a broad, ironical smile on his lips.

But suddenly he started back. An explosion had rung out, half an inch more and Père Moche would have received a bullet full in the face. Luckily he had foreseen the shot and ducked in time. With amazing agility, Moche sprang at his assailant, whom he hurled to the ground, keeping him down with a knee pressed hard on the fellow's chest.

"Brigand! Scoundrel! I don't know what stops me from killing you here and now!"

Who was this man Père Moche had mastered so adroitly? No other than Paulet, Nini Guinon's lover, the white-faced, pale-eyed scamp who had assuredly been completely sacrificed in the old usurer's sinister machinations. With calm ferocity the latter was now brandishing the revolver he had snatched from the apache's hands.

"One word, one movement," he declared, "and I blow your brains out, as you tried to blow out mine the day of the bank messenger's death. Villain! Murderer! Remember I hold your life in my hands, that I can do for you where I choose and when I choose."

"Scoundrel!" shouted Paulet, "you've robbed me of my doxy. What d'you think is to become of me now?"

"Fool! She wanted to be done with you!"

"Ah! if you hadn't hid her away, you old rascal, if only I could have seen her!"

But Moche ordered him to hold his tongue. It needed all his strength to keep the apache down. Paulet, savage and desperate, had managed with his right hand to grasp the barrel of the revolver, and was holding it away from his body. It looked as if he might renew the struggle, perhaps floor the old man in his turn. The two wretches fought furiously for some seconds, now one, now the other momentarily getting the upper hand. The two rolled over and over in the dust. At last Moche succeeded in gripping the young apache's throat between his powerful fingers, after forcing him to let go the revolver.

"Die, then," yelled Moche, "die, as you won't give in!"

"Oh! oh!" stammered Paulet in a broken voice, "Curse it, curse my luck! will no one save me?"

Suddenly the two combatants were dragged apart. In answer to Paulet's cry for help, someone shouted in a ringing voice: "I will."

The someone had picked up the revolver that had been dropped in the struggle and stood with it in his hand. Dazed and dumbfounded, Paulet gazed open-mouthed at his preserver, whom he did not know. Père Moche, for his part, saw that the person who had just intervened between them in the battle was none other than the servant at the restaurant who had waited at breakfast.

Moche stared at the man, scrutinizing his face with concentrated attention. Suddenly he broke into a cry:

"Fandor, in heaven's name!" he exclaimed, "you blackguard, I didn't recognize you before...."

At the name of Fandor, Paulet sprang up and ranged himself instinctively by the journalist's side. While Père Moche realized the time was not come to continue the discussion. Besides which, the landlord of *The Orange Blossom* now came running up from the penetralia of his establishment with very natural curiosity:

"What is up now?" he demanded, "I seem to have heard an explosion, like a revolver shot."

Mine host looked hard at the three men, standing there with torn clothes, all filthy and smothered in dust, but Fandor was ready with a plausible explanation. He gave his account with perfect self-possession:

"It's nothing, landlord, only the customer's car burst a tire just now and we've been helping to mend it. It was a case of creeping in under the chassis, that's how we're a bit dirty, but a clothes brush'll soon put that to rights!"

The landlord asked no more questions, and the four men returned quietly to the restaurant, but three of them were well aware that this tranquillity was only apparent. It was but a truce before the battle, for war seemed henceforth to be definitely declared.

24. Plots and Counterplots

It was nine o'clock, and the storm was at its height. The rain came down in torrents, the wind blew fiercely, lightning blazed and thunder bellowed. The streets were deserted, for a man must indeed have had urgent business to call him abroad on such a night.

Apparently such was Jerome Fandor's case, for the journalist was walking fast and resolutely under the pitiless downpour along the quays bordering the Seine in the direction of Charenton. As he fought his way against the gale, the belated pedestrian was growling between his teeth:

"Good lord! How my ears sting with the cold! and how pitch dark it is! Screw up my eyes as I will, I can't see a thing. All the same, I've got to get to Alfort. But shall I ever find the rendezvous in this darkness, I wonder! All the same, how right I was to attend the marriage of that fool Ascott with the unspeakable Nini Guinon! What a wedding! and what a crew! And old Moche! what a clever fellow he must be to keep this gang of scoundrels on the job, always promising the fellows money and never giving them the pay for the crimes they do at his bidding! Oh! he's one in a thousand, he is, the old moneylender of the Rue Saint-Fargeau! If I hadn't important reasons for not wishing him to see me, I'd just go straight, fair and square, to the abandoned quarry where the confabulation's to be between the 'Gasman,' 'Bull's-eye,' Paulet and the rest of that gang of ruffians. But surely I hear footsteps coming up behind me. Best turn off the road now and make to the right to get time to find a hiding place. Mustn't let yourself be seen, friend Fandor. True, all these fellows are your 'pals' and more or less well disposed, but beware Moche, if he spotted you, especially after yesterday's business, there'd be trouble, and that wouldn't help on poor Juve's affairs!"

All the while, as he soliloquized thus, Fandor was moving on as fast as he could in the deep shadows that helped to conceal him, sometimes crawling, sometimes walking. Still, he was the first to reach the rendezvous. It was a sinister spot. A sand quarry lay there abandoned, a hundred yards from the bank of the river. A strike of the quarrymen had been going on for a week, and there appeared no present likelihood of work being resumed. Fantômas' henchmen were aware of the fact and knew that nobody would come to disturb them. Besides, the river was close at hand, and if interruptors appeared, so much the worse for them! They would make a hole in the water, whether they liked a bath or no.

But the look of things would not have been half so grim if, moored by the shore, a dredger had not shown its huge, dark bulk on the black water, lifting to the sky its slanting spar with an endless chain running along its length carrying the great buckets that dredge up the mud and detritus from the bed of the stream.

A sound of footsteps. A cold sweat broke out on Fandor's temples. Like all truly brave men, he was not rash and deemed it foolish to risk his life without gain for anybody or anything whatsoever. Now it was very certain that, if he was seen by Moche, who knew him, and now treated him openly as an enemy, he would be denounced to the apaches, who would no longer take him to be one of their own crew and would dub him a traitor. A summary execution would be the sequel. But what would become of Juve then? Anyway, what was to be done now under these difficult circumstances? The intrepid journalist asked himself the question anxiously, calling up all his ingenuity and cunning to discover an immediate answer, for it was not hours now that counted, but seconds.

The footsteps came nearer. They were within a hundred yards, and the new arrivals would soon be able to pierce the heavy shadows that, luckily for Fandor, still hung, a protective screen, between them and the reporter. A happy thought! a really brilliant idea! Those great buckets (empty or full, what matter?) that swung in the wind along the dredger's spar, were they not observatories all ready-made, so excellently adapted to the purpose that assuredly it would never occur to the most suspiciously minded of the gang that a spy, however rash, should have chosen so perilous a hiding place. Fandor did not lose a moment. Rapidly and dexterously the young man hauled himself up by the chain and had very soon reached the highest point of the spar, where he settled himself, crouching down in the topmost bucket of all. By great good luck it was empty. From there he could both see and hear, while remaining entirely incognito himself.

He was only just in time. The apaches were arriving one after another in quick succession. "Big Ernestine" was the first; behind her came Paulet, the murderer of the bank messenger, the "Gasman," "Bull's-eye," the "Beadle," and other members of the gang, after them, five or six new recruits, whom Fandor only knew by sight, and who had as yet done little to get themselves talked about. These were whispering together under their breath. The rest seemed quite at home. They believed themselves as much alone as in their regular haunts, and their voices swelled to the loudest diapason of indignation.

"Eleven gone, and the dirty scamp's not come! It's too long the thief's been swindling us all with his promises he never keeps. Won't stand the cheat anymore, what say you, mates?"

"If old man Moche tries on another of his tricks tonight, I'll do him in tomorrow!"

"Hark there! What's that?"

"It's the old humbug, here at last! Oh, ho! His pockets are bulging with brass, that's why he's been so slow. It's too heavy for him, he can't walk!"—and the yells and imprecations broke out afresh.

A small, mean, cringing figure, his head almost buried in the collar of his greatcoat, his hands clasped in a suppliant attitude, the old usurer listened quietly to the recriminations that rose on all sides, guessing that for sure he would be in the tightest of tight places before long.

"Good day to you, mates all," he greeted the angry crowd, and said no more for the moment. But, after a brief pause, seeing looks of anger and suspicion scanning him from the soles of his feet to the crown of his head, he added in a whining voice:

"Beg pardon, but we'd be better elsewhere: suppose we adjourn to the deck of the *Marie-Salope* (the dredger) over there?"

All agreed. Only "Bull's-eye" slipped in a question: "There's nobody there?"

A general shout reassured him: "Why, who'd ever dare to come?"

Still, by way of further precaution, "Big Ernestine" climbed down into the lighter, moored in the wake of the dredger, into which the buckets when working emptied their contents. Another minute and the woman was up again, satisfied with her inspection, and declaring:

"All clear!"

But Moche now pointed out that they were wasting precious time, gassing without saying anything to the point.

"We're here to talk business, so let's begin."

The company took seats as they best could, some on the bulwarks, some on the deck-planks of the dredger, forming a circle in the middle of which Père Moche took his stand and the trial opened. "Trial" is the right word, for truly the speaker was pleading for his life before his judges seated round him, whom even a superficial observer would have found no difficulty in recognizing as ready to go to the most violent extremities.

It was the "Beadle" who undertook the prosecution. All the while brandishing before the face of the culprit, who stood impassive before him, his redoubtable clenched fists, the weight of which was familiar to all the onlookers and which without an effort could have felled the unhappy old man to the ground, he began with an artful reference that instantly won him the sympathy of his audience.

"Père Moche," he said, "you are come, and that is well, for it behooves us once for all to understand each other, us and you. You can see for yourself, that, among the chosen few of our band, one only is missing, poor "Beauty Boy," and if he has been nabbed, if he is in the stone jug, waiting till the bigwigs send him overseas, that is entirely your fault. I don't mean to say you sold him to the tees, but you left him without coin, without a yellow boy, without a stiver, and forced him to muck it somehow or other, so that. . . ."

A triple round of applause allowed the orator to take breath, which he did long and noisily, and to add another touch:

"Yes, if 'Beauty Boy' was pinched working the Yankees on the Trans-Atlantic boat-train, and he so clever fingered, it was because he didn't have the usual stuff with him. If he hadn't been forced to pick up just anything he could to fill his belly, he would never have. . . ."

Faces grew ugly, fists clenched, every eye glittered with murderous light. In his hiding place Fandor congratulated himself on his presence at this unexpected scene. Moche seemed to be racking his brains to find a way to exculpate himself. Still the old ruffian managed to conceal his distress, and it was without any great difficulty he succeeded in breaking in on the "Beadle's" eloquence and making himself heard instead.

"Come, come, you're never going to eat me, comrades? I've got a tough hide, you know, and you'd only get a bellyache. Now what makes you go howling at me when I'm your best chum? What have you against me, now?"

"The infernal cheek of the man!" snorted out "Big Ernestine," looking as red as a poppy.

"But come now, haven't I done everything I ought? Sure enough, Fantômas, who set us to work, don't pay us as we hoped he would. There's been some good business done, I admit, and without you, without us, it would never have come off. Coin's been handled by the chief, and it's all stuck to his fingers, we've not had a chance yet to touch it. But I'm not Fantômas! I'm only his lieutenant, and to pass on your complaint to him, I should have to know where he is. . . ."

"You don't know where Fantômas is? D'ye think we're going to swallow that hogwash?" vociferated "Big Ernestine."

"No, I do not know, my pretty dear, and if I did, I should have told you long ago, if only to satisfy your curiosity."

"It's not a plant, that?" asked the "Gasman," half-inclined to come to the old fellow's help.

"I swear it isn't! You think I know more than you do, and that my lot's more enviable. Nobody so blind as those who won't see. I tell you my lookout is just as pitiable as yours. He owes you your pay, well, he owes me mine, too. All I've been able to do for you is to hinder your getting disheartened and thinking Fantômas doesn't care for you anymore. Well, *I'm* convinced Fantômas still looks after us and thinks a deal of us. If we don't see him, if we have no direct news from him, it's because he has powerful reasons for acting as he does. . . . What, isn't a fellow like him cleverer than all the lot of us?"

"Hear, hear! Fantômas forever!"

"Well and good! Fantômas forever! . . . So then, I still deserve your confidence, eh? I was to come here to explain things. Haven't I come? Did I shirk away?"

"That's true enough, but where is the Chief?"

"Where he is precisely, he'd be a mighty clever customer who could tell us and be sure he was not mistaken. What is unfortunately certain is that he must have been put in confinement as from time to time we receive orders from the Santé prison, orders we have, in fact, always faithfully carried out. And all the same, with Fantômas, we are bound to look for the most amazing surprises. . . . Oh! if only we could see him!"

"We can if we want to!" declared the "Beadle" in a tone of conviction.

Everyone was startled at this bold statement spoken with such confidence, while Fandor felt his curiosity more keenly excited than ever.

"Why, yes, we can see him. If Fantômas writes from the Santé, that means he is there. If he's there, we must manage his escape, that's all."

"You're not a bit gone in the head, eh?" someone broke the silent pause of stupefaction that followed.

"I! not a bit of it. I've got my notion, and I'm just telling you what it is, and if you're not chicken-hearted, it'll come off. It's not so hard as all that to find a crack Fantômas can slip out of jail by. . . . Suppose we collar him as they're taking him along down the passages in the Palais de Justice to be examined, eh? We've done bigger jobs than that before now. Only. . . ."

"Only?"

"Only we must have a plan, and it's none too easy to find a good one. It's not to praise Moche I'm saying it, but there, he's a mighty clever chap, and can read a heap of big old books and write like a schoolmaster."

Moche was flattered and gave a little nod of the head, as much as to say they were quite right about him and the profundity of his acquirements. Then the "Beadle" seeing his audience banging on his lips, went on with redoubled ardor:

"Well, then, to my thinking we shall do nothing to rights without Moche. Let him make out a plan and we'll carry it through, dead or alive. I have spoken. Fantômas forever!"

"Fantômas forever!"

Looking on from his vantage point, Fandor was prodigiously interested in what he now saw and heard. For all the wealth of the Indies he would not have surrendered his place to anyone whatsoever. But suddenly the journalist felt his heart stop beating at a thought that filled him with consternation. He shuddered as he reflected on the apaches' new project. If, by any chance, this bold scheme of rescue which the gang proposed proved successful, it was not Fantômas they would lay hands on, but simply Juve! The fact was, the Fantômas of the Santé—Moche, indeed, must know this as certainly as Fandor did himself—was not Fantômas at all, but Juve, and once the police officer fell into the power of the apaches, he was irremediably lost, whether they took him for Juve or for Fantômas, their perjured and bankrupt paymaster.

Fandor had guessed right. This he gathered from the decision the artful old schemer now pronounced in half a dozen short, crisp words: "I'll take it on. Tomorrow we meet again."

"Where?"

"I don't know yet, I must think it over, and once my plan is settled, I will let you know by Paulet. Is that agreed?"

"Agreed!"

"Nothing more to do here then. Let's be off and have a cozy drink. It'll be warmer than here, what say you?"

"Now you're talking. Let's hook it"—and thus the sitting was dissolved. Threatening dire disaster to Père Moche at the beginning, it had ended finally in a blaze of triumph for that astute scoundrel.

Fandor found it hard to recover from his wonder and surprise. True, his poor body was aching and stiff and cramped, and his mind was feeling the numbing effects of this physical distress, patiently borne, but prolonged almost beyond human endurance. However, Fandor was young and energetic, and very soon, by dint of clinging to the chain and so stretching himself vigorously, he had restored the requisite suppleness to legs and arms and loins. He was making ready, grasping the spar of the *Marie-Salope*, to slip down to the deck when, looking before him, he caught sight of a shadowy figure returning hurriedly to the dredger. In a moment he was curled up once more in the bottom of the bucket, but by tilting this over sideways, he managed to secure a still better view than before.

It was a wise precaution, and it proved useful. There was no doubt about it, some member of the gang was coming back, after leaving his confederates under some pretext or other, to return to Paris by themselves. But who was it? and what was he after?

For all the cool presence of mind that characterized him, Fandor with difficulty stifled the cry that rose to his lips. It was Moche! It was indeed Moche, who, after accompanying the apaches for five hundred yards or so as far as the fork in the roads that lead in different directions to Paris and to Alfort, had announced in the most natural way in the world:

"I am expected at Alfort, so I must leave you here. I'm not in your bad books any more?"

"No, no! . . . tomorrow's the day?"

"Tomorrow or next day, not a day later. So once again: Fantômas forever!"

"Yes, Fantômas forever!" echoed "Big Ernestine," ". . . but only if he pays up and can prove he hasn't cheated us!"

"By God! yes, we'll keep our eyes lifting," added the "Gasman," completing the other worthy's meaning.

"Till we meet again!"

"So long then!"—and Moche, without rousing the slightest suspicion, had contrived to start back on his road to the dredger. What was he coming to do? Something underhand, evidently, for instead of advancing as the first time, walking quietly on his two feet, he was flat on his belly, crawling on the ground, as he had been doing for the last two hundred yards or more. Whose notice was the old scamp trying to evade? Doubtless it was one of the companions he had just left that he feared. Fandor was burning with impatience, albeit the temperature had fallen at the approach of the dawn, which was due in another hour. Moreover, a heavy, drenching rainstorm was beginning, accompanied by vivid flashes of forked lightning and reverberating thunderclaps.

On reaching the dredger, Moche abandoned his serpentine mode of advance and rising to his feet, stepped on to the deck and made straight for the winding-crank fixed at the bottom end of the spar, to put the buckets in motion. He took the handle in both hands and with legs wide astraddle and back hunched up, set to work to turn. Looking down at the old man from above, Fandor could not restrain a laugh.

"Sweat away!" he grinned, "I'll give you a dozen of champagne if you get the old machine to work . . . God in heaven! It is turning."

He had not time to say another word before he was pitched headlong into the lighter astern, among the rubbish that already half filled it and which, luckily for him, made a sort of cushion sufficiently yielding to break his fall. Nor had he time to get to his feet before the contents of the bucket that had previously hung below him, but was now suspended above his head as the chain revolved, came tumbling all over him.

"Bad luck again!" was all he said, as he shifted quickly a bit to one side, so as not to be fouled again if Moche went on working the crank, which had gone on turning without further application of external force. But what now? the avalanche had stopped. What did that mean? Peeping out through the cracks in the ramshackle bulwarks of the lighter, Fandor could get an excellent view of what old Moche might be at without any risk of being seen himself. What he did see was so singular that his face lit up with a broad smile. Something was afoot of so strange a sort as to force an involuntary exclamation from his lips. "The artful dodger!" he exclaimed. What the old usurer of the Rue Saint-Fargeau was doing was, in fact, extraordinary. He had stopped the crank at the exact moment when the first bucket under water rose from the depths of the dredger's hold. At this the old man was gazing lovingly, and it was only after he had cast a wary glance round the horizon and made sure there was no one watching his proceedings that he began groping in it with feverish eagerness. Fandor grinned like a Cheshire cat, chuckling to himself as he mentally apostrophized the old fellow:

"Oh, Moche, Moche, what a fool you are!—and just when you're thinking yourself the cleverest rogue unhung! What is the fellow after? By the Lord, he's hauling out of the mud an iron box, a cashbox. Full of yellow boys, I wager. Oh God, there's enough and to spare there to pay the greediest of Fantômas' regular workers for their trouble! Moche, my boy, if I wanted to play you a nasty trick, I'd go slap off and tell the gang what I've seen, and I promise you that, two bouts from now, when, they'd caught you, you'd be having a devilish bad half-hour! Luckily for you, I prefer, in Juve's interests, to find out what you're pro-posing to do with your treasure. Are you an honest agent, is it just a trust confided to you by Fantômas? Or, are you by way of robbing your master and all his confederates? Oh, ho! it looks as if the villain is preparing to answer my question himself."

For now, with a meditative air, Moche was pulling at his hideous red whiskers, one after the other. Then he took out his watch and made several unavailing attempts to see the time, for the night was still so dark he had to wait for a flash of lightning before he could read the hour, while the wind was blowing too violently for him to dream of lighting a match. When at last he was able to make out the face, a cry of annoyance broke from his lips: "Past three already!"—and without a moment's delay he started off at a run in the direction of Alfort, gripping under his left arm the precious box, which he had hastily closed.

Where was he off to? Fandor took prompt measures to find out, and the other had not gone three hundred paces before his steps were being dogged by the pursuing journalist. The pace was hot. It was plain that Fantômas' businessman was bent on completing before daylight whatever the job it was he had made up his mind to do. But to manage it he must make all possible haste, for, as Moche had noted, it was by now three o'clock in the morning.

"God Almighty!" Fandor swore, pressing on harder still, "what a racer the scoundrel is! . . . Where are we? We're clean through Alfort, and there's nothing else but that hovel ahead there. It looks deserted, but it's that way and nowhere else Moche is making across country. Aha! I think I'm going to know!"

Moche, in fact, was making straight for a tumbledown building that stood empty and abandoned in the middle of a wide stretch of waste ground, its shutters hanging from their hinges, its walls dropping to pieces, and a general look of poverty-stricken dilapidation brooding over all. Like a person familiar with the locality and having a perfect right to march in without knocking, he pushed open the door, a strong and heavy one. Still, the idea occurred to him that tramps might have taken refuge in the ramshackle hut for shelter from the cold out of doors. So he took his revolver in hand, and in he went.

The old usurer closed the door behind him. Then Fandor, who had been crouching to the ground, advanced with a thousand precautions, glued his ear to the door, made certain that the outermost room was unoccupied, and opening in his turn, made his way silently into the lonely house. Neither did he fail to hold his trusty Browning ready for action. At first he had some difficulty in making out just where Moche could be, but soon, noticing a feeble, almost imperceptible glimmer of light that filtered up through the floor, he realized that the old usurer was in a cellar, and had pulled to after him the trapdoor by which he had gained access. Fandor threw himself flat on the trapdoor in question and peeped through the cracks between the boards.

But what he saw went far beyond anything he bad expected. By the light of a lantern he had unhooked from the wall Moche, having first deposited his precious money-chest on the floor, was busy raising with infinite caution one of the paving stones in the north corner of the cellar.

"Evidently," the journalist thought to himself, "he wants to re-bury his treasure in a new place!"

And such was in fact the old reprobate's intention. In the hiding place he had opened up he now proceeded carefully to place the chest. Then he replaced the flagstone, then he scattered sand and dust all round the edges, so that it was soon quite impossible to guess that the stone had ever been disturbed.

Meantime Fandor had moved from his spying place. Moche was about to take his departure and he must not catch sight of the intruder. The journalist's first idea was simply to leave the ruined house before the old ruffian, but on second thought he realized that such a mode of departure was full of risk.

"Once outside, I shall be on the bare, deserted road, and Moche will inevitably see me—and that will never do!" But now a happy thought struck the young man—Moche, never for one moment suspecting the presence of anyone spying on his actions, would probably not trouble to search the rooms. All he himself would have to do would be to hide, let the old man go out first, then slip away after him quietly and in perfect safety.

A few minutes more and Fandor, concealed behind a forgotten pile of firewood, saw Moche emerge again from the cellar. The old fellow crossed the outer room, reached the door and went away.

"A pleasant journey to you!" grinned Fandor.

But the next instant a cold sweat broke out on his brow. Moche, after pulling the door shut after him, had locked it.

It was all the young man could do to keep back an oath: "A prisoner! I am a prisoner, by the lord Harry!"

25. Assault and Battery

Juve was a free man. The Judge of Inquiry, M. Fuselier, who had all along been skeptical as to the generally accepted theory of the identity of the police officer with Fantômas, but who had been rudely shaken in his faith in the detective's innocence by the startling coincidence of the wound found on the prisoner's arm, had bestirred himself with redoubled zeal and had instituted further searching investigations. The result had been the discovery that one of the warders at the Santé, Nibet by name, was in close touch with the Fantômas' gang, and having access to Juve's cell, had presumably seized an opportunity to drug the prisoner during the night and effect the cut on his arm that seemed to supply such convincing evidence of his being the same as the assailant of the unfortunate inspector of the Criminal Bureau at the Grand Duchess Alexandra's ball. Soon the conjecture became a certainty, albeit Nibet had disappeared, alarmed by M. Fuselier's inquiries, and Juve had been released.

He was now closeted with M. Fuselier in the latter's official room within the Palais de Justice and was receiving the friendly magistrate's cordial congratulations on the vindication of his character and his restoration to liberty:

"Juve, you are free. The fact is established, you are not Fantômas. Nibet is proved the culprit in the matter of your wound"—and with a spontaneous and charming affability the magistrate shook Juve cordially by the hand.

"But alas!" he proceeded in a less cheerful tone, "we do not know when we shall be in a position to announce the capture of another and a more terrible culprit."

Juve with equal seriousness replied:

"Pah! I ask you, sir, for a fortnight at the outside! It is more than a police matter for me now to arrest Fantômas, to unmask him at any rate and force him to flee. It is a personal matter.

Remember, all the time I have been in jail, I have no doubt my friend, my accomplice, Fandor, has been at work. I am going now to see him, and between us two . . ."

"Or you three," corrected M. Fuselier, "for indeed you must not forget, Juve, that you will have an invaluable helper in the person of Tom Bob."

But at once the worthy police officer's professional pride was up in arms. At the mention of Tom Bob Juve's brow contracted and it was in a hard voice that he answered roughly:

"Tom Bob! . . . well, it strikes me, folks make a deal of fuss about this Tom Bob, and for my part, Monsieur Fuselier, I am far from desirous of working with him . . . even . . ."

Juve stopped short, but the other craved an explanation of the broken sentence.

"Even what?" he demanded.

"Even," Juve resumed, "if I do deal with him, it will not perhaps be in the way you think, sir!"

M. Fuselier started violently.

"Oh! oh!" he cried, "oh, Juve! . . . is it possible? . . but no, it cannot be! you are mistaken."

Juve gave a dry little laugh:

"I am not mistaken because I am making no assertion, but this much is certain, that Fantômas this time is not acting alone. He had accomplices, and accomplices highly placed. Upon my word I confess that Tom Bob . . ."

But the other sprang up, unwilling to listen to such extravagant theories.

"Come now, Juve," he remonstrated, "you know the man yourself, you know Tom Bob personally. You are aware he is a famous detective, are you not?"

Juve wagged his head as he replied:

"Yes, I knew a Tom Bob. That Tom Bob I esteemed and admired and I do so still, but, sir, I am speaking of the Tom Bob who is now in Paris, who is a popular hero, the Tom Bob who boasts he will run Fantômas to earth, and who—mark this, it is an important point, believe me—who nevertheless never took the trouble to ask permission to see me at the Santé, when I was supposed to be Fantômas! There are but two alternatives: either the Tom Bob I speak of is my old friend, in which case it was only natural, I take it, he should have come to offer me the solace of his sympathy, or he is one of the . . ."

Juve stopped short again then, unwilling to say all he thought.

"However, time will show," he said. "Anyway, sir, you may be sure that all my energies from now on will be devoted to following up my investigations."

It was getting late. Since early in the afternoon Juve had been discussing with the magistrate the extraordinary incidents in which Fantômas' name once more figured so disastrously.

"Well, it's too late now to sign your discharge paper, and carry out the lengthy formalities required. So I am going to give you a provisional form of release and sign the formal document tomorrow. Will that suit you?"

Juve nodded, and was just opening his mouth to answer when a knock came at the door, and the magistrate bade the applicant come in.

It was a working mason who presented himself.

"Give you my excuses," he said, "but now, sir, can't we come into your room to fix up our scaffoldings?"

"Yes, yes, my man, just as you please?"

M. Fuselier got up, hastily arranged his papers, locking away some in drawers, anxious not to leave any compromising document lying about. He grumbled, "It's just killing. Here's a whole week I've never been left in peace with these building operations for enlarging the Palais. Every hour of the day I have workmen fussing around."

While the magistrate was speaking, in fact, five or six masons had entered the room. One of these made his way to the window, in front of which was a hanging scaffolding, where two more workmen were standing.

"All right, mates?" shouted the mason.

"All right it is . . . and you?"

"We're right, too—come on and see!"

And then next moment—the words were evidently a

signal—there followed an abominable scene of violence and horror.

From the scaffolding two more workmen had jumped down into M. Fuselier's room. Before they had time to gather their wits together, the magistrate and Juve were seized by the fellows, bound, gagged, and thrown roughly to the ground. M. Fuselier all but lost consciousness. Juve ground his teeth, fighting desperately, dealing blows left and right, a miracle of strength and courage. But what could he do against the odds? and he was quickly forced to submit.

"Oh! damn the fellow!" one of the masons swore, "it's a blessing we've got him tied! Now, sharp's the word, my boys! The beak on a chair, and tight up! Hold on with the tec, eh?" By "the tec," he meant Juve. Two men were kneeling on his chest, another was holding his head down on the floor, a fourth was cording his legs. Dazed and dumbfounded, Juve could make nothing of it all as he watched the bogus masons hurrying to obey the orders of the one who seemed to be in command.

"The beak on the chair, I tell you!" repeated the chief. A handkerchief was twisted round M. Fuselier's head, knotted ropes secured his legs, his bands were tied behind his back. Then two of the workmen took the unfortunate magistrate, one by the shoulders, the other by the legs, and carried him to an armchair. There he was seated and fixed firmly with ropes. Meantime his mates had finished tying up Juve.

But suddenly the amazing crew who had invaded M. Fuselier's sanctum stopped dead and stood motionless, afraid to stir. A knock had sounded at the door.

"Curse it!" muttered the "Beadle"—the chief of the band was in fact, that redoubtable apache—"here's something to queer our pitch!" Then, after motioning his accomplices to gather in a body at the door, he called out "Come in," in a quiet voice.

The door opened and the figure of a man appeared on the threshold. "M. Fuselier? . . ." he began, but the sentence was never finished. At a glance he had seen Juve's body lying bound and inert on the floor, he had even caught sight of M. Fuselier, helpless in his chair. Instantly doubling his fists, a marvel of coolness and courage, he hurled himself into the room and rushed at the "Beadle" with a hoarse yell. But behind the door stood massed the apaches, waiting. He had not taken two steps when a human swarm was clinging round his shoulders, blows fell thick and fast, arms and legs were hauled and mauled, he was down, he was choking, he was helpless. Like Juve, like Fuselier, in half a minute he was tied and bound, unable to move a muscle.

"Well, my fine fellow!" the "Beadle" now took up his parable, "here's someone I never expected! Why the devil must he come trespassing on our preserves? You know the man, eh? *You* know him, Paulet, don't you?"

The rest shrugged shoulders contemptuously.

Paulet, with his crooked smile, swore: "By God! Yes, there's no mistaking the beggar, it's Tom Bob, ain't it—the fellow that ran in poor 'Beauty Boy'?"

But the older apache had already resumed his gravity: "Yes, it's Tom Bob, the detective! I'm thinking if we should 'finish' him. But no, by the Lord! not worth the trouble, it ain't."

Thereupon the "Beadle" knelt down beside the detective's body where it lay and extended on the ground, took the unfortunate man by the shoulder and shook him roughly:

"Hi! detective, d'ye hear me? Yes? Good—now look and see how we stand. You wanted to arrest Fantômas, did you? Well, old man, it's *us* have laid hands on you. And if we don't finish you off, it's only to save worries here. Only, let me give you a bit of advice—by the next boat you'll have to hook it back to your own country. Got it?"

The man got to his feet again, and, a coward like all of his kidney, while Tom Bob lay helpless and incapable of offering the smallest resistance, he kicked him in the face again and again. Presently, tiring of the exercise, he broke off to add:

"There, I don't want to spoil your mug. What'd be the good of that? But what to do with the beast? We never figured to see *him* here. Bah! Let's just tie him up with the beak, it'll be company for him!"

But there was no time to waste. It was a good twenty minutes since the brigands had invaded Fuselier's privacy. True, at this time of day there was small likelihood of anybody coming to disturb the Judge of Inquiry. Still it was best not to delay—a surprise was after all a possibility to be feared. A night watchman, a court official, an usher might arrive at any moment. Like a general inspecting the dispositions made by his subordinates in command, the "Beadle" proceeded to make a rapid examination of the fastenings securing Fuselier and Tom Bob.

"Righto!" he declared, "they're hard and fast for the night, never fear!"

With a grin, he gripped Tom Bob by the shoulders and dragged him into a dark corner of the room, after which he seized M. Fuselier and turned him round with his face to the wall:

"They'll be bored worse than ever if they can't see one another! A pleasant time to you, gentlemen! . . . And the other, ready is he? you've got the sack?"

Yes, the other was ready. The chief might gibe and jest and enliven the proceedings with satirical remarks, but his men were not wasting their time. While he was speaking, they had executed the order previously given. The enterprise, no doubt, had been planned beforehand, and long beforehand. One of the apaches now unfolded a voluminous receptacle he had brought with him, a sort of extra big sack. Into this they bundled Juve, still bound, still incapable of the slightest movement. Two of the ruffians then picked up the sack, and carrying it to the window, dumped it on the hanging stage.

Finally, after turning the key in the lock to make security doubly secure, the chief addressed his men:

"Off we go! Let's hook it, mates, all that's left to do is to slip down by the scaffold ropes. Underneath we'll come on the masons' workshops. There's a watchman, of course, on guard there, but he's full up at this time of night; no fear of his waiting up. To get the gentleman away, we've the motorcar. Ah! by God! but it's a fine bit of work we've done this journey!"

It was three hours or more since the daring ruffians who

had found a way into the Palais de Justice had tried and accomplished their capture of Juve, whom they took for Fantômas. M. Fuselier was almost despairing. It was all too abominable. Just as he was liberating Juve, Juve had fallen into the brigands' power. The man was surely done for—and so keen was the sympathy the magistrate felt for the gallant officer, he almost forgot the grotesque horror of his own position in fear for Juve's fate. He was the more alarmed, inasmuch as, being reduced to helplessness, M. Fuselier realized quite clearly it would be long before he was set free, that there was practically no chance of his being restored to liberty before the next morning at seven or eight o'clock, the hour when the cleaners of the Palais would want to come in to put his room to rights, and surprised to find the door locked, would make enquiries and no doubt find means to enter the room by way of the window.

Nevertheless M. Fuselier was not without some fleeting gleams of hope. He had perfectly recognized Tom Bob at the moment the American detective sprang into his room and had, like himself, fallen a victim to the apaches. He could not see him, but now and again he heard him move. Tom Bob had not, like him, been tied on a chair, the wretches had left him stretched helpless on the carpet. Perhaps the detective was going to find a way to free himself? Very certainly it was he who was making those cracking, creaking noises he could catch at times. It seemed he must be dragging himself along the floor to try and break his bonds.

M. Fuselier was not mistaken. Battered and bleeding as he was, Tom Bob was giving proof of amazing energy. The apaches once gone, he had managed to crawl up to the magistrate's desk, and there, with infinite patience, being just able to bend his body, he was employed in chafing against the corner of the desk one of the cords that held him fast. It needed indomitable perseverance, the attempt to free himself in this fashion, but Tom Bob had never wanted for energy. Moreover, the task cost him agonies, every movement forcing the cords deep into the flesh, but he was not the man to be deterred by pain.

After prolonged efforts, Tom Bob at last succeeded in breaking the cord that confined his wrist. After that it was child's play to free himself altogether. In a very few minutes he had released his arms, then his legs, had then cut off the ropes and snatched out his gag. Barely giving himself time to inhale a deep draft of air, he hurried to the unfortunate magistrate's side and untied him. Then, at the end of his strength, he fell full length on the floor at his feet.

For many minutes, M. Fuselier and Tom Bob, now free, dared not risk a movement. Half stifled both of them, dazed and stupefied, they could only pant for breath. M. Fuselier was the first to recover his self-possession.

"Ah! Bob! Bob!" he groaned, "what a dreadful thing has happened to us! . . . Juve is surely done for!"

In a hoarse voice, forcing the words with difficulty from his dry throat, Tom Bob protested:

"Juve! d'you say Juve? But, Monsieur Fuselier, you are mad! You don't understand yet? . . . Juve is just Fantômas!"

"Nonsense, nonsense! If he was Fantômas the brigands would never have pinioned him as they did."

"Yes, they would, to put you on a false scent."

"But it was not worth their while, as he was free—I was going to let him go free."

"The wretches did not know that."

"He would have told them."

"Not before us!"

M. Fuselier shook his head emphatically.

"No, no," he asseverated, "I tell you Juve is innocent."

"And I," retorted Tom Bob, no less convinced it seemed, "I tell you the gang, thinking Juve, that is to say Fantômas, was definitely unmasked, resolved to deliver their Chief. They have delivered him and have so delivered him as to make you think they were treating him with brutal violence, merely the better to deceive you . . ."

M. Fuselier, suddenly recalling the words Juve bad uttered a few hours before concerning Tom Bob, grew thoughtful and gazed at the detective with eyes of sheer bewilderment.

26. Juve Hears Confessions

Hoarse, croaking voices were whispering together:

"Must get to work, half past two . . . day'll be here soon . . . hurry up, men . . . to business!"

As he heard the ominous words, Juve shuddered, brave man as he was. The police officer in the course of his adventurous life had gone through such ups and downs of fortune, taken part in such desperate struggles, confronted such dangers, that he was proof against all contingencies. Yet he could not help trembling, for he felt a clear and definite presentiment that his last hour was on the point of striking. The incidents of the evening before had astounded him, and despite his imperturbable coolness, the detective could not but shudder to recall the terrible hours he had lived through since then. In fact, what had occurred in M. Fuselier's room at the Palais and the brutal fashion in which Juve had been kidnapped, surpassed all limits in the way of fantastic extravagance. Not only had the gang of scoundrels taken him unawares, thrown themselves upon him, seized and pinioned him, in the very Palais de Justice itself, but they had actually carried him off by climbing down the scaffoldings running outside the windows of the building and got clear away.

Then Juve, gagged and bound, unable to stir a finger, had been pitched into a car which had been driven off at full speed without the officer being able to gather the faintest inkling of where he was being taken. Still blindfolded by a handkerchief tied tight over his eyes, he had been led into a house, where he had waited in silence and agonizing suspense to know the decision his abductors would come to regarding his fate.

As he recalled these events, his mind turned instinctively on what he had seen last, Fuselier attacked and terrorized, the last sound he had heard, the voice of the American detective, Tom

Bob, the man he dreaded and suspected. Then despair over-whelmed him at the thought of the ever-accumulating proofs of the persistent ill-fortune that pursued him.

In truth he was to be pitied! He had been captured the very day he had at long last regained his freedom, when, cleared of the dreadful accusations that hung over his head, he was about to resume the struggle with the help and cooperation of that mighty organization, that all-powerful combination, formed by the police and the Criminal Bureau together. Now, in a moment, as the result of an odious plot, a plot no man could well have foreseen, he found himself plunged once more into the dark depths from which he was just emerging.

All this was assuredly the work of Fantômas! This conclu-sion Juve had definitely arrived at in the course of the terrible night he had just lived through, the last hours of which were still slowly dragging out their weary length. He had clearly seen that, taking advantage of his own long detention in prison, adroitly profiting by the judicial blunder to which he owed his incarceration in the Santé, Fantômas had duped his con-federates and persuaded them that Juve was none other than the elusive brigand himself, and that it was actually Fantômas who was in jail. Yes, he understood the whole scheme now, and from information gathered here and there, he could guess what was going to happen. Fantômas, the real Fantômas, not content with exploiting honest people, had exploited the apaches into the bargain—and these latter were out to take their revenge. With amazing audacity they had carried off Juve, more than ever convinced that he was Fantômas. And Juve, now in their power, was about to pay the penalty for the grim brigand's perfidy.

As the night wore on, the noises the detective heard round him grew louder and more frequent. Evidently men were ar-riving at a rendezvous arranged beforehand, and their number increased as time went on, while new voices could be distin-guished demanding the immediate opening of the sitting. Pres-ently Juve felt someone was coming up to him, and the cords that held him fast were loosened and the bandage removed from his eyes. Mechanically the prisoner stretched his limbs, cramped by the pressure of the ligatures.

Juve found himself stretched on the floor of a square chamber with bare, whitewashed walls. By the light of a smoky lamp he saw he was surrounded by a score of apaches, with grim faces and surly, threatening looks. Some of these were unfamiliar to him, others he knew to belong to notorious criminals. By the chilly damp that exuded from the walls and the flagged floor of the place, as well as by the absence of windows, the detective gathered that he was confined in the depths of a cellar.

But his reflections were soon cut short. One of the apaches, the same who had untied him, now kicked a wooden stool towards him with the order: "Sit there, in the middle of us, and listen."

Juve suddenly sprang to his feet. With a desperate, senseless impulse—for indeed it was useless to dream of escape—he pushed away the wooden seat, drove back fiercely with his elbows some of those nearest him, and darting to the farthest end of the cellar, set his back against the wall with clenched fists and furious face, ready to offer a vigorous resistance to the first who should come near him.

Alas! this spirited show of defiance had no practical result, rather the contrary. Nobody thought of coming to grips with the officer. The apaches, seeing him leap away had first jeered, thinking it a fine joke that Fantômas—for one and all took Juve to be Fantômas—should try to give them the slip, now it was impossible. But then, by way of precaution, the men nonchalantly produced their revolvers, the women borrowed their lovers' knives and fell to polishing the keen blades on a corner of their red aprons.

Juve never flinched, but stood there impassive, waiting, though his heart was beating tumultuously. It was eventually the police officer's old acquaintance, the "Beadle," who, breaking through the circle gathered round the prisoner, stepped up to him, mocking and sarcastic, both hands stuffed insolently in his pockets. The apache was bent on heaping his scorn on the man he had looked upon as the "master," now a captive!

"So there you are, Fantômas," he grinned, "our chief, our trusty leader! the man who sets other folks to fight for him and pockets the tin, and never a stiver for his good pals!"

"Bravo! Bravo, 'Beadle'!"

With a wave of the hand, the apache silenced his comrades, signifying he had said nothing of importance yet, but he was going to begin.

"My friends," resumed the speaker, turning to his comrades, who stood listening eagerly, again and again interrupting his discourse by cries of enthusiastic approval, "yes, my friends, we may well say we've brought off a fine bit of business!"

"True for you," suddenly shouted the "Gasman,'" "and it's lucky we had smart chaps with us like the 'Beadle'"—and another burst of applause greeted the words.

All this while Juve had not stirred or opened his lips. Nerves and attention on the stretch, he had listened, understood, realized the appalling position he had to face. Meanwhile the "Beadle" resumed, emphasizing the facts, that were plain enough as they stood.

"Fantômas," he apostrophized the prisoner, "you're a sharp devil, I don't dispute that, but we are cleverer than you, seeing as how we've caught you. Well, I'm going straight to the point, I am: here's how it stands—Fantômas must shell out or croak! So look sharp and make up your mind, and tell us where the money is. You've got five minutes to answer, after that five minutes is up your silence will be your death warrant!"

To occupy his mind, to cheat his despair, Juve began to count mechanically, as if in a dream. There were left him, he told himself, three hundred seconds to live, after that he would face the final plunge, exchange time for eternity. Would they kill him at a stroke, or must he endure some of those dreadful tortures the apaches invent to satisfy their thirst for vengeance? Juve refused to think of it, that his courage might not fail him before the end.

Amid the deafening uproar that raged round him, the apaches were discussing, all clamoring at once, the sort of death Fantômas deserved. Juve, forcing himself to go on counting so as not to hear, continued speaking almost out loud:

"Hundred and twenty-five . . . hundred and twenty-six . . . hundred and twenty-seven . . . and twenty-eight . . . twenty-nine . . ." his voice never shook . . . "hundred and thirty . . ." he stopped dead. A mysterious voice had whispered in his ear, "Juve! Juve!"

The detective did not start. He stood quite still, his back against the wall. Where did the voice come from? He could not tell. All round him crowded the apaches, some actually hustling him with their shoulders, others crouching about his feet.

Meantime he felt someone trying to slip in between him and the wall, to hide himself behind his back. Inspired with fresh courage, he seconded the attempt, taking a short step forward towards the middle of the room.

The voice went on: "Don't turn round, Juve . . . and answer, for the love of God answer, tell them you are going to pay!"

Ah! that voice! and the tone and the words! Juve felt a sudden return to life and hope! his heart still beat as if it would burst his chest, but his mind experienced a prodigious relief. He guessed it was a friend come to save him, and one he could count on even more surely than on himself. He had recognized the voice of his old comrade Jerome Fandor!—Fandor of whom he had had no tidings for six months, of whom he had heard nothing, of whose very existence he had no assurance, since the day of their unexpected parting.

How came he to be there—just at the critical moment, at the risk no doubt of his own life, clearly with the sole intention of rescuing his friend from this most desperate of plights? Had Juve been cognizant of late events and known of the forty-eight hours Fandor had passed as a prisoner in the house at Alfort up to the time when the apaches had brought thither his fellow officer, he would not have needed to ask himself the question.

But neither did Fandor deem the moment come for explanations. His compelling voice still urged Juve to answer.

"Tell them—'I am going to pay'"—and Juve obeyed his mentor. Cutting short the "Beadle," who in ferocious triumph was counting out aloud the seconds left him to live—"Only twenty-five . . . only twenty-four . . . only twenty-three," Juve cried out suddenly, instantly grasping the part he must play, assuming a tone and attitude of dignity and high authority:

"Listen, you fellows. Fantômas is going to pay you!"

Bravos broke out on every side, and the ruffianly crowd, forgetting their rancor, now felt full of sympathy for the master who manifested so praiseworthy an intention. But next minute, this outburst of satisfaction was succeeded by a resumption of sour and suspicious looks.

"No humbug, eh?" muttered one.

"We've been done once before!" objected another.

"Fantômas," declared a third, "you will not leave this place before you've paid up!"—and to a popular air, the whole assemblage began to growl out the refrain:

"Money . . . money . . . money!"

But now, high above the hoarse-voiced, monotonous chant, there suddenly rang out like a peacock's scream a shrill, screeching voice, demanding:

"Fantômas, tell us where you have put the stuff?" Juve was losing his first fine confidence, and though to some extent reassured by the presence of his invisible ally, he began to fear he could not keep up the bold front he had shown so far. What was he to answer now?

Fortunately Fandor's voice again whispered words of counsel, and Juve, listening with one ear to what his trusty comrade was saying, brought out in broken jerks:

"The money . . . my lads . . . it's not far off, it's here . . . here in this very place, under the stone flags that pave the cellar floor."

The announcement was received with shrugs of incredulous derision and cries of

"You're humbugging us!"

Juve, greatly perplexed, yet obeying implicitly the instructions Fandor continued to whisper, went on:

"Stop your gab, you fools! Am I the master, or am I not?"

The rough, masterful words had their effect. A silence followed and Juve little by little entered into the very spirit of the part he was enacting literally impromptu. For sure, if ever

Fantômas had found himself face to face with his numerous accomplices, it would have been just so he would have talked to them.

The "Beadle," rather chagrined to see his prestige diminishing, challenged the individual he took to be Fantômas:

"Show us then where it is, take up the flags yourself! . . . But Juve stopped him with a gesture full of an impressive dignity.

"Fantômas," he cried, still prompted by his admirable coadjutor Fandor, "Fantômas scorns to work with his own hands, it is to you, you dogs, belongs the task of digging up the treasure you are going to divide among you."

"Proud beast!" growled the "Beadle."

But less sensitive, the rest of the apaches did not need twice telling. They were quite ready to obey the orders of the master whose high authority imposed itself upon them in spite of everything. "Bull's-eye" and the "Gasman" sprang forward and had soon raised the two first flags to find nothing underneath save sand. But taking advantage of the confused uproar that ensued, Fandor prompted again:

"Tell them to go on, tell them to raise the third stone, and you are saved!"

The detective gave the order Fandor suggested. The two apaches raised the last flag—and started back in sheer terror! An atrocious spectacle lay beneath their eyes, Juve himself, who had stepped forward to see, stood there transfixed with horror. The third stone covered a black hole in the ground in which lay a corpse half devoured by worms! The flesh showed the greenish hues of decomposition and exhaled a poisonous stench. The chest had fallen in, a mass of shattered bones and disintegrated, putrefying flesh, and from its midst gleamed the white, polished handle of a metal money-chest. Where the dead man's heart should have been a strongbox had been deposited. It was there the master had concealed the money destined for his confederates—a ghastly hiding place, a hideous repository!

Juve, who understood nothing and dared not so much as turn around to question Fandor with a look, yet retained his coolness. Henceforth an impassive spectator of the appalling scene, he stood waiting to become, when his friend should give the word, one of the heroes of the new scene that was now to be staged.

Again Fandor prompted, and again Juve gave the order:

"Whoever of you is not afraid, let him go take the treasure from the depths of the tomb."

The apaches gave a roar, but stood hesitating. All were bending over the gaping grave. Their eyes glittered with covetousness. Their grinning faces worked spasmodically in mingled repugnance and desire. Their hooked fingers twitched with eagerness to seize the shining handle of the treasure chest, the metal lid of which winked in the wavering light of the smoky lamps that supplied the only illumination in the gloomy cellar. But none dared to move. The apaches were afraid—for the first time!

But now the throng grouped round the hideous hole was pushed aside and an old woman, her face scarlet, her breath coming in gasps, advanced with arms akimbo to the edge of the grave.

"Why, what," she croaked, "what's the matter with you, chaps? to be scared of a dead man, for shame! Well, I'm only a woman, I am, but I'm out to show you cowards what pluck means. True as I stand here, this hand I hold up is going to dive into the fellow's guts and fetch out his gold heart!"

Her hearers shuddered as she carried out her gruesome purpose, remarking with a hideous laugh: "Why should I be scared of the good man? We're old acquaintances, we are . . . I was the one packed him in down there!"

Meantime the old harridan had deposited the strongbox at the feet of the man she too supposed to be Fantômas. Whereupon the apaches quickly found their tongues again and all bawling at once, demanded their fees in payment of the crimes they had committed. All that remained in fact was to open the little chest. The key was in the lock and an eager and obliging volunteer in the person of "Bull's-eye" came forward. The lid was raised and a mass of gold coins revealed.

Fandor, more and more well pleased with the turn events

were taking, had whispered to Juve:

"Let them share out the swag!"

But the journalist said no more, assailed by a new anxiety, for Juve had taken the game into his own hands and was preparing to speak.

"By the Lord!" thought Fandor, "what is he going to say? How risky, pray God he won't make a hash of it!"

Juve had drawn up his tall figure to its full height and with a sweep of the arm pushed away the apaches crowding round him. With a sudden jerk of the knee he upset "Bull's-eye"—this was his thanks for the man's zeal in opening the chest—closed the strong box and planted his foot on the lid.

"Not so fast," he cried, "hear me first, you fellows! The money is there, and it's good money. You can rest assured of that, but first of all, do as I tell you. Everyone shall be paid, each according to his deserts. You have worked for Fantômas, and Fantômas means to reward you in proportion to what you've done! Go on, my lads, and every man tot up his accounts: the bravest will come off the best. Let's sit down!"

A round of applause approved the officer's announcement. Yes, he was right, those who had done nothing much did not deserve much pay, the clever ones who had worked hard should get the richest prizes.

Juve marshaled his men in a circle round him, and Fandor, reassured as to his comrade's fate, slipped away and mingled unobtrusively with the crowd. A majestic figure, with flashing eye and commanding pose, the ex-detective played to perfection the role of the grim, mysterious Fantômas. The man's coolness was amazing, for did he not confront the possible risk that at any moment the true owner of that redoubtable name might appear before him? He went on:

"I am listening, out with it all I give in your claims, my friends; every man shall have his deserts!"

But to begin with a protest was voiced by all present. Nothing was to be paid away to the absent, the cowards, the shirkers, who had not dared to come—and by this they meant Moche, Père Moche, the gang's confidential agent, the man who no doubt had engineered the scheme to entrap Fantômas, but who from now on seemed of no more use and inspired only feelings of hostility.

Why yes, Juve saw no objection to sacrificing the old reprobate. "Père Moche," he cried, "shall get nothing, that I swear."

Another burst of acclamation. Then in the pause that followed, seven or eight voices were raised.

"It was us," they declared, "kidnapped the Minister, by your order, Fantômas. You remember, it was a devil of a job, we had to be mighty smart! . . ."

Calmly, impassively, Juve drew a memorandum slip from his pocket, "Your names?" he questioned coldly.

One by one, the apaches filed past the officer, giving in their names and their nicknames.

The "Gasman" made a bait before his superior: "It was me," he said, "set afire the beggars' refuge, while you were getting 'em aboard your car."

"Well and good!" pronounced Juve, ". . . and you?" he proceeded, turning now to the "Beadle."

"You know yourself, Fantômas, you know what I did."

"That goes for nothing. Say it over!"

"What's the good?"

But murmurs of discontent broke out. Why must the "Beadle" give himself these airs? All he'd have to do was to state his case like the rest, else he'd get nothing at all!

"Well," he let out reluctantly, "it was me did the trick about the Princess Sonia's jewels . . ."

But "Bull's-eye" broke in furiously.

"And what about me, 'Beadle'?" he growled, "didn't I see you at work—with your hands in your pockets? I was in that business, too!"

Imperturbably Juve noted down on his slip three significant memoranda: "Jewels, the 'Beadle,' 'Bull's-eye.'"

"Next," he called—and two women, "Big Ernestine" and another virago known as the "Panther," insisted on the master's hearing them.

"It was us," they clamored, "flooded the lake with petroleum, so as you could light up the blaze."

Juve, however, had a question to put. Would he get an answer? he hardly dared expect it. Still he ventured to ask:

"And the big things, eh? the Minister of Justice, who killed the Minister of Justice?"

But at this everyone burst out laughing.

"Devilish funny," they grinned. "None of your jokes on us, Fantômas! Everybody knows it was you."

Juve took heedful note of the information, yes, the crime should be set down to the account of the real culprit. He went on with his questions:

"And the bank collector? Who did the murder of the Rue Saint-Fargeau?"

A chorus of voices answered him: "Moche, it was Père Moche."

But one voice protested. Someone had sprung lightly over the gaping grave and stood before Juve. It was Paulet. The young apache with the light eyes and pallid complexion growled out:

"Moche never did anything but make his profit out of the crime. He robbed me of the money, as he's robbed me of my wench, to marry her to the rich Englishman. But as God's above me, I swear it was I, Paulet, all on my own, who did in the bank messenger!"

"Bravo!" rose the answering cry. "Bravo! It's you, Paulet, for the big prize!"

But now mother Toulouche, the hag who had hauled out the strongbox from the half decomposed corpse, emerged from the dark corner where she had been crouching ever since.

"And for me," she vociferated in her screaming voice, "why don't they question me? Ask me what I'm good for? Well, I'm going to tell you, whether or no. Hear me, Fantômas, and you, mates, too. The man who lies rotting there, down there in the fat, damp earth, the man who lies rotting there, bone naked, uncoffined, well, that's my work, mine! Fantômas," she persisted, "it was me did the hardest job of all. By Père Moche's orders, I sought out this man on the open sea aboard the liner *La Lorraine*. I boarded the big ship when the tug brought out her pilot to them. Slipping on deck when no one was looking, I crept down to the fellow's cabin. I had no weapon, and I was only an old woman against a man in the prime of life. Well, I was a match for him all the same. I sprang at his face, and with my bare teeth I tore out his throat! To stop his blood fouling the carpet, I licked it up with my tongue. The man fell dead without a cry. Then I sewed him up in a big sack, and when we got near port, I pitched him into the water. Next night, with Père Moche to help, we fished up the body, poking about with a long pole in the mud at bottom of the dock-basin. And for three days did I cart the carrion about, till I buried it with my own hands under the flags in this cave here! That's what I did, Fantômas, I, a poor old woman. Say, have I the guts, am I brave, or am I not?"

Without the quiver of a muscle, Juve had listened to the appalling confession of the hideous virago.

"This dead man," he asked in a low, broken voice, "who was he?"

But suddenly there rose an urgent cry of "Hush! hush!" The apaches had heard unusual sounds, the tramp of footsteps in the distance. By the wan, feeble light that filtered in through a grated opening on a level with the ground outside, the crowd could see one another's repulsive faces drawn with anxiety. Already half suppressed vows of vengeance began to be heard. Fandor was terrified. What was to happen next? Was Juve, after escaping the gravest of his dangers, finally to fall a victim to Fantômas' fury? Was it he, the real Fantômas, that was coming?

But Juve with superb audacity, an admirable effrontery, commanded:

"Silence, all of you, and don't budge! if it is Fantômas alone they are after, Fantômas will defend himself alone, if it is all of us they are looking for, Fantômas will be at your head to defend you and triumph over our enemies. Hush, do not speak, do not stir!"

Slowly Juve pushed through the throng and made for the door of the cellar. He tried to open it; it was locked fast!

"The key," he demanded. The "Beadle" advanced grumbling: "Here it is," he said, "what to do now?"

"Open," ordered the inspector.

"You are leaving us, Fantômas?" he was asked.

"I am keeping guard over you," replied Juve boldly. Then he left the cellar, but did not go away. Between him and the apaches now stood the heavy door secured by an outside bolt the officer had shot with his own hands.

Juve stood there listening. A posse of men was surrounding the house.

27. Juve's Bag

An hour or so before these events, while it was still night, the police officers on duty at the head Commissariat office at Alfort were roused from the peaceful doze they were indulging in by the unexpected arrival of an individual who seemed breathless and exhausted as if he had been running a great distance.

"The Commissary?" he demanded.

The sergeant shrugged his shoulders.

"You may be very sure he's not here."

"And his deputy?"

"He's away too, of course."

"Who is in command here then?"

The sergeant indicated himself.

"Well, if you must know, I am. Who are you? What do you want?"

Curtly, in measured tones, the man explained:

"Who am I! I am Tom Bob, American detective, specially known of late days at the Prefecture of Police and in the city for his war against Fantômas!"

The sergeant nodded and saluted. He had heard tell of Tom Bob and recognized the foreign police officer from the numerous descriptions and portraits he had read and seen of him.

"What can I do to serve you?" he asked.

Tom Bob told him: "You can . . . arrest Fantômas! . . . at this moment he is close by with his gang of apaches round him. They are all gathered, he and his confederates, in a deserted house, at the far end of the military road, right hand side after the second crossroads."

"I can see the shanty from here," announced the sergeant, "a wretched hovel it is, but who is it tells us . . ."

Tom Bob informed him curtly:

"*I* tell you, that is sufficient! . . . How many men do you have?"

"Eight."

"That's not enough."

The sergeant was getting alarmed: "I can ask for more from the Charenton office!"

"That's the thing."

The sergeant got into communication by telephone with his colleague at the neighboring police post.

"There are fifteen over there," he informed Tom Bob.

"They must all come," declared the detective, "Fantômas' band counts at least a round dozen ruffians."

The detective's requirements were transmitted from the Alfort office, and the fifteen Charenton officers promised to be there in a quarter of an hour. The gallant sergeant was greatly excited by the coming events. To avoid all doubt and make sure he was covered by his superiors, he asked:

"Monsieur Bob, shall you be coming with us?"

"Undoubtedly!" replied the American detective. But the sergeant was not satisfied yet.

"I have a great mind," he announced, "to go and inform the Commissary, he lives close by."

"You should have done that long ago!" Tom Bob said rebukingly.

Then, while the sergeant was issuing his orders, the detective sat down in the public office, lit a cigarette, and did not vouchsafe another word.

Before coming thus rudely to disturb the peace and quietness of the Alfort Commissariat, Tom Bob had been wandering up and down most part of the night in perplexity. On quitting the Palais de Justice, leaving Fuselier to make the best of his absurd plight, that ambiguous individual had realized one fact quite clearly, viz., that the magistrate had looked at him in a way that was decidedly disquieting. An extraordinary thing for him, Tom Bob's face had blanched somewhat under the magistrate's questioning look, but he quickly recovered his customary coolness. Stepping out on to the Boulevard du Palais, quite empty and deserted at this late hour, he hailed a passing taxi and offered the driver a handsome tip to drive him as far as the first houses of Alfort.

There the detective left his conveyance and plunged into the darkness of the silent lanes of the sleeping village. He entered a deserted house, and strange to say, a few moments later, it was not Tom Bob who reappeared, but Père Moche—Moche with his wig, his spectacles, his big nose, as soft and flabby as an india-rubber ball, and his red whiskers. It was Moche who was now making his way slowly and deliberately towards the building where two days before he had gone to bury the strong-box containing his money and where, without his knowing it, he had imprisoned Fandor when he double locked the door behind him on his departure. It was Moche who, hidden nearby, watched his friends the apaches one after another approach the house to which he knew that Juve, mistaken for Fantômas, had been brought. It was Moche who, as time went by and he sat watching how matters were going, fell to rubbing his hands in self-congratulation.

"No need," he thought to himself, "to go myself. I should only be risking the same fate as Juve. Now, what is happening? . . . it is three o'clock in the morning, Juve is on his defense at this very moment, they are demanding their pay, and he cannot give it them . . . I know my fine fellows—in ten minutes my sweet friend, the police inspector will be put to death, doomed as a Fantômas at once traitor and perjurer!"

Père Moche rose and set off at a run for the more central parts of the city. Suddenly he snatched away his wig and spectacles, pulled off his false nose and red whiskers—and, extraordinary to relate, instead of the old usurer's ill-omened face appeared the keen, refined countenance of the American Tom Bob. In a ringing voice the latter cried in defiance of men and gods:

"Goodbye, old Moche, goodbye, Tom Bob, I thank you both for lending me your fascinating personalities and enabling me thus to triumph over my opponents. Fantômas, my boy, you've worked to some purpose!"

Could anyone have overheard this extraordinary soliloquy, he would assuredly have been struck with sheer amazement, for if at a pinch sundry persons had come to suppose that Père Moche bore so close an affinity with Fantômas that possibly he was Fantômas himself, none could ever think that the detective, who had come to France under official sanction with the express object of hunting down the brigand, was in fact none other than that same notorious, ever evasive criminal, now better assured than ever against capture, seeing he was actually giving chase to himself.

Fantômas stood, a solitary figure in the far-stretching plain, thinking.

"I cannot rest satisfied," he muttered, "till I see Juve lying dead—as dead as a man can be! I must also," he went on, "for a few hours more keep up my role of Tom Bob. I shall score yet another success if by one triumphant cast of the net I contrive that the French police shall arrest the whole gang of my confederates . . . I should say Fantômas' confederates!"

Then it was that, calculating his time almost to a minute, the atrocious scoundrel had given the alarm at the Alfort police post.

Dawn was breaking fast. The officers from Charenton had joined the Alfort contingent and the united force was hurrying, Tom Bob and the Commissary at their head, towards the extremity of the military road where the mysterious house stood. The sergeant was issuing his instructions.

"You will surround the building," he ordered his men. "You will draw in the circle more and more, but taking cover to avoid accidents. Have your revolvers out, the brigands lurking there are terrible fellows. At the first suspicious movement, fire without a moment's hesitation."

Meantime Tom Bob, quite unruffled, was explaining to the Commissary:

"You know what happened yesterday—Fantômas released from prison, carried off by the apaches, tried by the villains, doomed and perhaps executed? . . ."

But Tom Bob broke off short with a cry of terror. On the threshold of the ill-omened house, at the opening of the stairs giving entrance to the cellar, stood a man motionless, with folded arms.

"Fantômas!" exclaimed Tom Bob. But the Commissary set him right at once.

"No, no! it is Juve," he cried, "Juve! Yes, we heard aright. The papers that gave the news yesterday spoke, the truth, Juve is innocent and a free man"—and the Commissary sprang forward towards the Inspector of the Criminal Bureau.

"Juve, Juve," he questioned, "what are you doing here? What are you waiting for?"

The officer replied deliberately, in a quiet voice, perfectly calm and collected:

"Why, my dear Commissary, it was you I was waiting for!"

"The brigands," went on the official excitedly, "Fantômas' accomplices—where are they?"

Juve pointed a finger at the door against which he leaned.

"They are there," he said, "inside there. It only remains for us to have them out one by one. How many men have you with you?"

"Twenty-three," the Commissary informed him.

After thinking a moment, "Yes, that is sufficient," Juve declared, "we can get to work."

The Commissary, a worthy fellow, once a subordinate under the friendly Inspector at the Criminal Bureau, could not refrain, despite the critical conditions of the moment, from expressing his delight.

"Juve, my dear Juve," he cried, "what a blessed thing! Your innocence is acknowledged at last. I am so glad, so very glad!"

But the good man never finished his congratulations. For some minutes ominous sounds had been heard coming from the cellar, and now a fearful yell broke out and a hailstorm of bullets, fired at point blank range from inside, pitted and pierced the door, fortunately a thick, heavy one. Nevertheless Juve was struck by two or three projectiles, spent balls luckily, otherwise the inspector would have been shot dead. He stepped back a pace or two.

"That spoils our game!" he muttered simply, "I suppose our fine fellows have found out at last that the Fantômas they held prisoner was none other than Juve, the police officer!"

"Sir," demanded the Commissary, consulting the Inspector with enhanced respect in face of the new danger, "how must we proceed now?"

Juve cast a rapid glance round the house. "We must parley with them to begin with," he declared—and in a voice he made big and authoritative, he challenged the apaches.

"You are taken!" he announced in peremptory tones, "surrender!"

The shouts redoubled, mingled with oaths of the most appalling profanity. The Commissary, all for making a quick end, suggested:

"For my part, I should make no bones about shooting them all down through the grated windows, if five minutes from now they haven't given in their submission."

But Juve was biting his lip, a prey to excruciating anxiety. At all costs firing must be avoided, the ruffians induced to surrender and a fight prevented. Doubtless Juve did not care a straw for the lives of the monsters who had come so near killing him, but he knew that among them was one, the least hair of whose head was sacred to him! But would the apaches give in, or must they be mastered by force or famine? Either solution was equally repugnant to Juve, always swayed by the same motive.

Meanwhile a crowd of the honest, hard-working inhabitants of Alfort, risen early as is their wont, had gathered round, naturally all agog with curiosity to see this quite unusual display of police activity round the old building that had always borne something of an evil reputation. The police, on being questioned, had not hesitated to say it was a matter of a gang of dangerous apaches they had just brought to bay. The louder the clamor of oaths and threats that rose from the cellar, the more excited and angry and impatient grew the crowd.

"Smoke 'em out!" rose the cry, and fists were shaken fiercely at the wild beasts' lair, as they remembered how in all the honest, hard-working population of Alfort there was hardly a soul but had suffered from the depredations and atrocities of the ill-omened gang, or at any rate, of similar gangs of marauders . . . They had them at their mercy, why not make an end? Already, in spite of the constables' efforts to keep order, the crowd was kindling round the walls dry vine shoots and wisps of straw: through the low grated window someone threw in a lighted brand.

Juve began to tremble, and once more addressed the apaches:

"Come now, don't go trying to be too clever. Surrender, I tell you!"

Then the "Beadle" spoke out in the name of all. In a quavering voice, a coward in face of the instant danger, the fellow whined:

"We're going to give in, Juve. Only protect us from the crowd, those dogs might easy tear us to pieces."

Juve made no show of insolent triumph. At a nod from him to the Commissary, a double line of officers, revolvers in hand, formed up either side of the entrance, while four men stood ready in the doorway to clap on the bracelets as the ruffians came out. A minute or two earlier the Commissary had caught sight of an army forage-wagon going by, and had requisitioned it to serve as an impromptu "Black Maria" for the conveyance of the sinister crew Juve had so opportunely arrested.

Juve held the heavy door of the cellar ajar. "One by one!" he ordered—and the apaches obeyed. "Bull's-eye" was the first to present himself, wearing a hangdog look and offering his wrists docilely for the handcuffs to be adjusted. Behind him appeared "Big Ernestine" with hard-featured face and rouged cheeks, casting black looks of furious defiance at the crowd that jeered at the streetwalker and her tattered finery. Next came the "Gasman's" turn, a tall skeleton with enormous hands. Then the "Beadle," shivering with fear. Paulet, paler than ever, his features drawn and distorted almost beyond recognition in sheer terror of the scaffold. Then Mère Toulouche, alone and utterly callous, who the moment she was outside, began to harangue Juve, the police officers, the Commissary, chuckling and grinning in hideous mockery.

All submitted to the same fate with a remarkable docility. But when the officers prepared to deal with the last of the unfortunates issuing from the cellar in this ignominious fashion and were going to slip on the bracelets, Juve threw himself impetuously before them.

"No, oh no!" he cried, "not that one, you shall not pinion him! Leave him to me, I will see to him. For, look you, this is the man who saved my life, Fandor!"—and to the amazement of all, Juve and Fandor fell into one another's arms in a long-drawn embrace.

For Tom Bob, he had vanished long before this!

28. The Decoy

It was broad daylight by this time and the morning, still a trifle chilly, gave promise of a very fine day. The tragic scenes just enacted had had, thanks to the radiant beams of the rising sun, an almost cheerful setting. As the forage-wagon, now transformed into a "Black Maria," was driving off, loaded up with the sinister crew so opportunely captured by Juve, the latter rubbed his hands, a customary mark of inward satisfaction with that officer.

"Good work Fandor!" he said—"and none too soon, neither! I was beginning to despair."

Fandor wagged his head sententiously.

"We should never despair, Juve, but all the same, like you, I confess this morning has held some surprise for us. I was just eating my heart out down in that cellar. I thought one time neither you nor I would ever see the light of day again! . . ."

But Juve was lost in a brown study. With head cast down and hands clasped behind his back, he paced a few steps in the direction taken by the army vehicle carrying the gang of apaches.

"We are going to the police station?" Fandor asked.

"To the station? No! We have something better to do."

Fandor stood with folded arms, fixing a look of interrogation on his companion's face.

"You are leaving all those fellows in the lurch?" he inquired.

"I am not leaving them in the lurch, Fandor! We shall catch up with them again before long; now at once, if need be. Only we have more pressing business. Never forget, my boy, that all those fellows are really and truly only supers. What we want now is to come upon the leading actor."

Fandor smiled: "The leader, Fantômas, eh? But I take it, Juve, that now, like me, you are no longer in ignorance who it is? Moche strikes me . . ."

Juve laughed too, a hearty laugh of triumph. After the terrible hours the gallant inspector had spent in his prison, after the depressing times he had known when everybody accused him of being Fantômas, he was at last nearing the final victory, the rehabilitation of his character, the arrest of the real culprits! It was in fact barely a few hours since M. Fuselier and his colleagues had recognized the fact that he was really Juve, and yet with marvelous skill and coolness, owing more to his own amazing boldness than to circumstances, he had succeeded in wresting the mask from a gang of the most dangerous criminals, accomplices of the ever-elusive arch-criminal himself. Nay more, he had pushed his investigations so far that the actual identity of Fantômas hardly admitted of further doubt for him, that he could feel confident the arrest of the *Lord of Terror* was now only a question of hours.

Taking Fandor by the shoulder, Juve spoke softly:

"By God! Yes, I know who Fantômas is! I even know twice over who he is!"

"Twice over? Juve, what do you mean?"

"You don't understand me, Fandor? Come now, you accuse Moche, don't you? You do this, by reason of the part he played with these apaches, and you are in the right. But there's more to follow. For Fantômas to be Moche was not enough. That travesty held good only for his confederates. Fantômas, to dupe all Paris as he did, believe me, was someone else into the bargain, someone I suspect, astounding as the thing may sound. And it is of this suspicion, Fandor, we must now establish strict, undoubted, indisputable proof."

Dumb with amazement at the cool confidence of the man, Fandor demanded in a stammering voice:

"Whom do you suspect then, Juve? Have you a scheme of investigation?"

Juve nodded his head gravely.

"I have more," he declared: "I have a fear."

"What do you fear?"

"Have you forgotten the corpse you showed me just now?"

Fandor started back in sudden agitation.

"What!" he gasped. "If I am to believe you, you already think you know . . ."

"The name of the dead man? Yes, by my faith! I do. Come with me."

The two men re-entered the ill-omened ruin where they had spent such tragic, such hopeless hours of agony. It was not without a shudder Juve gazed round the damp, confined cellar where, but for Fandor's quite unlooked for intervention, he would inevitably have met an appalling death.

"Fandor!" began his friend, "it is a hideous job we have to do. It is the grave there must give us up its secret. The unhappy man who lies in it, Fantômas' unsuspected victim, must rise up to accuse his murderer!"

The journalist was livid. A gruesome task indeed, this work of justice Juve proposed to undertake! For one who had so lately borne such torments of fear and suspense, it called for nerves of steel, an extraordinary strength of will, to confront afresh the dismal horrors of the exhumation he was bent on. The intrepid officer stepped up to the grim hiding place, which a few hours before the hideous hag, Mère Toulouche, had not feared to ransack in search of gold—gold Fantômas had buried there, and of which she claimed her share, boasting she had a better right to it than anyone.

Then, in the gloom of the cellar, Juve and Fandor bent over the gaping hole. A blast of pestilential gases struck them full in the face, the ignoble horror of what they saw forced them to recoil. Instinctively the two took hands, panic-stricken, yet resolved to prove their courage, to manifest at all costs that they had the right, the duty to break once again the repose of the dead man, who lay there in his unhallowed grave. The spectacle was appalling. The fleshless face, in which the eye orbits were two hideous holes, and the hanging jaw mimicked a dreadful grin, seemed to stare up at them with sightless orbs.

Bending low, Juve and Fandor, speechless, motionless, shuddering, anxiously scrutinized the unrecognizable features. Who was the unknown, this victim of Fantômas' villainy? After what grim drama had the corpse been laid in this secret grave, where once again his rest was to be disturbed, where Fantômas had not feared to deposit his treasure for safekeeping.

"The dead man is unrecognizable," pronounced Fandor, "it is impossible to know who and what he was. Bertillon perhaps, by his scientific methods, might discover. . . ."

But Juve interrupted the journalist with a rapid gesture, his agitation waxing greater every moment. While the other was speaking, he had leaned still closer over the grave and was examining the body with yet keener attention.

"Bertillon, say you? Fandor, we have no need of him and his system. I can guess the dead man's name! This is what I hoped—the dead man speaks, Fandor, the dead man denounces the impostor. The corpse we have before our eyes—why hesitate to say it, our conclusion will be confirmed by the Toulouche woman when we question her—is Tom Bob's, the unfortunate American detective Fantômas had them murder as soon as he knew of his arrival in France—yes, Tom Bob's, the real Tom Bob, for the Tom Bob everybody has known for months, the Tom Bob who was afraid to meet me, the Tom Bob who was seen at the Grand Duchess Alexandra's, the Tom Bob who only yesterday made pretense of struggling with the men who kidnapped me, you surely know his true name by now?"

Fandor, stunned by his friend's assertions, hardly dared articulate the name of terror, "Fantômas!" Indeed the journalist had good right to be terrified—and overjoyed too! If Juve was correct, if he was not deceiving himself, the triumph they were winning over Fantômas was even more complete, more brilliant than they had ever hoped for.

But the journalist was not convinced. Too many improbabilities seemed to him to forbid Tom Bob's being Fantômas, too many impossibilities rose in his memory to suffer him, unprotesting, to listen to Juve's assertions.

"I tell you, Juve," he brought out at last, "I cannot believe you. Tom Bob cannot be Fantômas, the thing is impossible!"

But Juve remained unmoved by the other's skepticism. "And why not, tell me?" he asked.

"Remember the messages dispatched from the *Lorraine?* . . ."

"Yes, Fandor, the messages dispatched by the real Tom Bob—the real Tom Bob whom nobody recognized in the train, because he had been replaced by the sham—the sham Tom Bob, who, being in fact Moche, knew the 'Beauty Boy' would be there, marked down his man and had the police arrest the apache—all the time a hundred miles away from recognizing his denouncer."

"But then, remember the attempted assassination at the Hotel Terminus. Tom Bob, the man you accuse, might well, like me, have lost his life there . . . so. . . ."

Juve smiled. "Silly boy!" he laughed, "why, don't you understand that this attempt, so miraculously frustrated, had all been planned by Tom Bob himself? My precious innocent, why, that was just the very best way of avoiding any chance of his being suspected. Look you, I wager, if we inquire, we shall find the occupant who preceded Tom was Moche—that is to say himself!"

But again Fandor objected: "I grant your explanation on this point, but here's another thing—if Tom Bob is Fantômas, why did he have the body of the bank messenger he had murdered brought to light?"

"Why, for the same reason, to impress people with his cleverness, my dear sir. . . . But what are you laughing for?"

"Because," returned the journalist, "I've kept my best argument for the last. Remember Fantômas telephoned, before witnesses, to Tom Bob. . . ."

But Juve knew better than to attach much weight to this last objection of Fandor's. The latter was very evidently convinced, if he could find no stronger argument than this to bring against his friend's theory.

"And do you remember this, my friend—how, a few days ago, they found in a garret at the Hotel Terminus a phonograph, the roll missing, hitched on to the telephone wires. After that, what else can you think of to say? or do you admit that Tom Bob is Fantômas?"

Fandor nodded, vastly impressed.

"I admit this, Juve, that you are now and always the king of detectives, and yet, there is a doubt still lingers in my mind"—

and pointing to the corpse: "Look here," he persisted, "you say this is truly and indeed Tom Bob's body—how do you know that?"

"By the finger"—and he drew Fandor's attention to the dead hand. One of the bones of the forefinger piercing through the discolored flesh hung down, with an uncanny, almost threatening gesture. The bone of the finger was slightly crushed and crooked.

"Mark that," said Juve. "In old days, once when I was working with Tom Bob, without knowing him at all well indeed, in the course of an investigation we were pursuing amongst certain anarchist associations, this unlucky Tom Bob came very near being killed by a bomb. Fortunately the explosion was not so violent as the assassins had expected. Still Tom Bob was severely hurt; his right hand was bit, and this finger damaged. The injury is therefore an unmistakable pointer, a bit of evidence that cannot be challenged. By God! sir, it will be easy enough for us to cable to the American Criminal Department and get the precise details from the descriptive ticket certifying Tom Bob's identity. It is only a question of hours. By this evening the dead man will have definitely avowed his name. By this evening, I tell you, we can be sure of having discovered the unfortunate Tom Bob, the real Tom Bob."

Fandor was already on his feet. Less inured than Juve to the sight of death, he felt an instinctive longing to get back to the light of day, to be gone from this noisome cellar that had been turned into a sepulcher.

"And now, Juve," he asked, "now, by your showing, what is best to do?"

Juve had likewise risen. Casting a last look at the corpse:

"Sleep in peace," he murmured, "sleep in peace, you shall be avenged!"

Then, turning to Fandor: "Now?" cried Juve in his clear, ringing voice, "now? Now, it is only left us for one time more to risk our lives! We must make all speed—you can guess to whose house, I imagine? and with what object? . . . My lad, the hour is come at last when Fantômas is to settle up accounts with us!"

Fandor involuntarily turned pale. Oh! that decisive moment Juve announced, with what anxiety he had been waiting for it all these long months! that moment they were now to know! What a joyful triumph they would both enjoy to grip Fantômas by the collar, the ever elusive Fantômas! The journalist could hardly credit the reality. He asked:

"Juve! Juve! Then we are going to arrest him, him the never-to-be-captured?"

Juve shrugged his shoulders, smiling, almost unmoved. "Yes," he replied, "we are going to arrest Fantômas! But can you guess, Fandor, where we are going to arrest him?"

"Not I!"

"For sure, you are losing your wits! Come, think! Tom Bob, at this present moment, must know we are hot on the scent and be thinking of disappearing. Now, is he the man simply to disappear without reaping the profits of his crimes?"

"Why, no!"

"Then, my dear man, all we have to do is to go to the grand duchess's, to Lady Beltham's, to seek the organizer of the famous subscription. It is heavy odds, don't you see? that Tom Bob, before disappearing, will want to get hold of the moneys collected for his benefit. The strongbox where they are locked up, that is the decoy, the bait, that is bound to attract him powerfully. It is beside it we must take him in our toils."

"Or shoot him down like a noxious wild beast," concluded Fandor, brandishing his Browning.

M. Landais, Minister of Justice, was that morning at nine o'clock clad in a very summary costume. Wearing a long dressing gown, gaping open over his chest, his naked feet thrust into a pair of slippers, unshaven, and only half awake, he was seated on his desk in his official rooms in the Rue Franklin. He held his telephone receiver in one hand, he was driving his secretaries frantic with a hundred contradictory orders, while at the same time worrying the unfortunate girl on duty at the Exchange out of her life.

"Hello!" called the Minister, "I'm asking you to put me through to the Prefecture. The Prefecture of Police? Yes! that's plain enough, surely. *Can't* you understand?"

Then he dropped the receiver, and swearing out loud a terrific oath, he yelled, as if to somebody behind the scenes:

"But, hell and damnation! the thing's outrageous! Havard has not been told about it! Else he'd be here!"

"You must remember, sir," observed a valet, who at M. Landais' summons had cautiously half opened the door, "it is barely a quarter of an hour since they went for him. If M. Havard was still in bed. . . ."

"Well, he had only to get up, eh? *I've* got up, haven't I? . . ."

But the Minister stopped abruptly. He had just got connection with the Prefecture of Police:

"Hello!" he called, "well, what news? . . . What? . . . What's that you tell me? Juve is dead? Good Lord! You are simply mad! . . . You don't know? They never do know anything at the Prefecture! We must make a change there!"

Trembling with agitation, he hung up the receiver again and, all alone in the room, began a perplexed soliloquy:

"Juve is dead! Juve is dead! That isn't true, for I was awakened by a message informing me that he was tied up at the Palais de Justice, along with M. Fuselier! But in that case. . . ."

Suddenly he stopped to listen. There was a knock at the door of his room.

"What now?" he yelled, "what is it? . . . Come in, come in!"

The same valet who had just before answered M. Landais' summons, again put in his head.

"It is a cyclist constable who would like. . . ."

"Tell him to come in, for God's sake!"

The manservant vanished, far from anxious to enjoy a prolonged tête-à-tête with his master, who was in the vilest of tempers. A second or two more and a police officer entered the Minister's office. He had no time to stare in astonishment at the great man's unconventional attire; the Minister was down on him instantly:

"Why, what is it now? Where d'you come from?"

The officer saluted respectfully.

"Sir," he was beginning, "I've come from the Commissary's office at Alfort...."

"From Alfort? Alfort, what the devil's up at Alfort? What do you want?"

"Sir," the man persisted, "they have just captured a dozen brigands ... a dozen accomplices of Fantômas."

"Who has captured them?"

"Inspector Juve, sir."

The Minister stood hesitating a moment. "Juve?" he said at last. "But that's impossible. Juve is dead!"

Losing all sense of the respect due to a superior, the officer, overwhelmed by the news, asked excitedly:

"Juve dead? Is Juve dead?"

But, paying no heed to the worthy policeman's emotion, the Minister proceeded:

"Or he is tied up in the Palais de Justice, since yesterday evening...."

"Tied up in the Palais de Justice? ... since yesterday evening?" stammered the officer, opening eyes of sheer amazement.

M. Landais completed the man's mystification.

"Certainly!" he affirmed. "He is tied up, because he is set at liberty! You can make nothing of it, my man? No more can I! ... And that's about enough! Clear out!"

The officer swung round on his heels as if to leave the room. Then, dead set on delivering his message, he repeated:

"Well, sir! Juve may be dead, or he may be tied up, or he may be at large. Anyway this much is certain, he has just arrested twelve apaches!"

And so saying, while M. Landais sprang to his instrument and began to ring up the Exchange again with frantic energy, the officer took himself off. Hardly was the door closed behind him before the manservant half opened it again cautiously:

"Monsieur le Ministre!"

"Go away! I'm telephoning.... Hello! Hello! Put me through to the Palais de Justice."

"Monsieur le Ministre!" repeated the servant.

"What is it, in God's name!"

"It's a lady crying in the anteroom. She says she *must* speak to you."

M. Landais looked up: "A lady? What's her name?"

"I did not quite catch her name, sir, but it's a princess, sir, it seems—the Princess Sonia. . . ."

"Sonia Danidoff? . . . What does *she* want now? Show her in."

But at that same moment the room door burst open with startling violence. It was Sonia Danidoff, who, beside herself with excitement, had forced her way, despite the secretaries' objurgations, into the Minister's private room. The unhappy woman was holding to her forehead a handkerchief, the muslin and lace of which were dyed red.

"Monsieur le Ministre!" cried Sonia, in a voice choked by emotion, "they wouldn't hear me at the Prefecture! Nobody would listen to a word! Make them do me justice. Look, I have just been the victim of a dreadful assault! The Grand Duchess Alexandra has disfigured me!"

Sonia Danidoff was exaggerating. With a tragic gesture she took the handkerchief from her forehead. On the pearly surface of the temple a cut was bleeding.

"Madam," said the Minister, who knew Sonia Danidoff very well, "it is the Commissariat you must apply at!"

"No, Monsieur le Ministre! They would not understand at the police office the importance of my wound. If I have come to you, it is to denounce an abominable piece of swindling! The Grand Duchess Alexandra, the organizer of the subscription for Fantômas' benefit, is Tom Bob's mistress! And it was on account of jealousy, because Tom Bob is my lover, that she flew at me."

For once the Minister quite forgot the courtesy due to a lady.

"The Grand Duchess Alexandra is Tom Bob's mistress?" he cried. "Why, what fresh complication have we here? And what do you want me to do?"

The door opened yet again, and M. Landais' private secretary came in, a very fashionable young man, very elegantly dressed and immaculately turned out.

"Sir," he informed the Minister quietly, "here is a fresh communication come from the Palais."

"What do they say?"

"It was not Juve, it was Tom Bob, who was tied up last night with M. Fuselier."

But Sonia Danidoff, hearing this, broke in, protesting: "Tom Bob tied up? What next! I have this moment run away from him. He was at the Grand Duchess Alexandra's! He is there now!"

"Tom Bob is at the Grand Duchess Alexandra's?"

M. Landais sprang to his feet once more. He clapped both hands to his head and vociferated in tones of desperation:

"Oh! I am going mad! I am going mad! They are all dead! they are all tied up! they are all free and at large! and there are twelve apaches arrested and the Grand Duchess Alexandra is Tom Bob's mistress. Don't, don't! It is too much! Let me be, give me a moment's peace!"

Once more the door opened. Calm, cool, collected, M. Havard entered the room.

"You sent for me, sir?" he asked. "Whatever is going on? I can't see one of your secretaries, the doors stand open for anyone to walk into your office. Your trusty servant even refuses to show me in, simply telling me to march straight into your private room! Is it a revolution?"

M. Landais cut short M. Havard's exclamations:

"A revolution? I can't say! It's just a story for a madhouse—the Grand Duchess Alexandra is a swindler! Juve is dead! Juve has arrested a dozen apaches! Tom Bob is tied up at the Palais! Tom Bob is running away! He's free and at large, he's at the grand duchess's! I tell you I've lost count of everything. I don't understand one word of it all!"

But seeing M. Havard's amazed look as he listened to the Minister's wild words, the latter realized he would do well to cultivate a little more calm of manner.

"Listen, Havard," he said, "I have really lost touch with things. Since waking this morning I have received twenty contradictory reports. It will be another dreadful panic in town unless we can clear all this up"—and the Minister told M. Havard the story of his morning as intelligibly as he found possible. All the time he was speaking, the Head of the Criminal Bureau listened quietly, nodding his head at intervals in silent assent. Where the Minister was all at sea, he, M. Havard, accustomed to matters of police, could make a shrewd guess at the truth, and it was in an unruffled voice that the police official finally proposed:

"If you think well, sir, I am going straightaway to Lady Beltham's?"

"To Lady Beltham's?"

"Well, the Grand Duchess Alexandra's, if you like it better."

"But what for?"

"To beg her—and Tom Bob, who is with her, by what the Princess Sonia stated—to come and make their deposition before you, and before Juve, who, I am persuaded, will not be long now in letting us hear of him."

For the Minister M. Havard's words were incomprehensible. Still he was too well assured of the ability invariably displayed by the Head of the Criminal Department not to agree to his plan.

"Go by all means, Monsieur Havard, but tell me, is it an arrest you are going to attempt?"

"No, Monsieur le Ministre, it is an invitation I am going to proffer, *but* I shall be accompanied by a dozen constables when I make it."

29. The "Ever-Evasive" Escapes Again

The Grand Duchess Alexandra gave vent to an exclamation expressive both of surprise and triumph, as she greeted the visitor who stood before her. The latter, dropping his eyes and assuming a humble, almost abject mien, the bearing of a repentant sinner, murmured:

"I am happy, madam, to return your greeting."

The grand duchess seemed skeptical. With panting breath, for she was greatly agitated, she questioned:

"Tell me, sir! tell me, Tom Bob, what fresh crisis, what pressing necessity obliges you to come to me like this?"

Tom Bob, for he it was, hesitated a moment before replying. Slowly he lifted his glance and fixed it on the grand duchess's face. The lovely creature and the wily detective looked long into each other's eyes.

The grand duchess? . . . Tom Bob? In truth, there was no need for play-acting between these two, they were by themselves, alone, without witnesses. They could avow to one another who they really were—she, Lady Beltham, the mysterious, the redoubtable mistress of the most abominable brigand in all the earth; he, that same brigand, Fantômas!

And now the tragic lovers, after a hundred changes of fortune, intentional or accidental, that had hindered their meeting, found themselves face to face and under untoward circumstances that forced them to exchange terrible, bitter speeches; for these two felt for one another at once an atrocious hate and an ineradicable love! Yes, in very deed, those two beings who were perpetually at daggers drawn, who had ever between them the most appalling episodes, the most fearful deeds and memories, were straitly bound one to the other by an unbreakable chain of love, whose links were riveted by the strongest of all implements, the crimes they had committed together.

It was in the drawing room of the mansion where dwelt the great lady who for all the world was the Grand Duchess Alexandra, but in reality was none other than Lady Beltham, that the painful interview took place.

"What have you come here for? What do you want?" demanded the lady, but Fantômas, in a hollow voice he endeavored to make cold and peremptory, but which only the more betrayed his anguish, only replied by another question.

"Sonia Danidoff," he asked, "what has happened to Sonia Danidoff?"

The brigand—he too was breathless with emotion—felt he *must* know the truth, his heart as a lover laid an obligation on him, an obligation that wounded his self-love, anxiously to question the mistress he had forsaken as to the fate which she, in her jealous rage, had reserved for the other who had now become the favorite. Lady Beltham fought hard against her agitation and the pain that tore her breast. She articulated in a voice that whistled between the clenched teeth:

"Sonia Danidoff! I wanted to kill her!"

Instinctively Fantômas doubled his fists and cast a look of menace at the speaker. He would have hurled himself upon his defiant mistress, but the latter with an air of sardonic insolence stood before him, a superb figure of defiance, and never flinched. Yes, she defied her lover. Fantômas dared not go near her. Yet curiosity, the craving to know what had become of Sonia, compelled him to hide his anger.

"What have you done with her? Where is she? Speak!"

Breathing all her hate in a dolorous cry, Lady Beltham wrung her beautiful hands, and groaning aloud, cried:

"Go, Tom Bob, go and ask the officers of justice, go and learn from the police the fate I have reserved for your mistress, and the opinion she now has of you!"

"Of me!"

"Yes, sir, of you!"

It was the brigand's turn now to tremble with apprehension, but such was the empire he possessed over himself, he was able to hide his agitation under a mask of smiling irony.

"Lady Beltham," he asked quietly, "so you have told the princess who I am, have you?"

Very certainly, Lady Beltham had not gone so far as this, for despite her jealousy, she still cherished for the outlaw one of those monstrous passions that are like consuming fires devouring women's hearts, fires that are only extinguished by death! Nevertheless the jealous woman suffered her lover to believe that during a scene of angry altercation she had revealed to her rival the ignominy, the baseness, the crimes of the man whom the too trustful Sonia Danidoff had thought well to choose as the object of her heart's desire.

Fantômas bit his lips and his eyes fell, while Lady Beltham demanded in a questioning, defiant tone:

"And why should I not have told the princess who you were?"

Receiving no answer, she proceeded, smiling in her turn with a show of scornful dignity:

"You are afraid, it seems, that knowing you in your true aspect, she might cease to feel for you the fatal infatuation that consumes her? Poor princess! poor pitiful passion! . . . What matter the faults, the vices of the man a woman loves, when she truly loves him? Fantômas," the sobs were rising to her lips as she went on, "I ask you, have your villainies, have your crimes silenced in me the fond feelings I entertain for you? Have I, for all the hideous life of blood and terror I live because of you, have I ceased to love you?"

Fantômas broke in:

"You profess to love me, madam, to love me still, and yet you harass me with your threats. . . ."

Lady Beltham interrupted in her turn:

"Hate, Fantômas, is it not another form of love?"

But the outlaw shook his head sadly.

"Madam," he declared, "I have lost all confidence. Trusting to appearances, you have doubted my loyalty—I have proof of it, I know it. Perhaps your distrustful attitude has gone for much in that I have shown towards you. . . ."

"What do you mean?" demanded Lady Beltham, "have you not, many times over, tried to kill me? Remember, Fantômas, the evening of the Pré Catalan!"

"You were there, madam, and I knew it. But recollect how, by an accident contrived by me, your car could not be started, a circumstance which saved you from the accident in the lake."

"Say rather," protested Lady Beltham, shuddering, "that hitch, that breakdown, seemingly providential, enabled you to start back alone and unhindered with the Princess Sonia Danidoff."

Fantômas shrugged as he avowed with a cynical grin: "Little I cared for her love, it was her jewels I was after. You see I have nothing to hide from you!"

"Scoundrel! Ruffian!" screamed Lady Beltham. "So that is the alternative you offer me—to find my satisfaction in your thievish instincts to appease the horrid jealousy that stabs my heart. No, it must end, Fantômas, a life like this has become impossible, you must make your choice. Choose between us two, the princess and me. I do not mince my words: I bid you think of the consequences!"

A flash of rage flamed in Fantômas' eye, but today the pirate, the outlaw had clearly no chance left to show himself, as usual, the master, the tyrant, the despot, who commands, and all men obey! He must condescend to parley, and in a choked voice he muttered:

"Let us leave that for the moment, Lady Beltham, let us leave it. More serious events are brewing, are imminent!"

The great lady laughed sardonically.

"Why, yes!" she sneered, "I don't doubt that, if you are here, it is evidently. . . ."

Fantômas cut her short.

"Lady Beltham," he assured her, "our plans have been frustrated, the scheme I had built up is crumbling to pieces. Since yesterday Juve bas been free and triumphant. . . ."

"Juve!" cried Lady Beltham, thunderstruck, "is it possible?"

Fantômas nodded in confirmation.

"Juve!" reiterated his agonized mistress, "why, then it is the same existence of anguish and fear and never-ending alarms will begin again, but worse than ever."

"Yes, Juve is at large," insisted Fantômas. Then he added: "But as you were saying just now, Lady Beltham, I think it must all end—yes, and soon."

"What do you propose then?"

Lady Beltham stopped suddenly. The bell of the house telephone that communicated with the porter's lodge had just rung. Mechanically the great lady unhooked the receiver and listened. She was going to say no! to the question asked by the servant speaking from the other end of the wire, but Fantômas, without the smallest scruple, had appropriated the second receiver.

"Ask him up, madam," he gave his orders, "you cannot do otherwise, you must!"

Lady Beltham obeyed and gave the required answer to the servant:

"Ask Monsieur Ascott kindly to come upstairs. Show him into my rooms."

In the midst of that Parisian oasis formed by the Parc des Princes, Lady Beltham had for some months been in occupation, under the name of the Grand Duchess Alexandra, of a magnificent mansion standing in the middle of a vast park. The front of the house was approached by great gates of wrought iron, dividing the boulevard from a fine graveled drive that swept round a lawn before the main entrance. Behind the building was a short cut leading from the offices and opening into a deserted bystreet; this could only be reached after crossing an orchard planted with fruit trees, a spot of quite a countrified and unpretending aspect. The path connecting the house with the exit into the bystreet was completely overshadowed by a double row of clipped yews, a relic of a garden of an earlier date, and throughout its length were ranged a number of beehives, giving this part of the garden a homely and utilitarian appearance, a charm that was at once restful and picturesque.

While Lady Beltham was awaiting the visitor whom, at

Fantômas' unexpected order, she had decided to receive, and was endeavoring to restore to her features, distorted by the agitations she had gone through, some appearance of calm and composure, the monstrous malefactor, who had for months duped all Paris, passing himself off as the American detective, Tom Bob, slipped away softly into the adjoining room, under pretext of an intention to listen to the conversation the wealthy young Englishman wished to have with the lady he doubtless still took to be the Grand Duchess Alexandra.

But anyone who could have seen Fantômas when alone in the room would surely have suspected the man of some more sinister motive. The brigand did not stay near the half open door, shielded though it was by a heavy curtain. With preoccupied air and a brow wrinkled in anxious thought, he stepped up to the window, and long and carefully scrutinized what lay outside, if by any chance he might see under the shadow of the trees some suspicious figure, some symptom of unknown danger.

Ascott was shown in by a footman to the grand duchess's apartments. The Englishman appeared, his features drawn with anxiety, his limbs twitching in uncontrollable excitement. With a hurried bow, he sank into a chair.

"Excuse me, madam," he stammered. Then going straight to the point, he asked:

"Tom Bob is here, is he not? Oh! I beseech you, tell me. I must see him."

So agitated was the young man he never noticed the look of terror his words brought to his hostess's face. Hearing it said that Tom Bob was with her, she all but fainted, but recovering her self-possession:

"Who told you that?" she demanded: "What do you want with him?"

Then, without waiting for an answer, she questioned further:

"But tell me, what has happened to you?"

Ascott faltered in broken words that betrayed his confusion of mind:

"A calamity, madam, an appalling calamity has befallen me

and still crushes me."

He drew from his pocket a crumpled telegram, the tears welling to his eyes:

"Read, madam," he cried, and could not articulate another word.

Lady Beltham glanced through the message. It announced that, in a motorcar accident, Ascott's father, the well-known peer and member of the Upper House, and his. son, the young man's eldest brother, had been killed! The tragedy had occurred in Scotland, in the Highlands, without a soul in sight!

Ascott was sobbing bitterly. "When I heard of this terrible blow, madam," he declared, "I had a presentiment, nay, all but a certainty, that the death of my loved ones was not due to mere accident. For, I must tell you this, I am the victim of a hideous plot, a prey to the most poignant anxieties. Madam," he went on with an effort, "I was married quite lately, as you know. . . . I married an 'unfortunate,' an abandoned creature. . . . I am the victim of Fantômas' villainies, who showed himself to me under the repulsive guise of the old usurer known by the name of Père Moche. The monster of superhuman guile has me in his toils, which he draws tighter and tighter every day! The wife he made me marry has run away, she has robbed me, ruined me; but that is nothing, would be nothing at all, did I not guess that my father's death and my brother's must be yet another outcome of a plot contrived by Fantômas!"

Lady Beltham was in a better position than anybody to realize that the rich Englishman must be right. Assuredly, the further she went, the more she would hear set down to her baleful lover's account the most appalling revelations.

Ascott, harking back to his first idea, again demanded an answer to his question, adjuring her to tell him where Tom Bob was.

"I *must* see him," he urged, "I must see him and speak to him. Tom Bob is the only person on earth, madam, who by his perspicacity, his adroitness, his admirable detective skill, can extricate me from my difficulties, and put me in a position to avenge my relatives' deaths. Tom Bob, madam, is the man who must fight Fantômas!"

Lady Beltham was like to die of distress and perplexity. No doubt, she had but to open a door to bring the young Englishman face to face with the bogus detective. But was it her duty to act so? Ought she not rather to enlighten Ascott, to tell him that Fantômas and Tom Bob were one and the same, just as Père Moche and Fantômas again were one single and identical person! This course was what her conscience bade her take. But would duty triumph over love?

Mechanically, moving like an automaton, without knowing yet what decision she would adopt, for, if she felt pity for Ascott, she burned with an ardent love for Fantômas, the great lady advanced slowly into the room where the brigand was. But next instant, horrified, she sprang back, though not without having first double locked the door of communication.

What she had seen must have been something to cause both terror and despair, for Lady Beltham turned deadly pale, her splendid arms beat the air, she staggered and fell flat on the floor in a dead swoon. The look she had directed into the adjoining room and which had, in fact, determined her fainting fit, had passed unnoticed by the unfortunate young Englishman, too much preoccupied and agitated to observe the details of what was happening before his eyes. But now, seeing Lady Beltham's condition, he hurried to her side and endeavored to restore her to consciousness. His efforts proved vain, and shocked and alarmed, he rang the bell in the anteroom and called loudly for help.

Servants appeared in answer to his summons. Lady Beltham was laid on a couch and restoratives applied. In ten minutes, by slow degrees, the unhappy woman began to regain her senses.

But suddenly the tense silence was broken by the sound of shots. Lady Beltham shuddered and grew paler than ever.

"Great heavens!" she asked, "what is happening?" Ascott could not tell her. The servants gathered about their mistress stood rooted to the spot in dumb bewilderment.

Fantômas, when he left Lady Beltham waiting to receive Ascott, had his plan already cut and dried. The desperate villain realized that the game was up, beyond redemption. Unmasked so far as Moche was concerned, he was no less so in his incarnation as Tom Bob—but only in the minds of Juve, of Fandor, and of Lady Beltham.

For one brief instant the criminal had debated with himself what course was best to adopt. The moment was surely near at hand when he must either take flight and disappear, or play his last desperate card, defy the world and maintain that he was indeed Tom Bob and no one else. But would that suffice?

Still, Fantômas would have risked everything on this last chance, had he not had an opponent as cunning as himself, and now free to act. He knew, in fact, that from one minute to the next he might find himself face to face with Juve—not Juve, the ordinary adversary he had been before, but Juve proved innocent of the crimes he was accused of, Juve his character rehabilitated in all men's eyes, Juve with power and authority fortified by the priceless, invaluable collaboration of the whole police force of France. After coldly weighing his chances of victory against those of defeat, Fantômas decided for flight.

Still the hardy scoundrel did not go at once. Examining the room where he was, he noted a safe embedded in the wall. An evil mille crossed his pallid lips. Cynically he muttered:

"So the Grand Duchess Alexandra has constituted herself treasurer of the fund for the good souls who were for subscribing Fantômas' million! Fantômas," he went on with a vile grin, "would be a simpleton indeed not to pay to himself what is meant for him."

Evidently the ruffian knew the secret of the strongbox. Was it not he, in fact, who had advised Lady Beltham to purchase it? Fantômas opened the safe, drew out its contents in handfuls, stuffed his pockets full of gold and notes.

For a moment he was disturbed in this twice infamous robbery by the creak of an opening door. He looked round, startled and confused, but he could see nothing, the door had been closed. And Fantômas, never knowing that his last act of brigandage had so profoundly shocked his mistress that she had fallen fainting to the floor in the next room, went on with his thievery.

With infinite precautions, five minutes afterward, the thief was creeping surreptitiously down the back stairs. Gaining the deserted offices, he found an open window, and leapt into the garden behind the house. He had his good reasons for not leaving by the front gates. Cowardly, like a traitor, like a wild beast pursued by hunters, like a criminal hiding after a dastardly deed, he glided into the deep shade of the pleached alley, muffling his footsteps, revolver in hand, ready to resist the first attack, confident of escaping the most ingeniously laid trap.

Then he halted for a second. The hot sun of this summer afternoon pierced the heavy overhanging foliage and threw on the ground a hundred black, dancing shadows that patterned the mossy carpet and dazzled the eyes. But the robber's keen ear had caught a suspicious sound and he stopped to listen. Was someone spying on him? Instinctively he told himself:

"Juve, since yesterday a free man, and by a miracle escaped from the hands of my confederates, is perhaps at my heels?"

Then came a cry of rage! Suddenly, emerging from the bushes, a man had sprung at his throat. The man was Juve!

Fantômas fired, without a tremble of the outstretched arm, at point blank range. But the ball never reached its aim. Piercing the thick roof of greenery above, it was lost in the sky. For at the same instant he had caught sight of Juve and taken aim at his heart, Fantômas was attacked in the rear. A formidable blow across the loins upset his balance and the villain measured his length on the ground. Boiling with rage, he pressed the trigger and shot off at random the four remaining charges—quite without effect. The bullets struck no one. Plowing up the soil, they raised a thick cloud of dust, and that was all.

Juve had leapt upon his assailant instantly. Kneeling on the man's chest, he held him down, both hands gripping his throat. Looking up, Fantômas could see his face, and Fandor's beside it. He was done for! His two implacable enemies had him in their power.

Hours ago officer and journalist had planned his arrest. Instead of hurrying off to find M. Havard, as the latter hoped,

Juve and Fandor had sworn to themselves to set off at once, hot foot, on the track of the atrocious villain. They had been well advised in going straight to Lady Beltham's, for no sooner did they reach the neighborhood of the house in the Parc des Princes than they saw Fantômas slip in. Thereupon, making sure the outlaw would inevitably try to escape by way of the hidden pathway behind the building, they ensconced themselves in the deepest shadow of the trees and waited.

Their foresight was rewarded. They had the brigand hard and fast. In one second, with amazing dexterity, Juve had his prisoner handcuffed. With his hands thus linked together in front of him, Fantômas was harmless, helpless, impotent. With a vigorous push Juve forced him to his knees, then to his feet. Gripping their captive by the arms, Juve on one side, Fandor on the other, the two, without a word—they might surely have found too much to say, and thought it best to hold their tongue—dragged off their redoubtable prisoner towards the door at the far end of the park.

Fantômas was deep in thought:

"Once they get me as far as there, once they drag me over the threshold of that door, once I leave this garden, it is all up, I am done for!"

With amazing coolness the extraordinary man analyzed the situation, and in two seconds drew his conclusion. He had a hundred yards still to go along the tree-shaded pathway. Before that hundred yards was traversed, he must find a means of escape—or else. . . .

Any display of physical force was impossible! any exertion of strength would have been in vain. Juve and Fandor held him fast, each with a grip of steel, their strength doubled by the furious anger that tightened their muscles and the triumph that swelled their hearts to have captured the scoundrel. Nor could Fantômas dream of eluding their vigilance or asking any favor of his captors. The pitiless ruffian could hope for no pity!

Only the last fifty yards remained, and Fantômas had devised nothing yet.

But suddenly a gleam of ferocity flashed in his eye. With a

sudden spring, he threw himself to one side of the pathway, shouldering back Fandor who was on his left, dragging Juve on his right after him. Next moment, with a lightning dart neither officer nor journalist could anticipate, the brigand had fallen on two hives and kicked them over.

True, Juve and Fandor, instantly hauled him back to the middle of the path, but yells of agony now burst from their lips. The bees, disturbed in their peaceful labors, exasperated at the earthquake that had befallen them, rose in angry swarms and swooped down on the three men! Burning for revenge, the insects in their hurrying thousands fell upon their enemies!

With the hand left free—for they would not loose hold of Fantômas—Juve and Fandor strove instinctively to parry the attack, to sweep away the clustering swarms. But this made things worse, the number of the aggressors was only multiplied. Now about their faces whirled a buzzing, eddying cloud of infuriated creatures!

Fantômas, on the contrary, who had had a second or two's time to think what course was best to adopt after upsetting the hives, forced himself to stand absolutely still, refraining from making the slightest movement, barely stirring lips and eyelids. And the bees, in their blindness, never attacking the villain who was their real enemy, directed all their efforts to the two who, from the weird gesticulations they indulged in, seemed the most redoubtable foes.

Stung in a thousand places, Juve and Fandor shrieked in agony and, overmastered by the pain, let go their prisoner.

The latter, following the same tactics, dropped to the ground, burying his face in the grass by the side of the pathway. There Fantômas lay as still as death, while Juve and Fandor fell victims to the angry bees, all the more because they waved their arms wildly about and tried to defend themselves.

Beaten at last, the two martyrs abandoned all efforts to resist and rolled on the ground in transports of insufferable pain!

Two hours after, Juve and Fandor were discovered lying under the trees in the garden of the grand duchess's house.

They were unconscious, half dead, their faces so disfigured by the bees' merciless stings as to be unrecognizable.

As for Tom Bob-Fantômas, *he* had disappeared. Once again that monster of iniquity was at large. . . .

Would he add yet more atrocities to the long list of his crimes? ? ?

THE END